The Glitter Box

The Glitter Box

Pat Tito
&
Pat Bellavia

Writers Club Press
New York Lincoln Shanghai

The Glitter Box

Writers Club Press
an imprint of iUniverse, Inc.

For information address:
iUniverse
2021 Pine Lake Road, Suite 100
Lincoln, NE 68512
www.iuniverse.com

ISBN: 0-595-13876-4

Printed in the United States of America

To all senior citizens who refuse to grow old, especially Mel Brooks

Chapter 1

A double line of tears marred Annie O'Neil's perfectly executed makeup as one hand surreptitiously removed a topaz brooch from Cissy Raven's coffin while the other swiped at her eyes with an embroidered linen handkerchief. With a single deft movement, a honeyed shimmer of brilliance slipped inside the sleeve of her cuffed, black wool coat. Just before the gems were hidden from sight there was a winking spark of red and gold fire. Annie looked down at smudged linen in annoyance. Wearing mascara was a definite mistake, she thought fleetingly. I'll end the afternoon looking like a disreputable clown or an aging hooker with an unsteady hand.

"My God, you stole Cissy's brooch," Julia Devlin hissed, shocked at her best friend's action. "You're a....a grave robber. Pin it back on her dress. Hurry."

"Do be quiet?" Annie hissed. "Mr. Gibbs will hear."

"Annie, how could you?"

"Ladies, please. Family members are already assembled in their cars. We're late for the cemetery services." Martins Gibbs was flustered over the delay. It went against his better judgment to allow Cecelia Raven's two dearest friends to remain in the chapel until the very end but the three woman had been inseparable for almost fifty years, since they were ten as a matter of fact. And Mrs. Raven's daughters had given their okay for the two to remain with the deceased for a last goodbye. But enough was enough. Everyone anxiously awaited an end to this mournful day. Martin firmly believed the healing process couldn't begin until this last rite was over, not to mention the more important fact that his hemorrhoids were acting up again. The itch was beginning to drive him insane and all he wanted was to sit and soak in a hot tub. He awkwardly wedged his rather portly torso between the women, determined they would not be delayed another minute and firmly closed the lid of the casket. "You must go to your car if you're continuing on to the cemetery."

Annie and Julia clung to each other as they made their way to the chapel entrance crying copiously. Annie slid into the driver's seat of an emerald green Lexus, a treat she bought herself with some of her late husband's insurance money. She missed Jack most of the time but there was nothing she could do reverse the heart attack that killed him so she thought she might as well enjoy what he left because sooner, rather than later, she would be joining him in a heavenly afterlife, if indeed there was such a thing. After all, how many good years did one have once they reached the age of sixty? The older Annie grew, the more flippant she became over death. Death was a situation she couldn't control and she vowed when her time came she would make the transition gracefully. Her car was third in line behind the hearse as she switched on the ignition. Poor, dear Cissy had less than sixty years since her mind began faltering over a year ago. Quiet, warm-hearted Cissy should have lived at least another decade or two but fate intervened and dealt a low blow. Who would have thought the three sharpest minds in high school would dwindle down to two? Friends for a hundred years was their motto, which sounded lame now. Cissy broke the circle through no fault of her own.

Julia looked ready to explode as she locked her seat belt. "I couldn't believe my eyes when I saw you snatch Cissy's most prized possession right off her lace dress. Never in all the years I've known you would I think you capable of such a loathsome act. For God's sake, why?"

Her surroundings came sharply into focus as Annie wiped her eyes again. She put the car in gear and they made their way to Mount

Oakwood Cemetery. What the hell was wrong with Julia; Julia the instigator of most of their crazy schemes, Julia who accepted any dare? What was happening to them these past two years that their natural verve began dwindling? Dear Lord, don't let her turn into a prim and proper prig, she prayed. "Cissy told me to do it."

"Have you lost your senses? Cissy's dead, gone, finito. You know that as well as I do."

"Cissy told me to do it," Annie repeated stubbornly. "She told me the topaz would lose its beauty underground and she wanted the glow to live on, to be appreciated by others."

"Sometimes I wonder if you or Cissy had Alzheimer's. Annie, what if Martin Gibbs noticed the brooch was gone? Can you imagine the ruckus?"

"He didn't. I wouldn't have taken the chance if I thought he'd see."

"You can't have known that for certain."

"It was a gut feeling, Julia. We'll discuss this later, after Cissy is laid to rest."

"At least take the damned thing out of your sleeve before it falls on the grass and everyone knows you've robbed the dead. What a stir that would cause."

A few short prayers by the priest, a final blessing and Cissy was gone forevermore, unless you counted memories of which there were thousands, ever since fifth grade, on into high school and then throughout their married years and the trauma of widowhood. Cissy was always the timid member of the trio, the more cautious and level headed. If Julia could be described by only two words they would be daring and cunning and Annie's would be flamboyant and outspoken. Cissy was sense and sensibility. To be killed by an eighteen wheeler and tossed into the air like a targeted clay pigeon was a ludicrous death for a woman who had always been careful about crossing streets, careful about every move she made in life. So maybe it was better that God took her before Alzheimer's destroyed her totally. Cissy would have hated that. And thank God Martin Gibbs had been able to make her presentable in death after the fatal accident. Not to see Cissy one last time would have been unbearably sad.

Cissy's older daughter caught up to them after the brief service. They hugged silently for a long moment. "You're coming back to the house for lunch aren't you, Aunt Julia, Aunt Annie?

"Dear Amanda," Julia answered, "we couldn't bear it, not yet. We have to handle our grief in our own way. You'll forgive us if we simply slip away quietly?"

"I understand," Amanda said quietly. "You were such a close trio. I'll call you when things settle down then."

Annie swept through the cemetery's ornate, iron gates at a sedate pace. "I think this calls for a two martini lunch. We can't spend the rest of our days mourning because we don't know how much time we have. Yes, a martini should disperse my grief."

"You know I hate martinis," Julia snapped.

"Two Manhattans then. I'm flexible."

Chapter 2

A doddering waiter, who might have been put to pasture a decade ago but was sorely needed now that the restaurant was short-handed, led the two women to a quiet corner table overlooking a rose garden at the Orchard Inn. Neither woman spoke until the man deposited two frosty glasses in front of them and shuffled away. Rather than study a lengthy, overpriced menu they ordered the day's special, grilled salmon.

Annie placed the brooch on the table. Four honey-hued stones, two large, two smaller, comprised a butterfly's wings, the center of the stones a deep gold with a tinge of red that melded into darker amber at the tips. The wings were surrounded by the tiniest of diamonds, as was the body of the butterfly itself while its antennae were fragile wisps of gold. Cissy had bought the piece as a fortieth birthday treat for herself. Twenty years ago when she spotted it in a jewelry store, she simply had to have it, damn the cost. She purchased the brooch on a time payment plan that took three years to pay off. As a ray of sunlight moved a centimeter to the right, it alit on two of the stones, which suddenly sprang to life, overpowering the small diamonds, turning them into a golden hued border for the magical winged creature. The topaz pieces were perfectly matched stones from Brazil, or so the jeweler told Cissy at the time.

Not able to take her eyes away, Julia picked up the intricate piece of workmanship and held it up to the light. "Cissy always said when she looked into the stones she could see the sun. I would laugh but there is a fiery gleam in the center. You shouldn't have done it, Annie. It's a desecration to Cissy's memory."

"Nonsense. Cissy would have appointed us legal guardians of the topaz if she knew her life would end suddenly. She never made out a will, never knew what hit her. Her children are too sentimental sending this magnificent jewel into oblivion. The topaz didn't die, Cissy did." Annie removed her one-carat engagement ring and the small circlet of diamonds that was her wedding ring. She set them next to the brooch.

"What the hell are you doing now?" Julia asked.

"Will you stop being so negative today and look at the play of light? We swore we would never get crotchety, so don't start."

Julia obliged and stared as the gems. She removed her own wide band wedding ring and half-carat ruby stud earrings, adding them to the small pile. The combined reflected radiance was staggering. "Amazing. These gems could hypnotize me." All right, maybe Annie hadn't committed a crime after all. Mining gemstones was grueling, sweaty work so why should they put be back into the earth from whence they came? She replaced her ring and earrings, scolding herself for thinking along Annie's lines, even if it was an innocent momentary slip. She could not condone her friend's action.

"Do you remember what we wanted to do when we were in high school, Julia?"

"How could I forget? We were going to study gemology and travel to South Africa and pluck diamonds from the beaches of Namibia. And after we found diamonds we were going to go to Australia, to search for black opals at Lightning Ridge. If that didn't work out, we were going to become cat burglars. Typical grandiose plans of teenagers with wild imaginations who never have a thought for the consequences."

"We were fascinated by the beauty nature produced millions and millions of years ago. We wanted to capture that beauty for our own."

Julia thought back to those carefree days when every thought of the future was filled with adventure. They made hundreds of exciting plans for their future but the gemstone dream had never really died; pushed far back to the recesses of the mind perhaps but never discarded. "We came to our senses, thank God. We met our future husbands and gave up those silly dreams for marriage, babies and making a home for our families. We lived good lives and our husbands, bless them, left us enough to live comfortably. We should be thankful for that. Neither one of us wanted wealth beyond our imagination and gems represent wealth. We're not materialistic people."

"It I had a hoard of gems I wouldn't sell them. I'd take them out every day and enjoy the play of light and fire. Imagine me running my hands through precious gems and watching them cascade like a sparkling waterfall. Julia, I still have all the notes we wrote back then."

"You saved that old junk?"

"They're somewhere in my attic. I'm going to dig them out. And I still have that old treasure chest I bought at Mr. Lemmer's garage sale when we were seniors in high school."

"You saved that ugly piece of battered tin that wasn't worth the dollar you paid?"

"A beautiful piece of antiquity, Julia. I lined it with black velvet and placed the glass ring I found on the street twenty years ago inside. Now I'll have real gems in the chest."

"Dozens of people we know would recognize Cissy's pin. It was one of a kind."

"Not if I take the stones out of the mountings."

"They're set in eighteen carat gold."

"I'll get rid of the setting."

It was no use admonishing Annie when she was lost in one of her fantasies. Once Annie's fixations took over they could last for days, weeks, even months. She would make one more attempt to bring her back to earth. "What you should do is go back to the cemetery and bury the brooch."

"Really, Julia, do you expect me to go to the cemetery in the dead of night with a shovel and dig Cissy out by the light of the moon? What would be my excuse; that I thought she should be buried with all her worldly goods like a queen in ancient Egypt?"

"I don't mean you have to dig six feet, just a few inches down, somewhere near the headstone so it can be buried near Cissy where it belongs."

"No. Cissy would haunt me if I did something so stupid. She told me that with her thoughts as she lay in her casket."

"The dead can't convey their thoughts."

"Who can prove that? There are people who are extremely receptive to wave lengths of thought and I must be one of them."

"Cissy's brain cells are dead. Even when she was alive they were half dead since that dreadful disease began taking over."

"I know what I heard in my mind. Julia, what happened to our dreams? What happened to us these past two years? Describe what we have now."

"We have grandchildren who look up to us for wisdom." Julie closed her eyes. "And my focus now is babysitting whenever my daughters ask. Being with my grandkids is fun. It is fun isn't it? But I have to admit they get on my nerves a little if they're around more than a full day. That's my fault though. I don't have the stamina I once had. I run out of ideas to keep them amused. Okay, babysitting isn't adventurous and neither is baking for church sales, grocery shopping every Tuesday at ten in the morning like clockwork or crocheting enough coverlets to keep an entire block warm. "But we go to Vegas twice a year."

"And play quarter slot machines like robots. We sit for hours pushing little buttons until our circulation gives out. Sometimes coins fall into the tray but most of the time the machines suck up our money. We turn into crazed, obsessed women in Vegas, miss our flight home and have to take the red eye, which makes us irritable for days afterward."

"We play bingo every Wednesday night and get upset if it's canceled because of a holiday. I don't know why I let you talk me into going in the first place. I hate bingo."

Annie was surprised. "I only started going because you didn't want to go alone. I detest bingo."

"You do? I only suggested it because I thought you enjoyed it. I despise bingo, especially when some woman yells out that the caller should shake the balls. It makes me want to fall through the floor. Such a crude statement."

"We should go back to our original dreams now that our kids are grown and our husbands are gone."

"Oh be sensible, Annie. I don't think we're physically fit to mine in the wilds of Africa. Besides, they have better methods these days. They move tons of earth with heavy machinery to get at a few measly stones and conglomerates have all the gem bearing areas tied up. We would be shot out of the mining area for trespassing or x-rayed to the point of radiation poisoning."

"Mining was plan A but rough stones aren't as pretty as ones that have been cut and polished. We should switch to Plan B and become jewel thieves. We could build up a collection centered around the topaz."

Julia snorted. "Yes, and then we could go on to Plan C and become astronauts, then plan D and study brain surgery and then Plan E and fight oil well fires or join the circus and fall in love with a trapeze artist. Oh God, we did fall in love with a third rate trapeze artist once. We even fought over the fool. I can't believe we were so stupid."

"We were sixteen and at the time he seemed dashing."

"Can you imagine being married to him now? He's probably shoveling elephant manure and we'd be sewing spangles on costumes."

"No, we would be fortune tellers. So are you going to tell anyone what I did today?"

"I should because it was wrong but you're my best friend. I couldn't squeal on you."

"What if I keep on stealing? Would you turn me in?"

"You were caught up in thievery because you couldn't bear to see Cissy's topaz lost forever but that was simply a wild impulse done on the spur of the moment. Of course I'm not going to turn you in."

"I've been thinking about where my life is going ever since Cissy died. My son, daughter-in-law and granddaughter live in Seattle and because they live so far away, I only get to see them two or three times a year. Other than those visits my life is falling in a rut. I want to change that."

"And how would Allan react if he knew his mother was a jewel thief? He would be appalled."

"I'd like to think he'd see the humor in the situation. Allan and I love nothing better than a good laugh." Annie thought back to the time before her son started high school, when he was still young enough to enjoy her company on any adventure. And he enjoyed her company because she was enthusiastic about everything he wanted to try. They white water rafted in Colorado one summer, Jack trying to show signs of encouragement from the riverbank because he was afraid of water, afraid his wife and son would drown. All three of them sky dived the following summer, in tandem with instructors because they didn't have enough hours to jump solo. They shunned beginner runs in Vail because they were too tame. She liked to think Allan gained confidence through her daring, that he wasn't afraid because she never showed signs of fear although there had been times she was afraid. She never feared taking a risk though. Neither did Jack for that matter except for his fear of water. And Julia was the same up until a few years ago. Had she put away her memories of deep sea diving in Mexico, swimming across a raging river to save that damned ugly dog of hers, taking karate lessons at the age of fifty and almost gaining a brown belt? "Didn't Cissy's death prove anything, Julia? Why should we be taken for granted because we've reached our so-called golden years? Where is it written that older women have to be old?"

"I think you're a little drunk from those three Manhattans. You'll come to your senses once the liquor's worn off. Give me your car keys; I'd better drive home."

They stopped in the ladies room before they left. The room was empty. Annie stared at herself critically. "I'd have to stop dying my hair. Everyone would remember a redheaded thief. I'm still kind of trim although my waist has thickened just a little. And my eyelids are beginning to droop a bit but that's only to be expected at my age. All in all, I'm agile enough to make a fast getaway."

"It's time you put an end to flaming red dye anyway. It doesn't suit you. You look like a matronly Raggedy Ann doll, or Bozo's the Clown's girlfriend."

"Well, you should talk. Everyone stares at your blue-gray hair. Your head looks like a silver bullet enhanced under blue neon lights. It's a wonder space aliens don't hone in on the glare."

They were ready to engage in another one of their minor disputes but started laughing instead. "Come on, Annie, I'll take you home and you can lie down with a cool cloth on your head so you don't get a hangover."

Chapter 3

Heavy layers of snow accumulated over Cissy's grave, all traces of her headstone lost until spring thaw. The cemetery was desolate with only a handful of red, artificial bouquets piercing through a field of white. She wasn't forgotten but the blustery frigid weather made short visits to the cemetery impossible. Life went on for Annie and Julia much the same and yet different in some ways. Cissy was always the peacemaker and as weeks passed, the two women found themselves at odds several times.

Whenever Julia came over to Annie's house unexpectedly, Annie would put away the stacks of books she was studying. All of them pertained to gems, minerals or crystals. Whenever Julia spoke of the new hobby, Annie changed the subject adroitly.

They went on vacation to San Diego for two of the coldest weeks in January, lying in the sun, shopping and spending two full days in La Jolla, browsing in quaint shops and eating lunch at colorful outdoor cafes. Imagine that when Chicago and the surrounding suburbs were blanketed in dirty, icy slush. Once they were home, tan and relaxed, life settled into the old routine again. They got together three times a week for lunch or dinner and took in a movie instead of the boring bingo games. However enjoyable the outings were, Annie seemed distracted although she denied it vehemently whenever Julia mentioned it.

Tracy, Julia's oldest daughter, popped in after dinner in early February, bursting into the kitchen like a burgeoning tornado. "Mom, you won't believe the deal Tim and I got on a trip to Fort Lauderdale. The airlines are having another price war and we can both fly for the price of one ticket. And Tim's aunt is letting us use her condo. Seven glorious days in the sun. I was jealous when you called from San Diego but now I'll have my turn."

It felt so good to see your offspring happy and excited. A mother always hoped her children always saw the good side of life and never had to suffer through any tragedies. Losing their father four years ago was bad enough. "That's great, Tracy. Little Lori will love playing in the sand and wading in the sea. Three is a good age for a little girl to get acquainted with the shore. You and Molly loved the beach when you were that age."

"But that's the problem, mom; we can't take her. The condo doesn't allow children. They have some stupid rule barring them because the condo association says kids wreck everything and upset the seniors who own all the condos. You've got to watch Lori, mom. Please say you will. Tim and I haven't been away for longer than one night since before the baby was born."

Well this certainly was a stunner. Julia had never watched Lori for longer than one night before. "I'm not sure I can keep up with her. She's such a spitfire."

"She really won't be any trouble, not now when she's getting into cartoons. You'll hardly know she's around."

Julia sighed. Tracy always had a glib tongue, chattering away a mile a minute so a person couldn't think straight while she was getting her way. "When were you planning on leaving?"

"Tomorrow afternoon."

Julia was taken aback. "You couldn't give me any more notice than that?"

"We didn't hear about the deal until last night so we booked immediately. And Tim had to talk to his aunt."

"I think it would work out better if I came along. I could still watch Lori and stay at a hotel with her but you and Tim would be around in case it got to be too much."

"But the entire idea of a vacation is to get away from responsibilities for a few days. I mean, we'd love to have you but…well, Tim and I were thinking along the lines of a second honeymoon. If daddy was alive he'd say yes in a minute."

Because he wouldn't be the main caretaker, Julia thought. He'd tickle the baby under the chin for a few minutes then leave for the golf course or meet up with his cronies and come home just in time to tuck Lori under the covers. Mel never did take an active part in bringing up his children. When he worked, he had no time and when he retired, he pursued his hobbies relentlessly. Who would have thought such a virile, strong man would succumb to terminal cancer that killed him two months after the diagnosis was made? "I don't know, Tracy."

"Please, mom, I don't ask you for much. It's not like you have anything important coming up."

My life is important, Julia thought. Maybe to everyone else it seems trivial but the older I get the more precious the days become. I never would have dreamed of asking my mother to watch my girls for a week. She would have refused. If I had a little more notice I could accept the idea gracefully. "All right, Tracy, just this once."

Tracy threw her arms around her mother and planted kisses all across her face. "Thank you, thank you. I'll bring Lori over in the morning so I can finish packing."

Dawn hadn't tinged the sky yet when Julia's doorbell rang. It was only five-thirty in the morning and Tracy's plane wasn't leaving until three in the afternoon. Julia hated rising before the sun but put a smile on her face for the baby's sake.

The first day was precious. She had a number of projects planned to keep Lori amused but Lori preferred lying on the couch and watching cartoons. Julia cuddled next to her on the sofa taking in the delightful aroma only a child emits, kissing her round little cheeks, curling tendrils of soft blond hair around her fingers. She worried when the baby only ate a half bowl of soup for dinner. An hour later Lori chucked it up all over herself, the sofa and carpeting. Julia felt her forehead and fetched a thermometer. Lori had a temperature of a hundred and one. Thank God Tracy left the phone number for the condo. She tried calling every hour and finally Tracy answered a little after midnight. There was more than a tinge of worry in Julia's voice. "Lori's listless and has a temperature. She can't keep anything down."

Tracy must have had a few too many drinks because she had the audacity to giggle. "Don't get all up in arms, mom. Just give her baby aspirin. I put some in her suitcase."

"You knew she was coming down with something and left anyway?"

"It's only the sniffles. She'll be fine in the morning."

"What is she throws up the aspirin?"

"She won't. Will you stop overemphasizing? Got to go, mom. Tim's waiting on the beach. We're going for a moonlight stroll."

It was four days before Lori was herself again and that was only because Julia had taken her to the pediatrician for an antibiotic. She tried calling Annie several times to see if Annie wanted to keep her company but there was no answer four days running. How strange. She intended calling again in the evenings but fell asleep with Lori every single night. Did Annie get an emergency call from Seattle and fly out there on the spur of the moment? But she would have called if that were the case. Something terrible must have happened if she flew out west without calling. Another thing to worry over.

The last thing on Annie's mind was babysitting or talking to Julia. She couldn't think of anything except her mission and it made her a nervous wreck. Talking about doing a deed and actually doing it were two different scenarios. But she had made a promise to herself and intended keeping it. If she didn't, she knew she would lose her drive for the different and daring in life. Time to get into action or sit back and turn into an old lady. She couldn't call Julia and tell her she was about to dabble in crime. Julia would only try to stop her.

It was the seven longest days of Julia's life. She loved all three of her grandchildren with all her heart but at the end of seven days she was at wit's end. Lori had cried almost the entire last day for her mommy and daddy and nothing would calm her hysteria. The whines continued, drumming into her head until she had a raging headache. She practically shoved everyone out the door at six that evening when Tracy and Tim returned, desperately needing a nap

At nine, her other daughter Molly called. "Mom, you remember that I'm leaving for the three day seminar in Atlanta tomorrow."

Julia stifled a yawn. "I remember. Have a good time, hon; see you when you get back."

"I tried calling earlier but there was no answer."

"I took a little snooze. Must have been out like a light if I didn't hear the phone ring."

"The company announced today that some of us could bring spouses along. An entire department canceled out and they had extra plane tickets. Derek is excited about going so I thought you could watch the boys. It's only for three days."

"Molly, I haven't recuperated from taking care of Lori. She was sick and kept waking up all hours of the night. I'm exhausted."

"You did it for Tracy so why can't you do the same for me? My sons are older and practically take care of themselves. Grandmothers are supposed to love babysitting."

Julia groaned. Where was her gumption? She had absolutely no qualms about speaking out her mind to anyone else so why couldn't she do it with her daughters? Even before these two unexpected trips they had been demanding more and more of her time. It was now up to two or three evenings a week, some overnighters. Her grandchildren were becoming fixtures in the house. Where was her life heading?

For the entire three days the boys were bored…bored with everything she suggested. They hated the movies she rented, hated the ice skating rink, which was brand new and had every modern convenience, hated what she cooked, hated being forced to bed at ten. Both boys, who were normally little angels, turned into obnoxious little brats right before her eyes.

After those ten grueling days Julia slept for fourteen hours straight before she felt up to par. She had talked to Annie on the phone the other night but with the bickering going on between her grandsons, trying to hold a normal conversation was impossible.

She dressed and got in her car to have lunch at Annie's. Damn, the tank was empty. She prayed all the way to the Mobil station that she wouldn't run out of gas. "Fill it up, Murph," she told the owner."

"Shouldn't be out driving in weather like this, Mrs. Devlin. Lots of slippery patches below the snow. Women your age should be sitting by a nice cozy fire reading a book."

This was the last straw. "I'm a damned good driver, Murph, better than most of the twenty year olds around here. I've never been involved in an accident and I don't have any tickets on my record. I'm far from being a senile, old lady."

His face turned crimson. "Didn't mean nothing by that remark, Mrs. Devlin, just thought you'd be more comfortable staying home on a miserable day like this and have your girls run errands for you."

"I can do nicely by myself, thank you." She wanted to burn rubber pulling away but it was treacherous in spots.

She hugged Annie tightly after taking off her coat. "God, it's good to see you. I don't think we ever missed seeing each other for ten days straight in our entire lives. I called a few times but you were never home. Did you go to Seattle?"

"Lord, no. I was shopping at some of the outlying malls. Drove to a different one six days in a row and got home late every night."

"But we have excellent malls here. Why did you drive so far, especially in the weather we've been having? What did you buy? Let me see."

"I just browsed."

"All that way to window shop? It must have taken you hours with the snow we've had lately. You must have a bad case of cabin fever."

"Come in the kitchen, I have coffee and apple pie."

"How marvelous to be served. I'm so tired of cooking and cleaning up the mess afterward I could spit."

Annie thought Julia was walking directly behind her but she came into the kitchen a minute later carrying the treasure chest. "Saw this old thing on top of your china cabinet. I'd like to see the topaz again. It might bring a little sunshine in on a gloomy day. I hate overcast skies."

Annie yanked the chest away. Sit down, I'll take the stones out."

"Annie, what's wrong with you? I'm perfectly capable of opening the box myself."

"You didn't want to get involved. What you don't know won't agitate you."

"Why would I get agitated? Oh my God, have you started? Please tell me, Annie. We've never had secrets."

"You'd only disapprove."

How could Annie not blurt everything out immediately? They always did that, always. Maybe she had been too stern over Cissy's topaz. "I swear I won't. Annie, we're best friends. We've never kept anything from each other, not since we met in grammar school. I swear I won't say one negative word."

Annie handed over the chest then poured coffee.

"Oh my," Julia cried out after opening the box. She took out a diamond tennis bracelet."

"The diamonds are small, only one carat total weight. The bracelet was selling for three hundred dollars so the stones must be poor quality."

"Did you…?"

"Yes."

"How? How did you manage? Where?"

"I'm starting out small as you can see."

Julia was overcome with surprise, barely able to believe Annie was treading dangerous ground without her. "Tell me everything."

"I went to various malls for six days. At the first there was a costume jewelry outlet and I bought a big bag of fake costume jewelry."

Julia fingered the bracelet. "Then is this real or not? Maybe it's better if you fill the box with glittery fakes. But you said three hundred."

"The bracelet is real enough. The next day I drove out to the big mall near Quincy. I went to the jewelry counter at one of those discount stores where it's always crowded and I asked the clerk to show me the tray of tennis bracelets and when she was distracted, I substituted a fake for the real one. Another customer was clamoring for attention so the clerk didn't pay much attention when I said I wouldn't be buying after all. The tray was still full when she returned it to the case and that was all that mattered."

"Annie, what if she remembers you? I'm not being negative I'm only trying to help. They might have discovered the fake by now and give out your description."

"I was in disguise."

"How clever. What did you wear?"

"I also bought a bunch of clothes and wigs that first day, in various thrift stores, the kind I normally wouldn't wear. I was a peroxide blond bitch with false eyelashes, ruby lips, heavily rouged cheeks and wearing a flamboyant red coat. They say when you're in disguise you should always have a focal point, something witnesses will remember vividly. But it can't be part of the real you or you'll blow your cover. The red coat and heavy makeup were my focal points."

"I wish I could have seen you." Annie peered down into the box again. "Oh, I almost missed this ring with a yellow stone."

"Citrine, with a four hundred price tag but it does sparkle nicely doesn't it? Another mall, another crowded store. There's a half-carat diamond stud earring in there too. I must have dropped the other one. Julia, I have to confess I was nervous substituting fakes for real but I think I'm over that now. I went to a few other malls but the right opportunity didn't present itself. I made a rule that I wouldn't take unnecessary chances just for the thrill of adding a jewel to my collection. If I don't feel confident, I'll back off."

"You've actually made a beginning, an opening move. I think I'm proud of you. You ventured where eagles fear to fly. Is that how that old saying goes?"

"I suppose you're going to try and talk me out of what I'm doing at every opportunity now that you know what I've done."

"No, I promise. If what you're doing makes you happy then carry on." Julia laughed. "And if you get caught I promise I'll visit you every other day in jail."

"I will **not** go to jail. By the way, I'm going to have to back out on our Vegas trip in March."

"You can't, we always go twice a year."

"We've been there six times and six times we lost most of our money. I'm going to fly to New York instead."

"Another heist?"

"New York is big time and I'm not ready for that. I'm going to walk the diamond district, to get a feel for quality and quantity. Millions and millions of dollars worth of gems are on that block and overlapping into the adjacent streets. Half the diamonds mined in the world wind up in New York. It's an expensive city and I don't want to dig too deep into my nest egg for two trips in one month."

"I could go to New York with you. I've never been there."

"You'd hamper my style. I mean I'd love having you along, Julia, but I'm not going there to sightsee or shop. I'll be too busy taking in the layout so to speak."

"I understand, really I do. You can tell me about the Big Apple when you get back."

Julia was depressed driving home. She would love to see New York. While Annie was checking out 47th Street she was capable of sightseeing on her own. She wouldn't be a hindrance or curb her style in any way. And Annie couldn't walk the streets at night. They could see a hit show or have elegant dinners in the evening, even discuss what Annie had seen and planned. It was unthinkable that they were growing apart instead of bonding more firmly than ever now that it was just the two of them. Are my feelings hurt? Damned right they are. Annie had a new, exciting project even if it was criminal and here she was losing her identity day by day.

Chapter 4

Julia wasn't in the house five minutes after seeing a movie with Annie the following week when Tracy called. "Mom, Molly and I have to go out to dinner Friday. The guys are going bowling so it would be a perfect time for us to get together for some girl talk. We'll make it easier and bring the kids to your house."

They don't even have the courtesy to ask anymore, Julia mourned. Don't they think I'd like to be included in their get-togethers? I'm being treated like a servant, a doormat. This has to stop before it snowballs into one request piling atop another until I'm buried in other lives and lose my own. "No," she answered bluntly.

There was shocked silence on the other end. "No? Why? You'll be home anyway."

"I will not. Annie and I have started taking classes and we plan to travel more. And we've joined several clubs so I won't have much free time. And you can tell your sister I'll only baby sit once a week, all three kids at once so you'd better coordinate. And that's only when I won't have other plans."

Mom!"

"And I'll need two weeks advance notice when I do babysit."

"I can't believe I'm hearing this."

"That's a definite, Tracy. You and your sister can both hire babysitters the rest of the time. You gad around far too often for mothers of young children. Think back and you'll remember neither of your grandmothers were at my beck and call; they were too busy. You're probably itching to call Molly and tell her I'm off my rocker for not wanting my grandkids around night and day but let me assure you I'm perfectly sane. I have miles to go before I sleep, Tracy. Keep that in mind."

Julia felt invigorated after she hung up and turned on a cassette of Latin music. About time I took a stand. I'm free; free to soar. But where do I soar? I didn't join any new clubs, didn't register for classes, don't have any travel plans. She picked up the phone again. "Annie? Count me in amigo, whole hog, all the way, till death doth part us from our dreams."

"You're absolutely sure?"

"Never surer of anything in my life. Call the travel agency and get me on your plane. What else do I have to do?"

"Call the Hair Net tomorrow and get us two appointments. We're going to do something about red and blue hair."

"It's as good as done."

"And get your ass up to your attic and start digging out all the old costumes you've saved over the years so we can see if we'll need anything."

"Even the harem garb?"

"You don't have to bother with those. We're not going to walk the streets of New York dressed as concubines. Julia, I'm so excited that you want in."

"I'm excited, nervous and scared silly but still looking forward to tomorrow and the day after that and the week and months after that. I'm so happy I want to sing. Hell, if I want to sing I will."

Annie held the phone away from her ear as Julia burst into Happy Days Are Here Again. Thank God Julia never wanted to pursue a singing career. Her voice even made the neighbor's dog cower under the bed.

Chapter 5

"Why are you smirking?" Annie asked as she and Julia waited to board their flight to LaGuardia.

"Even after two weeks I can't get used to your new look. I know the red hair had to go, thank God, but that tight, frizzy mop makes you look exactly like thousands of other golden agers who insist their perms last at least six months to a year. Identically coifed women are on all the tour busses, at bingo, eating at low priced buffet restaurants. I think you'd look younger if you reverted back to your original brunette shade or maybe just a shade lighter."

"Later. Right now I want to look like thousands of other seniors. I want to blend in with a crowd, become invisible so to speak and what better way to disappear in a crowd to look like everyone else. I have to admit you look much better with medium ash brown hair. I don't think of you as Captain Nemo any more."

"He had dark hair."

"Whatever, but whenever I saw that blue tint I thought of Captain Nemo or Darth Vadar. Only someone from another planet would be acceptable with a silvery blue head."

"Annie!"

"Sorry. They're calling our flight. This is it, Julia, your last chance to reconsider. If you want to back out, do it now."

"Are you backing down? Not me. I've never been so excited about anything in all my life. I wake up in the mornings raring to go, fall asleep with plans running through my head. Some I reject, others I cultivate. Our gem collection will be a small and silent protest against the DeBeers monopoly. Don't ask me what they have to do with my feeling but I've just discovered I don't like monopolies and they've been controlling diamonds for a long, long time."

"I hardly think we'll be stealing thousands of carats or causing a worldwide shortage."

"Annie, what if by some slight infinitesimal chance we get caught; I mean just the tiniest of chances? If we're put in jail do you think those fierce women there, I think they're called dykes, will try to molest us?"

Annie laughed until tears streamed from her eyes. "I honestly don't think they'd be interested in us except in a grandmotherly way. And if they decided they lusted after older women, my advice would be to pick the toughest one of the lot and leave everything else to fate. On the other hand, think of some of the interesting stories we'd hear; tales of abuse, seduction, betrayal, misplaced justice. It would be ten times better than a soap opera. Anyway, we're not going to get caught. That's another one of my gut feelings."

"Actually I feel the same. In fact, I feel invincible. Annie, if an opportunity presents itself in New York we will take advantage of it won't we?"

"Thank God you're back to your old normal self again. I was beginning to lose hope thinking you were ready for a rocking chair and daily doses of fiber in your diet to keep you regular. Yes, if an opportunity comes our way we'll go for it but don't get your hopes up this soon. We're still novices at the game."

"My quality of life has improved tremendously since I made the monumental decision to join forces with you. Seeing my grandchildren only once a week makes me appreciate them more. I took a stand and Molly and Tracy know I mean business. I have my life back again, Annie. I don't know how it got away from me in the first place."

"No talking about thievery once we're on the plane. You never know if someone's eavesdropping."

"I know that. Annie, give me credit for having a very intuitive and devious mind. You have to admit that some of the plans I've come up with are brilliant, past and present. Wasn't I the one who got Otto Baldwin to confess he was filching a few dollars from the collection basket in church?"

"Don't start me laughing again or I'll pee in my pants. Only you would stand outside his bedroom window in the dead of night during a blizzard and pretend you were the ghost of Christmas past."

"And remember when Mel started flirting with that floozy he worked with? I nipped that in the bud."

"By saying you just happened to see a positive herpes test result on the woman while you were at the doctor's office."

"He barely spoke to her after that. I don't think Mel ever cheated on me but male menopause was causing a roving eye. I had to do something to remind him he was a married man."

They settled into their room at the Rhiga Royal Hotel on West 54th and walked over to 47th Street since the weather was almost balmy. "It's certainly a bustling area," Julia remarked. "And look at all the men with dark coats, hats and fetlocks."

"What?"

"Fetlocks, those curls hanging down around their ears."

"Peyes, Julia. I think fetlocks have something to do with horses."

"Well, you studied Hasidic diamond dealers, I studied diamonds. All the important dealings are conducted on the upper floors behind tight security. Street level is strictly for tourists."

"And that's exactly what we are, tourists. We'll just walk along very slowly and browse…and keep our eyes and ears open. You never know what we might pick up." They stopped at each store window for at least ten minutes admiring the array of gems for sale.

"A feast for the eyes," Julia purred. "I can almost feel them running through my hands." They crossed the street and would have been perfectly content window shopping for the rest of the afternoon if it wasn't for the hawkers trying to entice them into stores.

"Best price on the street," one man cried.

"Go to Bergman's," another said. "He buys for less therefore sells for less."

"I can get you a good discount at Brookman's," another chimed in. He handed them a card. "Just mention my name and you'll automatically get twenty percent off."

Annie tried to maintain a polite smile. "I'm really getting annoyed with all this bullshit."

They ignored most of the sales pitches and found themselves standing in front of a window displaying trays of emeralds, sapphires and rubies, along with diamonds naturally. "Don't look now, Annie, but some strange looking little man has been watching us for the past ten minutes or so."

"Where is he?"

"Look in the mirror in the display. You can see him standing across the street, by the lamppost. He's wearing a long black coat and hat but he doesn't have those curlicues. I saw another man walk up to him and try to talk but he brushed him off and kept staring at us. Annie, he's crossing the street, right in our direction."

Annie stared into the mirror. "My God, he took his hat off. Is he wearing a fright wig or is that his natural hair? If he comes near us I'm really going to be pissed. We've had enough sales pitches for one day."

"I'll handle it. I'm very good at cutting obnoxious people dead."

The obviously nervous man bounced from one foot to another as he stood before them, his eyes darting up, down, left, right. Was he a crook looking to see if the police were nearby or was he simply a twitcher? Words shot out of his mouth in a sharp staccato; harmless bullets of sound shooting through the air. Several expressions crossed his face as though he was auditioning for a silent movie; hope, anxiety, fear, joy. "I can tell you ladies won't settle for anything less than a colossal bargain but you won't find any bargains in these stores. Oy, the mark up you wouldn't believe. If you deal with an honest man on the street, like me, you'll be amazed at how low I can go. You'll be the envy of all your friends, the talk of your social set. I have the very thing for two attractive ladies; one carat white diamonds, flawless to the naked eye. Technically they're white VVS. Five hundred dollars each. With the right setting, they'll dazzle the eye. Or you can buy two and have perfectly matched earrings. Three I have left, the others were snapped up almost before I could take them from my pocket."

Julia gave him one of her imperious glares. "We're not interested in buying diamonds from a street seller."

"Ah, women who prefer gems of color perhaps? I knew it, knew you prefer something unique. I was saving them for another customer but the worm an early bird catches. So I show you two Colombian emeralds instead. Grass green, slightly over one carat each."

"Can you look into their depths and see the future?" Julia asked.

The man's hands flew above his head and then he clutched his heart. "What? What? A prophet I'm not. I sell gems."

"Will they blind snakes like the legends say? Will they make me an eloquent speaker, quench the passion that threatens to overwhelm me night and day? Will they bring harmony into my chaotic life?"

"I get it; a kibbitzer. Okay, okay, no interest in emeralds. Sapphires, that's it. You must be looking for sapphires. I don't have any on me but a couple I can get if you give me ten minutes."

Annie was getting tired of his spiel. "Okay, we want a diamond."

"Good, good. We're in business because I have just what you're looking for."

"D loupe flawless, twenty carat, brilliant cut."

His eyes almost popped out of their sockets, his mouth hung open as he spun once and came to a halt. "Oy, the lady doesn't want a diamond she wants a miracle."

"If you have one on you we'll purchase it immediately. Money is no object."

"A stone that size doesn't appear on the street like a bagel from a street vendor."

"Then fuck off, you little runt, before I scream." Annie tried to keep a straight face as his arms flapped wildly; a prelude to liftoff?

"Okay, okay, I'm gone." He scurried off. "Meshuggeneh," he muttered to himself as he sped down the street. "Crazies." He stopped at the corner and looked back. There was something about those two. Did he like the feeling that swept over him or was it a dire warning that he would have the misfortune to meet them again. "Dybbuk," he pleaded, "more trouble I need like a hole in the head."

Julia started giggling. "You shocked the hell out of him."

"It'll make his day but I forgot one of my rules in the heat of the moment. He won't forget me. I should have politely told him no and ended the conversation quietly. It's time we left the district. We'll come back tomorrow dressed differently."

Chapter 6

Instead of returning to 47th Street the following day, they strolled along Fifth Avenue stopping to study gems in the windows of internationally known jewelry stores. Walking into Tiffany's, they were greeted by a cold-eyed, snotty bitch dressed in black from head to toe who watched them like a hawk as they went from one display case to another. The salesmen weren't much better no matter how coyly Julia smiled. "They wouldn't be so smug if we walked off with a good portion of their inventory," Julia whispered.

"Not yet, Julia, but perhaps some day."

On the third day, they returned to the diamond district dressed in polyester pantsuits, flat shoes and modified bee hive wigs. Their objective was to study the side streets that branched off 47th where the diamond flow had spread in recent years. They were about to return to 47th when they spotted the odd little man who tried to sell them diamonds talking to three women and a man, obviously tourists who were avidly listening to his spiel. "He probably wouldn't recognize me in this get up but it's better not to take chances," Annie said as she pulled Julia back. "Let's call it a day and visit Ellis Island or the Empire State Building."

On their fifth day, they sat in a small crowded coffeehouse in the district. "I think we've seen all there is to see," Annie remarked. "We can't get into the upper floors where all the wheeling and dealing takes place and we certainly can't gain admittance into the Diamond Dealers Club. You have to be a member and no one can sneak in.

Their security cameras are top notch and they have more locked doors than a maximum security prison. But we did get the feel of things while we were here didn't we? I have a better understanding of the business now. Let's go get some coffee."

"That odd little man never came near us again. He never recognized us in our disguises because we must be artists in that area." Julia stopped talking and motioned for Annie to be quiet as she cocked her head to hear every word a man in the next booth was saying.

"Look, there's Tsvi Frenzel, the Israeli macher. Insolent momzer. He's got old Holdheim on the verge of apoplexy, teasing him with flawless two carat pinks. A dozen dealers would sell their souls for them but Holdheim would sell his mother. Frenzel's going to leave him hanging until tomorrow, just before he leaves for Israel and Holdheim will have a nervous breakdown before then thinking Shermer will wind up with the pinks. See how Frenzel looks down on everyone else because he had the good fortune to get his hands on a thirty carat blue last year. The sale made him a millionaire, not that he wasn't one before the blue fell into his greedy hands. Bloom said he thinks Frenzel brought something special with him again this trip."

"Another blue?"

"Could be."

Julia threw money on the table. "Hurry," she whispered as she got up to leave.

"What were they saying?" Annie asked. "I only heard a word or two, something about pinks."

"We have to follow that man standing by the curb. This could be our golden opportunity." Julia repeated every word she heard as they watched the Israeli dealer walk down 47th, nodding or saying a few words to other Hasidic dealers. He appeared to be in his fifties with salt and pepper hair and a neatly trimmed beard. The quality of his black suit and hat was richer then the others on the street.

Annie was puzzled. "I'm not sure if he's Hasidic. His suit is black like the others but it looks very expensive and well cut. It could be an Armani. And look how he wears his topcoat thrown over his shoulders, like an old time Italian don. I'll bet he acquired that look from watching the Godfather. Do you remember the corrupt don young Corleone killed because he was demanding too much protection money from his fellow immigrants?"

"I guess every nationality has their egotists."

"Look," Annie said. "His right hand just went up to his left breast pocket. That's where he must have the diamonds stashed. That's the third time I've seen him do that."

Julia stopped suddenly. "I saw him before. Yes, at our hotel. Annie, he must be staying on our floor. He came out of the room next to the elevator on Wednesday morning. He glanced our way and I thought he would hold the elevator for us but he didn't and the door practically slammed in our faces. I thought that extremely rude; sticking his nose up in the air and pretending we weren't there. He deserves to be robbed for his lack of common courtesy."

"I didn't pay much attention so I don't remember his face."

"Well, I saw and that's him. Forget following him, we have to get back to the hotel before him. He leaves for Israel tomorrow and evidently he's keeping some guy on the hook until then."

"I'm sure he doesn't leave himself open to attack but we do have the element of surprise working in our favor if we work fast."

Julia waved down a taxi. "He just walked into that restaurant with another man. That means we have time to prepare, just in case the window of opportunity opens. But what if he puts the diamonds in the hotel safe?"

"Not many people trust those safes because clever thieves can get at them. But if he does, all we've lost is time." Their adrenalin was flowing.

"I'm so excited," Julia said.

"From this point on we stay cool."

Julia stood at the window looking down at the street through a pair of binoculars while Annie finished her disguise. "It's him. He's getting out of a taxi. Naturally he wouldn't walk, not with diamonds on him. He practically threw money at the driver. If he wants to be treated like royalty he should have hired a limo."

"Okay, if he's not upstairs directly it must mean he's putting the diamonds in the hotel safe. In that case we call it off. I think we have everything we need."

They opened the door a few inches and peered down the hall toward the elevators. After another minute there was a distinctive ping as the elevator stopped on the tenth floor. "Move when he closes his door," Julia said quietly. "I'll be sixty seconds behind you."

Annie's face was tinged dark olive, her cheeks rounded with puffs of cotton she had stuffed inside her mouth. Thick heavy gauge stockings were padded as was the middle of the black uniform jacket she wore. Long, black bangs hung beyond her eyes and partially covered the tinted glasses she wore. The black hair ended in a thick bun at the nape of her neck. As soon as she heard Frenzel's door click shut, she hurried down the hall carrying a tray covered with a napkin. Balancing it with one hand she knocked.

"What is it?" Frenzel asked with annoyance."

"Room service."

"I ordered nothing. You have the wrong room."

"From a Mr. Holdheim to be sure," Annie said with a thick Irish brogue. "And didn't he say I was to deliver the treat to his good friend personally?"

There was a burst of laughter and the door opened. "So Holdheim thinks he can bribe me with delicacies. He'll learn he's wrong."

"Excuse me, sir?"

"Never mind, put it on the table." He was impatient for her to leave.

Annie laid down the tray. At that moment Julia walked in holding a blood-stained towel to her face. She wore a billowing silk robe and a cascade of copper curls hung down her back. "Help," she cried. "Somebody please help me." She swayed as she came closer to Frenzel and just as she appeared about to fall he reached out his arms. Julia kicked out in her most practiced karate move hitting him hard in the groin. Haven't done that in a few years, she thought. Can't kick as high as I used to. Before Frenzel could clutch his crotch, Annie slipped a pair of handcuffs she had pulled off the tray around his right wrist, clamping the other end to the bedpost. Julia yanked the other arm back with a painful twist and did the same with a similar pair of cuffs she had enfolded in the towel. Fortunately they had brought the handcuffs to New York along with old clothes and other miscellaneous paraphernalia. The handcuffs were from the time she and Mel were prisoner and bounty hunter at a Halloween party. In a matter of seconds, Annie pressed duct tape over Frenzel's eyes. The last thing he saw when he looked up was a dark wart near his assailant's nose. The wave of pain began subsiding but only a little. He wanted to double over but couldn't because he was secured in an upright position. Pain or not he tried to kick out with his leg but couldn't. Before he could cry out, another wad of tape was slapped across his mouth.

Julia reached into his breast pocket and pulled out a square of folded paper. She raised her hand in a victory sign. Annie patted the other inner pocket and pulled out another packet. Frenzel was struggling to stand and free himself from the cuffs. The bedpost shook alarmingly. A few more strong tugs and he would crack it.

Annie wiped off the tray quickly while Julia took care of the door knob. Suddenly Julia stopped and whispered in Annie's ear. "Can tape carry legible prints?"

Annie shrugged her shoulders. She didn't think so and she had been careful to grasp only the edges of the tape. In any case, it was too late to think about that now. If she pulled the tape off Frenzel's eyes he would get a better look at them. If she pulled it away from his mouth he would yell. "Mazel und brucha," she said in a gruff voice before opening the door and peering down the hall. It was the traditional Jewish conclusion to a successful deal. The hall was empty. They had devised an alternate plan if guests or hotel workers in the hall. Julia simply would have kicked Frenzel again and they would wait until the coast was clear. Julia gave the knob another swipe with her robe and they scurried back to their room on winged feet.

Once they were locked safely inside their room they worked without talking. Julia went directly to the bathroom and began cutting up the wigs, flushing hair and netting down the toilet. Annie threw her foam padding on the floor and Julia began hacking at that. Thank God hotels have first class flushing systems, Julia thought as she worked the scissors at a furious pace. Annie had left the thrift store uniform jacket in Frenzel's room. She only wore a t-shirt beneath that held the padding in place and a black skirt when she left. She hung the skirt in the closet where it matched a beaded jacket. Next she popped the tinted lenses out of the glasses and replaced them with clear glass, putting the tinted glass inside a wash cloth and smashing it down with the heel of her shoe. The shattered glass was thrown into the toilet. While Julia continued cutting Annie stepped into the shower and washed away all traces of dark makeup covering her face, neck and hands. The ugly wart dissolved and went down the drain like a dead cockroach.

Not even stopping to inspect the contents of the two briefkes, Annie opened them and let the contents drop into a bowl of vegetable soup room service had brought up earlier. None of the food they ordered had been touched; soup, a club sandwich along with a pot of coffee and two cups. The tray they left in Frenzel's room had been taken from another floor earlier. It had been set outside a guest's door and they simply removed the dishes and claimed the tray as a necessary burglary prop. If Frenzel had lifted the napkin he would have found a ball of cheese and crackers they had bought at a small market the previous day for a late night snack. Julia's towel had also been left in Frenzel's room, not bloodied but saturated with ketsup from a plastic dispenser. If any hairs clung to the towel they would be red and curly. Annie took out another pair of smaller scissors and helped Julia snip. “I hope this doesn’t clog up the plumbing system.”

“Cut as small as you can but it should be okay. This toilet has the power of a whirlpool.”

The last thing Julia cut was the voluminous filmy robe. Loud voices could be heard in the hall along with running feet. Frenzel’s outraged roar rose above the other voices. Julia and Annie put their ears to the door.

“Two women,” Frenzel shouted, “one dark and fat with black hair and an ugly wart near her nose. She spoke with an Irish accent. I only saw red curly hair on the other before I was kicked. She was tall, six feet or more.”

Could they have been men dressed as women?” another voice asked.”

“Yes, of course. They must have been men because they were too strong to be women. I was a fighter in Israeli wars and could easily have subdued two women. They might have been IRA. Bastards are always stealing to further their cause.”

“Please come back into your room, Mr. Frenzel, or we’ll have other guests milling around the hall gawking and creating a three ring circus.”

“They took me by surprise. I could have snapped their necks if…”

“We’ll get to the bottom of this.”

“He called you fat and ugly,” Julia said, outraged.

“And so I was.”

“And how could he say I was six feet tall? I’m only five feet eight inches.”

“He was looking up from a crunched position so you must have looked like a giant.”

A half hour later there was a knock on their door. Julia settled herself in bed atop the coverlet holding a half eaten sandwich in her hand. The television was on covering the evening news. Annie walked over to the table, dipped a spoon in the soup and carried it with her to answer the door. "Who is it?" she asked sweetly.

"Police."

"Oh dear." She left the chain on and opened the door an inch. "Can you show me some identification? My son warned me to be cautious in New York." Satisfied it was really the police, she unlatched the chain. "Sorry, but strange cities make me nervous."

"You did the right thing," the officer said. "Better to be safe than sorry."

Annie went back to the table and placed the spoon in the bowl of soup. She picked up a cup half filled with cold coffee and took a sip. "Why are you here?"

"Did either of you hear or see anything unusual in the hall earlier?"

Annie paused to think. "No, but my friend had the television on and I was soaking in a hot tub for at least thirty minutes. We must have walked ten miles today, sightseeing, shopping. My feet are throbbing."

Julia went over to the table and put down her sandwich. "Did something terrible happen?"

Always keep hotel guests calm and never tell them the entire truth, Officer Dankin reminded himself. "There was an incident in another room down the hall."

"Annie, I told you New York isn't safe. We should have gone to Vegas like we planned. It's sin city but the security at the Mirage is first rate." She turned to the officer. "What exactly happened? Was someone murdered?"

"No, ma'am, nothing that serious."

"If you won't tell us, it must be serious. We have theater tickets for tonight. Will it be safe to leave this room?"

"Perfectly safe. You didn't see or hear anything?"

"Neither of us left the room when we got back late this afternoon. We were too exhausted. And all I heard were sirens, probably from a fire truck, and some horns honking."

"Sorry to disturb you. Enjoy your stay."

"I'm not sure we can if crimes are committed right here in the hotel. Do you swear it wasn't a murder?"

"I swear. I doubt the intruders will be back but keep your door dead bolted tonight."

They waited another thirty minutes before picking gemstones out of the soup and placing them on a napkin. Julia put her fingers into the bowl and squeezed vegetables to make certain no gems were left behind. "Look at the dazzle, Annie. But we'll still have to give them a proper washing when we get home."

There were forty diamonds on the napkin, thirty nine actually along with a red stone. "I'd say they're two carats each and the larger red stone must be a ruby," Annie said after holding it to the light. "I thought that man at the restaurant said pinks. These are all white."

Julia giggled. "Maybe he was wearing rose colored glasses." She brought out a large tube of toothpaste and began stuffing the gems inside, poking them down deep with a letter opener. She washed the opener in the bathroom before replacing it in her purse. "We should get dressed. Those tickets were expensive."

The hall was quiet and deserted when they left. They never noticed the little man from 47th Street following them.

It was after midnight when they returned after enjoying the famed musical and a late snack. Julia walked up to the desk clerk. "We're a little leery about going up to our room alone. A policeman told us there was an incident on our floor earlier."

The clerk was most solicitous. "I'll have one of our security guards accompany you."

"Tell him he'll have to check every possible hiding place before we bolt the door." She leaned closer and whispered. "Was someone murdered in the hotel?"

"No, ma'am."

"Then at least tell us what happened so we don't spend the entire night imagining strange noises."

"A guest had some articles stolen from his room."

"How frightening. Annie, I don't think I'll be able to sleep tonight. I can't wait to get home."

Velvel Chavivi ducked back behind a pillar rubbing his hands in glee. This was far better than the play, which he didn't enjoy, not to mention that the price of his ticket was horrendously high even though he sat in the balcony.

Chapter 7

For the exorbitant prices the hotel charged, Julia insisted they stay until the last moment before checking out. An Iranian cab driver got them to LaGuardia fifteen minutes before departure, which was barely enough time to check and in and run down the terminal to their gate. Out of breath, they found a man sitting in the center of their row of seats. A wide brimmed hat hid his face as he slumped in his seat. "Do you mind moving over so we can sit together?" Julia asked. There was no response. "Excuse me, but you're supposed to be at the window."

Velvel Chavivi pushed up his hat, eyes twinkling with mischief as he grinned impishly. "The two lovely ladies wanting a big diamond. So we meet again. God, do they not look much better today? Such an improvement over baggy clothes and foolish wigs, although you did look beautiful at the theater. Sit, you should sit. The flight attendants are glaring, the engines humming and we're ready to fly like a much too heavy bird."

"Why are you on this plane?" Annie questioned angrily after crawling over him and buckling in. The last thing she wanted was a scene on a crowded plane so she tried to keep her voice low.

"Why? Funny you should ask. Because this is America and I happen to be flying to Chicago. Nervous I get on airplanes so if we talk, time will fly just as we fly. Since disaster is my best friend, I always fear the plane will go into a tailspin and we'll hit the ground with a big boom or lose a wing or engine. And I never sit by the window because it might pop and into the jet stream I would be sucked, just like a vacuum cleaner picking up dust."

"That's just dandy. I've always wanted to be on a plane with a born loser," Annie said sarcastically. "Look, we're not going to buy your diamonds. They're probably cubic zirconias."

Velvel held his chest, as though to keep his heart from popping out with indignation. "A dishonest dealer I'm not. When I say I have a one-carat diamond without flaws to the naked eye, I mean exactly that. Ask anyone on 47th and they'll tell you I'm an honest man."

"Since we're headed in the opposite direction you know we can't do that."

"True, true but may a fire burn my heart if I lie, God forbid. I'm going to Chicago to negotiate not sell. I am Vel."

"How unusual. What's the full name; Velcro, Velveeta, velcome?"

He broke out in peals of laughter. "A sense of humor. No greater asset can a woman have than a sense of humor. The full name is Velvel Chavivi, seller of precious gems. My card; one for each of you." He handed them business cards with a theatrical flourish.

"I have a feeling this is going to be a flight from hell," Julia muttered. "You followed us to the theater?"

"I did that. I saw you coming out of the hotel where a certain Israeli was kicked in an unmentionable place and noticed smirks on your faces, like cats who swallowed canaries. Why a cat would swallow a whole canary I don't know. Better they should say a cat that swallowed sweet cream. Anyhow, I had a feeling it would be worth my while to keep both eyes on you. A robbery took place at the hotel but the thieves were sloppy. Feh, I should keep the mouth shut before I bore you."

"On the contrary, do go on," Annie insisted. "We lead such quiet, mundane lives. You're beginning to pique my interest with this cloak and dagger mystery."

Velvel smiled smugly. "Happen to know one of the cops on duty who told me what went down. Seems two ugly bruisers robbed a fellow dealer from Israel, big ugly bruisers who disguised themselves as women. At first Frenzel thought they might be connected with Irish terrorists but later changed his story. One of the thieves gave the traditional Jewish good luck and blessing words just before he fled. You are enjoying this?"

"Immensely."

"Now the sloppy part. The crooks only got half the goods. Frenzel had two more briefkes of pinks taped to his chest. Normally a dealer chains them to his wrist but who am I to say how he should conduct business?"

"Pinks? Sorry I don't follow you."

"Pink diamonds, Australian pinks, all approximately two carats each. Professionals they weren't. Professionals would have known Frenzel's full inventory before they attacked. They would have tortured him for the rest once they had him subdued."

"Poor man. I hope he's grateful they didn't get everything."

"Grateful he's not, but rich he is and so his loss will be covered. My question is do you have the red."

Both women stared in disbelief. Julia's nostrils flared in anger. "Are you accusing us of theft? Two women against one strong Israeli? No wonder I think you're mad. You are."

"I should apologize when I know what I know? You didn't do bad for amateurs."

"That's it, we have a nutcase sitting with us. Annie, let's see if we can find different seats. There might be some in back. We have to tell one of the attendants there's a lunatic on board."

"Okay by me. The captain can radio the police in Chicago and they'll have an armored car waiting when we land. An armored car, no, I mean a squad car. But after they detain and search you, what a bonus they'll find. They have special x-ray machines and diamonds give off an iridescent glow. Call the attendant. I should press the button instead?"

"I refuse to talk to a lunatic."

"Fine, then we sit as quiet as a rat."

Two flight attendants wheeled a cart to their row. "Coffee," Vel ordered "and some of those peanuts you always pass out. Airlines must buy a million pounds of peanuts a year. No peanuts on the planes and the market would collapse, peanut farmers would starve and the country go into a depression. Ladies? Coffee?"

"Nothing," Annie snapped.

"Scotch on the rocks," Julia ordered between clenched teeth.

Velvel shrugged. "I'd pay but I'm a little short."

"You certainly are."

"Of cash. The last of my money bought the plane ticket."

Not another word was spoken for the rest of the flight although Velvel was itching to continue the conversation. Several times he clamped his hand over his mouth to keep words from pouring out. So these two women were tough cakes, no cookies. No matter; he would hound them until he had an answer to his question.

The women waited for him to leave the plane first and he waited for them to leave. It was a standoff. Flight attendants had to ask them to disembark. Velvel ran to keep up with them, his short legs pumping. "Didn't want the captain to call the police did you?" he panted. "Means I'm right. Okay, okay, no cops. I'll follow you day and night, Julia Devlin and Annie O'Neil."

Annie slowed her pace. "How do you know our names?"

"My secret. I'll follow you, camp on your doorstep, sit with you when you're with your friends, ring your doorbell when you have company, chant outside your window, bang a drum. I only want to know if you have the red. You say yes, we talk business."

"We don't have the red. Now go away."

"I can tell by your eyes you're conning me. Good thieves you may be but good liars you're not. Who would have thought two women would rob Frenzel? Oy, he must be in a frenzy. Frenzy Frenzel." He laughed at what he thought was a good joke while Julia and Annie glared without amusement.

"Julia, I think we should bump him off once we're away from the airport. His passing won't be a loss to mankind."

"The sense of humor again. Love it, love it."

The woman turned away but a horrendous clatter stopped them again. Velvel had slipped and crashed into a metal luggage cart. They heard a loud thump as his head hit the steel bar.

"Oh my God," Julia cried. "He's bleeding. Annie, run into that bar and get a towel or something from the bartender." Julia put the jacket she was carrying against the gash. "Stop thrashing about, you're only making it worse. What's the matter with you; do you have ants in your pants?"

Velvel winced and looked at Julia with sad, soulful eyes. "Ants? Wouldn't I feel ants crawling if I had them in the pants? Oy, there's blood. I'm going to die and never see my younger brother again. Tell Avram I love him, that I thought of him in my final moments. I knew something bad would happen. Always does. God, why do you keep heaping calamities on me, a poor man who tries to keep all six hundred and thirteen Mitzvot commandments, although I only remember a few?"

"For God's sake you're not at death's door. Lie still; here's Annie."

Annie knelt on the floor and wiped off the wound with a wet towel. "It's not too bad; the bleeding's almost stopped." She looked up and saw a dozen people standing around. "What are you gawking at? He's fine." She pulled at Velvel's arm. "Get up before a gaggle of security guards come asking questions."

He popped up like a jack in the box. "Right, right, no cops. Already I feel better." He looked up at the ceiling. "I won't be dying today, God."

They led him to a table at an isolated dim corner of the bar. "Three brandies," Annie told the waitress.

"I can't pay. Stop."

"I'm buying. Will you stop fluttering about like a nervous hen?"

"Okay, okay. Why this about turn?"

"About face."

"Yes, yes. Sorry. You suddenly help me and I ask why? You could have left me lying at death's door and fled. It would take me weeks, months to find you although I think I have your addresses somewhere, from the hotel register."

"Basically we're Good Samaritans."

"Nobody ever treated me with kindness before, not one person in my entire life." Velvel took the towel away from his head. "I'm healing already." The waitress set a brandy in front of him and he took a long swig. "I've never tasted brandy but it has a kick I think."

"What do you mean no one's ever been good to you? What an exaggeration. You mentioned a brother you loved. Parents? Lots of people must have been good to you. Why are we listening to you anyway?"

Velvel seemed ready to cry. As he sipped more brandy he relaxed somewhat and stopped bouncing in his seat. An inner peace swept over him because he was in the company of someone who cared. God, didn't you give me a sign that these two would come into my life again? "My father died when I was five and so I don't remember him much. My mother had to find another husband or we all would starve. She had no idea Solomon Saltzman was cruel when he came sniffing after her. Solomon liked no one, not even God himself. He especially disliked me from the day he moved into our apartment. And when I got older, he threw me out of the house, disowned me. My mother never protested. If she did, she knew she would get thrown out too. You see, I was the runt of the family and my two older brothers used to enjoy beating me. I was their practice punching bag."

"Was Avram one of them?"

"No, Avi is the youngest, the good brother."

"You love him don't you?"

"I did, I still do. He was always a great little guy but he had to obey the others or get a few klops on the head. Not easy klops but hard ones. Solomon had powerful hands."

Julia ordered another round. "I can't imagine anyone being put out on the street. What happened?"

Velvel talked for almost an hour. His stepfather, Solomon, was a diamond cutter on 47th Street. Since machines were taking over the majority of that particular phase of work, not many people came to him with roughs. He sometimes sold on the street on consignment since he didn't have the fee or sponsor to join the Diamond Club. If he was lucky enough to make a sale he earned a five percent commission but that didn't happen often. He was a good cutter but all the important work went to men who rented working space. Solomon couldn't afford rental so what cutting was given to him was done at home in a corner of the kitchen.

Solomon decided his youngest stepson, Avram, had the skill to carry on tradition and so Solomon nurtured the boy's talent, often saying Avram would be the family's salvation since the two older boys were shmos. He never noticed that Velvel listened avidly to everything he said concerning diamonds; their history, cutting, polishing, faceting. The mild dislike Solomon felt for his stepson turned ugly when Velvel was ten and tried to sell a stolen garnet to a fence. At the time, Velvel thought he was helping the family make ends meet since they were behind in the rent, utilities and barely had enough food on the table. His ears were boxed and he was hit across the back ten times with Solomon's belt. Solomon's rage lasted for days as he yelled incessantly at Miriam. He screamed that marrying her was the biggest mistake of his life, and her four brats should have been drowned at birth. Solomon thought himself a prize catch although no women in the area would have him. Everyone but Miriam knew he was prone to attacks of violence and abuse and it didn't take much to set them off. He often said to

Miriam that she should kiss his boots for saving her and her kids from the poorhouse.

"One day fortune smiled on the Chavivi family," Velvel continued. "Solomon's uncle brought over a ten carat rough for cutting. There was a visible flaw but if it was cut properly, into a pear shape, it would end up a dazzling four or five carat stone."

"Half would be lost?" Annie asked.

"Losing half is common. Solomon's eyes were failing but never would he admit it to anyone. He took the commission but planned for Avram to cut the diamond. They studied the stone for weeks and finally it had to be done since the uncle was getting impatient. Cleaving would take place the next morning. Avram lay in bed next to me that night, trembling. He knew he would ruin the stone and shatter it into a thousand pieces. He was terrified that if he made a mistake Solomon would kill him. I mean really kill him, not talk about it. My mother wrung her hands and cried, hoping all would go well because to see Solomon in a temper was worse than having a plague descend."

"Ever since I was five I studied gems, in books, with the dealers on 47th, whoever would talk them with me. While Solomon slept, I studied the diamond for hours every night. I knew every grain, could put my mind inside it. I knew exactly where it should be cleaved. Near dawn, Avram was so nervous he kept throwing up. I said I would do the job before anyone woke and Solomon would be none the wiser. I stole into his bedroom and removed the diamond from beneath his pillow and brought it into the kitchen. Everything was ready. Just as I was about to strike, Solomon barged in. He yelled and my hand slipped. The diamond shattered. I watched as it broke into a thousand pieces. If Solomon went into a crazy rage when his dinner was cold, you can imagine his fury over the diamond."

Velvel's tale had Julia and Annie in tears. Here was a man in his sixties, certainly not tall, dark and handsome but yet sweet; an innocent among the snarling wolves of the world. "You poor thing," Annie said sympathetically.

"Solomon beat me and threw me down the stairs, disowned me, said I was dead. He would have had men sit shiva for me but somewhere in life he lost all religion. He claimed to be Hassid but I know he was godless. I was twenty at the time, forty-five years ago and I still shudder whenever I think of that day. For fifteen years every spare dollar I earned went to repay the debt to Solomon's uncle."

"Your stepfather should have been horsewhipped," Julia said angrily.

"There it didn't stop. His cruel words made me the laughingstock of 47th Street. Over the years I was able to bring myself up a bit, never with anything important but enough to make a living. Jewels, especially diamonds, are my love, my reason for being. Banished from the gem industry, my heart would shatter, like the diamond I ruined."

"Surely you must have friends."

"People I know in the industry, not friends. To Solomon and my two older brothers I was dead. My mother couldn't help or she would have been beaten. When Solomon went out we would look at each other, her in the window and me on the street. She would beckon for me to come up for a minute but I would not take the risk. Solomon forbade her to go out unless he was with her. Have you ever lost your entire family? When you lose your family you lose your very soul."

"But you must be doing well now. You sell diamonds."

"Some but everything I touch turns to disaster. The girl I was to marry ran off with a garment cutter three days before the wedding. I was twenty-one and my heart broke. I found jobs outside the industry and was fired every time, never because it was my fault but because disaster is my middle name. I sold cars and although I had no driving lessons, one day the manager insisted I drive a car from the lot into the showroom. He said even a fool could drive a few feet. Suddenly no brakes and I crashed through the window. Not my fault I said but the owner said otherwise. I worked in an ice cream factory and bitter chocolate was labeled sweet. Thousands of gallons I ruined and the boss chased me with a giant paddle. I sold pots from door to door but they were so heavy I tripped down the stairs one day and ruined them all. Had to pay the distributor more than I earned. I could go on and on but talking of my failures is depressing. I think I'm getting drunk because I never tell my secrets. A little wine I drink now and then, never hard liquor."

"How much money do you have on you?" Annie asked.

He reached into his pocket and spread some bills on the table. He tried counting them but his fingers fumbled.

Annie counted instead. "Nineteen dollars."

"And some change in the pocket."

"Where did you intend sleeping tonight?"

"I don't know. On your lawn I thought, or maybe on a porch if you have one. My coat is warm."

"Why am I doing this?" Annie asked as they sped down the Kennedy Expressway in a cab. Velvel's head was resting on her shoulder as he slept.

"Do you want me to stay with you tonight?" Julia asked.

"It's late and your daughters will call or come over. I'll take the poor soul in but you'd better come over first thing in the morning so we can straighten out this mess."

Annie shut the spare bedroom door. The cab driver had helped drag Velvel inside the house and he was still sound asleep under a down comforter in the spare bedroom. Julia had been worried about leaving and Annie waved her off. "What harm can he bring? It's the least I can do after the way I insulted the poor man in New York. How was I to know he didn't have a friend in the world, no family, an abused childhood? I'm a sucker for a sob story. But I don't understand why he's so hot over a red. Can't he just call it a ruby and not get so dramatic? My garnet's the same size and you don't see me running around in a tizzy."

"He was going to call the police on us."

"He wouldn't have done it. It was a show of bravado."

"At least promise me you'll lock your bedroom door. The man may be a lunatic with a good line."

So here she was alone with a man she barely knew, yet one who seemed very familiar, like an old friend. Why was she such a pushover for strays? Annie laughed. Even through the closed door she could hear Velvel's strange snore. It reminded her of an old song she heard when she was little; Chiri Chiri Bim. She shut the lights and went to her room at the other end of the hall. Tomorrow promised to be an interesting day.

Chapter 8

For a moment, Annie was disoriented when she woke to the smell of coffee brewing. Did she leave the pot on last night? Then she remembered a man with the strange name of Velvel Chavivi was in her house. She quickly put on a pair of slacks and a sweater and ran her fingers through her hair. "I'm getting to like this do, she said to herself as she glanced in the bathroom mirror. "No fuss, it practically takes care of itself."

Velvel grinned from ear to ear as she entered the kitchen. "Good, good, you're up. Coffee's ready and I made oatmeal."

"I hardly ever eat oatmeal. In fact I didn't know I had any in the house."

"Healthy it is, and cheap. Barrels of oatmeal went into our mouths when I was young but ours was plain, made with water. Today I add sugar, cinnamon and a little applesauce to sweeten it up. Look, there's Julia at the back door." He hurried to open it.

"I see you're safe and alive," Julia said to Annie as she sat down. "I worried all night."

"About me?" Velvel asked indignantly. "A hair on Annie's head I wouldn't harm."

"It wasn't her head I worried about. Oh sit down, I was only joking." Julia poured herself a cup of coffee while Vel placed a bowl of oatmeal in front of her. She took a spoonful. "This is delicious. All right, we're not here to test breakfast cereals. Let's talk business. Velvel, let's say you're right and we were the ones who robbed Frenzel. If we were to admit it what would you do? Remember this is only supposition."

"My stepfather used to say never lie but don't tell the whole truth either. I believed that but I'm going to level with you. I have to know if you got the red. Frenzel's not saying anything except that he still has the pinks, which are worth a fortune. So does he still have the red or is he holding out because he found a higher bidder? On the day he was robbed I was on my way to see him, to ask if I could sell the red on a consignment basis. I think I could have gotten a quarter of a million more with an anonymous buyer I happen to know. I even would have gone down to a five percent commission. He probably would have thrown me out but I had to ask. It would make my reputation secure forever."

"Why is the damned red so important? It's not that large a gem. Don't tell me you believe that ruby has special powers, that it can bring you health, wealth and wisdom?"

Velvel jumped up, arms flapping. "Ruby? Ruby? You think my buyer would be interested in a measly three carat ruby? Everybody sees a red stone and they automatically think ruby. The red is the rarest of all diamonds, a blood red diamond. There are less than twenty known reds in the entire world and they're all smaller. I'm talking about blood red. Most of the known reds are a deep pink or purple tinged, classified as red."

Annie was dumbfounded. "I've never even seen a picture of a red diamond. I didn't think there were such things. The books I read mentioned white, yellow, brown, pink, blue and light green. But then I've been pouring through old books that mainly featured the historical gems. Does Queen Elizabeth have a red? She has just about every kind of gem there is and they're all huge."

"No, no, even she doesn't have a red. If you have it, I can sell it for you at top price. My cut would be commission and expenses to California.

Frenzel was going to sell it to Holdheim for a cool million. I can get two million, maybe more."

"Oh my," Annie said. "Two million for a small diamond? Richard Burton bought a diamond for Liz Taylor for a million and it was gigantic."

"Aha, but it wasn't red. We're talking rare here, as rare as you can get with diamonds. The commission would be my salvation. Haven't been selling much of the good stuff lately, if you want the truth. As we speak, they evict me from my apartment, even though it's a dump. I'll be lucky if I can reclaim my clothes when I get back to New York, if I ever get back to New York. One lucky break is all I need."

Julia and Annie looked at each other then nodded. "Okay, Velvel, we overlooked the pinks but we still got a nice haul, not bad for our first joint effort."

"You never did this before? Amazing."

"Well, I did manage a couple of smaller pieces," Annie admitted, "but that was before the golden opportunity arose. Julia, did you bring the toothpaste?"

"Toothpaste? Toothpaste? A crucial moment and you want to brush your teeth?"

"Velvel, I'm surprised your mother didn't name you two-two but I guess she didn't know because you weren't born talking."

He ran his hands through his hair making it spring up every which way. "Tutu? Why are we talking tutus here? I'm beginning to think we're from two different planets. A ballerina outfit, toothpaste? You two don't look crazy but maybe you are."

"The number two, Vel. You have an endearing way of repeating a lot of your words twice. It's rather charming. That and putting some of your sentences backward."

"Because I had to leave school at an early age. I wanted to be a genius but Solomon wouldn't allow school, saying it was a waste of time. Instead I had to find coal and potatoes at the railroad yard, because it was free if you ran fast enough."

Julia laid the tube of toothpaste on the table and began squeezing it out from the bottom.

"Okay, we brush our teeth and than get to business."

Red and white striped paste began snaking onto the table. "Dig in, Velvel. They'll start popping out any second."

"You've hidden them. Very nice although I think it wouldn't get you past Customs."

Annie brought out a pan of sudsy water and Velvel began dropping diamonds into the pan gently. Thirty-nine. The red. Where's the red?"

"There's a lump at the opening of the tube. It must be stuck. I'll get scissors and cut it open."

"No, stop, you'll damage it. Here, let me do it. Come out and catch the light, beautiful red," he crooned. He took a considerable amount of time cleaning off the gem then pulled out a loupe from his pocket and began examining it. "The most wondrous diamond my eyes have ever seen."

"We probably wouldn't have been successful miners after all," Annie moaned. "We don't know enough. We thought it was a ruby."

Velvel passed over his loupe. "Look and get inside it. Pretend you walk through crystal corridors trying to find your way out of a maze. Turn it all ways and look for internal reflection, the satin finish. The greater reflection comes from the table facet. You know, if a diamond is exceptional, it will talk to you."

Julia took the loupe. "Staring at it too long could make me dizzy," she said with admiration. Annie thought the same.

"Okay, enough. Are you ready to decide if I can sell this red to the man I know?"

The women didn't quite know how to tell Velvel about their goal. "Velvel, we didn't rob Frenzel for money. We were following a dream."

"You were going to return these?"

"No. Annie and I have always been fascinated by the sparkle of gemstones. We always said we were going to collect a boxful just so we could stare at the radiance. We never planned on selling any of our collection. It's all for personal pleasure."

"The first job you pull, you manage to hit a bonanza worth over two million and you're not going to sell? Do my ears trick me?"

"We stole over two million? Annie, I'm overwhelmed" They grabbed each other and began dancing around the table.

"What did you think it was, chopped liver? The others are two-carat blue-whites, all investment quality. Frenzel doesn't deal in inferior goods. I think I'm going to kill myself. To be this close and yet so far. I came all this way for nothing. Oy, oy."

"Will you excuse us, Velvel? Julia and I want to talk something over. We'll go into the living room."

He hardly paid attention to them as he continued staring the red diamond.

Chapter 9

"A person has to love Velvel even though they've only known him for a short time," Annie declared once they were in her living room. "He annoyed me on the plane but yet when he began telling his life story, I was drawn to him. I can't begin to imagine a child being thrown out into cold, harsh world. It's inhumane. You know how I feel about abuse, Julia, how we both feel. It makes me want to kill. Don't let me get started on the subject or I'll get in my car and run down the first scowling man I see walking down the street. Let's see if we agree on a course of action here."

When they returned to the kitchen thirty minutes later it was as clean as a whistle; dishes washed and put away, fresh coffee brewing. The diamonds lay on one of Annie's indigo blue napkins Velvel had placed on the table, the magnificent red set in the center with the whites surrounding it, paying homage. Velvel's eyes pleaded. "I was thinking maybe you could lend me enough for bus fare back to New York. I'll pay it back, with interest. On that you have my word. You don't know me well but my word I never break."

Julia set the treasure chest on the table and opened it. "This is what started it all."

Velvel pulled out the tennis bracelet first. "Poor commercial diamonds, heavily flawed. Same with the stud." He looked at the ring. "Nice citrine but common. A brighter yellow would be worth more." He held the four topaz stones in his hand and studied them longer. "Good topaz; Brazilian."

"How do you know where they came from?"

"Only Brazil produces a deep honey color with just a slight tinge of red."

"The diamonds we took from Frenzel will look magnificent with the other jewels in the box. Velvel, can we ask you a few questions?"

"Okay by me." He stared down at the gems as he talked, a long farewell to his dream.

"Where is your family?"

"Mama and Solomon died in a tenement fire. As my stepfather's eyesight failed, he lost the better part of his income, not that it was all that much to begin with. He switched to selling full time and more often than not he got screwed, a few times by some dishonest goyim dealers. He couldn't see that well even with his loupe. My brothers and me did our best to support the folks. I mean I'd give Avi some gelt to throw into the kitty and the rest pitched in what they could. To make a long story short, there was a fire one night and they didn't make it from their walk up apartment on the fourth floor. Happened a long time ago. Maybe if my brothers were home they would have had a chance but it was only ten at night and they were out."

"Where are your brothers?"

"After the fire the two older brothers took off. I hear Jacob is set for life in Florida. He took the bus after the funeral and never came back. Went into the real estate business and did well. Herman did well too. Married a rich but homely woman and wound up owning supermarkets in Connecticut. Three years ago he died. Heart attack. I hear his wife and three children moved to Pennsylvania. Jacob and his wife have no children. A showgirl she was and didn't want to ruin her figure."

"And Avram?"

"Avi stayed in the business. He lives in London. We talk on the phone often. He's an arbitrator for the Diamond Trading Company in London. Ten times a year they hold sightings for two hundred and fifty international cutters. They each buy a box of carefully selected diamonds that could be worth anywhere from two to twenty million or more. You take what you get or you never get invited back. Nobody's allowed to quibble over price except for diamonds weighing over fourteen carats. If a dealer feels the asking price is too high, that's where Avi steps in. He negotiates for the syndicate."

"Sounds like a monopoly run by the mafia."

"No, no, that's what they call the operation. In their case a monopoly is required. Without DeBeers, the industry would be in chaos with prices going up and down like a yo-yo."

"If you say so. What would you do if you got the commission from the red?"

"First thing I'd get a decent apartment; small and nothing showy since I'm not home much. Then I'd book a flight to London. I keep promising Avi I'm going to get there one day but I never do. He thinks I'm doing well and I don't want to tell him different. Does this mean you're going to let me sell the red for you?"

"No."

"Oh. Then you can lend me enough to get home?"

"No."

"Okay, maybe I can stick out my finger on the highway and someone will stop and let me in their car."

Annie picked up the red diamond. Once she and Julia walked with their eyes through its complexities with a loupe and saw the fire from within, they knew it was much too worthy to be put in their old treasure chest. It was a gem never to be forgotten or laid aside as inconsequential, a gem waiting eons of time to be born and when it was, its birth was phenomenal. "We're giving this to you. Whether you sell it or keep it is your affair. It's an offer of friendship."

"Giving? You're giving me over two million in goods? No. I can't take it. All I need, all I want is the commission on the sale."

"We can always send it back to Frenzel."

He held his hands over the glow, protecting it. "No, no, Frenzel doesn't deserve this. He steals and it's no crime to steal from a thief."

"He actually goes out on capers?"

"Capers? I don't know that word. He steals from independent miners that come to him with stones. He pays far less than they're worth but most of these men are poor and desperate. He goes to South America three of four times a year and pays peanuts for the gems he picks up there. He commits thefts of omission by not giving those miners a fair price."

"Then it's all settled. You'll take the red. It comes with no strings attached."

"No one gives away something that precious."

"We do. You've met two unique women, Velvel. What we originally planned was to fill our treasure chest with beautiful glitter, not rarity. As long as our stones are genuine, such as garnets or zircons, we'll like them. On the other hand, your reputation is much more important than our pleasure."

"I would have to repay you in some way but I can't help you steal. It would lead to disaster, which follows me like a shadow. I'd trip a burglar alarm, a ventilating fan would suck off my disguise, my feet would get caught in a grate when I'm trying to escape."

"We don't want you to steal." Annie picked up nine of the whites. "Take these too."

He backed away, horrified. "No, no."

"We need your help with these. Take one of the whites and exchange it for some red stones. We want red because it adds a little color to our collection. The reds you find don't have to be expensive. Garnets would do nicely. That leaves us with thirty diamonds for the treasure chest. We want you to sell the other eight so we have ready cash on hand. Never know when we might need it. We have homes and some money in the bank but cash isn't readily accessible. What we need is an emergency stash."

"Okay, okay, that I can do."

"And there would be times we might need your expert advice on what we get."

"You're going to continue stealing? You got a haul that could set you up for life and you're going to continue anyway?"

"We have a goal."

"You have to fill the whole box? Do you have any idea how many stones it will take?"

"We may never fill it to the top but we're certainly going to try. So when we get our hands on more goods, could you look at what we have? We're not going to keep a written inventory but we would like to be knowledgeable about our little treasures."

"Let me think a minute; my brain is scrambling." There was a long pause. "I can do better than that. I can steer you in the right direction. I know where half the good stuff in the world is. But I don't think you should tackle museums, fine jewelry stores or the Crown Jewels in England. Even the experts can't get at them."

"We won't do any more dealers either. New York was a lucky strike. But neither will we go back to places like Service Merchandise and Walmart. Then you'll be our advisor?"

"Yes, yes but I can't accept the red. How about we split the proceeds?"

"Don't make us angry, Velvel. We said it was yours. When we give a gift we don't like to haggle over it. Just bring us back some garnets, or anything red. And normally we wouldn't ask you to sell the other eight but ready cash might be necessary one day."

A flood of tears formed in Velvel's eyes. "Fortune is finally smiling on me. When I first saw you on 47th and you told me off, I got angry but when I turned around and looked after you, I noticed the aura around you both. That kind of aura only clings to a handful of people."

"What aura? Are we phosphorescent?"

"No, no. It's as if there's a golden glow hovering around you."

"Halos?"

"No, no. The sky was dark and ominous and yet in my eyes you seemed to be walking in the sunlight. I'm not a man of flowery words so I can't say it better. Okay, so I'll be the best gem advisor in the world. Call whenever you need me and I'll be here in hours even though the plane makes my stomach jump. Nobody ever treated me good. Why me?"

"Because you're a very lovable man and I think we were destined to meet, to make up for the family you didn't have."

"I..."

"Not another word, the subject is closed."

"To Los Angeles I go but..."

"No problem, we'll finance that part."

"On a loan basis. I insist on that. I should leave now."

"Stay a few days. You don't want your potential buyer to think you're overly anxious to dump the red. You have to take time for strategy and we'll help with that. We're very good at plotting."

"You can stay here," Annie offered. "We'll fit you out with some nice conservatives clothes and then you can fly west. The long black coat has to go though. It makes you look like Dracula. But if you insist on keeping it, to look truly Hasidic, then you should grow two long curls at the side of your head."

"Had peyes once but they kept dipping in my soup. Same with the beard, which once flowed down my chin. Had to scrub it every time I ate, like I was washing dishes. You really like me. I can't get over it. I thought I was unlikeable. Are you by some chance Jewish?"

"No."

"Goyim ladies like me. Then all goyim ladies aren't evil temptresses. You see, my real father was Hassid and I wanted to take after him and go to yeshiva classes but it was forbidden by Solomon. Maybe it's better that I didn't go because I would never remember all the commandments. The first of 613 is to go out into the world and multiply and I haven't done that so right at the beginning I was doomed."

"Julia's staying overnight and we'll have a pajama party. We'll make popcorn, watch old movies or stay up all night and talk if we feel like it."

"Pajama party? I've never been to one."

"We used to have them all the time, all girls naturally but what the hell, we're older now and we promise we won't seduce you."

"Always joking. Never have I been in a house where laughter bounces off the walls, where happiness is normal." Velvel looked upward. "Thank you, God, for letting me experience this."

Chapter 10

Velvel tripped coming out of the spare bedroom wearing pajama pants that were eight inches too long. He scrambled up in an instant. "Usually sleep in my underwear but can't do that here, not with two woman in the house.

"Jack, my late husband, was a much bigger man but those will have to do until the stores open tomorrow. We were so busy today I never thought about clothes."

"Is this what a real family does? All laughing and pitching in to get things done like you making dinner, me tossing the salad and Julia in charge of desert?

"Not all families but a lot of them. Naturally there's heartache now and then but there's more fun than grief over the long haul."

"Being with a family makes me want to sing. Should I? No, better that I don't. What movie will we watch?"

"I thought To Catch a Thief would be appropriate."

"I only saw three movies in my life. One was Bambi when I was young and crawled into the theater through the ventilator. I cried for the deer. Another was Frankenstein which frightened me so I slept under the bed for two weeks. The last was something about a big throat. Saul Hirschner took me. Only ten minutes I stayed. They allow such scenes on big movie screens nowadays? I was so astounded I closed my eyes as I ran from the theater and almost fell from the balcony. I'll make popcorn."

"Fine, but first put this plastic tablecloth around your shoulders."

Velvel laughed. "Every time I think things are back to normal you start another crazy game. Am I to be a tent or will you wrap my body in plastic and toss me in a river?"

"I'm going to give you a haircut."

He put both hands to his head. "No, no, not a good idea. A haircut lasts me a long time; I'm not ready for one yet."

"Listen to Annie, Velvel. When you go to California you want to look successful. And you can't look like a made man wearing a dusty, long black coat with your hair poking out in all directions. Annie's just going to tame it down a bit."

"It won't stay down. Don't you think I tried keeping it down all my life? I was born with springs instead of hair."

"I'll bet you never used mousse."

"That chocolate stuff?"

"No silly, hair mousse. And I'm a very good stylist. Jack never went to a barber because he said I was the best and even to this day when I visit Allan, my son, or he comes here, he asks for a haircut. Trust me, Velvel. I wouldn't let a member of my family look foolish and you've become a bona fide member of my family."

Thirty minutes later Velvel studied himself in a mirror and smiled. "I like it. I look distinguished. Yes, that's the word, distinguished."

"You have a full head of wiry hair and I doubt you'll ever go bald. The trick to keeping your type of hair in check is to keep it shorter and nurture it, style it in place every morning. I'll teach you before you leave."

"I'll make the popcorn now. Annie, Julia?"

"What?"

"Never had a pillow fight. Solomon would have killed us if we did that. Could we have one later?"

"What a neat idea. We haven't had one in years. We'll toss pillows, tell ghost stories in the dark before we fall asleep and say a prayer that we continue to be just as happy as we are now. Do you go to temple, Velvel?"

"I wanted to and if my father had lived I would have been a true Hasid. And if I was a true Hasid, I wouldn't be here with you because they don't believe in mixing with Goyim. But if I was a true Hasidic, I could go to the Rebbe and present my kvitl, that's a petition. I would ask him to chase away the dybbuk that follows me."

"What is a dybbuk?"

"A devil, a mischievous sprit. The one assigned to me makes certain my life never runs smooth. He brings disaster instead. But if I was a true Hasid I would have to follow too many rules, more than I can remember. You don't understand my religion, Julia and Annie. For some people it's…it's so much. It buries you in rules and regulations and when I was out on my own, I sort of put it to the back of my mind. Besides, God lost track of me. I fell between the cracks."

"God never loses track and sometimes religion is in the heart not in a temple or a church."

Julia picked up a pillow. "Now, you varmint, I'm going to make you eat feathers until you surrender." She began pummeling him, chasing him from room to room. Velvel knocked over a lamp as he ran but Annie assured him it wasn't expensive, that it was all her fault for getting wild.

"The lamp I broke," he cried. "I'm a clumsy fool."

Annie laughed. "Velvel, say I broke the lamp."

"No, I broke it. You were nowhere near it."

"Just say I broke the lamp not the lamp I broke."

"There you go again. I did it, me, no one else."

"Never mind, it was a piece of junk anyway. Velvel, if I ever try to correct anything you say again, tell me to mind my own business. Now I'm going to clobber you."

A pillow split apart and feathers floated around the living room, a feathery snowfall coating the floor and all the furniture.

Velvel needs a childhood, Annie thought sadly. Julia and I will make sure he has one even if he is sixty-five years old.

Chapter 11

They drove Velvel to the airport five days later, the happiest five days in his life, he thought as he gazed at them with love in his heart. He had a family. They went out to dinner or prepared lavish meals at either Annie or Julia's house. They went dancing one night where he took turns with them on the floor. He especially liked cavorting to fast music since his body always moved in double time anyway. Whenever he danced with Hassidic men, he became so enraptured with niggunim, the wordless melodies and clapping, that he often went into a trance and did a somersault or two as the others cheered him on. They rode bicycles down secondary roads, shopped till they dropped and stayed up all hours talking. He kept them enthralled as he explained diamonds, telling him how he matched countries with stones just by looking at them through his loupe, Namibia coast, Zaire, Siberia, Sri Lanka; each country producing different hues and structure systems within a diamond. He was a walking encyclopedia when it came to other gems as well. Beneath the big city facade he wore like a plate of armor, he was just a little boy at heart.

"Are you sure you can trust the man you're seeing in California?" Annie asked as they reached the terminal.

"I can trust him. He came to New York two years ago to buy twelve matched Kashmir sapphires. Brought them to Moe Brendmeer's place for a second opinion. Moe wasn't sure because he's not into colored stones. I happened to be there because I sometimes sell on consignment for Moe and I asked if I could take a look. The sapphires were good but they weren't Kashmir. Kashmirs are the best. They were from Brazil and irradiated."

The women looked puzzled.

"Heat treated to give them a deeper fuller color. So the man was grateful and said if I ever had anything of interest I should see him first, that top dollar would be mine for anything I brought him. He calls once in a while but so far I haven't had anything important to show him."

"What if doesn't like the red?"

"Even a blind man would like the red. When I called the other day he asked how soon I could be out. So I stretched it and said not for another four days like you told me. Waiting will kick up his appetite. Besides I was having too much fun to fly off immediately. Never woke up to the smell of rolls baking in the oven, birds singing. Never played Monopoly or built a snowman. And to think there was a late snow just to impress me." He looked in the rear view mirror. "And look at me. I look like a macher, a successful man."

"Because you are. Will this potential buyer let it be known he's got a red? Word could get back to Frenzel."

"No, no, his lips will remain sealed. He's Oriental, a Japanese. What do they say about Orientals? They're…"

"Inscrutable."

"That's it. Japanese are buying up gemstones like they're popcorn and they're very sly when it comes to buying. Maybe they plan to corner the market one day and drop a bomb on DeBeers. Not a real bomb but one that will explode the diamond market. They snap up everything; smuggled, legal, stolen. Once a major stone gets inside Japan, it's never seen again unless they want it to be seen."

"Don't let him take you, Velvel, or we'll have to go out there and kick him where it hurts most."

"And you would do that for me wouldn't you? Don't worry, everything will go like clock chimes. I'm under your protective aura."

"I think you should be inscrutable as well. Stay cool."

"I will, I will. I'll be Charlie Chan."

They waved goodbye at the United terminal and Annie drove off. "Julia, I feel like I have another son. Isn't that strange? I think of him as our little boy."

"I know what you mean. I never had a son but if I did, I wouldn't mind if he was like Velvel. Rejected by so many people. I'm glad we gave him the red."

"Julia, I've been thinking. We should take turns keeping the treasure chest. What if you wake up in the middle of the night and need to see sparkle to cheer you up or what if you need some splendor on a gloomy day?"

"I don't mind coming over to your house. After all, you're the one who got us started."

" We share equally. One week I'll hold it and you take it the next. Okay? Yes, it's okay. "Lordy, I'm starting to sound like Velvel."

"As long as you don't keep repeating yourself it's okay. With him it sounds good, with you it would drive me up a wall."

Chapter 12

Velvel's flight encountered turbulence over the Rocky Mountains. But what else could he expect? Every time he boarded a plane something went wrong. His was sure his personal dybbuk spent all his spare moments plotting ways to scare him at every turn. Ah, but when he was on the plane with Julia and Annie, his dybbuk had been frightened off. So the spirit wasn't invincible after all. The captain's voice came on the intercom and he calmly told everyone to fasten their seat belts. Less than a minute later, the plane bounced and skimmed through the air at thirty-five thousand feet. Velvel broke out in a sweat, gripping the armrests until his knuckles turned white. This plane is not going to crash, he said to himself, not while Annie and Julia's protective aura envelops me. His eyes darted around and he spoke out loud. "You hear that, dybbuk? Steady, steady," he ordered the aircraft. "Pilot, don't let the dybbuk take possession of your hands and wits." He spread out his arms wide, keeping the plane in balance and almost elbowed the woman sitting next to him in the eye.

She grew quite irate. "Sit still or I'll slam some of my tranquilizers down your throat."

The turbulence subsided after another few minutes, due only to his influence he decided.

First things first. He wasn't going to run to Toru Yakasawa's office like an unprofessional schmuck, not with a deal of this magnitude. He took a taxi to the Bank of America and opened an account with one hundred dollars of the money Annie lent him, telling the clerk there would be more transferred by wire. He was supposed to go directly to Yakasawa after arrival but when the bank business was taken care of, he went to his hotel, unpacked and ordered lunch from room service. Just as he finished the phone rang. "Mr. Yakasawa, you call at my hotel? What? You said noon? I thought our appointment was for three o'clock. Well, since I'm late anyway, do you want to postpone until tomorrow? Oh, you're flying to Tokyo tomorrow? Okay, what do we do? A limo? Ten minutes? Fine, I'll be waiting for your magical vehicle."

Velvel settled into a plush seat and poured himself a brandy from the car's amply stocked bar. He was acquiring a taste for brandy ever since his girls introduced him to it. Fast work, he thought smugly. If I didn't have the red I would have been riding in a taxi with a faulty motor and then kept waiting for hours."

Toru Yakasawa shook hands with a man he barely recognized. Gone were the atrocious clothes, the nervous fluttering of a bird trying to escape a predator, a head of hair that looked fried from a major electrical shock. Mr. Chavivi had indeed undergone a dramatic transformation. Perhaps he was more then he seemed. "Can I offer refreshment?"

"A brandy I'd like." Can't have more than two, Velvel warned himself. More than two and my head will be befuddled. Can't screw up the most important day of my life.

They settled in chairs placed around a low table. "You brought the red?" Toru asked.

Velvel reached into his pocket and pulled out a velvet pouch. Diamonds broke out of imprisonment and shimmered in a fiery glow on the cloth Yakasawa provided. There was no red. Yakasawa's face was devoid of any expression but his words were terse. "I see no red diamond, Mr. Chavivi."

"I had it, I had it." Velvel turned out his pants pockets but only crumbs fell to the floor. "Don't fret my friend, it's here somewhere." He took off his jacket and turned those pockets out as well. "Well, what do you know? Not here. Keep calm." He unbuckled his pants next and let them fall to the floor.

"Mr. Chavivi," Toru Yakasawa said in astonishment. "What are you doing? I will not have this flagrant display in my office."

As he examined his pants, Velvel spotted a tiny hole in the left pocket. He looked perplexed. How could new pants have a hole in the pocket? "The dybbuk is playing his tricks again." The red must have fallen out while the whites stayed in the pouch. He had lost it. The magnificent gem had been entrusted to him and he lost it. Gottenyu, he thought. What will I do? Bulvon, oaf, dolt. You are all of these and more. There was only one thing to do and that was to kill himself. He ran to the window to throw himself out but the windows were huge slabs of thick plate glass. He backed up to gain momentum and flung himself against the glass. It didn't shatter and he bounced backward hitting the floor with a loud thud.

Yakasawa was furious. "Out. Get out of here."

Velvel didn't hear him because his head was swimming with alternate plans. Hari kari. He wasn't sure how it was done; something to do with a sword through his stomach. There were no swords but there was a letter opener on the desk. No, that would be too painful.

"Time to say a little prayer, Mr. Yakasawa. Do you pray to Buddha or is it Zeus? No? Maybe Allah?"

"I'm a Christian Mr. Chavivi; I pray to God."

"Right, right. What's his name in Japanese?"

"God. You're trying my patience. Leave."

Toru Yakasawa's assistant walked in then and tried not to gape at the visitor with skinny legs standing amidst a heap of clothes on the floor. He was instructed never to show emotion in front of foreigners so he lowered his head and ducked when a shirt came flying in his direction. Velvel stood in the center of the hand-woven carpet in shorts, socks and shoes, his hair puffed out like cotton candy. He removed his shoes.

"Leave immediately," Toru thundered.

Velvel put down his foot and winced. “Ouch.” His fingers felt down into his sock and he smiled beatifically. “A red I promised and a red you get. Imagine that, falling from my pocket right into my sock.” He handed over the blood red diamond as a wave of relief swept through him. How proud Julia and Annie would be that he hadn’t lost the diamond.

Toru Yakasawa took out a loupe, all trace of anger gone as he examined the gem. “Remarkable, truly unique. I have seen only one other similar to this but it had a tinge of violet; nothing like this fire. Word is that a similar stone was being sold in New York. The asking price was two million.”

“Plus commission.”

“Yes of course. I offer two million two.”

“That’s what Holdheim was going to pay.”

“And I once said I would do better if something came along didn’t I? Two million, five.”

Velvel moved the smaller whites to the center of the table. “These are part of the deal, nine stones, two carats each, D flawless.”

“I don’t buy small stones.”

“The seller insists or the deal is off. One hundred eighty thousand for the white lot. If you don’t take the whites, they’ll sell them and the red to another interested party.”

Toru sighed heavily. Anything to get the red. “Satisfactory. Which method of payment do you prefer?” He would have haggled down to his original offer but at the moment it seemed prudent to get this bumbler out of his office and the diamond safely tucked into his safe. This wild man was capable of smashing it to pieces with one move.

“Two million three wired to my account, two packets of cash, one containing two hundred thousand the other the price of the whites.”

Toru politely asked his assistant to handle the matter. “Mr. Chavivi, will you please put on your clothes? It is not fitting that you pace the floor in your underwear.”

Velvel talked of diamonds in such rapid fire words Yakasawa couldn't follow everything he said. His assistant returned in less than fifteen minutes with two manila envelopes. It was the longest fifteen minutes of Toru's life. Brandy had spilled onto his priceless carpet, his precious Monet was hanging precariously and a sculpture was barely saved from toppling against a plate glass window. He had been forced to follow Chavivi around the room lest this deal cost him ten times more in damages. "Would you like to count it?" he asked.

"No, diamond dealing is based on trust."

"Here is your transfer receipt. You'll find everything is in order."

"Mazul und brucha," Velvel beamed as they both bowed. Velvel lost his balance and his forehead cracked into Yakasawa's. "It was a pleasure doing business with you, Mr. Yakasawa."

Toru adjusted his eyeglasses. I'm sure you have other pressing business as do I. You will let me know if other items of interest come to you in the future?"

Velvel couldn't tell this man that if Annie and Julia got their hands on something big the answer was yes. "First choice you will always have, my lord. You see, good fortune is in my future. Now why did I say that he asked himself? Think of something more appropriate or this rich man will think you're a dunce. "The moons of Jupiter have aligned with Mars and for anyone born on October 17th, my birthday, a profitable decade is forecast, especially when Pluto begins a new rotation moving away from a black hole." He had heard something similar on the radio once.

"I beg your pardon?"

"Astrology, Mr. Yakasawa. The day should never start until you talk to your astrology."

The first thing Velvel did after returning to his hotel was to call his brother in London. "Avi, it's me. How you doing?"

A tall, lean, good-looking man with dark hair and olive tinged skin shed his usual restraint and shouted in surprise. "Vel, where are you? Don't tell me you're finally here in London?"

"Actually I'm in California and I hate it. Too hot. The sun is blinding me. Must be the peasant blood we have that thrives in zero temperatures and blizzards."

There was a booming laugh. "You'll never change. You'll be cracking jokes on your hundredth birthday. When are you coming over?"

"How does next week sound, or two weeks at the most?"

"Perfect. Want to get in on the sightings?"

"Really? I can do that?"

"I've been promoted to second in charge. I can do almost anything within reason."

"Mazel tov. Is it okay if I bring two women along? They're really great gals, Avi, you're going to love them."

"Two? One isn't enough for you?"

"No, no. Romantic I'm not. Well maybe I am involved but not like you think. We're more like one happy family."

"I'm sure you are."

"Serious I am."

"If you love them that's good enough for me."

Velvel went shopping before boarding a flight back to Chicago.

Chapter 13

Annie and Julia were deep in thought in Annie's kitchen. There were pressing matters to be resolved and each of them deliberated the best way to handle the situations. "Which is more important?" Julia asked. "Mrs. Bishop down the street is going to lose her house if she doesn't come up with back taxes by next week. The poor dear is ninety-one; losing her home would be the death of her. She loves that old place."

"How much does she owe?"

"Twelve thousand give or take a few hundred. The county let her slide by until now but they won't let it slide any longer. She's used up her savings and her social security and Bart's small pension barely lasts from month to month."

"I could sell the Lexus and get a jalopy instead. The Lexus was a vanity purchase."

"But Diedre Scott, the little girl we've grown to love, needs new treatments and they're only done in Canada. The family is short fifty thousand after the fund raiser. The longer she waits, the less her chances of surviving."

"Do you think Velvel will get enough from the sale of the diamonds?"

"Maybe his contact won't buy them. I know Velvel will sell them eventually but it might be too late."

"In the meantime I can sell the car."

"I can sell the two paintings Mel bought. I don't know what they're worth now but he paid eight thousand ten years ago. They must have risen in value."

"Keep thinking. If we do come up with enough for both causes, I want the donations to be anonymous."

Velvel knocked on the front door, performing a little shuffle as he waited for it to be answered. "Julia and I were just talking about you and here you are. I thought you'd be gone at least a week. You said your mysterious buyer liked to deliberate. Come in, let's not stand in the doorway."

He gave Annie a hug while Julia swept in from the kitchen and began planting kisses on his cheeks. This is what it was like to have a family, to be loved. "When was I ever cuddled? I don't remember. I must be in heaven."

"What happened? You have a smug look of success on your adorable face."

Velvel beamed at their attention. "I've never been treated with such respect as the Japanese buyer bestowed on me. It's all due to you."

"Nonsense, you deserve respect. Did he buy the red?"

"Did he buy the red? Yes and the whites." He followed them into the kitchen where he took a napkin from a holder on the counter. "Okay, okay, close your eyes." There was a dramatic pause. "Now open them."

Julia and Annie stared down at a dazzling array of gemstones. "Velvel, there are ten; red, yellow, orange, green, black. Two of each color."

"Garnets. You said garnets and garnets I got. Five carats each. The green is the best, demantoid out of Russia. You can tell by the horsetail swirls. I'll show them to you later with the loupe. The reds are Bohemian, the orange from Nevada, the black is called mellanite and the pale yellow is essonite from Ceylon. That's what you got from the sale of one white." He opened his palm, which held two huge stones. "Blue topaz; one is thirty-five carats the other thirty-eight. Not the kind you find in your local jewelry store. These are Brazilian, to keep the gold topaz company. The blues are a gift to my special ladies. No, no, don't protest. Protests are not acceptable."

"You couldn't have bought all these garnets from the sale of one diamond."

"Got twenty thousand for each white and that buys a lot of garnets. If you wanted poor quality, I could have bought a hundred. And here's the proceeds from the sale of the other diamonds." He pulled hundred dollar bills from an envelope and fanned them on the table. "Now what else should I do? I must work to repay your kindness."

"I'd better explain our concept of friendship," Julia began. "It's what kept Annie, me and another friend, Cissy, who died recently, firmly bonded. We never had rules, never had to explain our actions to one another. We were like one person and yet we lived individual lives. If the three of us made plans to go on vacation and one dropped out at the last minute there were no recriminations, no hurtful words, no attitudes. If one of us was short of cash the other two paid the way. When we were flush, we shared. That's what we did with you. We shared, no questions, no strings. We asked for your advice but we'll love you the just the same if you decide not to give it. You don't have to jump over barrels for us. We may ask for something but you have every right to refuse."

"Got it, got it. But you have to let me do just one more thing, as a friend. And if you're a friend, you can't refuse. Passports you have?"

Annie and Julia looked at each other in bewilderment. "Yes, but we've never used them. We went to get them on a whim a few years back because we thought we might take a trip abroad."

"Good. To London we go, to visit my brother, to visit the greatest stockpile of diamonds in the world. Next week. More time you'll need?"

"We're not going to…?"

"Absolutely no stealing? After one job, you should rest. My treat all the way. While we're there you can learn, fill your eyes and heads until they feel they can hold no more, meet new people, see new sights, drink in pubs, walk the same streets as royalty."

"What fun," Annie cried. "Actually we could be ready in an hour but next week is fine. Yes, next week is good because we won't miss a ritzy birthday party at the country club on Saturday."

Julia laughed. "It should be a riot. Nora Semple's husband is throwing Nora a surprise sixtieth party and she's going to be totally undone since she's been passing herself off as five years younger for years. She was in our class at school so we know her real age. Her husband, Jim, has gone bonkers ordering everything with a big six zero emblazoned on it."

"Nora's had a face lift," Annie added "and a few tucks here and there. I wish you could go with us, Velvel. You could wear a black cape, walk in with a woman on each arm and act mysterious."

"An apartment I must find and settle my affairs in New York. I'll see that you get on a plane from Chicago to New York and we'll go together to London from there, any time after your important party. Okay?"

"I don't think it's smart to show our faces in New York again."

"Right. So I'll fix it that you don't have to leave the airport. You hop off one plane and hop on another. I can stay the night so let me take you to dinner, to the fanciest restaurant you know."

Julia clapped her hands in delight. "You can wear your old black coat and devilish hat. I had them cleaned."

"You told me they were ugly."

"For California. Tonight we'll sweep into The Cave, your coattails flapping and your hat pulled down low. Everyone will wonder who the mystery man is."

"I like it. I'll speak with a foreign accent."

"French?"

"No Yiddish."

Chapter 14

New outfits were the ticket for Nora Semple's sixtieth birthday bash. Although both Julia's and Annie's husbands had been members of the Raintree Country Club for years, the women saw no reason to continue paying exorbitant dues for a facility they seldom used. Mel and Jack had been avid golfers so the club was considered a necessity in their lives. The couples often had dinner there on Friday or Saturday nights but with their men gone, they soon tired of the food served and the conversations which usually centered around golf, tennis and who was cheating on their spouses. The money they would have spent on dues and fees was used for travel and a new kitchen for Annie while Julia put down payments on homes for Tracy and Molly. They could have lived more affluent lives had they hoarded the money in their bank accounts but both felt money was invented to be spent, wisely or foolishly. What was money if you couldn't enjoy it?

They were exuberant the night of the party. Mrs. Bishop's taxes had been paid and the dazed woman didn't know who to thank except God. And little Diedre was leaving for treatments in Canada on the coming Monday. Her family had thanked an anonymous donor in the community paper since an unmarked enveloped filled with cash had been left in their mailbox. They had helped when help was needed and still had one hundred thousand dollars in their emergency fund. And best of all, Velvel had decided to stay and join them. Annie had called Jim Semple and asked if they could bring a guest and he assured her there would be an extra place setting.

"Think of it as a costume party," Annie said as Velvel dressed, "with you the center of attention. No mousse on your hair, let it spring out in all its glory. The black suit I think, with the white collarless shirt." Velvel had decided to grow a beard and prickly black hairs jutted out from his chin, springing in every direction to match his unruly hair. "I do wish there were more and they were longer so I could braid them," Annie lamented. You could make a fashion statement. There, you look magnificent, rather mystical, like Rasputin."

The look on Nora's face as a hundred people yelled surprise was well worth the price Julia and Annie had paid for their new finery, gowns they probably never would wear again. Julia looked regal in emerald green satin. It was straight cut with a slit that reached above the knee and had long sleeves. Julie felt her legs were still pretty damned good but the slightly wrinkled skin on her arms and neck had to be covered. Annie's gray, feathery, lightweight wool went well with her silver gray hair that had lost a little of it's spring. Because she missed her red tinted hair, she wore a long red stole around her shoulders, which brought a rosy glow to her cheeks.

"I don't want to sound vain but we look better than Nora," Julia said as they settled at their table, "even with her face lift."

Nora was still standing inside the doorway, frozen stiff as a statue with shock and dismay. A deep flush suffused her face while her mouth was a terse slash of red, a gargoyle's grimace. When she had the composure to look around, she saw hundreds of colorful balloons with the number sixty on them and two huge cakes; one a six and the other a zero. She closed her eyes in horror as young men dressed as lottery balls, depicting sixes or zeros pranced around to the music of Bessame Mucho, handing out favors; bouquets of six chocolate roses wrapped in foil and tied with golden ribbons. Jim stood behind her beaming with pride. A waiter passed and Nora grabbed a drink, gulping it down in one long swallow. A second drink quickly followed the first.

Nora was clad in a long, exquisitely cut, black Donna Karan gown. Diamonds sparkled around her neck by way of three strands of them set in platinum. Her ears, wrists and two fingers held more of the same. The glitter only emphasized the anger she vainly tried to keep in check. Nora usually steered away from scenes and this would be her greatest test. She strongly believed that creating a scene was vulgar and though she could cuss with the best of them in the privacy of her home, in public she was a true lady. A crystal glass seemed to be part of her ensemble since she held one in her hand all night. The eyes that had shot out daggers at Jim earlier now seemed glazed.

The guests sitting at Julia and Annie's table could only stare at Velvel, who swung his arms and hands wildly every time he spoke. They weren't quite sure if he was related to Julia or Annie or if he simply walked in unannounced. But he made them all laugh so they didn't ask Jim Semple whom he belonged to.

Julia was in the ladies room when Nora stumbled in, bouncing against one of the cubicles in a rush to get inside. She barely made it. The sounds of retching were obscene in the opulent marble and crystal lit room. Disgusting, Julia thought. There's no uglier sight than a drunken woman who can't handle liquor. The cubicle door was open and Nora knelt in front of the toilet. She groaned and threw up again. "I'm going to kill Jim for this humiliation." She heaved again and fell against the toilet seat. Julia watched in fascination as the clasp of her necklace came undone. She rushed to Nora's side just as the necklace plopped into the bowl. "Nora, don't flush…" Too late. Nora had pressed the handle. Julia moved with the speed of a hummingbird and just managed to catch the edge of the clasp before it went all the way down the drain. In fact, she had to fight suction to pull it up again. "Nora," she cried. "Your necklace…"

Several other women hovered in the background not knowing how to handle the situation. They came closer to Nora who was now sitting on the floor, her legs spread out in front of her. "Call for help," Effie Worthington yelled.

"Get a plumber here," another shouted.

Julia patted Nora's head. "Nora, you…"

"To hell with the necklace," Nora screeched. "I hate the fucking thing almost as much as I hate Jim for putting on this three ring circus."

Well, in that case, Julia thought. She let the chains slither down the bosom of her gown. Yuck. It was wet, cold and probably covered with vomit. All for the cause since the ungrateful bitch didn't want it anyway. She left Nora and the others to get back to the party.

The band broke into a spirited hora since several of the guests were Jewish. Velvel's eyes lit with delight. Hasidic Jews were known for their frenetic spiritual dancing and although Velvel had never been a true Hasid, he never forgot his roots, the many hours spent with Hasidim he knew at prayer. Two couples tried to keep time with the beat but failed miserably. Velvel shot onto the floor, fingers snapping, head laid back as he gazed at the ceiling in supplication. His feet floated along the floor as the band increased the tempo. Faster and faster he twirled never once opening his eyes to see where he was going. He was back in the days of religious ecstasy, his body becoming a blur of motion as onlookers stared in awe. With the lively music approaching the final notes, he defied gravity by twirling like a top. The increased momentum sent him off to the side where he tripped into several human lottery balls. They tumbled with the force and rolled across the floor taking Velvel with them until they crashed into the table holding the cakes, which tumbled atop them. Coming out of his trance, Velvel stuck a finger into the frosting and tasted it. "Delicious," he cried. "Let us eat cake."

Several other guests joined him on the floor poking hands in what was to have been desert; white cake with black cherry filling and cream icing. Nora let out a piercing scream as she saw a dozen of her friends kneeling around frosted lottery balls and a weird man dressed in black.

Needless to say, the party began breaking up. A maintenance man had taken out the toilet but couldn't find the necklace even after using rods and hooks. Jim Semple wandered around the ballroom looking like a lost soul, wondering why his wife was seething as she staggered around breaking balloons with long perfectly manicured fingernails. Everyone else was having a marvelous time.

"I think it's time to leave," Annie suggested as Nora collapsed in a heap in the center of the dance floor. "This will be known as the party of the century. Too bad beautiful diamonds went down the tube."

Julia put her mouth next to Annie's ear. "Didn't have a chance to tell you with all this hoopla but my deft fingers caught the piece just before it was sucked into oblivion. I was going to return it but she screamed right in my face saying she hated it. Her loss is our gain."

"Excellent reflexes," Annie praised.

"Let's go to my house so I can get the loot out of my bra. And I have to take a shower before I start smelling like a drunken skunk."

"How many diamonds would you say are on that piece."

"A whole bunch. Jim spared no expense."

"It's rather like winning a lottery isn't it? They helped Velvel up off the floor. "Snap out of it, darling, the party's over."

"I did good?"

"You were born to party, Velvel. It's your true calling and I think you're just beginning to realize your potential. Everyone can tell you're a bon vivant."

Later they learned there were twenty-five one carat diamonds in the necklace. Velvel appraised them as excellent quality worth about three thousand dollars each. They asked him to sell the diamonds whenever he found the right opportunity. Their emergency fund was back to its original figure.

Chapter 15

"London? You're going to London tomorrow? Mom, why didn't you say anything sooner?"

"If I remember correctly, Tracy, you and Tim took off for Florida with only a few hours notice. And another thing you should keep in mind is that I'm free and unencumbered. I cooked this wonderful dinner tonight because I'm not sure how long I'll be gone and when I'll see my little angels again."

"Who's all going?" Molly asked.

"Annie naturally and a new friend of ours. Actually he's paying for the trip."

"A man is taking you?" Molly was thunderstruck. "Who is he?"

"His name is Velvel Chavivi and we met him in New York; a darling man. I wish you had a brother like him."

"You're going with a young man? A stranger is treating for a trip to London? This is absolutely the goofiest thing you've ever done. Don't tell me he's the one who created the scene at Nora Semple's party. I hear the entire older crowd at the country club is up in arms."

"Nora created enough scenes to keep gossip mongers going for months. Velvel only danced and fell into the cake. Annie and I feel quite comfortable about traveling with him."

"Annie was always wild and so were you. Only Cissy could keep you in check. Who is this Velvel? The name alone is weird."

"Tracy, not another word. Never in my life have I bad mouthed your friends and you've had some doozies, especially when you were in college. Did I ever say anything about the boy who was in a rock band and had snakes tattooed all over his arms? Did I ever talk about the bald cult leader?"

"I was young and foolish, going through a stage."

"Then I'm old and foolish and we're even. And Velvel's not that young; he's sixty-five. When I said brother I meant you could love him like a brother. In many ways, he's like a young, underprivileged boy. He stayed at Annie's for a few days when we got back from New York and again before he left for home."

"There'll be a scandal brewing any minute now. He must be a gigolo out to get your money."

"Really, dear, how could he possibly want our money if he's paying for the trip? He's as good as gold. We're going to London to meet his brother."

"My God, are you or Annie planning to marry him?"

"No, he's only a very close friend. I'll call every few days so you know I haven't had my throat slashed by Jack the Ripper."

"This is not a joking matter."

"I think it is. In any case I'm a grown woman who has always believed in freedom of choice. Let's change the subject before the children think we're arguing." Julia turned her attention to her grandchildren. "Guess what's for desert darlings? Your favorite, Mississippi Mud."

Annie only had Allan to tell of her upcoming trip. "In case you try to call, I'll be in London for a while."

"That's great, mom. Finally going to get that passport out of moth-balls? I'll bet a hundred bucks you get one of those stoic palace guards to laugh."

"I wish I could. Sometimes I wonder if the British have a sense of humor. Maybe they do but it's different from the American brand. Allan, what would you think if you heard something very strange about me?"

"You're always involved in strange doings. Granted you've slowed down these past couple of years but you've always been a very interesting person. Remember when a cop took you to jail after a Halloween party? He tried to give you a ticket and you gave him some lip and he locked you up. There you were in a cell dressed as Cleopatra."

"I was only ten miles over the limit and policemen aren't infallible. His radar meter was out of sync."

"And the time you let all the dogs out of the pound because you insisted they weren't being treated humanely?"

"And they weren't. My action got enough publicity to bring in the authorities."

"So what are you planning for the Brits? You going to swim the English Channel or rob the Crown Jewels?"

Oh, how I would love to, Annie thought. "I think that's beyond my capabilities."

"Nothing's beyond your capabilities. Give the queen my regards."

"I'm so glad I raised a son who's not stuffy and conservative."

"And I'm glad I raised a mother who dares to be different."

You don't know the half of it, Annie thought as she hung up.

Chapter 16

"Did your pilot stop off for lunch in Cleveland for two hours?" Velvel asked impatiently. "Arrogant flyboys think they run the world. We must hurry. Why was your flight delayed? Never mind, we have to run all the way over to the international terminal. Passports? You have your passports? Wait, do I have mine? Yes. Not a minute to lose."

"Velvel, you can't stop dead in your tracks every time you start a sentence. You said we had to hurry."

"Did I stop? Maybe I did."

Julia and Annie were amazed when they walked into the jumbo jet. "First class? We've never flown first class."

"Nothing but the best. Anything you want is yours on this trip. You want the Queen's autograph? We'll storm the palace gates. You want to see Henry the VIII? We dig him up. Wait, I have something more important on my mind. Avi, my brother, thinks I'm bringing along two women who…this is too embarrassing. Oh well, in for a pound, in for an ounce. He thinks I'm bringing two girlfriends so can you pretend you're crazy about me?"

"We are, Velvel."

"I mean in love with me, no not that kind of love but…"

"Like we're after your body?"

"Yes, yes, that's it. Could you? I've been giving him a line for years and now I have a reputation to prove. He thinks I'm a regular ladies man."

"Tell you what we're going to do. We'll melt over your every word, swoon every time you look our way, touch you whenever Avi's looking."

"You don't have to overdo it."

"We'll do the right thing, I promise."

"Good, good. First day after we have dinner with Avi I'm going to take you to the Tower of London to see the Crown Jewels. Then we're going to the Diamond Trading Company for a private sight. Your eyes will be blinded by dazzle."

"They'll let us in for a sighting?"

"A private one just for us. After all, Avi's a big shot there."

Julia and Annie were startled at the difference between Velvel and his brother. Avi was tall, dark and extremely good looking with a quiet air of distinction while Velvel was short, thin and excitable but they decided they'd take Velvel any day over his younger brother. Avi had tears in his eyes as they hugged and kept patting each other on the back although Velvel had to reach up to return the embrace.

"Vel, you sly devil. And here are your two women. Leave it to you to have two girls at a time not one like the rest of us."

Annie and Julia took hold of Velvel's arms. "He's quite a man," Julia said sincerely. "I don't know what I'd do without him. When he's away I can't wait for him to call."

"And I wouldn't mind if he moved in with me permanently," Annie added. "My house comes alive when he's there."

"And you aren't jealous of each other?" Avi asked, puzzled.

"We've been friends too long to be jealous. It's always been our theory that one person doesn't own another. We've reached a point in our lives when every minute is precious and I believe Vel was put on earth to make women happy."

Velvel slapped his forehead. "Forgot, almost forgot to tell you. Since Avi came to England he's called Adam Chapman. You see…never mind just remember to call him Adam unless it's just us."

"Okay."

"See, that's what I like about them, Avi, no rules, no regulations, no explanations required."

And so the evening progressed; a great deal of laughter, reminiscence between the two men, talk of their work."

"How is it that you came to England while Velvel stayed in New York and two other brothers went to Florida and Connecticut?"

"Our mother died in a horrible way. Vel told you about that didn't he?"

"Yes, so tragic."

"After they were buried I was so angry at the slum landlord I wanted to kill him. Me who was taught from the day I could comprehend that doing physical harm to another person was one of the worst sins against God. That day I found the owner of the tenement and thrashed him, beat him to within an inch of his life. When I came to my senses and saw him on the ground bleeding, I panicked. I had done that? I was raised to be peace loving."

"When I was young I thought I would be deeply religious," Velvel added. "But as I got older, diamonds took over my mind. I think my falling away began when the Rebbe told the boys we should sleep with our hands in our sleeves so we wouldn't touch impure parts of our bodies."

Avi laughed boisterously. "Vel never could never sleep that way. His arms flailed even while he was sleeping and I should know since I slept next to him and usually got a klop in the nose twice a night. Vel couldn't stand his hands in his sleeves and I couldn't fathom the idea of being ruled by to many rules to count. I was too busy dreaming about seeing the world. Anyway, to get back to my story, the man I hit pressed charges and there was a warrant out for my arrest. Vel was the one who had an offer to go to London to work for the Diamond Center. He gave me his ticket and made me to go in his place."

The women looked at Velvel. "You never told us that."

"Nothing, it was nothing. On the streets I work best. I make enough money using my mouth. Being cooped up in a building all day would have made me crazy. Besides I don't like some of the dealers who get invited to the sightings. I would have screwed up and given them bad parcels and the center would have fired me. Avi always had more patience."

"He saved my life," Avi said proudly. "If I went to jail, I would have died. The thought of being locked up is a nightmare. Some day I hope to repay my brother. I keep asking him to come and work with me in London but he loves New York too much to leave."

"You made me proud," Velvel complimented as he dropped Julia and Annie off at the Park Court hotel. "You don't mind that I stay with Avi?"

Annie sighed. "Didn't we tell you there are no rules in our friendship? Everyone comes and goes as they please."

"Right, I remember. I'll pick you up at eleven tomorrow to see the Crown Jewels."

"You should spend as much time as possible with your brother. We can manage on our own."

"The sights begin in two days so he's very busy. After they're over, he'll take a couple of days off."

Velvel was more excited than any of the tourists as they went into a chamber to view the Crown Jewels. He was also more knowledgeable than the tour guide who was getting annoyed as people stopped paying attention to him and listened to Velvel instead.

"Look, look," Velvel gushed. "The Russian Kokoshnk tiara, four hundred and eighty eight diamonds. Count them, no that would take too long. It was designed to look like a peasant's headdress. All of the ladies in this room should have their picture taken wearing a tiara. Guide, can we borrow this for a minute?"

The rotund tour guide puffed with indignation. "Absolutely not. The pieces never leave their case."

"A few pictures is all we want."

"No." The guide dived to get him away from the display before alarms sounded.

"Okay, forget that idea. Here are the Greville chandelier earrings. They have every modern cut of diamond there is. You name it, they got it; pear, emerald, brilliant, all of them. A gift to Princess Elizabeth from her parents but she couldn't wear them because she was afraid to get her ears pierced. Up to then she never wanted it done but once she took a gander at these beauties, hoo-haw, her mind she changed. Probably stuck the needles in her lobes herself. Enough of them, look over here. Queen Victoria's collet necklace. See the bigger diamonds? Eight to eleven carats each of the finest. Wait, wait, here's the Lahore. Perfect, absolutely perfect."

He passed up a case. "Lots of pearls here. Don't like pearls much, they don't sparkle. He hurried to the next exhibit. "Ah, these are children of my favorite, the magnificent Cullinen. Here are the Cullinen III and Culinen IV, out of the original, which weighed in at 3,106 carats. Frederick Wells found it in a shaft wall at the Premier mine in Africa while he was diddling. Experts said it was part of a larger diamond that had broken off. They never found the other part but can you imagine a diamond that originally must have weighed six or seven thousand carats? It was the papa of diamonds. If I could only find the other piece I'd die the happiest man in the world. No, how could I be happy if I was dead? Premier probably put the other chunk through the crushers without realizing what lay in those slabs of rock they dynamited. Never understood why they have to blast diamonds out of the rocks. Finding them lying on a beach in Namibia was much easier. But they're blasting there too now. Every time they blast and crush, some diamonds are lost. Progress, I hate progress."

See that pear drop in the Cullinen III? Over 94 carats and the one hanging from Cullinan IV is square cut, over 63 carats. The most valuable pieces owned by the queen." Vel hopped from one case to another marveling over what he saw. The crowd followed him, totally entranced with his monolog. The guide stood at the back, furious. The little half pint was trying to take over his job. It was time to put a stop to this charade. They had to practically drag Velvel away at closing time.

On the next day Velvel crowded in every possible tourist attraction available because he had other plans for the following day. They rode on a double-decker bus, cruised down the River Thames where the wind tore at his unruly hair until it doubled in volume and spiked up straight in the air. They shopped at Harrods, stood outside Buckingham Palace for the changing of the guard. Velvel scurried from one man to another, examining their uniforms. "I'd like a hat like that. If I had a hat like that I'd be a foot taller." Annie prodded him toward a tea shop although he kept looking back. "Think of the stir I'd create if I walked into one of your fancy parties with a hat like that."

"Velvel, we're exhausted. Can we sit for a while and enjoy a cup of tea?"

"Didn't I say you could have anything you wanted? Let me tell you what I have planned for tomorrow. We're going to browse through every antique shop in London. Sometimes a person can pick up a good semi-precious stone for peanuts…no pounds. Why do they call their money pounds? It doesn't weigh a pound. One pound won't buy you a one pound halibut."

Annie and Julia groaned.

The day before the sightings began, Avi arranged for a private room. He was followed into the room by two guards, each carrying a box, one large the other small. The weight of the boxes was duly noted on paper and the guards left.

"Even though you're family, Vel, and I hold a position of authority, I still have to abide by the rules." He turned to Annie and Julia. "The weight has to be exactly the same when the boxes are taken back to the vault. If it's off by even one gram it's panic time." He opened the smaller box. "These are roughs, what the dealers will be buying tomorrow. Over two billion dollars worth will go out this year. These happen to be near colorless with very slight inclusions."

"They look like chunks of glass," Annie said. "There's no sparkle and they're sort of gray."

"The outer skin. When they're cut and polished they'll look like what I'm about to show you next. These need romancing; faceting and polishing because people aren't going to mount and wear roughs as adornment. Rough diamonds may look like ordinary pebbles or rocks but they're anywhere from fifty million to three billion years old. How's that for antiquity? Now it's time to see the finished product." He closed the small box and opened the larger. "As I told you earlier, these are flawless. They're earmarked for special purposes; promotion, advertising, television commercials. All are three-carat investment quality stones. There are several different cuts; you might like to examine the new lighthouse cut."

Julia and Annie could only stare in awe as the gems caught the light and reflected every color of the spectrum. Their fire seemed to come from deep within.

"Keep in mind that every diamond is unique, much like fingerprints. Prices vary greatly in the diamond industry, anywhere from five hundred dollars a carat for the poor quality up to fifty thousand a carat. These are the latter."

Velvel never took his eyes away. "This box is worth millions."

"Have a billion to be exact. Now you'll understand why the box has to be weighed carefully before leaving the room. I never get over the thrill either, especially when you consider diamonds are similar to coal. They're both crystalline carbon but to be a diamond, they have to go through more tortuous stages. Go ahead, Julia, Annie. You can run your fingers through them. They'll feel a trifle oily."

"Doesn't feel that way to me," Annie said rubbing several of the gems between her fingers.

"With a little practice you can feel the difference."

"What do you do when you get away from all this magnificence? Do you have a family?"

"Vel and I shied away from marriage although I'm seeing a fine woman I met here. And I'm hardly ever away from diamonds. Even on holidays I have them on my mind. Last year I spent three weeks in Zaire, poking through the mines. This year I'm going to Australia, to the Argyle mine. Want to see if I can find one of their cognac diamonds. Their browns weren't selling well until they changed the names to champagne and cognac. Personally, I prefer stumbling upon a rough. I keep thinking I'll be the one to find a rare flawless diamond over a hundred carats in weight and it will be named for me. I sometimes dream I find one of the most rarest of diamonds, a vivid orange."

"And would it be the Chapman diamond?"

Avi laughed. "Maybe the Chavivi Diamond. I'm sorry I changed my name but when I came here, they insisted. Show's over I'm afraid. It's rather hectic with the sightings tomorrow."

As Velvel tried to replace his handful of diamonds into the box they slipped and fell to the floor, a shower of flashing raindrops. Fortunately the floor was carpeted. "Oops, didn't mean for that to happen. Now you see why I sent Avi in my place. No harm done."

They all got on their hands and knees to recover every last diamond that had fallen. Heads bumped as they searched.

"Did you notice something in there, Julia?" Annie asked once they were out of the building. Those old myths aren't true at all. One states that if you're guilty of a crime, a diamond will dim and if you're innocent, it will shine brilliantly. We're guilty and none of those diamonds grew dull."

"Because you're pure of heart," Velvel said. "A diamond denotes purity."

"I'm glad the scale tallied when Avi had them taken back to the vault. If it hadn't, I'd die of embarrassment if I had to be strip searched."

"They don't make mistakes here. "Okay, ladies, on to the antique shops to see if we can spot any treasures. And tonight we'll have dinner in a castle."

"You never cease to amaze me, Velvel. You've never been to London and yet you know everything about it."

"A few good tips from Avi. I want to make this trip memorable for you."

They walked for miles, Velvel skipping ahead of them because he was sure there would be a treasure in the next store or in the one after that. He passed up fine antique furniture as though it was old junk, only asking to see costume jewelry. At a small shop that was barely eight feet wide, his eyes turned crafty as he looked through a cardboard box of old brooches, bracelets and necklaces. He picked up strands of jet beads. "How much for this?"

"Twenty pounds," the man answered without blinking an eye.

"Two much. I can carve the same from lumps of coal. You have to come down on the price." Velvel was acting up again, pacing from one end of the store to the other.

"You'll have to excuse him," Annie explained. "He tends to get hysterical and the only way to stop the bouts are for him to breathe in the fumes from burning jet."

"The devil you say," the owner answered. "Hysteria or not, the price is still twenty pounds."

"I could buy a pint bottle of tranquilizers for that," Velvel said sarcastically. "Okay, okay, forget the jet. How much for this dirty looking bracelet with a missing stone?"

"Five pounds."

"Too much. I'll give you three."

"Four."

"Okay, but I'm being taken." Velvel handed over the money. When they were outside, he did a little dance. "It's brown tourmaline called dravite. Worth a lot more than four pounds. A couple hundred in American dollars. He had the stones popped out in an instant. "For your collection. I knew I'd find a bargain. Now we can stop visiting the shops. We found our lucky piece."

They were wandering around a castle just west of London after a superb dinner, straying away from the other diners who were in the library with brandies. "Look, Velvel, a suit of armor. I always wanted to have a picture taken with a knight in shining armor," Julia said wistfully. "I suppose a photo of the armor alone will have to do."

"You want a picture with a knight in armor you shall have it. Just help me get into this tin can."

"Will you really do this for me?"

"No problem, just give me a minute here. Medieval warriors must have been midgets. Even I'm having a rough time with this." Velvel struggled with the pieces but they were finally on after a great deal of clanking.

"En guard," Julia cried as she grabbed two swords and handed one to Velvel.

"It's sharp," he warned.

"You're practically bulletproof. En guard. Annie, get a picture of this."

Velvel backed up as Julia advanced, thrusting out with a great deal of flourish. Velvel parried and leaped up several stairs. He tripped over his own feet on the tenth step and came crashing down with a great deal of noise. "Oops," he said as he lay on the marble floor below. "No harm done. I'm okay."

Several men came rushing out of the library. The florid faced lord of the manor was livid. "What's going on here? That armor dates back to the sixteenth century." He yanked it off Velvel piece by piece. "Out. All of you out and never show your faces here again. Howard, get those swords."

They laughed as they returned to the city. "Old grouch," Annie said. I detest people who don't use the treasures they own. It's like Myra back home. She never allows anyone in her living room because she claims it cost a fortune to decorate. Why have a living room if no one can sit in it?

Who cares if there's an expensive French sofa? A sofa was meant to be sat on or it wouldn't be a sofa."

Over the weekend Avi took them to visit a friend who owned a cottage near Brighton. Annie and Julia had no idea why it was called a cottage when there were fifteen rooms but it was fun playing croquet, having tea and scones in the afternoon and wandering around the countryside. They refused breakfast kippers. Fish didn't seem the proper thing that early in the morning.

The weekend over, Velvel planned to spend the last three days with his brother while Julia and Annie wandered off on their own at a more relaxed pace. Their visit to London came to an end much too soon.

Velvel had a surprise for them as they waited at LaGuardia for the connecting flight to Chicago. "I don't know how to say this," he muttered. "I should just say it straight out. I will. Avi gave me something before I left." He reached into a pocket and pulled out two rings. "He said I ought to give my girls—oy, this is embarrassing."

"Out with it, Velvel. You don't have to be embarrassed around us."

"He said it would be appropriate to give my two girls a ring and handed me these. They're identical, white gold set with eight gray diamonds, each a quarter carat. The grays aren't priceless, in fact they're pretty common."

"Velvel, they are priceless. Thank you." They kissed his cheeks soundly until he turned beet red.

"It's a friendship symbol, because I can't get romantically involved with Gentile women?"

"Yes, we'll wear them always."

"Ah, not when you're doing a job. Someone would remember them."

"No, not when we're doing a job."

"I've got a handle on something promising. I should know more in a couple of weeks."

Later, Julia's daughters were to remark that their mother and her friend were both engaged to the same man.

Chapter 17

I've signed up for advanced karate classes," Julia said one day in early May as they drove home from dance class. They were taking polka lessons. Since they hated regimented exercise they felt dancing the polka covered all flexible parts of the body. Such a stomping pounding dance. Such fun. Polish people were so carefree, leaving their troubles at home to dance, drink and be merry. "I must say my quality of life has improved tenfold since we made the decision to take charge of our lives again."

"I always took the bull by the horns," Annie answered, "but then again my family lives halfway across the country." She deftly swept by a truck in a no passing zone. "I now realize that we let ourselves slip into middle age without realizing we were giving up our daring-do because our children expected it of us. Well, not so much Allan because he's not around but I'm a second mother to Tracy and Molly and they both gave us such withering looks whenever we did anything out of the ordinary. I'm glad that's behind us."

"You should take karate lessons with me."

"You already know the basics, I don't."

"It's a good skill to have. You never know when we both might need to handle ourselves with strength. I can't kick as high as I used to but my instructor says I still pack a hell of a wallop."

"Okay, sign me up but when am I supposed to fit it in? I just signed up with the jewelry making craft shop. Can't give that up because I can buy semi-precious stones for next to nothing. I never knew that many minerals could be faceted. I love obsidian when it's polished. If I gaze at it long enough it looks like a snowfall against a dark sky."

"We can't give up volunteering at the hospital either. The children look forward to our visits. Maybe we could forego gourmet cooking classes."

"Now there's an idea. If we keep on sampling the dishes we make we're going to turn into butterballs."

"Swimming takes care of that along with the polka dancing. We're as slim as willows these days."

"I have to put a hold on everything for a week, Julia. Allan, Jennifer and Caro are coming to spend a week for Mother's Day."

"Tracy's cooking for all of us and since the grandsons have a school break, I thought I'd take them into the city for a few sights. They've never been to the Sears Tower or Navy Pier."

They each made separate plans. Annie loved nothing better than having her son home again, not that Jennifer wasn't welcome. She was a darling girl and Caro, her seven year old granddaughter, was the real treasure of her life. Time to spoil her again.

Julia got ready for the special day set aside for mothers. Molly and Tracy were sure treating her differently these days. She was now included in their get togethers and when she had time, she joined them. I wasted almost three years," Julia thought to herself. "No, I didn't. The years weren't wasted at all they were simply different. Life runs in cycles anyway and the excitement's returned full force. And maybe I needed those few years of rest to be able to cope with what was forecast for the future.

Chapter 18

"Gram, can we dress up in the old costumes up in the attic while mom and dad visit their friends?"

"Of course, Caro. What a splendid idea. I have boxes and boxes of old things up there. Let's see, you can be a lion. Your father was a lion one year for Halloween."

"And a ballerina?"

"Yes, I believe I can manage that. Your grandfather dressed as a ballerina one year."

"Grampa?" Caro giggled. She didn't remember Jack that well but often looked at photos of him.

"He was in one of his silly moods."

They spent hours up in the attic trying on dozens of costumes. With each change of outfit, they stood in front of an old cheval mirror admiring themselves and putting on silly skits. Caro was a skeleton, a lion, pumpkin, witch and ballerina. Annie loved the mess they made as they rummaged through more cartons.

Suddenly Caro cried out in delight. "Look, gram, I found a tiara, just like the one queens wear. I had a tiara once but it was plastic and cracked in half. I love tiaras."

"This one is made of metal so it's more durable. Would you like to keep it?"

"Can I?" There was awe in the little girl's eyes.

"Yes. Let's take it downstairs and clean it up again. It used to sparkle nicely when I dressed as Queen Victoria and your gramps was Prince Albert at the country club costume ball one year."

They sat at the kitchen table cleaning of the headpiece. "It's sparkling again, gram. Oh no, there's a jewel missing."

"So there is. Must have fallen out somewhere."

"A tiara isn't real unless all the jewels are in place."

Annie was hit with a perfect idea. "Indeed not. You wouldn't be a queen with a missing jewel. I think I can fix it. Find the tube of glue under the sink." Annie returned with one of the whites she had taken from Frenzel. "This should be a perfect fit."

"It shines brighter than the others. Is it a real diamond, gram?"

"Who's to know real from unreal these days? They made such good imitations. Fashion changes so often by the time you grow up, real might be false and false will be real. Tell you what, Caro. You might want to keep this always and check it out again when you're a grown woman like your mother. Maybe you'll be in for a surprise."

Caro placed the tiara atop her head. "I'll keep it always and forever. You're a magical grandmother."

There were tears of joy in Annie's eyes. "Thank you, my queen. Now what would the queen like for a snack? Royal french fries? The emperor's cookies? Or how about the frog prince's chocolate layer cake?"

Annie rummaged through her treasure box humming These Are A Few Of My Favorite Things, substituting her own lyrics; children and winter and jewels in a basket. Would Caro ever find out her grandmother was a thief? There was that possibility. If she ever did, would she understand that everyone marched to a different drummer, everyone had their favorite things, their favorite dreams, their individual goals?

Chapter 19

Fencing, your neighbor said you were fencing," Velvel groaned as he paced across Annie's front porch. "Stabbed in the heart you could have been, your life's blood oozing out."

"Dear Velvel, when did you get in? If you had called I could have picked you up at the airport."

"Two hours ago and for two hours I have a lump of worry sticking in my throat. Why? Why do you do such foolish things? Isn't stealing exciting enough?"

"We're having so much fun. Don't destroy it by being a sourpuss. We've already learned to polka so we had to find a replacement for the time slot."

"You couldn't learn to tango instead?"

"Dear man, we already know that dance and fencing is job related. What if someone comes after us with a sword one day? We can assume a stance, parry and thrust."

"All my life I try to avoid disaster and you two seduce it, seek it out."

"When you look for trouble, trouble runs away and hides. It's only when you run from it that it pursues you."

"If only I could believe that."

Annie opened her door. "I believe strongly that everyone makes their own aura. Come inside, Velvel. I'll make us dinner and you can bring me up to date."

Velvel sighed in contentment two hours later. "Latke. My mother used to make them because potatoes were cheap. But we had no sour cream or applesauce. And the steaks here were right off the hoof. Now that I'm eating better I'm going to get a potbelly. How would a man with skinny legs look with a potbelly?"

"You move around so much, you burn off all the calories. Now what have you been up to since London?"

"Julia should be here so I don't have to repeat myself. But I repeat myself a lot anyway don't I?"

"I'll call her and we can have desert together."

Julia arrived twenty minutes later, swinging Velvel into a merry polka as she hummed one of the tunes from dancing class. Velvel caught the knack of the steps in less than three minutes. "Enough," he said after a while. I could dance like this until I go into a frenzy because it's so much like our music but I bring good news and bad. What do you want first?"

"Get the bad news over with so we can forget about it and enjoy the good news instead."

"Always optimistic. Frenzel came back to New York to sell another lot of diamonds, all whites this time. But that's not all he brought. In Tel Aviv he had an artist draw sketches of the thieves; you, Julia, and you, Annie."

"Oh my God. We didn't think he had enough time to get a good look at us. Do we have to flee the country, seek asylum in Switzerland or the Cayman Islands?"

"Not to worry. That was the bad news but now the good. I brought copies of the flyers they're passing out in the district."

Annie and Julia burst out in peels of laughter. "He made me look like a gorilla." Annie laughed harder.

The sheet of paper was divided into four sections; one showing Frenzel's interpretation of how Annie looked as a woman and another as a man. The same was done for Julia. Annie had worn a black wig but the hair in the female sketch was more like a basket of snakes set atop her head. Annie liked to be charitable when it came to people's looks but the woman in the sketch was ugly as sin. As her late husband would have said, she could scare away a nine day rain. When it came to Frenzel's interpretation of the male counterpart, the result was even more atrocious. "He either saw me as Bushman, Medusa or a Neanderthal. Probably a combination of all three. And I did not fake a wart the size of a dime."

"Look at me," Julia laughed. I'm a woman and man without a face. In one I have hair longer than Lady Godiva and in the other, I'm a bald faceless ogre who stands over six feet tall."

"The bad news wasn't so bad after all." Velvel said. "But I had to make a point and that is you're wanted women in New York. Frenzel will never rest until he finds the two who robbed him. You should quit while you're ahead."

"Not until we good and ready," Julia answered stubbornly.

Velvel shrugged helplessly. "Okay then, I have more news. I didn't tell you that when we were in London I bought a rough from the Diamond Center. They usually don't do that but Avi pulled strings. Ten carat rough, same size as the one my stepfather was to cut. I've been working on it every spare minute and this is the result." He opened a pouch and a diamond fell into his hand. "Royal cut, one hundred fifty four facets. Tedious work but the results are magnificent. The more facets you cut, the bigger the stone appears. And I won a bet with myself; only lost forty percent in the cutting. Pretty good, nu? No, it's a masterpiece."

"It's a work of art," Julia said turning the stone to catch every possible reflection. Color shot out and bounced around the room leaving a rainbow on the wall.

"A diamond has to glow from within, every facet must reflect the next or it loses brilliance. Showed this to a man I trust and he offered plenty for it."

"Are you going to sell it?"

"Never. It'll carry it with me for luck."

"That would be really courting disaster. Someone could rob you."

"Only you two know. I feel my stepfather is looking down from somewhere, wishing he had chosen me to cut his diamond. It would have made my career."

"If he's not, he should be. Velvel, you're better than Michaelangelo, better than Rembrandt."

"Wait, wait, I almost forgot. Looking at a diamond makes my mind jumble. If you still insist on adding to your collection, I have something that may be of interest. I tried to remember easy marks so you won't be in too much danger."

"You've pinpointed another possible heist? How thrilling."

"I shouldn't tell you this but if I didn't you would only go off on your own and try to attempt an impossible. Can you visit Dallas for two weeks or so? Three would be better but it can be done in two."

"We can go anywhere we like, especially for jewels."

"There's a filthy rich woman who lives on a ranch as big as Rhode Island just outside Dallas. She's about your age but there all similarity ends. Every year she heads a ritzy charity ball where they raise millions for worthy causes. The woman's late husband, may God rest his generous heart, gave millions upon millions and never missed it. Made his fortune in oil and real estate. Shame he had to die helping put out an oil well fire but he always insisted on keeping his hands in the dirtier side of the business. The wife is another story. She inherited those millions but she's not very charitable. But in memory of her husband, the committee still honors their name. Every year for the ball she wears her most fabulous jewels and flaunts herself over the others. It's said she has a walk-in safe in her house. This will be her ruby year. Last year it was diamonds and the year before that, emeralds. Next year will be the sapphires. She has so many jewels, she alternates."

"I like the idea of taking jewels away from a tight-fisted woman," Annie said gleefully.

"So she'll be wearing the ruby necklace with a large pear shape fifty-six carat pendant. Two dozen five-carat rubies make up the circlet around the neck. All the rubies are surrounded by diamonds and none of them are small. There are two wide bracelets, drop earrings and three rings. Her hand will be so heavy she'll have trouble keeping it from falling into her soup. She also has a tiara to match but I don't know if she'll have the chutzpa to wear that too. She calls herself the queen of Texas."

"How can we get invited to the ball or get to that safe?"

"You can't unless you donate a hundred thousand dollars and that's only for the cheaper seats. And you definitely can't get into the house. You can only get what she's wearing that night."

"But how?"

"Patience, I'm getting to that. She has an older chauffeur, in his seventies. Sometimes he carries a rifle. Been with the family for years. The lady in question always leaves the ball immediately after dinner. She enjoys making the grand entrance, having a few people fawn over her, sits for a few bites and makes a grand departure. That's where you come in."

"Snatch the goods outside?"

"No. Well, yes, but not right outside. There's a long stretch of road from the ranch gate to the house, a little over a mile of private road."

"She'll be decked out in a fortune. Won't the police escort her home?"

"They haven't done that yet. But you have to get her before she enters her house, which is wired better than a bank vault. If you get to Dallas a week or two early you can get the lay of the land and see if there's a chance of success. If not, you have to give up the idea and we'll find something else."

"We'll give it a shot, Velvel. What's this cheapskate's name?"

"Sukie Rae Fremont."

"**That** Fremont? One of the scandal sheets had a story on her a few months back written by one of her former servants. He really did an expose saying the dogs ate better than the servants, that Mrs. Fremont threw a fit if a slice of bread was wasted. The coffee grounds had to be used three times before being thrown away. How did you get all this information on her jewels?"

"Mordecai Birnbaum has relatives in Dallas and he visits them often. He tells everyone in the district stories about Dallas. I could come with you. Maybe you'll need my assistance."

"That's sweet but we don't want to get you involved. You can rest assured we'll never implicate you in our crimes."

Chapter 20

Julia was designated driver from the Dallas airport to their motel. They had rented a mid-size, gray Ford Taurus, a very inconspicuous car suitable for two older women. "Let's get everything straight in our minds," she said as she expertly maneuvered through traffic. Both women were excellent drivers but Julia always had the greater sense of direction. She had only studied a road map for a few minutes and knew exactly which was the best route to get them to the Holiday Inn on the fringes of Dallas proper. "We have nine days; we change motels every three days."

"We wear our dowdiest clothes except for the special night," Annie added.

"We act a little befuddled, not so much as to draw attention to ourselves though. I'll develop a slight limp."

"And I'll be a little palsied."

They were dressed in thick-heeled, low shoes, print cotton dresses with cardigan sweaters topped by a set of faux pearls. It was threatening rain so both wore plastic rain bonnets, the kind sold by the thousands for under a dollar at every discount store. They both wore tinted reading glasses, which hid the true color of their eyes. The handbags they carried were black vinyl with short straps, the kind depicted in cartoons where elderly women drove off mashers with a sound wallop.

The desk clerk at the Inn was most friendly as they checked in. "How yah all doin?" he asked in a deep Texas twang. "Welcome to Texas. Let's see, you're from…here it is, Pittsburgh."

"Yes, a dreary city this time of year," Annie answered. "As soon as we landed we knew we chose the perfect vacation spot. It's warm, sunny and everyone we've met so far is so gracious."

"Cause you're in the friendliest state in the nation. We're known for our warm hearts. How long you plan on stayin?"

"Three days. We're going to drive all over the state. It's so huge we don't know if three weeks is anywhere near enough. Dallas, Houston, Austin, Galveston, Padre Island, Waco. Lordy, we'll be tuckered out in no time with all that gallivanting."

"Need a little help with the routes?"

"Oh no, thank you. We have it all mapped out nicely. My son has that new Rand McNally program on his computer. It's amazing how all the points of interest along the way pop up in an instant. We have more sights to see than anyone could imagine. Now, young man, if we could just have our keys we're plumb tuckered out after the flight."

"Sure thing. You enjoy your stay now and take lots of stories home."

"Why thank you. I'm sure we'll take home enough stories to keep our friends at bingo wide-eyed for years."

They unpacked very little. "Time to drive to Sukie Rae's ranch and learn where the roads lead."

"There it is," Annie pointed out forty minutes later. "The Golden Clover and if this fence we've been passing for the longest time and if the land inside it all belongs to Sukie Rae, she owns her own fiefdom. You're going right in? I thought we were just going to drive around the property."

"You can't drive around property like this. God only knows where it begins and ends. We have to find a good spot to ambush Sukie Rae and we only have two shots at it; one on the way in and one on the way out today." Julie turned into the private road.

They were halfway to the house when Annie pointed excitedly. "Right up ahead. Finally we see some thick bushes. We should be able to hide in them. Everything we passed on the way to the ranch so far is barren. I was beginning to give up hope unless we land on top her limo by helicopter. That's one thing we haven't tried in our lives. These bushes should give enough cover."

"If the bushes aren't heavy enough we can always pull tumbleweeds around ourselves."

"No, this is fine." The house finally came into view. "Wow, will you take a look at that? The population of a small town could fit comfortably in that house."

A young man who looked to be in his thirties rode a horse toward them. He dismounted and came over to Julia's side of the car. "Can I help you ladies?"

"My, are you a real cowboy?"

"Ranch hand, ma'am."

"Thank goodness we've finally come upon another human being. We've been driving for miles and didn't see any signs of civilization. We need directions."

The ranch hand laughed. "You've probably been riding past Mrs. Fremont's spread for a spell."

"All this? Then where is the Ewing Ranch?"

"Ma'am?"

"J.R. Ewing's place. You have no idea how we loved that show. Every week we watched it faithfully. It was such a sad night when it ended, sadder when J.R. got shot but he pulled out okay. I felt I was part of the action even though I was sitting comfortably in my living room."

"The Ewings aren't a real family."

"You're mistaken young man. Our friends back in Pittsburgh said they visited the Ewing ranch."

"Well now, I think I know what you're talking about. There is a ranch where some of the shows were filmed. I think it's a tourist attraction now. Bout thirty miles north of here."

"Lordy, we must have made the wrong turn."

"I can show you around this ranch a little. Don't think Mrs. Fremont will mind as long as we stay away from the house."

One man saw them and one man was more than enough. Best that they leave before someone else came along. "That's very nice of you but you see it wouldn't be the same. We have to take pictures of the place where J.R., Bobby and Miss Ellie lived."

"And Sue Ellen," Annie added. "She was my favorite. Poor thing taking all that double talk from her conniving husband. I almost stood up and cheered when she started showing some spirit. Sorry to trouble you but we'll have to be on our way. If you'll just point us in the right direction."

"When you come to the end of the private road, make a left. About seven miles down make another left and you'll start seeing signs pointing the way."

"You're so helpful," Julia cooed. "I swear all we meet is friendly folks in Texas."

Julia and Annie were relaxing in their room late that night. "So what do you think of my plan?" Julia asked

"Excellent but there's nowhere to hide the car on Sukie Rae's road. We shouldn't use the rental anyway. Tomorrow we'll drive around and see where we can stash it."

"It'll be a hell of a long walk if you park it anywhere outside the private road. The nearest secondary road must be five miles away. Granted, we could walk it there but we wouldn't get far after the job's done."

Annie's eyes lit with an idea. "A motorcycle, Julia. Allan taught me how to ride one that summer he was home from college. We drove our bikes all over. He had a Harley and I only had a cheap rental but I kept up with him. Not with as much flash and dash but with a flair of my own."

"That was twenty years ago."

"It's the same principal; once you learn how to ride a bike you never forget even if the bike has a motor."

"Are you sure?"

"All I'll need is an hour's practice. I can put on a disguise when I go to the shop. Yes, that's it; a biker's outfit, all leather and a helmet. And if I add dark glasses no one will be able to tell I'm an older woman. I'll buy a cheap used one since we'll be dumping it later."

"I'm game. God, I haven't worn tight leather in years. I should get some of those clanking chains that hold a lot of keys."

"No showy accessories and definitely no chains. They could get caught in the gears and you'd be strangled. What if I had to drag you along a highway, the chains sparking like fireworks so everybody would notice us? We keep everything simple, remember? Fireworks. That gives me an idea. We have a lot of shopping to do."

"I was only fantasizing."

"In the next days we shop and pick up things for this job and maybe the next. We're going to drive around until we know every road as well as we know our area back home. We'll be prepared for every contingency. I realize nothing's perfect but we have to be as near perfect as possible."

"Neither rain, nor sleet, nor dead of night will keep us from Sukie Rae's rubies."

Chapter 21

In almost total darkness, only an occasional gleam from Annie and Julia's eyes could be detected as they sat on the ground in between prickly bushes lining Sukie Rae's private road. "Are snakes indigenous to Texas?" Julia asked. "That's all we need; to be punctured by rattler fangs after we've come this far."

"I'm not sure if snakes are nocturnal creatures. Make a little noise every few seconds so they stay away."

"We should prop more tumbleweeds around the motorcycle."

"Julia, we spray painted it matte black so it would blend in with the night. Besides, it's dark as pitch out here. The only way anyone's going to see the cycle is if they focus powerful spotlights on it. I don't think I've ever been in such darkness in my entire life. This must be what being in a grave is like. It would be nice if the moon cooperated and peeped out once in a while."

They were dressed in black leotards, turtleneck shirts and fleece jackets. On their feet were calf length boots. They had stowed their helmets on the cycle handlebars and black knit hats covered their heads. Black gloves covered their hands and their faces were smeared with black makeup.

"What time do you have, Julia?"

"Nine-thirty."

"Cocktails from seven to eight followed by dinner which should be over before ten. Sukie Rae should be back here by ten-thirty. Damn, the wind's picking up." Twenty minutes later they heard thunder in the distance."

"Annie, how are we going to light the rockets if it's raining?"

They had planned to startle the chauffeur by aiming harmless rockets at the limo. He would stop and Julia would keep him immobilized while Annie took care of Sukie Mae. If the car door was locked, they had a crowbar to pry or smash it open. A smoke bomb lit inside the car would blur the victim's vision after Annie had the jewels safely in hand and they would be off. It would take at least two or three minutes for the chauffeur and Sukie Mae to make their way out of a smoky car, clear their throats and watery eyes and call for help. All Annie and Julia needed was a five minute head start. Annie would then drop Julia off at the car while she drove another two miles to the river where she would send the motorcycle flying, hopefully into deep water. If by some chance the river wasn't deep enough, the cycle would be left there anyway. The dealer who sold them the bike couldn't possibly recognize Annie and there would be no prints left behind because they wore gloves. The spray paint was bought outside of Dallas on one of their exploration forays at a Walmart store and Annie had dressed in men's clothes for the purchase. If Sukie Mae had a police escort or any ranch hands came out to meet them, the operation would be canceled. They swore they would only steal if they had a good chance of success.

Forks of lightning ripped the sky and a sudden deluge broke loose from ominous, roiling clouds. "Damn," Annie swore, "I feel like I'm under a shower."

"More like a waterfall. I'm shivering. How am I supposed to keep a steady hand? I never remember it raining this hard back home except for that one time in 1977. Could we be struck by lightning?"

"Better lie flat on the ground just in case."

They were in the center of a maelstrom. One flash of lightning hadn't cleared from the sky when another fought for dominance. Bursts of thunder shook the ground beneath them like a burgeoning earthquake. "Do you hear something?" Julia asked.

"How can you hear anything in this din?"

"I thought I heard something close by."

"The rattlesnakes running for shelter."

"Now I hear horses."

"It's probably ranch hands checking to see if the cattle are stampeding. Or maybe they've been electrocuted and a massive barbeque will get under way come morning."

"This storm could delay Sukie Rae. She might decide to stay at the ball until it blows over."

"She has to come home sometime." Annie held her hand above her eyes to keep out the rain. "Look, headlights are coming this way. And I just heard that noise too, like something skittering away. Are there wild animals in Texas?"

"They have everything here and it's all bigger than anything we know. It could be a rodent the size of a pig. Here take two rockets. Hurry."

Sukie Rae was continuing a barrage of complaints to her chauffeur that had gone on since they left the hotel where the annual ball was being held. "For all that Bo donated year after year you'd think the committee could approve real food instead of all those dainty morsels they call a meal. I don't get out that often but when I do, I'd like to bite into something with substance. Bad enough Maria barely sets a decent table. She must be skimming from the household money. I'll have to go over the accounts again tomorrow and it'll take hours. Oakie, I can drive better blindfolded."

The lanky, gray-haired former ranch hand grimaced. "It's the storm, Miz Fremont. Can't see five feet in front of me." Jim Oakes gripped the wheel harder in anger. Old battleaxe, he thought. Maria did the best she could with the measly food allowance doled out to her once a week. At least the hired ranch hands ate good or Buzz Temple would have pulled all his men out in one fell swoop. Why the hell did anyone stay with Miz Fremont? Well the Mexicans didn't know better. Thought they were getting a decent salary at first but it didn't take them long to find out otherwise, which is why they quit in a hurry and always had to be replaced. He and Mrs. Siefert, the housekeeper, were the only long standing employees with almost thirty years of service each under their belts. Everyone else who worked in the house or on the grounds took flight when Bo Fremont died. And Mrs. Siefert handed in notice the other day. Two more weeks and she would retire on her social security and the nice inheritance Mr. Fremont left her in his will.

After Bo Fremont's death two years ago Miz Fremont turned into a viper and cut expenses to the bare bone. Servant's lights had to be out at ten, heat lowered in their part of the house so that on cold nights they had to wear coats to bed. Cheap, starchy food filled their stomachs instead of wholesome food. Time for me to retire too, Oakie thought. Should have retired nine years ago when I turned sixty-five but the ranch was my life and it was a good life when Bo was alive. Well, I have an inheritance as well and it's time to look into one of those pretty retirement communities or even a nice apartment away from this harridan.

"Can't you drive faster, Oakie? These damn jewels are weighing me down, my feet are killing me and I desperately need two fingers of bourbon and a hot tub. You should have seen some of those women at the ball, Oakie. In my opinion, they're anorexic. And the gowns they wore were sinful; barely coverin their bodies. I don't know what this world's coming to. God is going to smite all those whores of Babylon for their lascivious ways."

Probably jealous cause they're beautiful, Oakie sneered. Nobody's gonna take you for anorexic since you put on all those pounds since Bo's death. Everybody else on the ranch is losing weight the way you work em. Yes, it was definitely time to retire.

Annie and Julia were ready for action. Everything was precisely thought out with a main plan and alternates. When the rockets wouldn't ignite they ran for the limo doors. Good thing the car was barely rolling along. They planned to hit the windshield with a crowbar if the door wouldn't open. Before they could act, there was a blur of motion off to their right. Was it a black panther trying to avoid being hit or a baby horse?

Velvel jumped in front of the car and took a diving leap onto the hood. His face slammed against the glass flattening his features into a grotesque caricature. Multi-forked lightning defined the black sky and shattered it into segments of stark stained glass. Sukie Rae let out an ear splitting scream that overshadowed the next roll of thunder. Oakie lost control of the car, slammed on the brakes and it slid, tilting into the drainage ditch across the road. God, Oakie thought fleetingly, I've killed someone. He glanced up once, saw a demon from hell staring at him and shut his eyes again.

The car door had been locked but when Sukie Rae's body shifted hard she inadvertently grabbed the handle for balance and pressed down on it, which caused the door to fly open. A double pair of hands roughly yanked her out. Julie and Annie hadn't been expecting such a heavy load. They lost their grip and Sukie Rae plopped into mud. She sank down into it several inches and there was a great sucking sound as mud entrapped her in its sticky grip. Before she could think, those same hands were tugging at her jewels, pulling them away none too gently. "Oakie," she screamed again, "I'm being robbed. Stop them. Help me."

Jim Oakes' head had hit the window but he wasn't knocked unconscious. It appeared that way because he was praying that he hadn't killed someone or that he hadn't driven into a specter from the beyond. Now he smiled. So Sukie Rae was being robbed. About time she got her comeuppance. He closed his eyes and kept his head against the wheel, grinning. What he couldn't see he couldn't tell the police.

Sukie Rae screamed on, fighting the thunder for dominance in sound. "My tiara. No, you can't have my tiara."

Julia and Annie hadn't noticed she was wearing one although Julia thought she saw a gleam of light when Sukie Rae fell into the mud. They flipped her over and there it was beneath her.

The woman's screams were getting on Julia's nerves. They had enough to deal with because of the storm and some unknown banshee flying from the bushes. "Shut up," she growled "or I'll ignite you like a torch."

Sukie stopped in an instant.

It took a little force but the tiara was pulled up and shoved inside Annie's jacket. It was then they noticed Velvel standing on the side jumping up and down. Somehow the electrical charge of lightning made his hair stand on end even though it was wet. "Perfect," he cried in delight.

"Quiet," Annie hissed as she went for the motorcycle. She turned to Julia. "Let's move it."

"I have to see if the driver's okay," Julia said stubbornly. "I thought the car would simply come to a stop. It'll only take a second." She reached over the back seat and pressed two fingers against Oakie's neck. "Come on, where's the pulse?"

"Go," Oakie whispered. "Get the hell out of here. I'm okay."

Julia jumped back, startled. She ran to the motorcycle and jumped on behind Velvel. "Okay, go."

"Hold tight," Annie shouted. "Don't know if it'll hold three of us. If we don't get stuck in a quagmire, we'll be home free." Gravel spewed as the wheels caught hold.

Julia's rear end barely had clearance over the wheel and she hung on for dear life. "Velvel, how could you?" she shouted in his ear.

Annie executed a sharp turn out of the ranch drive. "We're going to die," Velvel whimpered. "Into a field we'll fly and vultures will eat us for breakfast."

"Quiet, Annie has to concentrate. She hadn't ridden a motorcycle in years."

Finally they came to a halt at the car. Julia hurried Velvel into the back seat. "There are some wet towels in a plastic bag. Toss them up front. And put on one of those rain bonnets; your hair is ghastly. At least you got rid of the beard. Maybe you can pass for a woman if we're stopped." She tore off after Annie who was twenty yards ahead.

The narrow river that had been tranquil only hours ago was now a raging torrent. Seconds after the motorcycle hit the water, it disappeared from view. "We have one exactly one minute to clean up," Annie instructed as she wiped black makeup from her face. "There's a streak across your chin, Julia. Hurry." They pulled yellow ponchos over their heads, dropped their boots, hats and helmets in the plastic bag and slipped into low-heeled shoes. They crammed everything into the plastic bag and Julia sent it flying into the dark water.

Annie finally breathed a sigh of relief. "Drive at a sedate pace. Remember we were sightseeing and got caught in this awful storm. Velvel, lie down on the back seat and don't say a word till we're safely in our room."

"Something's poking me. Let me just find it." There heard the sound of a match being lit.

"Velvel, no."

Billows of smoke invaded the car. Velvel bobbled the smoke bomb trying to push it out a window. He finally succeeded but not before nauseating smoke filled the car. Julia had to drive with her head out of the window, tears streaming down her face while Annie navigated from the other open window. The wail of a siren could be heard in the distance. "Switch to plan B," Annie gasped, "the long way back."

Chapter 22

They sat around the motel room in pajamas after taking a hot shower to chase away the chill of the night. Velvel's clothes were sopping wet and spread across several chairs. He wore Annie's terry cloth robe instead. "Tell me I did good," he pleaded. "I helped, I know I helped."

"What possessed you to interfere without giving us any warning? You scared the hell out of us. I thought there was another set of thieves out for Sukie Rae's jewels and we were going to have to fight a duel over the spoils. And even though I know there was an intruder, I couldn't stop the operation in mid-stream. You made me so crazy I forgot the driver carries a gun. Forgetting an integral part of the plan is the first step towards making a mistake."

"I didn't want you to be alone. Texans are tough, even the women. Figured three was better than two."

"Just how long were you lurking in the dark?"

"Only a half hour."

"How did you get there? I know you didn't walk. Oh my God, there's a car back there that will lead the police right to your doorstep and eventually to us."

"Stupid I'm not. Besides, I never learned how to drive. Don't need to in New York. I rode a bicycle to the ranch."

"A motorcycle?"

"No a regular bicycle, no motor, no noise."

"All those miles?"

"My legs were pumping all those miles. I feel like someone stole my legs off my body."

"Velvel, you must promise, no you must swear on the holy Torah that you'll never do this again. You must not get involved in our escapades."

"We're not friends any more? You're mad? You don't want me around?"

"No, we're not mad. You can still get involved in our escapades but not in the actual robbery. Now swear."

"Okay, okay, I swear by the holy book."

"The driver wasn't knocked out after all," Julia said. "I felt for a pulse and out of the blue he told me to get out, that he was okay. Scared the hell out of me."

"He was on our side?" Annie asked in astonishment. "I'm getting very puzzled."

"Only goes to prove Sukie Mae doesn't deserve those jewels."

"You see," Velvel interrupted. "It's that aura of yours. It's protecting you, and me along with you. Now can we look at the haul?" He unfolded a towel where the gems were drying out after their shower. "Look at this," he said reverently. "You got the tiara. I can't believe you got the tiara. Ugly workmanship but the rubies and diamonds are beautiful."

"Start popping out the stones, Velvel. How long will it take?"

"I can have them out in no time, just let me look at this huge ruby through a loupe before I start. I knew it, knew it; Burmese. Best rubies in the world."

"Julia, do you have the padded bra ready?" Annie asked.

"Yes." She began stuffing rubies and diamonds in between foam rubber padding. "I'll wear the bra to bed, under my pajamas."

"Tomorrow, well really today since it's after midnight, you drive Velvel to the airport before dawn. About seven, I'll go to the restaurant, order breakfast and tell that nice waitress that you've overslept but you'll be joining me shortly. You should be back by then and we'll say loud enough for anyone to hear that we're continuing our tour and driving on to Austin. Once we get there we can fly home. Velvel, take my keys and wait for us at my house."

"What a haul," he kept repeating. "I can't believe you got the tiara."

"Velvel!"

"What, what? Oh the key. Okay, I'll be waiting at your house."

They switched the channels on the television to see if the robbery was on the news but there was no mention of it.

Chapter 23

"I know what I saw, Sheriff, and nothin you say will convince me otherwise." Sukie Rae's face was flushed with anger as she sprawled in an oversize chair in her living room along with Oakie, Sheriff Dane Robard and one of his deputies. She wore a feather-trimmed, red robe and matching mules, all traces of the mud that coated her body earlier gone. Her hand held a water tumbler half filled with brandy. "I had one glass of champagne at the ball and one glass does not constitute a drinking binge."

The sheriff wished he were anywhere but here. He had dated Sukie Rae a couple of times when they were both in high school and they used to go at it hot and heavy at least once a week. Thank God he hadn't been foolish enough to propose marriage while he was in a sexual frenzy. Being married to this buzzard would be pure hell. "Miz Fremont, maybe you better start from the beginning again. This just doesn't make sense."

Sukie Mae sighed with impatience. "We were driving home from that god awful charity affair. I told Oakie he was driving too fast what with the weather and all but he didn't heed my warnin. Maybe he's losin his hearing with age. Out of nowhere, a bat slammed into our windshield, a bat with the face of a human. It glared at me with wild, red eyes and I thought I'd die of fright. The thing must have had suction cups on its...whatever they have; black claws I'd guess because it clung to the window like glue, until the car tilted."

For the past two years Sukie Rae had been calling the station for the goldarndest things. She accused her cook of trying to poison her but it was later discovered she had ladled into a pot of starch meant for the living room doilies. She had seen it on the stove, poured herself a bowlful and wolfed it all down. And just last month she called and insisted he shoot a horse that bit her. The ranch foreman refused to do it so Sukie Rae called him instead. He had the horse taken away in a trailer and gave it to a grateful rider, later assuring Sukie the deed was done. She called if planes flew too low over her land, if the state road outside her property had one tiny pothole and now human bats. Oh Lord, was she after him again? "Miz Fremont, no little bat has a human face. It's impossible."

"Who said anything about little? This bat was huge; black wings flapping behind him, glaring at me with devil eyes like it wanted to suck out my life's blood. Oakie can back me up on that part of the story. Tell him, Oakie."

Jim Oakes was thoroughly enjoying his brandy although Mis Frement had been a little stingy when she tilted the bottle his way. He was going to play this story for all it was worth. "Fraid she's right, Sheriff. Strangest thing I've ever seen. First I prayed I hadn't hit a man and then I saw that hair-raising creature stuck to my windshield. Wasn't more than a few seconds but I got a good look at it." He had to hold back a loud guffaw. "For all I know, might have been one of those vampires you see in movies. Eyes twice as big as normal, mouth wide open. I'm not sure but I could have sworn it had fangs. You see them, Miz Fremont?"

"I sure did. Two big teeth on either side of its mouth."

"Or it might have been the rain distorting images," the Sheriff offered.

"No sir, real people don't have wings like a bat's and I seen those wings flappin like it wanted to fly away but couldn't."

"Oh for God's sake, can we just go on with the details of the actual robbery?"

"Maybe the robbers scared off the bat and if so, then I'm eternally grateful because bein robbed is better than having all the blood sucked out of you," Sukie Rae resumed. "Two big hefty thugs, strong as ox. One wanted to suffocate me in mud but I fought back like a demon, especially when I knew they were taking the tiara. One threatened to set me on fire. Bo paid a fortune for that piece of jewelry and now it's gone. He's probably rollin round his grave this very minute. When he gave it to me, he said I'd always be his princess. Told him I'd rather be a queen and that's what I was, still am."

"Can you describe the thieves?"

"All I saw was black clothes, black faces and black hands. Must have been darkies, or Ninjas. As soon as they had my jewels, they were off. Didn't see anything cause my eyes were slathered in mud but I did hear a roar."

"Car? Truck?"

"How could I tell? I told you I was blinded. Did you see anything, Oakie?"

"I sort of passed out then. Nasty bump on the head."

"Yes, that's right. They got away somehow."

The Sheriff felt like a fool but he had to ask the next question. "Was the bat one of the robbers?"

Sukie Mae spluttered. "How many times do I have to tell you the bat was on the windshield and the robbers were at the side of the car?"

"So did you find an injured bat lying on the road before we got there?"

"Am I talkin to a cottonwood? It must have flown away. When it hit the car, it must have been stunned. Maybe it was their familiar."

"Their what?"

"Familiar. You know, like a cat is a witch's familiar. The darkies must use bats. Maybe it has something to do with voodoo and black magic."

The deputy had to step out of the room as Sukie Rae's story got wilder by the minute. He was ready to laugh but the sheriff glared and he figured he better take himself away from the scene.

"We'll check around after first light," Sheriff Robard advised. "Are you going to offer a reward?"

"Reward? I never thought about that. How much does a victim usually offer?"

"Maybe twenty five or fifty thousand. If that doesn't bring results you can go higher."

"That much? The way I see it, you're the one being paid to catch thieves. The jewels are insured so I won't lose out any way, except for the sentimental value of that tiara. Besides, I pay enough in premiums for that jewelry to feed half of Dallas. You just do your job, Sheriff, and everything else will fall in place. Oh my God."

"What?"

"What if they come back for the rest of my jewelry, the stuff still locked in the safe? I couldn't stand up to that brutal treatment again."

"We'll have a patrol car stationed here the rest of the night."

"As a big taxpayer in this county I demand protection for longer than one night. Why can't you stay here?

The sheriff paled. No way. He'd rather face a crazed killer. "Maybe some of your men could help patrol the area. We're kind of shorthanded."

"Excellent idea. Let them earn their pay for a change. Oakie, take your hand away from that bottle. One brandy is more than enough."

"Hope they do come back," Oakie muttered. "Hope that bat sticks to you like glue and doesn't let go." He left the room grinning. Sure sounded like the thief that felt his neck was a woman. He'd like to give her a big hug.

Chapter 24

"I demand the thieves be apprehended," Tsvi Frenzel shouted to Captain Rourke at the precinct station near the diamond district in New York. "No one gets away with stealing from me. What do you have here, real policemen or boy scouts?" Three months had gone by without any progress whatsoever in the case. "I've ordered another twenty-five thousand flyers at my expense. My expense. The least you could do is distribute them all over New York and the surrounding suburbs. You certainly don't expect me to tack them up personally."

"We're doing everything humanly possible," Captain Rourke answered tersely. Who the hell did this arrogant, foreign bastard think he was issuing orders and ultimatums like he was the commissioner? Every other day the man was in demanding that the entire New York City police force be put on the case. When he was in Israel, he called every day asking for progress.

"And those sketches should go out on the wires. The damned thieves could be anywhere in the country or outside the country. Have you contacted Interpol?"

"I said we're doing everything."

"You can add that I'm offering a quarter of a million dollars reward for the identity of the thieves. Let's get moving on this before the case runs cold."

Incompetents, Tsvi Frenzel thought as he stormed out of the station. I'll pass word about the reward throughout the district myself. Better that I get my hands on the thieves than the police find them and treat them with kid gloves. I'll smuggle them out of the country, into Israel where they can rot in the desert and suffer the torture of the damned.

Holdheim almost slammed into Frenzel as he emerged from his office building. "Any news on the red yet, Frenzel?"

Why was this gnat of a man bothering him day and night? If he had the red he would be shouting the news from the rooftops. "No," he answered through clenched teeth.

"Personally, I thought your sketches weren't all that good. I see thousands of people every year and never have I seen any that looked like that black-haired brute. And you can't do a sketch of a faceless woman with red hair. Makes no sense. Maybe you'd better stop thinking about the robbery for a few days and try to refresh your memory so you can have a more accurate sketch drawn up."

"And maybe I should never do business with you again, Holdheim."

The older man shook his head. A man should never be robbed of the product of his livelihood but what was done was done and Frenzel had received the insurance check. Rumor was running rampant that Frenzel was making his family miserable because of the theft, taking it out on them instead of moving forward, which would be wiser. Could it be true that Riva Frenzel was sporting bruises on her face from her husband's hand? Men who lifted their hand in anger against an innocent woman deserved punishment.

Chapter 25

"Your bra, Julia?" Velvel asked.

"I beg your pardon?"

"I meant no offense, please believe me but your bra…the rubies. You make my face go as red as the stones."

"I was teasing. Just give me a minute to change."

Velvel examined each and every ruby and diamond. "Exquisite. It was a shame taking them from their ornate settings. Did you dispose of them?"

"They're lying along a busy highway right outside of Dallas; platinum and gold debris. After I threw them out the car window, we turned around and headed in the opposite direction. I have to tell you the robbery was all over the news those last two days in Texas. The announcer said Mrs. Fremont was prostrate with grief over her loss. I love the word prostrate; so old fashioned and appropriate. People don't use distinctive words nowadays. Can you just imagine the heightened drama when Sukie Rae Fremont said I am prostrate with grief?"

Annie laughed. "Another announcer said the thieves used a life-sized bat as a decoy. Couldn't figure out what he meant at first but then I realized he was talking about you, Velvel. They thought you were a bat."

"Impossible. Was the lady drunk or near sighted? Do I look like a bat to you?"

"Your coat sleeves must have been flapping in the wind. Time to divvy up the goods."

Velvel was horrified. “None for me. You’ve given me enough. I never have to worry about money for the rest of my life. I helped because you’re my friends.”

Who was this man they felt they knew so well and yet didn’t know well enough? He explained his early years but what about the ones that followed? He had a fiancee once. Was his heart broken when she ran off with another man? Did he still dream about their life together? Did he have other girlfriends later? A man couldn’t work constantly with no outside interests. He would have to open up more if they were to fully understand him. Maybe one day when he had a few brandies he could fill in the missing pieces.

“Get off your high horse, Velvel,” Annie teased. “You must have a commemorative piece. At least select one of the rubies. We insist.”

He picked up one of the smallest.

“No, take the big pear shaped.”

“The one over fifty carats? Under no circumstances could I do that.”

“Then this one. I think it was in one of the rings. Ten carats I’d say.”

“Twelve and a half.”

“It’s yours in remembrance of batman and his two hoods.”

“A man at the bat I’m not but I’ll accept to keep you happy.”

“Yes, or we’ll be very angry. One more thing.”

“Yes?”

“Never again try to help us in our work.”

“Only if you promise you’ll tell me what you plan. I couldn’t stand being left out in the cold.”

“We’ll tell you but then you’ll have to sit on your hands.”

“My hands? Oh I see, another joke.” He slapped his forehead. “Of course you’ll tell me because I’m the one who’ll pick your next mark.”

“Not until the end of summer. We’re taking a hiatus for July and August. No one wears heavy jewelry in the summer.”

Chapter 26

"Cursed flying machines," Velvel muttered. "They must wait for me to board so they can scare me into an early grave." Velvel was sitting in Annie's living room in early October. "We were forced to emergency land in Cleveland and had to wait three hours for the door to be fastened properly. I went mad but it wasn't my fault. I took the microphone from the woman's hand and said for the price we pay to fly, the plane should sing, massage our backs, pop corn from the exhaust and be on time."

"You poor dear. I can tell something went wrong," Annie said, "because your hair's standing on end."

"It was moused nicely when I left. So I waited in a bar having one of those brandies you got me to like and then a man wanted to punch out my lights. What lights? I asked. A lamp I'm not. Does that mean my eyes? God forbid my eyes go, I have no life. One of the televisions was out of order and a mild argument broke out. Half the people wanted to watch the football game and the other half the president's speech. One fool began taking a vote and when he came to me I voted for the Home Shopping Network. Once in a while you find a good bargain. He thought I was mocking him and raised his fist. Big fist it was, almost the size of the football in the game."

"Oh, Velvel, did he hit you?"

"Lucky for me he was flying in the opposite direction and had to run to catch his plane. If he was on my plane I know I would have been flung out the door at thirty thousand feet."

"If you spread out your coat you could glide down."

"What? What? Oh another one of your little jokes."

"Don't think about what could have happened. You're safely here. So how did you spend your summer vacation?" Julia asked.

"Vacation? Never have I taken a vacation in my life. I hardly know the meaning of the word."

"You're really out of touch at times. It's a standard question for school children every September. I really wanted to know what you did all summer."

"In school I was made to stand in the corner or else my knuckles were rapped with a ruler. And Solomon made me quit when I was twelve. No one asked about summer vacations because no one could afford a vacation. Walking into another neighborhood was a vacation if you didn't get beat up on the way."

"Then you must come on a vacation with us one day. You keep your nose to the grindstone too much."

Velvel smiled. He would love going away with his two friends. Whenever he was invited to visit them, he couldn't wait to book a flight even if airplanes were his nemesis. "Where would we go?"

"Somewhere warm I think, right after the New Year; Hawaii, the Bahamas, Cozumel."

"I don't know if I'd like that. You would expect me to swim. I can't."

"We could teach you. Julia and I are excellent swimmers."

"You do everything well. You would expect me to put on a bathing suit and that I refuse to do."

"Why ever not?"

"Because I have skinny legs. No one has seen my legs in fifty years."

"You're just riddled with hang ups aren't you? No one would pay a bit of attention to your legs."

"No bathing suit."

"Okay. You can sit on shore and watch us water ski."

Velvel looked heavenward. "You see, God, they skim across water too, just like you."

"Or maybe we could go to Vail in the winter and ski in the snow."

"Now you expect me to fly down a mountain and break every bone in my body?"

"We'll decide later. You can pick the place. Now tell us how you really spent your summer."

"I worked. What else would I do?"

"But you have enough money to relax, to take it easy."

"A man must keep busy and what better way than to be gainfully employed at a job he loves. I almost forgot. Frenzel stayed away all summer but he was back last week. He upped the reward to three hundred thousand."

"Goodness, he really wants revenge doesn't he?"

"No chance he'll ever know the truth. The only one who could tell him is me and my lips are sealed." He clamped his across his mouth to prove his point. "Not even nails driven into my body would force me to tell. Wait, wait, I brought you presents."

They sat close to him on the sofa waiting expectantly. "We adore presents, Velvel."

"Maybe a little light in here would help. It's starting to get dark outside." He turned on the nearest lamp and gawked. "God, tell me I'm hallucinating. There are diamonds on your lamp. Why are there diamonds on your lamp?"

"It's a surprise. Look at how they sparkle under artificial light; better than Austrian crystal."

"You have diamonds on your lamp."

"They're just secured lightly with a dab of rubber cement. It'll wash off in a jiffy when I have my fill of looking at the sparkle. I'll keep them on until it's Julia's turn to hold the treasure chest."

"Anyone could walk in and see diamonds on your lamp."

"They wouldn't think they're diamonds, just some fake brilliants. You have no idea how much I enjoy sitting in this room reading a book and glancing up to look at the lamp. I read a few paragraphs and they seem to start calling me for attention. A little red winks out, then blue, and green. It's like a rainbow begging to be admired."

"I better look away or I'll go mad thinking of how someone could rob you and walk away with a fortune."

"Then pretend you don't see the lamp."

"Really, Velvel," Julia admonished. "If we don't worry about them why should you? I let my granddaughter play with the treasure chest last week. She almost swallowed one of the whites."

"She played? She played with real jewels?"

"Yes, and it kept her amused for two hours. I should have thought of it sooner."

"Crazy, you're both crazy but who am I to interfere? Oh yes, your surprise." He opened one hand. In it were two deep blue stones. As he turned them around the color changed to purple then deep pink. "Tanzanite from Mount Kilimanjaro where they were first discovered. It's a fairly new gemstone."

"I read a little about Tanzanite," Julia said as he took one of the gems in her hand. "If a man wears tanzanite it strengthens his genitals."

Velvel's face turned beet red. "Why do you persecute me with your silly myths?"

"Somebody must have believed in them; I didn't pull it out of my hat. They're beautiful, Velvel. Thank you. One for me and one for Annie. You're so sweet."

"And now surprise number two." His other hand held two rectangular cut stones. The tips were red turning to green at the other end. "Watermelon tourmaline. I knew you had nothing like it in your collection."

"Tourmalines are for people who think of life as one big adventure. How appropriate."

"I thought they were for people who seek peace."

"How dreary. I like the adventure bit better." They showered him with kisses until he hid his face behind a decorative pillow.

"Okay, okay, enough. Before we get down to business tell me how you spent your summer vacation. See, I catch on quick."

"We managed to add a few stones to our treasure box. Nothing as magnificent as these though."

"Tell me."

"We did another switcheroo in Milwaukee when we drove up for the Polish fest. Got two zircon pendants. They're kind of red with a brownish cast. Here I'll show you."

"Not bad," Velvel said. "Thai zircons."

"It always amazes me that you can pinpoint the country of origin."

"Sri Lankan are best but these are very good. What else?"

"They had a jewelry show at the Rosemont Horizon. We said we were never going to do a job that close to home but it was so easy we couldn't pass up the opportunity. I created a distraction while Julia slid a tray of aquamarines into a bag. Naturally we hid the stones until we could recover them safely, after the hoopla died down. We came out with twenty aquamarines ranging from two to five carats." Annie dug into the treasure chest. "Here's one."

"American, from Maine," Velvel diagnosed. "The best are from Brazil but we're seeing more and more Maine specimens. Good quality."

"If you hold one in your mouth you can call on demons to answer your questions and they won't harm you."

"Oy, don't even joke about demons. They can appear like that." He snapped his fingers. "If you call them, they appear and hover around for the rest of your life. Eventually you fall under their evil spell. I never called on one and yet one was assigned to me without my permission."

"Oh all right, we won't put any in our mouth."

"What was the distraction?"

"Oh that. Nothing spectacular but it worked."

"Tell me. You have to share your experiences."

"I set off a few bombs," Annie said calmly.

Velvel's eyes opened wide in surprise. "A bomb specialist you've become?"

"Now really bombs; M80's."

"Rocket missiles?"

"Didn't you ever light fireworks when you were a kid?"

"I held a sparkler in my hand once. It was so beautiful, like living diamonds but then it started my clothes on fire. Someone rolled me down the street to put it out. My hair was singed for months."

"We drove to Indiana one Sunday I bought firecrackers. M80's are pretty powerful. I strung ten together, spaced so they'd go off at ten second intervals. Practiced in the woods first."

"You are an explosives expert."

"Jack taught me how to do it one Fourth of July twenty or twenty-five years ago. Of course he had smaller firecrackers so Allan couldn't get hurt. Anyway, it caused quite a commotion and Julia was able to snatch the aquamarines."

"So impressive. I wish I could have been there."

"It's better that you weren't."

"Now we get down to business, okay? Have you ever been to New Orleans?"

"No, but we've always wanted to go. We had plans four years ago to fly down for Mardi Gras but we got a better package deal to Vegas to we went there instead. New Orleans sounds so romantic; Creole cooking, Cajun music and voodoo."

"Never talk about voodoo. That's worse than dybbuks."

"Spoilsport. All right, no voodoo."

"A woman in her late twenties lives in a magnificent house in the French Quarter. Her name is Claudia Fanchon. She's married to a man in his mid sixties, Louis Fanchon."

"Was it a love match or did she marry him for his money?"

"How can I know that? A mind reader I'm not. Among other magnificent jewels, Claudia has a magnificent set of sapphires; circlet necklace, three bracelets, drop earrings, several rings."

"Oh, marvelous, we don't have any sapphires yet."

"If you're going to keep interrupting I'll seal my lips with tape."

They knew he wouldn't ever do that. To stop Velvel from talking would be to destroy him. Julia apologized. "Sorry. Tell us more."

"For the past five years the Fanchons have hosted a party in November. It's called the Winter Fete. People practically beg on their knees for invitations. It's the party of the year, a winter Mardi Gras but one held in a private home. Everyone is required to wear costumes or they aren't allowed inside. One hundred people are invited, not more, not less so now you see why invitations are impossible to get."

"I hate to interrupt again but I must. Can we somehow snag invitations?"

"No, but I have an idea. A woman I know lives in New Orleans and she caters the event. It's not a sit down dinner but food and liquor flow all night long. Waiters serve drinks and waitresses carry trays of food around non-stop. Every twenty minutes a different appetizer is served. The caterer I know will hire two extra women if I recommend them. She owes me a favor."

Annie looked at him mischievously. "You sly thing. Who is this woman?"

"She's my…my former fiancee."

"The one who ran off with the garment worker?"

"Yes, yes, but he left her after ten years so she filed for divorce and married again; a shrimp fisherman from New Orleans who died five years later during a storm at sea. He was washed overboard."

"How terrible. Maybe not so terrible after all. Do you still love her, yearn to hold her in your arms again, make passionate love?"

"Stop, stop, it's nothing like that. I helped her out a little after the fisherman's death when she needed capital to open up the business.

She's very successful. I've been paid back although I wouldn't accept interest."

"And?"

"And what?"

"Do you still love her?"

Velvel rolled his eyes. "No, no, she has four daughters who help her run the business. What would I want with four daughters and a bossy wife?"

"Do you know other women, Velvel?"

"Certainly I know other women. I know you two don't I?"

"I mean intimately as in the bible saying knowing a woman?"

"Gotenyu, have you no shame? You shouldn't be so forward with intimate questions."

"Just a hint, Velvel. Please?"

He turned around and around in circles before he answered, not wanting to lie to his friends. His face turned crimson as he tried to stop words from escaping his mouth. "Yes, for one night or maybe two, that's all. A man can't sleep with his hands up his sleeve every night."

"Good. I thought you might be a eunuch."

"Is my voice high? Do I sing like a canary? A eunuch I'm not."

"Now we have a surprise for you. We're going on a hayride."

"I'm going to ride hay? I have allergies."

"You're going to love it. We'll drink apple cider, sit around a campfire and roast hot dogs."

"Kosher?"

"I'll bring pastrami in case they're not."

Chapter 27

"Dear Vel spoke so highly of you," Florence Stern gushed as she led Annie and Julia into her orderly office.

Julia and Annie were at a loss. Velvel was only supposed to give Florence their fictitious names and say they were neighbors. "What exactly did he say?" Julia asked.

"Why that you hail from Brooklyn. I spent a lot of time in Brooklyn with my first husband and then we moved to Queens, which is when our problems started but that's a long story. Vel said one of you used to date his older brother in high school. I think that would be Jacob and that you're both widows now. He said you like to work for a few weeks and use the extra money you earn to travel, to see the country. That's exciting in a way but I'd rather stay put."

Annie shuddered inwardly. Velvel should thank his lucky stars he didn't wind up with Florence. She had no idea what Florence looked like in her younger days but now she was three times Velvel's size and from what she'd seen so far, a dedicated motor mouth. With both of them jabbering a mile a minute one would never know a moment's silence. They would have spent their lives together vying for center stage. She had to give credit where credit was due though. From what she could see, the business looked modern and prosperous. Florence had taken an old store and refurbished it from top to bottom, putting in gleaming stainless steel and white tile. There was a walk-in refrigerator, freezer, restaurant sized stoves and a half dozen ovens. Immaculate, white tables ran the length of the room and dozens of pots and pans of every size hung neatly on hooks. Four women were busy mixing and shaping dough. Florence's daughters? A heavenly aroma graced the air. Annie sniffed appreciatively.

"We're catering a club luncheon today but my girls can handle it while we talk. Chicken Kiev, rice pilaf, spicy, stuffed mushrooms and for desert, lemon and raspberry tarts."

Annie's mouth began to water. "So, can we work for you for three weeks? That should give us enough money to drive on to Sarasota, Key West and Daytona Beach."

"Of course. I promised Velvel didn't I? How I love that man. He's always there when I need him."

And what about you? Annie thought angrily. Where were you when he needed you? Oh forget about it she told herself. He's better off without her.

"The party season is upon us and we're going to be swamped until the end of May. Even if you can only work three weeks it'll save me hiring young girls who don't know a thing about serving properly, who worry more about meeting men than the job they're being paid to do. Vel says you've done this type work before."

"Hundreds of times. We love seeing fine homes which is why we developed an interest in catering."

"Let me jot this down. You're Antoinette Osterman and Jane Dorfman. Jewish; that's nice."

"Half," Julia answered. "Our fathers were Jewish but since our mother's weren't, we never knew too much about Jewish traditions. Our fathers were too busy to care."

"How sad. A mother carries on the Jewish line. How odd that both of you had Jewish fathers and Gentile mothers."

"It's what brought us together in the first place. We were considered outcasts in our neighborhood."

"You must have lived among strict Orthodox."

"Not everyone was Orthodox but most were."

"You can start tomorrow if you like."

"Are cooking duties involved?" Julia and Annie didn't want to be assigned kitchen duties. Their goal was to serve not be stuck in this building. If they were forced to cook they would have to find a way to ruin everything they put their hands on.

"My girls and I are in charge of cooking and baking. I have secret recipes and wouldn't like them bandied around. I couldn't be in business long if everyone knew my special ingredients. There are some dishes that have to be heated once we're in the client's home but that doesn't involve cooking them from scratch. Let's see, we have a bar mitzvah tomorrow afternoon and a convention dinner in the evening. Almost forgot to tell you but Saturday's our busiest day so could you take Monday and Tuesday off, unless there's an emergency and we all have to pitch in?"

"We will get to see fancy homes won't we? It's what we enjoy most about catering, probably because we have such drab little apartments which we can't give up, because of rent control."

"We work in some of the finest homes in New Orleans. As a matter of fact, in two weeks, the Fanchons are throwing their annual party. Money is no object there. When you see that house you're going to drool."

"How divine. We can go home and daydream about some of the American palaces we've seen this trip."

"Let me just find two of those application cards to fill out. I'll need your social security numbers and addresses for tax purposes."

Julia looked ready to cry. "Velvel told us…well, I wouldn't want you breaking the law but he said you could stretch things a bit in our case and pay cash. If we declare what we earn on our little domestic jobs the government starts taking away some of our social security money and it, oh, it's so horrid. Then we have to scrimp and there's barely enough for food and…"

"I suppose I can do it this once," Florence said.

"We wouldn't want to get you into trouble."

"Damn government. They eat us alive with taxation. You don't see politicians scrimping do you?" Florence asked. "They fly off on junkets all over the world, waste money left and right never taking into consideration that it's our money footing their excesses."

Annie charged into the conversation with vigor. They couldn't easily give false tax information and possibly get in trouble later. "Did you hear about that Senator from New York who spent ten thousand dollars on a tea service for his office? Ten thousand for a teapot, cups and saucers. Why I bought mine from Woolworth's for under twenty dollars."

"Really?" Florence asked. "I write protest letters to Washington on wasteful spending. I hadn't heard about the tea set."

"Well, Mrs. Stern, I have dozens of similar stories."

"Please call me Florence. Not Flo though. Flo sounds like the tide, or plumbing problems."

"Florence, one Senator from Nevada flew out several of his colleagues to Tahoe just last month for a wild party. I know the woman who had to clean up afterward. She never saw such goings on in her life. Half naked women, liquor being spilled left and right, flowers in the pool, a five-piece band. Naturally, we taxpayers get the tab."

Florence was all ears. "How do you hear these things? This is much more exciting than what I hear. Deborah," she called out. "Bring in a pot of coffee and a few of the tarts. I'm having a meeting. Let me just jot down some notes. Tell me more."

Annie had seen something similar about a senator in the Godfather movie and every once in a while there was an article on government waste in the Enquirer or the Star. She racked her brain to recall some of the other things she read while standing in line at the supermarket and if that wasn't enough, she would use her imagination.

They winded things up two hours later. Florence felt she had hit the mother lode of useful gossip. "I hope you found a suitable place to stay while you're in New Orleans."

Annie gave Julia one of her looks. "Actually, we found a lovely bed and breakfast near Charles Street. Very reasonable and clean. A Mrs. Dumont owns it."

"I know her; very lovely woman. I was going to say if you hadn't found anything yet I do have a spare bedroom."

"You see, Antoinette," Julia said. "We should have come here first."

"It's not too late to change your minds," Florence said eagerly.

"But we paid in advance and I'm afraid we wouldn't get a refund. But we can come in half an hour early and chat for a spell over coffee before the workday begins."

"Thank God," Annie said once they were outside. I was running out of government stories."

"Really, Annie, a grant for the study on mating rituals of frogs?"

"That was real. I read it somewhere."

"The medicinal benefits of ostrich feathers?"

"I stretched that a bit because I was running dry. I have to get some of those tawdry magazines or maybe I can dream up more by tomorrow morning."

Velvel called them that night. "You see, didn't I promise I would stay out of your way? I'm here, you're there."

"How did you know where we're staying?"

"Talked to Florence and she looked up the number. You're the best thing that happened to her since the microwave oven."

"I don't mean to butt into your life," Julia said, "but you're far better off without good old Flo. She's not your type."

"Don't ever call her Flo. She gets like an outraged bumble bee if you do."

"We know."

"And didn't I tell you she wasn't the woman for me any more? I tell you and tell you but you still see romance where there is none. She's a friend who ran into bad luck a couple of times. Together we would have been a double disaster. Things are fine for her now."

"I'll apologize profusely the next time we meet."

"There's still time to call everything off. You don't have to work for Florence."

"We can take it for three weeks. Velvel, do you know of any Senators or Congressmen who send money down the toilet?"

There was dead silence for a minute. "Who's so crazy that they flush good money down the toilet? Your questions always they amaze me."

"Never mind. Has Frenzel backed off yet?"

"Backed off? His flyers are littering the streets. Every time the wind kicks up, I get a drawing of you slapped into my face. Naturally it doesn't resemble you in the least but still I know it's you."

"For a Hasidic Jew, he sure doesn't turn the other cheek. He got his insurance money so why won't he quit?"

"Who told you he's Hasidic?"

"Isn't he? He looked like the others."

"He didn't have peyes did he?"

"No, but I thought he was more modern."

"He dresses like them whenever he comes to America. In Israel, he wears wild colored shirts and shorts. Never puts a hat on his head in Israel unless it's to protect his head from the hot sun. He lives in a big fancy house, drives a new car and never goes to temple."

"So why the pretense?"

"You couldn't figure? Because he wants to be deeply religious like them but he's filled with greed. Clothes don't make the man, Antoinette Osterman. I like the name I chose for you. Very classy."

Chapter 28

"Annie, we're working our asses off here. I must have wrapped five hundred asparagus spears in dough."

"Rebecca needed to get away for a few days so what else could we do but offer our services? Florence really works her daughters. I have to admit I never thought of dipping asparagus in lemon butter and giving them a filo coat. They're delicious."

"Because you kept testing them out I had to do an extra twenty-five."

"I wasn't standing around watching you know. I par boiled so many tomatoes I got a steam facial in the process."

"Only two days till the Fanchon party and we still have things to buy. We have to leave early today no matter how much Florence insists we stay later for a chat. Her whining is driving me up a wall. Yesterday I wanted to slap a meringue pie in her face."

Florence burst out of her office like a summer storm. "Any more news on our government today, girls? Letters have been literally flying from my computer."

"I think we've reached the billion dollar mark, Florence. The Senate has recessed for a week."

"I have a stack of protest letters to mail. As soon as I come back, we'll start making salmon strudel. Eileen and Rebecca had to drive to Baton Rouge and cater a small party there."

"Salmon strudel?"

"You've never tasted anything like it. It's so good it makes you want to cry when you bite into it."

"Imagine that," Annie said when Florence left. "I've had all kinds of fruit strudels but never salmon. I wonder what she uses in the recipe."

"You're going to have it emblazoned in your mind because we have to put together fifty. When I get home I never want to lay eyes on mounds of food again."

Chapter 29

"This isn't like any costume party I've ever seen at the country club," Annie said passing out yet another tray of crab puffs. The Fanchons had ordered thirteen rounds of varied appetizers served in such quantity that six would have amply fed a regiment. They were serving the third round, already having gone through mounds of shrimp toast and miniature chicken kabobs. "We had funny or historical costume parties at the club but everyone here looks gruesome. It's like fright night."

"Ghouls, voodoo priests, demons, devils, fallen angels, phantoms. The worst is that walking dead man because he really looks like a corpse. I expect him to start looking for a coffin any minute. Thought he was going to bite off my hand when I handed him a puff. Did you see him, Annie? Even his eyes look washed out and dead."

"Probably on drugs. Oh lord, Florence is signaling the shrimp boats are ready." There were three other women serving, temporaries Florence had called in, and still is was difficult keeping up with voracious appetites. "Don't their stomachs ever fill? They have to stop eating at some point unless they're bulimic."

"Claudia, our beautiful hostess, must be bulimic. She's had six of everything and still keeps packing it away. She can't weigh more than a hundred pounds."

"You got a good look at the sapphires?"

"Very stunning with her moon goddess costume. She must be a couple of pounds heavier with them on; necklace, earrings, two bracelets, two rings."

"Granted, she's a beauty but I still say she's an air head. All she does is giggle and say the most inane things. Someone asked her about water reclamation and she answered that as long as there's enough to fill her pool she doesn't bother her head with it. And she looks utterly ridiculous when she claps her hands like a schoolgirl every time another guest walks through the door. Reminds me of Shirley Temple in her heyday."

More guests arrived and in two hours the party was in full force. The appetizers almost flew off trays, grabbed by eager fingers. They were serving the twelfth round, bite size pieces of filet mignon wrapped in bacon bread. Julia and Annie had a few minutes respite. They caught their breath in an alcove off the hall. "I've had my eye on Claudia all evening," Julia said quietly. "After every round of appetizers, where she scoffed down six or seven, she went to the bathroom, the one off the library which is off limits to guests. I stood outside the door and the toilet flushed several times. She has to be puking up everything."

"Then we change the plan accordingly," Julia decided. "We strike on the next bathroom visit. We'll move toward the kitchen and then change course in mid stream."

"Is everything ready Julia?"

"As ready as it will ever be."

"You are so amazingly clever. You must have an astonishing degree of foresight."

Round twelve of the appetizers were diminishing when Claudia unobtrusively made her way to the rear of the house. Julia and Annie slipped between guests and sidled after her. They still carried their trays but left them on a credenza just before entering the hall leading to the library. Thank God the guests are using four other washrooms, Annie thought. But still, one or two who knew the layout of the house might sneak in here. And thank God she had a chance to study the rooms when they arrived that afternoon to set things up.

Julia turned the knob while Annie peeked down the hall. No one was in sight. Claudia is a fluff head, Julia thought. Didn't even bother to lock the door behind her. There was no need now to pound on the door and cry emergency. There Claudia was, just as she thought, kneeling on the floor with her head over the toilet bowl as she retched. Julia made a quick sign to Annie who slipped in silently and locked the door behind her. What with the racket she was making, Claudia didn't hear a thing.

Annie clamped a piece of flypaper over Claudia's eyes. There was a drawerful in the kitchen and she had a feeling it would come in handy. No duct tape this time, in case some hotshot sleuth made the connection. Julia held Claudia firmly down as Julia began winding strong twine around and around her body until she was firmly affixed to the toilet. Claudia was too stunned to move.

Julia broke into her best imitation of Dracula. "I vant your jewels. After I take zem you will count to five hundred before you zound the alarm or I vill bite your neck until you die. You understand?"

Julia giggled. "Oh, it's a game. What fun. Is that you, Gregory? Personally I don't mind if you bite my neck but can you do it later, when Louis is asleep? You've never bitten my neck but please don't leave hickeys or Louis will be furious. Do I start counting now?"

"Yes."

Julia and Annie looked at each other, both thinking the same thoughts. Dumb broad. In a few seconds they were back in the midst of the party, passing out the rest of the appetizers on their trays. The trays emptied quickly and they hurried to the kitchen waiting for the final round, which were just coming out of the oven.

Suddenly everyone was assaulted by ear piercing shrieks. Florence dropped a tray. Her daughters' mouths hung open. This was Annie's cue. She screamed louder and longer than Claudia. I could get an Oscar for this, she thought. Not many female actresses can scream well.

Florence didn't know which way to turn. "What is it? What's happening?"

"A man just ran past the window," Annie cried. "He was wearing a ski mask."

"Where? I don't see anything."

"He ran towards the back of the house. That is the back isn't it?

Several guests ran into the kitchen checking out the commotion there and herded the workers into the ballroom where all signs of merriment ceased. Some people milled around not knowing what to do while others stood silently. A woman came from the direction of the library. "Claudia's all entangled with the toilet." There were gasps of astonishment. "No, don't go back there; it's too crowded. Louis and two of the men are with her."

Several other women screamed as playing cards shot out of thin air and began landing on them. "They're all aces of spades," one cried.

"The death card," another screamed.

The lights flickered then suddenly it was dark. The howl of a wolf pierced the stillness. Panic mounted as people began bumping into each other as they tried to escape.

"We sure as hell didn't have anything to do with this latest development," Julia whispered.

"I told you these people were weird. No, there can't be anything supernatural afoot just because of costumes."

Several guests flicked on their lighters but suddenly the lights came on again. An older woman standing next to Julia held her hand to her chest. "This is all Anne Rice's fault."

"Who's Anne Rice?"

"The writer. You've never heard of Anne Rice?"

Actually Annie and Julia had read all her books.

"I knew the minute she walked in that something terrible would happen. Success has gone to her head you know. All those books about witches, demons and vampires have made them come out of hiding. Now she must have unloosed a fifollet and this house will never know peace again."

Annie was at a loss. "Feefoolay? Is that a French candy or a stripper?"

The woman was highly indigent. "You definitely are not familiar with New Orleans. There are impish, mischievous fifollet and evil ones. This one might have both characteristics." Two women standing to the other side of the woman picked up the story and sent it winging down to others. Soon the entire room was buzzing.

"Somebody call the police," a man shouted.

"What can the police do against this demon?"

Claudia walked into the ballroom clinging to her husband and sobbing. "The vampire ordered me to stay quiet. He said he would drain my blood. I felt something sharp on the back of my neck; his teeth". She sobbed louder. "Oh, Louis, do something."

Julia suddenly remembered she had small manicure scissors in her pocket for emergency purposes. When she leaned over Claudia in the bathroom she must have nicked her.

"Darling, there were two vampires here tonight and they both left a half hour ago. They came with Anne Rice. Whoever did this is real enough."

"There is a tiny mark on your neck dear," an Egyptian queen said peering down at Claudia.

"Louis, I told you he was real. A vampire is loose."

The walking dead man shouted out. "Everyone should walk in front of a mirror. We'll catch him then."

The lights flickered again. Just before they became bright, clouds of glitter floated down on everyone. "It's still in the house," one woman whimpered. "Now we're all marked. It will be able to find us wherever we are." She looked at Julia and Annie. "Why are you staring at me?"

"Glitter isn't necessarily an evil sign. Look, it's quite pretty."

"Just where are you from?"

"Brooklyn."

"Well, no wonder. May I remind you this is New Orleans? Where are those hors d'oeuvres? You'd better get back to your posts. And where are the bartenders? We all need a stiff drink to calm our nerves."

People walked about shimmering in the light from the chandeliers. "It looks like a room full of diamonds," Julia said in awe.

"Say that when you're walking down a dark deserted street and wispy phantoms torment you." The overwrought woman turned away and began moaning to her friends. 'New Yorkers indeed. They'll soon find out New Orleans is nothing like New York."

Annie and Julia went back to the kitchen, sparkling winks of glitter in their hair and on their black uniforms. Florence followed them in a few minutes later. "The police are here trying to restore order. We're to wait in the kitchen so there'll be less confusion. The bartenders were sent to another room and the guests have to sit in the ballroom. I swear I've never seen anything like this."

"We thought it was part of the party theme," Julia said.

"Lord no. Mrs. Fanchon's sapphires were stolen."

"Really? This was a robbery? I don't know that I want to stay in New Orleans. I'm getting frightened. Robbery, evil spirits, howling wolves. I want to go home."

"It's not like this normally. I mean there are voodoo superstitions and odd customs but not many take them seriously."

Annie and Julia stood in a corner, feigning fear. Florence and her daughters began straightening up the kitchen although they couldn't capture all the flecks of glitter they had carried in on their clothes. The air sparkled here and there with the movement of the ceiling fans.

"We're doing just fine, Annie praised. "It'll soon be over; stay cool."

"A bat threw the glitter, Annie."

"What are you talking about? I didn't see a bat."

"Up on the landing. I saw an arm, or rather a wing but not the face. Just when the lights flickered a whole mess of the stuff was thrown and then the fans did the rest by scattering it around.

"I never believed for a minute that evil was afoot. Oh no!"

"It can't be. Velvel wouldn't dare break his word. He made a solemn promise."

Chapter 30

It was Julia and Annie's turn to be questioned by Sergeant Philip LaPlaca. "Ladies, please sit down. There's no need to hide in a corner. Just a few questions and you can leave."

Julia trembled. "I'm almost afraid to move."

"Mrs. Stern explained that you were frightened but there's no need. It's after the fact."

"A woman out there said evil was afoot, that it wouldn't leave this house for weeks, that spirits were commonplace in your city."

"I heard several people say the same but robbery is not committed by spirits. Mrs. Fanchon's sapphires were stolen along with Mrs. Roche's pearls. Never heard of a spirit craving jewels."

"There's always a first time. My God, was Mrs. Roche tied to a toilet as well? We heard that's what happened to Claudia Fanchon."

"Mrs. Roche was standing among the other guests. Never left the ballroom. With all the commotion, she didn't realize her pearls were gone."

Annie looked down at her hand. "Oh, what if the crook took my wedding and engagement rings? I've worn them for forty years. I should turn them around so no one notices the diamonds."

Sergeant LaPlaca looked down at the half-carat stone set in Annie's engagement rings and the circle of minuscule diamonds in the wedding band. "I'd say he was after bigger fish, ma'am."

"But these are priceless to me, sergeant. My late husband saved for a year to buy them. We want to go back to New York. We may have muggings and shootings but our crimes are committed by real people not wicked goblins."

The sergeant was beginning to get annoyed. "Mrs. Stern said you saw a man run past the kitchen window. Can you tell me more about that?"

"It was right after that dreadful scream, just a few seconds after, or a few minutes."

"Try to be more specific."

"Not more than a minute. I came into the kitchen to start serving the next round of appetizers, a barbeque concoction that would make your mouth water. Florence was just taking them out of the oven and we heard Mrs. Fanchon scream although I didn't know it was Mrs. Fanchon at the time. The ribs had fallen to the floor and created a terrible mess and…"

"Let's not worry about incidentals. Get back to the man."

"It was just a flash you know. I happened to be facing the window and a figure ran past. Couldn't tell if it was a man or woman but I'll call it a man to make it easier. He had on one of those black knit hats, you know, the kind that pull down over the face with holes for the eyes and mouth. Let's see, I was standing right here and the top of his head came right where the upper section of the window begins. I'm afraid I screamed too and that's when Florence dropped the tray, or maybe it was before. But all those weird things didn't start happening until after the man ran off so where does that leave us?"

"We're checking the guest list now. You were serving all evening. Can you come into the ballroom for a few minutes and see if there's a newcomer among them, or one who was here, disappeared for a while and returned?"

"Of course." Annie still clung to Julia's arm.

Some partygoers were sitting, others were milling around. In a corner a small man was waving his arms; Florence trying to calm him."

"Anything or anyone here that looks out of the ordinary?" LaPlaca asked.

"We were so busy," Julia began, "we can't bring people into focus. They look a little different now with their masks off. I recognize the ghoul, the mummy, the Egyptian queen. The zombie hardly moved all night. At first I thought he was a statue." They were getting closer to the fluttering bat, Florence Stern and Louis Fanchon.

Velvel looked right through them without any sign of recognition. "If you told me there was going to be voodoo rites I wouldn't be here. Only for you, Louis, did I put aside my fears and dress in this ridiculous costume you ordered. I am a businessman not an actor in a movie, a seller of gems not a cult member. Thank God the diamonds weren't taken."

"The sapphires are just as valuable."

"Feh, only diamonds are important to me. Anything else is second best."

Another police officer came up to them. "You had an invitation?" he asked Velvel.

"An invitation? Invitation? Do you think I enjoy devils and gobbledegooks?"

"Mr. Chavivi is an honored guest," Louis Fanchon explained. He personally delivered the diamond choker I bought Claudia a few weeks ago and he's cutting a matching diamond for a ring. We were discussing that most of the night."

"I have enough trouble with dybbeks in my heritage," Velvel, shouted, pacing back and forth. "I don't need other people's evil baggage. Never in all my life have I seen anything like this. A chill wind swept over several of us standing near the stairs. My hair stood on end and I had to pat it down again. You felt it didn't you, Louis?"

"Yes, I believe I did. Anyway, lieutenant, Mr. Chavivi is here at my personal request. He's a highly respected diamond expert from New York."

"Sorry, Mr. Chavivi, you're free to leave. Everybody here looks so damned suspicious. Mr. Fanchon, we have Gregory Lukas in the library.

Mrs. Fanchon did think it was him in the lavatory. I believe he's played tricks at some of your other parties."

"Well, yes, he's a practical joker but not a thief; at least I don't think he is. Let me accompany you when you question him."

"Sergeant LaPlaca, do you think we can leave too?" Annie asked. "I was supposed to take my medication an hour ago. I can feel palpitations and the doctor said…"

The last thing LaPlaca wanted to hear was another boring monologue. "Of course, sorry for the delay."

"Can you walk us to our car? It's a rental and anybody could have a key." She turned to Florence. "Florence, I hate to bother you at a time like this but can we still take some of the cream puffs, and maybe just a few of those sweet sour ribs that were meant for the last round of appetizers? We haven't had dinner and I don't think we can stop at a restaurant now. It would be too unnerving if we had to look over our shoulder constantly."

"You poor dears," Florence cooed. "By all means, fix up a plate. I'm so sorry. I've been working you to the bone tonight haven't I?"

Julia carried a tinfoil pan of ribs while Annie toted six huge cream puffs on a paper plate. "Oh dear, some of the glitter's floated onto the food. I don't think it will do any harm though. I've eaten worse. Would you like a cream puff, sergeant?" Annie poked her finger into a blob of whipped cream. "Someone stuck an olive in this one. How rude. Oh, is this a hair? Still we can't let them go to waste." She picked up one of the pastries and took a dainty bite. "I swear I'm famished." She held out the plate. "Are you sure you won't have one?"

"No, thank you. I'll walk you to your car now. We have a long night ahead of us."

Annie babbled as they walked to the rented Chevy Cavalier. "Do you think we'll have to stay in the city until the case is closed? We were planning on touring Florida in three days but if we're ordered to stay what can we do but…"

"I don't think it will be necessary. Florence said you're staying at Mrs. Dumont's place. I doubt we'll need you but if we do, I'll call you there."

"Such a lovely woman. We would have liked to talk to her more but Florence has been so busy. You see, we were practically neighbors in New York although we lived there at different times so I'm not sure if that qualifies as neighbors or not. Such a hardworking woman. We've been assisting in catering for a few years now, so we can get enough money to travel a bit. Do you know we've visited twenty-seven states so far? We hope to make them all God willing."

"I'm sure you will. Now if you'll excuse me."

"Are you sure no one's lurking in the back seat."

"Positive."

"Then will you please check out the trunk?"

"No one's going to…"

"Pretty please?"

LaPlaca took the keys roughly and opened the trunk. "Only a spare tire and a jack."

Julia started the car with a horrible grinding of gears. "I don't know why all cars do this when I start them up. They don't make them like they used to. I remember an old '63 Plymouth I had that ran like a charm."

LaPlaca ran back into the house.

"We should have been actresses, Julia. Remember the applause we got in the senior play? That was another one of our dreams. I don't know if I could take the hot lights though with the hot flashes that come upon me at the most inconvenient times. I have to get out of this padding," Annie said as she squirmed in the seat. "I'm sweating bullets. Julia, who took the pearls? I don't think Velvel would have."

"I took them, when the lights went off. I had my manicure scissors in my pocket, just in case they were needed and I snipped them right off that crow's neck. She never felt a thing. My hand was as light as a feather. I hope I never get palsy."

"So where are they? I know they couldn't be sitting inside the cream puffs; there's no room. I almost bit into a sapphire right in front of Sergeant LaPlaca."

"And aren't you glad he didn't accept one?"

"How could he after I poked my fingers in them and added extra glitter from the floor?"

"Some men will eat anything."

"The sergeant seemed to be a meticulous man. The pearls, Julia."

"They're sitting under the barbeque ribs."

"Won't they stain?"

"I'm sure there must be some kind of solution to clean them properly. Anyway, we don't like pearls."

"I know but the window of opportunity flew open. We'll find use for them and if not, what's a treasure chest without a few pearls?"

"You're right. Why didn't Velvel acknowledge us?"

"It's Florence's problem right now. Maybe she's a jealous harridan. He wasn't supposed to be here anyway. And I must remember not to add any details about the suspicious man I supposedly saw run past the window. Any more than I've already said and the police will start picking up innocent men."

Chapter 31

As much as they hated to go back and face another barrage of questions on government spending, Julia and Annie were forced to show up for work the following morning. They had promised Florence three weeks and three weeks she would get or it might appear suspicious. The second reason for hating to return was that smelling and seeing mounds of delicious food was much too tempting.

"The police learned the principal buyer from Winston was at the party," Florence announced as soon as they were settled with coffee and fresh cinnamon doughnuts. "He was there trying to talk Louis Fanchon into buying a one of a kind diamond pendant. Don't ask me why he was dressed as a zombie but that ghastly makeup made him look highly suspicious. The police questioned him for hours. Thank God they didn't suspect Vel because he would have gone berserk. He only flew in to deliver the necklace and was invited to the party at the last minute. Dear Vel wouldn't steal a stick of gum."

"By the way, Florence, the cream puffs were sinfully delicious," Julia praised. "Did I detect just the barest hint of nutmeg?"

Florence beamed under the praise. "Just a pinch along with another spice I won't divulge."

Annie patted her stomach. "I'm afraid I made a pig of myself with the ribs. You should enter your recipes in contests. You could win a fortune in prizes."

"But I'd have to write out my recipes and give them to strangers. I'm glad you enjoyed them because no one touched the deserts after the fracas and the last course of appetizers wasn't served either. My girls took the left-overs to the homeless shelter. There were bits of glitter here and there but it made the cream puffs look rather festive. I do hope no one complains of stomach pains."

"I swallowed some glitter myself and as you can see, I'm fit as a fiddle," Annie said seriously.

"I'll certainly need your help today putting together a full meal for the Delta Men's Club but my girls will handle the serving tonight. It's only for fifty people. I'm afraid the Botanical Club canceled for tomorrow, not because of the robbery but because their founder died. She was ninety-four and lived a productive life but respect demands a period of mourning. It looks like today will be your last day unless you'll reconsider and stay on in New Orleans longer. Our calendar is full starting next week."

"It's been a joy working for you, Florence. You're such an innovative woman. All this work and still you set aside time writing to Washington and keeping everything in tip-top shape here."

Annie kicked Julia, conveying the thought that she didn't want to get started on government waste again.

"Any more hot tips on our country's leaders?" Florence asked brightly.

"Only one small item I just remembered last night. Senator Hershell spent twenty-five thousand of our money bringing in an aerobics instructor for his staff. He said something to the effect that they would work harder if they were physically fit. When I saw the woman's photo in the Globe, I thought to myself those men are going to sweat off more calories lusting after that blond than working out."

"Oh, I will miss you. Are you sure you can't stay another month?"

"We'll use our extra two days sightseeing here and I suppose we'll have to call Sergeant LaPlaca and see if he needs us for further questioning. Regretfully, we have to pass on your kind offer, Florence, or we'll never see Florida and we have to be home for Thanksgiving. It's such a special holiday. We're going over to my cousin's house in rural Massachusetts. You know, over the river and through the woods to cousin's house we go. We always sing that song on the train."

When they were in their car Annie nudged Julia. "I tried calling Velvel several times. Either he's not back in New York or he's avoiding us. I have at least a dozen questions when I find him."

Annie and Julia were looking for a good restaurant the next day, a place that personified the charm of old New Orleans. "I feel dowdy and old in these clothes, Annie. I can't wait to get home and dress normally."

"We are old."

"Not old old."

"We can't change our appearance until we're out of state. There's a nice restaurant across the street. It has tons of that intricate grillwork and romantic balconies. Look, that man just knocked down one of those street persons. Now why did he do that?" They hurried across the street.

"Damned panhandlers," the man roared. "Go and get a job like the rest of us. And don't ever put your hand on my arm again or I'll break it."

The younger man was lying on the sidewalk. "Sir, I swear I didn't mean any harm." He tried to get to his knees and collapsed again."

The older man stood over him menacingly. "What's that on your face? Do you have that queer disease? Your kind should stay out of decent folks' sight."

Julia stepped between the two. The older man was dressed in a business suit and an impeccable white shirt with gold cufflinks. The younger wore jeans and a flannel shirt. "Leave him alone," she ordered.

He was ready to kick out when her words stopped him. "You're sticking up for this scum?"

"As a matter of fact I am. What are you going to do, hit me? If you do, your ass will be in jail before you can say Jean Lafitte."

Annie was helping the younger man to his feet. She raised her head and snarled at the bully. "Go about your business. We heard this man apologize and that should end the situation."

"The police should round them all up and ship them off somewhere where they can fornicate to their heart's content and die off so we can have a God fearing world again."

Julia began poking his chest. "And a God fearing person should show compassion for those less fortunate. Go away or I'll give you a karate chop."

"Damned do-gooders," he swore as he turned away.

"You're shivering," Annie said when at last the young man was able to stand. "Where's your jacket?" It wasn't hard to discern the victim must have been quite handsome at one time. He was so painfully thin and his complexion was rather gray beneath the stubble of beard, which made him look older than his actual years.

He looked down at his feet, painfully embarrassed. "Sold it the other day. Thanks for helping me up. I got a dizzy spell."

"Why did that man push you down?"

"Because I asked him for some change. Look, ma'am, I'm not a beggar." Tears filled his eyes. "Oh God, why can't this just be over? I swear I never begged for anything in my life, not until a few weeks ago."

"When did you eat last? And what's your name since I can't keep calling you young man."

"George, George Bernard."

"You still haven't told me when you had a decent meal."

"I'm fine now. I'll be on my way." He looked around. "Cops see me talking to you, they'll haul me off to jail. Thank you again."

"George, I will not let go of your arm until you answer my question."

"Yesterday, maybe the day before."

Julia took his other arm. "We were just going to have lunch here. You'll join us."

He tried to pull away but they were too strong and he was too weak. "They wouldn't allow me inside. I'll be on my way."

"Of course they'll let us in. We're paying customers. Come now. A hot meal under your belt and you'll be able to think better."

A host greeted the two women courteously. "A table for two?"

"Three."

He noticed George standing behind them and was ready to walk him firmly to the door. "I'm afraid this…this man isn't welcome here. He's not properly attired."

George pulled away again but was still helpless under an iron grip. "I don't care where you seat us," Julia said in her nastiest tone, "but you'll find us a table for three and send a waiter over pronto or you'll have a lawsuit filed against you as big as the state of Louisiana. Our guest is quite presentable. He may need a shave but so do half the men in this country." There was fire in her eyes as she dared him to defy her.

"Perhaps one of the small private rooms?"

"That would be just dandy and the service better be as good as if the governor and his wife were dining with us."

They were led to a small room in one of a dozen alcoves. Each had a balcony outside the window and was furnished in exquisite taste. The waiter seemed agitated as the women glared at him. He shrugged his shoulders and presented menus with a flourish.

Julia rattled off her order. "You can start us off with a pot of tea and three bowls of soup. Do you like onion soup, George?"

He nodded, miserably embarrassed.

"Three onion soups and hot, fresh rolls. While we're eating that we'll decide on entrees."

After George had eaten every drop of soup, Annie and Julia stopped talking trivialities. "There. You're looking much better. Still a bit pale but at least you don't seem ready to pass out on us."

"I…I don't know how to thank you."

"Fiddle. One thank you is sufficient. Any more than that and it gets boringly repetitive. Now, George, would you like to tell us why you're out on the streets? Of course if you're a very private person and would rather not say we'll talk about the national debt or foreign affairs." Goodness, Annie thought, he has the saddest eyes I've ever seen; like a lost puppy. "Are you an alcoholic or a drug addict?"

"No. Never did drugs and all I drank was wine or a beer now and then." George was so embarrassed he barely whispered. "Ahh…that man on the street, he was right. I do have…Aids. I shouldn't be here with you. I really feel better now, good enough to walk a mile. When the bad times come I get a little weak but they come and go."

"Oh, for heaven's sake, do sit down. We're not going to catch it from you. And I did notice a spark of delight when the waiter said veal stew was the special."

"My mom made the best veal stew in the world. Even after I was out on my own I used to dream about sitting at her table and having veal stew and corn bread."

"Is she gone?"

His eyes grew sadder if that was possible. "No, ma'am, she didn't die. Family didn't want anything to do with me after they learned I was…"

"Gay, George. You can say it. It's not that difficult and we're very modern women who flow with the times."

"After they learned I was different, they disowned me."

"How horrid. Your father, brother, sisters?"

"My dad was the worst. He would have taken it better if he learned I was a murderer. I have one brother; big time jock. He's ashamed. My mom's ashamed too."

"Isn't there anyone else, someone you love; someone who loves you?"

His eyes glazed and became distant. "Charles and I were together, ever since the year after college. We had ten years together before he died eleven months ago."

"Aids?"

"Yes."

Annie felt George would slip away if she didn't change the subject. So you went to college. Did you graduate?"

"With honors, ma'am."

"You don't have to keep calling us ma'am. I'm An…Antoinette and this is Jane. I would have liked to finish college but after two years I met Jack and all of a sudden, I found myself married. But that's a long, tedious story. What was your major?"

"Business at Ohio State. After the family feud, Charles and I moved to New York. I was a commodity trader and did very well. Money began coming in left and right. I helped Charles buy a flower shop because he wasn't happy working for a design house. He was fantastic when it came to artistic work. The shop clicked right from the start and the next seven years were very good to us. Don't they say luck runs in segments of seven years; good and bad? Then Charles' health started deteriorating. Looking back, it seems like one day life couldn't be better and the next it couldn't be worse. Started cutting my hours to take care of Charles and after a while work didn't seem important. It didn't phase me when I was told I needn't come in any more because by that time Charles…"

"Please don't talk about it; we understand."

"New Orleans was Charles' city. I brought him home to be buried. All he had was a grandmother and she's gone too, buried alongside him. I learned I had Aids three months before Charles died but I never let on. He was going through enough without worrying about me."

"How bad is it?" Julia asked.

"Nice ladies like you don't want to hear about this."

"Really, George, if we didn't want to hear we would have walked over you when you were lying on the sidewalk. Try to think of us as family, just for today. Now, how bad is your case?"

"Doctors say I have six months, give or take one or two. After Charles died, I stayed on in New Orleans and found a few jobs, mainly at minimum wage because they would let me go when a bad spell came on and

I couldn't work. When I felt better I'd get another job; washing dishes, janitorial work, whatever I felt I could handle. Lately I haven't felt up to putting in a full day. Everything might be okay for an hour or two and then whammo, I'm knocked for a loop. If I don't have a job, I don't have health insurance and you can't get health insurance until you've work for a prescribed number of months. I guess you could say I'm caught in a vicious circle."

"Maybe your family had a change of heart."

"No chance of that, absolutely none. Funny how you wish your life was over but yet you get hungry, tired and you go on for another day and then another. There was a time when I'd rather die than ask for a handout and yet that's what I've been doing these past weeks. Goes to show you the will to live is the strongest force in the universe."

"Aren't there hospices that would take you in?"

"The charity ones are full, with a waiting list that'll go on long after I'm gone."

"Private places?"

"I'm out of that league."

"Which are the best here in New Orleans?"

"Hope House I'd guess. There's another called Brothers that's more reasonable. Went there to see if I could work off my stay but it's the same old problem, a waiting list. The activists say we shouldn't hide our sexual preference anymore but there's still a hell of a lot of prejudice."

"Tell us about Hope House."

George's eyes glowed. "Haven't been inside but it's a reconstructed mansion. They have twenty bedrooms, on-site care, extensive grounds with magnolia trees, a pond. I walked past it once and it looked like heaven, at least at this point of my life."

"That's where you should be."

"At two thousand a week? No ma'am…I mean Jane. That's for the guys whose families have money."

Julia and Annie looked at each other and nodded. "What would you like for desert, George?"

"Nothing, thank you. It's not that I don't enjoy deserts. At one time I could devour an entire pecan pie but too much food doesn't sit well lately. The waiter keeps popping his head in here so I'd better leave. I can't begin to thank you enough and if there was any way I could repay the favor I'd…"

"If you thank us once more, George, I swear I'll wash your mouth out with soap. Best you sit here for a few minutes while Jane gets the car. It's parked in a garage two blocks from here."

"Ma'am, you don't have to drop me off anywhere. Right now I don't have a place, a permanent address, so I'll just go on now that I'm feeling better."

"Try to be quiet and conserve your strength. When you talk too long you get a coughing jag."

"But where are you taking me?"

"To Hope House. Where else?"

Chapter 32

Julia spotted a discount department store on the way and pulled into the parking lot. "I'll just be a few minutes. Stay and talk to Annie." They both couldn't go in and leave poor George alone. She had an idea he would flee the coop. Probably thought they were two old crackpots. Who else would befriend a sick panhandler? No, he wasn't a panhandler, just a man who met misfortune and didn't have the strength to pull himself out of a hopeless abyss.

The meal was the best thing that happened to him in days, George thought. For weeks he had been living from day to day, begging for change whenever he could get up the nerve, which was usually at the moment of collapse. More often, he searched through trashcans near fast food restaurants to see if anyone left a few fries or soda in a cup. He knew he was getting on these ladies nerves by saying thank you too often but what else could he say to two angels of mercy dropping out of the blue? Maybe they were real angels but he didn't have the sense to see beyond their polyester suits and old-fashioned hairdos. He wanted to bawl his eyes out in gratitude for the meal but they'd only get angry again. And now they were going to try and get him into Hope House where he could work to pay for his stay. Could they really get him in? He could help in the kitchen or do odd jobs for a few hours a day, until another bad spell came up. If he had a million dollars, and he would have that if he had stayed in the commodity business, he would have left it to these women in his will. They just plowed into problems as though it was no more than whipped cream barriers.

He closed his eyes in gratitude and said a silent prayer of thanks. The back of the car felt more comfortable right now than a king sized featherbed in a palace. Since he was thrown out of his furnished room, the park or doorways were his bed, until a cop came along and shoved him out. And I used to scoff at middle class America, he thought. In retrospect, it was the richest life in the world. It was part of middle class America that was helping him now.

Julia returned to the car with a cartful of bags and a suitcase. She and Annie began removing tags and packing things into the case.

"What do you have there?" George asked when he saw a package of men's underwear.

"Well now, you can't go into that fancy place with just the clothes on your back can you? By the way, what happened to the rest of your clothes?"

"Someone stole them in the park a couple of weeks ago."

Julia opened the largest bag. "Put this jacket on, George, there's a bit of nip in the air. I don't know why I thought New Orleans was balmy all year round."

"I can't…"

"The jacket goes on, George. I'm your drill instructor. Any back talk and you'll be severely reprimanded."

"Yes, ma'am."

"Now we're off to magnolias and a duck pond. Let me see, I think I make a right after I get out of the parking lot." Julia merged into traffic with an expert hand, weaving expertly through three lanes.

"You sure know how to handle a car, Jane."

"You should see me open up on a highway. I always said I'd make a good getaway driver but Mel, my late husband, forced me to drive at a sedate pace. Whenever I was alone though I let it rip."

"I've never met women like you. Don't get me wrong but usually women your age, well, they walk around with tight disapproving lips and crab about anything that doesn't go their way."

Both women laughed. "Antoinette and I have a rule. If one of us gets ornery, the other will slap her soundly. I almost reached that point but she snapped me out of it."

"Why are you so sure Hope House will accept me without paying?"

"Just leave everything in our hands. We have a magic touch."

George was filling out a questionnaire while Annie and Julia sat in the director's office. Adam Schuldt looked to be quite friendly and compassionate about the men under his care. He had kind brown eyes and both women decided to like him on the spot. "We trust you won't disappoint us by telling us there's no room for George Bernard. It's vital that he be admitted today because if he isn't, well, I'd hate to think of the consequences. He's a very sick man."

"No, I'm not going to tell you that." Adam answered.

"Just call us Jane and Antoinette. We hate formality."

"Actually, there's a bed available in a semi-private room and another in a private room because...well, I think you know the circumstances regarding availability. I'd like nothing better than to provide our service without charge but we hire the best caregivers and the upkeep of the house doesn't come cheap. There are some volunteers but they can't handle everything. Our goal is to keep our patients comfortable and pain free and occupy their minds when they're not bedridden. Some people say Hope House is a strange name for a place where men are dying but by hope, we mean the hope of an end to physical suffering, the hope of not dying alone, the hope of a peaceful end. Other homes get grants, we don't. There have been donations here and there by grateful families and through those donations we were able to lower the fees. We have a specialist on call twenty-four hours a day, nurses around the clock, therapists, counselors. Our patients can order meals they like best, within reason. A volunteer band comes in once a week. Sometimes it's jazz, blues, whatever the majority votes for. We have an activity director, religious services. We're trying to get government funding and when we do, we're thinking of expanding. There's quite a lot of land to build on one or two additions. Unfortunately, until that time comes, we can't lower the fees any further."

"We'll leave six thousand today, to get George started. As soon as we get to our bank we'll make arrangements to pay by the month."

"We only accept payment by the week. Under the circumstances..."

"I understand," Julia said. "We'll call once a week because we're from out of state and naturally we'll fly down to see George now and then."

"I take it you're relatives."

"Yes, George's godmothers."

"I'll leave a name and number," Annie said, "in case of emergency. I'd prefer that you keep that information confidential."

"Of course."

"Now, can we see the private room? I think he'll prefer that." They examined the room, which was bright and sunny, and best of all, it overlooked the pond. "George will like this. He had a pond near his home in Ohio where he used to fish when he was young."

"He'll be up in a few minutes. You can see that he's settled and then we're going to run some routine tests."

George was escorted upstairs via an elevator since many of the patients hadn't the stamina to climb stairs. "Well, what to you think?" Annie asked.

"I would have taken one of the closets. I don't know how you managed to talk them into accepting me but you've worked a miracle. If you sold away my soul, I'll accept the penalty."

"Nothing that drastic. Oh dear, you're looking pale again. This entire day has been too much for you."

"I feel one of my bad spells coming on but to sleep in a real bed tonight cheers me up no end. I may not look it but I want to jump with happiness."

"It's definitely time for you to take a nap. We won't come tomorrow because you have some tests scheduled but we'll be here the day after. We'll have to leave for home then but you're in good hands."

"I have to thank you again, even if you wash my mouth out." They gave him a loving hug. "Get stronger, dear George."

Chapter 33

It was ten in the morning when Julia and Annie walked into the foyer of Hope House again. They made inquiries for George to the pretty young woman sitting at the reception desk. Adam Schuldt came out of his office before they could walk upstairs. "Can I see you for a minute? It'll only be a minute because I'm afraid George is going to run out of here before that. Becky, call me if you see George Bernard coming down the stairs."

"He wants to leave?" Julia asked. "The other day this was his idea of heaven. What went wrong?"

"I don't know and that's the problem. He refused to tell me. A few minutes ago he was in my office going over his admission papers to see that everything was in order and all of a sudden he became very angry and left the room."

"We'll just catch him upstairs and find out what's wrong."

George was attempting to tie his shoes, struggling with the laces as he bent down, which made him dizzy. He was obviously out of breath.

Julia tied his right shoe. "Would you like to tell us what brought about this change of heart? You were so happy to be here the other day. Didn't they treat you well? Isn't this place what it seems?"

It took some minutes for his breathing to return to normal. "You forked down six thousand dollars to get me in here, with a promise of more to come. I can't, I won't accept that from you. You're not going to waste your money on a lost cause, a dying man."

"Is that all that brought about this tantrum?"

"All? Isn't that enough? Do you realize what this would add up to in six months, seven?"

"Yes, we know how to add. We also know what it would take for a year or two years. It's our money and we can spend it however we like."

"Then answer one question truthfully. Are you rich?"

"We're rich in countless ways but if you mean financially, no. We're comfortable but not wealthy."

"I'm not going to let two wonderful women waste their money on me. It's the same as setting it on fire or throwing it down the drain. I'll be okay without this place."

"Oh, do sit down, you're working yourself into a state of exhaustion. Should we tell him the truth, Julia?"

"Julia? You said her name was Jane."

"What do names matter? Before I say another word, we must have your solemn promise that what we tell you goes no further, not to one single person because if you spill the beans you'll send us behind bars for the rest of our lives."

"What kind of wild story are you going to concoct now?"

"The truth. We're not in the habit of lying to our friends and you are a friend; a new one but still a friend.

George managed a weak smile. "You have my word."

"We can afford this place because it isn't our money that's footing the bill. To put it simply, we came to New Orleans to pull a heist and we were successful. What we're spending on you is a form of celebration for a job well done."

George laughed so hard he went into spasms of coughing and choking. It took several minutes for the spell to abate.

"You find this amusing?" Julia asked with a snarl.

"I'm not making fun of your statement but it's totally off the wall. Two kind-hearted, compassionate women pulling a heist? Wouldn't you find that hard to believe if you were in my shoes?"

"I suppose it does sound ludicrous."

"Extremely."

"I don't know if you heard about the robbery at the Fanchon house on Saturday."

"Someone left their newspaper in the park Sunday. I picked it up and read it to pass time. Made me feel like I wasn't a vagrant, that I was sitting on a bench for relaxation."

"We stole Claudia Fanchon's sapphires."

A million dollars in jewels?"

"More like eight hundred thousand but the media always exaggerates."

"You walked in, picked up almost a million in gems while a party was going on and then walked out with no one questioning you, stopping you?"

"It was more complicated than that but to put it simply, yes."

George frowned. Were they both loose in the attic? But they had already given six thousand for his stay with their promise of more to come. What the hell was happening? Maybe he was still shivering in the park and having delusions.

"Annie, let's show him some proof."

"Well, most of them are stitched into our clothes but I'll see what I can get at easily." Annie removed a quarter pound box of chocolates from her voluminous bag. "The bottoms of the chocolates are cracked but pressed together firmly again." She split one open, took out a tissue and wiped off a ten carat Kashmir sapphire. "Here's one from the necklace. Don't tell me you want to see them all?"

"My God, you are telling the truth. I'm not laughing any more."

"I'd offer you a chocolate but I'm afraid you wouldn't find the centers digestible. Do you want the others opened? It's very clumsy patting them in place again."

"No, no, I'm a believer. How long have you been doing this?"

"Less than a year actually and this is our third major haul. There were a few smaller ones but they were insignificant. Don't ask any more questions, George; the less you know the safer we'll be."

"Then you really are rich."

"No, we were telling the truth on that point. We don't sell any of the goods. Well, we did sell a few but that was for a good cause. We simply find them pretty to look at. It's always been our dream to have a magnificent gem collection and we followed up on that particular dream. We realize what we're doing is a crime but we would never steal from a person who couldn't afford to lose a few paltry possessions. And only one or two of these beauties will pay for your entire stay. So you see, on one hand we commit crimes but on the other, we're in a position to offer help where help is needed."

"Modern day Robin Hoods."

"Not really. We're a little greedy because we intend hanging on to most of our gems. So now you see why you've got to keep our little secret. You have the power to bring us down."

"I'll take the secret to the grave."

"Thank you. Now is it settled that you'll stay?"

"Yes."

"Thank goodness we didn't have to go searching for you. Our plane leaves in two hours but we'll call every few days to see how you're faring."

"You must be angels in disguise."

"Far from angels. We could tell you some stories that would curl your hair. But there's one thing you should keep in mind, George. It was meant for us to come here to New Orleans because we were meant to meet you. The lure of precious gems brought us but there was a deeper purpose ordained. There are no random happenings. Every person we help might go on to do great things for this tired old world and a ripple begins that could go on for years and years."

"I'm afraid you picked a loser in me. I don't see any greatness in my future."

"You never know, dear boy. Stranger things have happened."

"Some day, will you tell me your whole story; like a bedtime fairytale?"
"We'll see. Now rest."

Chapter 34

"Sargeant LaPlaca, two women here to see you."

"Young and gorgeous I hope?"

"Ahhh...well, if you go for babes just like good old mom they'll fit the bill. Antoinette and Jane. Wouldn't give their last names because they said you know them."

"Oh, Christ, tell them I'm out on a case, or better yet that I'm on vacation."

"There you are, Phil," Julia said sweetly. "We just followed this nice young private so he wouldn't have to walk back and forth. I always remember my father saying policemen all have bad feet. I guess it goes with the territory or do you think it might be that men with bad feet join the police force? It must be a paradox like who came first the chicken or the egg."

LaPlaca was trapped. An old saying came to mind; you can run but you can't hide. "What can I do for you?"

"First of all, we have to tell you that you missed out on a terrific treat the other night. Florence's cream puffs were as light as a feather. And the bits of glitter on top didn't cause one second of discomfort."

"Yes, but I have to watch my cholesterol."

"Have you caught that dastardly thief yet," Annie asked.

"Not yet but the crime will be solved. We're working on a number of leads."

"That's the reason we're here. We thought we might be needed as material witnesses. Florence Stern said we could work for her for as long as we like. I suppose we can put off our Florida tour and Thanksgiving back home. We'll give our all for the cause if we must. If you insist, we could look at all your mug shots."

"You said you didn't see the thief's face."

"No, I didn't, but maybe I can come up with something by the shape of the head or his height if you measured the space from the ground up to three inches above the bottom half of the window."

"I doubt that will help, Antoinette. You're free to start your tour. As a matter of fact, you can leave whenever you like."

Annie planted a wet kiss on his cheek. "Why thank you. You know when you reach your golden age you don't know exactly how much time you have left in this world so you have to make every minute count and we did so want to see Busch Gardens, the sunset at Key West, which is supposed to be breathtaking, and the Home Shopping Club headquarters. We'd love to see Disney World but I'm afraid that's far beyond our means. Friends were telling us everything is so expensive there. I believe a plain old burger cost Millie Rednick over six dollars. Millie's a friend of ours."

"I'm sorry to rush you off, ladies, but the captain's called a meeting and I'm running late."

"Well, hurry along then. Should we call if we think of anything further to add to our testimony?"

"Splendid idea. Be careful driving."

"Could you just see us out the door, in case that thief is stalking us? If he is, he'll think we came here to give evidence that will convict him."

He took each of them firmly by the arm and hurried them out of the room. God, what did it take to get rid of them? "Where are you parked?"

"A very polite captain said we could park out in front if we were only staying a few minutes. At first he wasn't going to allow it because it is a no parking zone but when I explained we were key witnesses he gave us permission."

"Have a pleasant journey."

"Do you see anyone suspicious lurking about?"

"What? No, all's clear."

Again Julia started the car with a loud grinding of gears. "Drat. Phil, do you think we should get this checked before going on?"

"Sounds fine to me. My car does the exact same thing. Goodbye."

Julia and Annie were laughing so hard Julia had to pull over to the curb. "I swear if I ever met two women acting like we did back there I'd strangle them."

"Did you see how badly he wanted to get rid of us? I was going to invite him to lunch but that might have been going too far."

"We're leaving New Orleans with the police department's blessing and that makes me feel good."

"Drive girl, drive."

Chapter 35

"What are you doing in New York? You can't be in New York. God, tell me this isn't happening." Velvel's door was open but a heavy linked chain blocked entry.

"Well that's a hell of a welcome for your two best friends."

"You should have warned me you were coming so I could discourage you. New York is dangerous for you. My place isn't as nice as your homes."

"We didn't fly to New York from Louisiana to inspect your apartment. Are you going to let us in or not? We're tired and I'm carrying a bagful of Chinese take out that's burning my arm. One of the cartons must have collapsed and I feel a hot, oozing sensation."

"It was you who called a half hour ago and hung up without saying a word?"

"How did you know? We wanted to check and see that you were home and surprise you."

"I heard Chinese sing-song in the background. Again I tell you can't be in New York. Why won't you listen to me?"

Annie's smile turned into a frown. "Have we come at a bad time? Is there a woman in your apartment? We didn't stop to think that you might be taking your hands out of your sleeves and making whoopee with some sexy lady."

"Woman? Are you mad? I never bring a woman here. Actually I don't have a woman that often. I exaggerated a bit. In fact I can't remember when I last had a woman." He unlatched the chain. "You shouldn't be in New York because Frenzel's here, staying at the Royal Rhiga Hotel. "

"Really, Velvel, we're only here for one night. We're not going to the diamond district and we're not staying at the Rhiga. In fact we don't know where we're staying because we flew here on the spur of the moment and forgot to make a reservation. We called a dozen hotels from the airport and all of them were booked because of some convention and the United Nations being in session, so we thought we could bunk in with you and have another pajama party."

"I only have one bed."

"A double?"

"No one."

"I don't know if you're putting us on or if you've never learned the complete English language. Do you have a double size bed?"

"There, you see it. The sofa opens into a bed. Is it a double? I don't know. I went to a department store, asked for a sofa bed and bought the first one I saw."

"I suppose we could all squeeze in if we didn't move around much. You could be in the middle."

"Me in bed with two women? Have you no shame?"

"I suppose it's a little bizarre. We'll sleep on the floor."

"Ladies can't sleep on the floor. I'll sleep on the floor and you take the bed."

"Chinese, Velvel. We're starved. Let's eat and then we have a favor to ask. And while we eat, we have a bone to pick with you."

"I thought Chinese took out all the bones from their food. They can't have bones clanking in their stir fry."

"Don't try to put us off with your double talk. You swore you wouldn't interfere with our New Orleans job. You made a promise and broke it."

"Me break a promise? Never. I had a legitimate invitation to that party so I wasn't interfering. And I didn't do anything while you were busy thieving. I spent most of the night talking to Louis about diamonds. When I left New York, I didn't know I would be invited to the party."

"Your hand threw the glitter."

"Because it was a party. I thought Louis told me it was an early New Year's Eve celebration so I thought, why not? Festive I felt."

"You made the lights flicker and go on and off."

"I might have done that because I was so excited over the fact that Louis wants to commission a diamond belt for Claudia. No one I know has a diamond belt, no one I know has enough matched diamonds on hand to make such a belt. It would take a year to gather everything together and have a craftsman follow an intricate design. Wouldn't you be excited and maybe let your hand slip a few times if you were part of such a deal?"

"You do have a way of getting yourself out of a jam. So how come you pretended not to know us?"

"So the police wouldn't suspect a conspiracy. I told Florence to keep her lip buttoned or you would probably faint and collapse because of your condition."

"What condition?"

"I didn't go into details. Not to worry."

"Was it you who howled like a stricken wolf?"

"Could be. Everyone looked and acted weird so I thought I should join in."

"You did a superb realistic howl. A shiver went up my spine."

"When I was young, Mr. Zimsky, who lived downstairs, howled every time the moon was full. He moved in when I was five and one night I heard the most disturbing noise. I ran to my mother in fear and she said Mr. Zimsky was a little soft in the head. Every time I saw him I thought his head was like oatmeal. For years I wanted to touch his head but I was too afraid."

"So he just kept on howling?"

"After a while everybody got used to it."

Velvel put down his napkin a half hour later. "Unusual but good. The only Chinese food I've ever eaten were egg rolls."

"Sometimes it seems like you were raised inside a plastic bubble. You should be more daring in life."

"Daring? Don't I dare the fates every time I get on an airplane or subway train? I was on the subway two weeks ago and you know what happened? I'll tell you. There was something on the tracks and the driver came to a sudden stop. People who were sitting fell to the floor and people who were standing fell on top of them. I bounced up and hit my head on the roof. I'm daring enough when I associate with you. Not that I don't love it. I do love it."

Annie walked around the studio apartment. "Your work area?"

He was proud to show them the tools of his trade. "I can go through every stage right here at home; cleave, cut, polish. I have a scale to weigh to the nearest gram, a refractometer, ultraviolet lamp, grinder, sawing disc, lathe. Avi was able to sell me a few roughs and I've been working on them at home in the evenings."

"Don't you ever relax and watch television?"

"Don't own one and don't want one. Here, let me show you something. I'm almost finished with a Ceylon cut. Sixty-five percent was lost but I have a 3.5 carat diamond, very small inclusions with only the barest tinge of yellow."

"You're following in your stepfather's footsteps aren't you?"

"It's what I've always wanted."

Annie took out the pearls and the large sapphire pendant that had once hung around Claudia Fanchon's neck. "We're going to need more cash so could you find someone who won't ask questions to sell these for us?"

"I never deal in pearls so it would look suspicious if I started now but I know a man who will buy them, no questions. Why do they have pink stains on them?"

"We probably didn't get all the barbeque sauce off."

"Oh? So why should I ask how they came to be barbequed? Maybe you thought they would taste good? Maybe it was your way of testing them to see if they were real. Did you put them on a grill or in the oven? Don't answer. I'm better off not knowing. I can do two things with the sapphire." He took out his loupe and examined it thoroughly. "Definitely Kashmir. Deep blue, no inclusions, slightly milky. I'd say this sapphire is worth close to two hundred thousand dollars. So I could sell it to my Japanese contact but he's in Tokyo and won't be back for a month or I can cleave it and make two sapphires, or maybe three."

"We'll opt for the California connection as long as you won't get in trouble. We can wait four or five weeks."

"If the plane doesn't crash, it's as good as done. Do you need money immediately? I can give you whatever you need. By rights it's yours anyway."

"Let's not go through that again. A month is fine. We met a nice man in New Orleans and decided to pay for his care. Poor George didn't want to accept but when we told him the cost of his medical care was coming from a heist he came to terms with our offer."

"You told a perfect stranger?"

"Not perfect; I imagine he has his flaws just like everyone else."

"Stop, stop. You're driving me crazy. There you go teasing fate again. One word from this stranger's mouth and your fate is sealed."

"He won't tell."

"Oh? You'll bet your life on it?

"Yes. It was meant that we meet him, Velvel, just like it was meant that we meet you."

"I guess it's okay then. It is isn't it?"

"That's enough serious business for one night. We learned a new game. We can play it before we go to sleep."

He instantly forgot his sense of doom over Julia and Annie revealing a secret. "I'll get into my pajamas."

"Here's how it goes," Annie began. "It's much like telling a story but far more exciting and hilarious. I start by saying the first sentence of the story, then Julia adds a second and you pick up the third. We keep taking turns until a full blown story emerges."

"I got it, I got it. Begin," Velvel instructed.

"A woman dressed in black came running down the street, out of breath and obviously frightened."

Julia continued. "She paused for a moment, listening for the sound of footsteps behind her." Go on Velvel."

"I like this game. Let me think. The footsteps were those of doom because she carried the Hope Diamond in her pocket."

The story didn't end until two in the morning and it was so scary Velvel wound up sleeping in the middle after all, with two walls of pillows separating him from the women. It was such a tight squeeze Julia and Annie half hung over the bed. Luckily the armrests of the sofa kept the upper parts of their bodies in place.

Chapter 36

Samuel Holdheim and Tsvi Frenzel were having coffee in Holdheim's office after concluding a successful sale. Frenzel had just sold thirty of Australia's finest champagne diamonds for a half million dollars. "I'm going to see if Velvel Chavivi will cut two of these champagnes for me," Holdheim said. "He would do a brilliant job on the two largest. Royal cut I think. It would bring out their luster to perfection."

"Chavivi?" Frenzel laughed. "He trips over his own feet when he walks. Passing cars splash him when he waits to cross the street because he doesn't have enough sense to back away. The old timers still snicker when they tell the story of how he shattered his uncle's diamond."

"His luck has changed recently. As a matter of fact, he's earning a good reputation. It started when he cut a ten-carat stone he bought overseas. I think his brother may have talked the syndicate into selling him the rough but Chavivi won't say. Nusbaum saw the finished piece and said it was a work of art. Some months back, I heard a rumor that he was going to ask you if he could sell the red at a lesser commission. He would have taken it right from under my nose without an apology. By the way have you heard anything yet?"

Frenzel's coffee spilled as he slammed down his cup. "Why do you keep hounding me about the red? If I got my hands on it again you'd be the first to know. And that rumor you heard can't be true. Chavivi knows I would have given the red to charity before I'd let him handle it. The fool probably would have dropped it down a sewer when he bent over to tie his shoe. He's a bumbler, Holdheim."

"I gave him the assignment of selling the diamond necklace Petrov designed. Twenty brilliants, sixty baguettes and one large pendant that can be removed to change the look. He sold it to Louis Fanchon in New Orleans and got more than I asked. Earned himself a respectable commission on the sale. Funny thing though. Fanchon invited him to his annual party and while he was there Claudia Fanchon's matched sapphires were stolen, bold as brass."

"Chavivi was there when it happened?"

"He wasn't a suspect, if that's what you're getting at. He was with Louis Fanchon all night. Louis hates the parties his wife throws but he goes along with anything she asks. He's besotted over her. Anyway, he and Chavivi discussed gems all evening because Fanchon felt like a fool dressed as a werewolf. The police suspect a friend of the family but can't prove it."

As soon as Frenzel was back in his hotel room he called the private detective he had recently hired because the police were still clueless. Only last week they had physically ejected him from the station because he was demanding his rights. "Mr. Zim, find out what you can about a robbery that took place in New Orleans last week at Louis Fanchon's home. I want the information by tomorrow." Frenzel wanted to slam the phone against Zim's head. "You can fly out later. Get what you can by fax and phone. Do I have to tell you how to do your job?"

The next evening Frenzel sat at the desk in his hotel room marking off salient points. Twine had been used, not duct tape. Claudia Fanchon had been secured to the toilet with twine. She never saw the thief because her head was facing down toward the toilet. Why was she in that position? Probably upchucking too much liquor. A family friend was suspect because Claudia thought he was playing a game. In any case, there had been two others in the bathroom with Claudia Fanchon. More than a dozen guests said the robbery was committed by a supernatural force. Rubbish. Every robbery was committed by a human hand.

Frenzel picked up the phone. "Zim, check out major jewel thefts for the past six months. No, only the ones where an individual was a victim. Don't bother with jewelry stores. I know it will take time. I have to return to Israel but I'll be back in six weeks. I'll expect a full report then."

Chapter 37

"Only two weeks till Christmas and so much to do," Julia said with a sigh. "I'm glad we decided not to pull any jobs until after the first of the year. I can't plan properly with all the shopping still to be done."

"We should go out and see George before Christmas. It must be lonely having no family to turn to during the holiday season even though he's made friends at the home. We could fly to New Orleans and return the same day."

"Yes, let's. I always say if it's important enough you can always find extra time. He sounded so weak on the phone."

"Allan and his family are coming for Christmas and I've invited Velvel here. I know he doesn't believe in Christmas but he should see how much it's enjoyed. I'll have a party one night and you can bring your family. Maybe your daughters will finally realize neither of us is romantically involved with Velvel."

Julia was busy marking two calendars; one for herself and one for Annie. "That fills every hour of the next two weeks. Let's sort through our treasure chest and pick out some two carat or less stones. We don't want to risk the bigger ones being traced. I love your idea of spreading good will."

"We can fit in the good will while we're shopping; killing two birds with one stone so to speak. And we'll have to pull out those old clothes again for New Orleans."

"Tell me we're not going to visit Florence."

"Julia, you know I want no part of that woman."

"You sampled and resampled everything she cooked. I thought you might have ideas of stuffing yourself again."

"It took me four weeks to take off the weight I put on working for her. I'm not about to put myself through that torture again. I'm going to have a fresh tree again this year. I saw a perfect specimen on Deland Murray's property, better than any I could find at a tree market."

"He'll shoot you." Deland was one of the founders of the country club and had an enormous spread of land. His mansion was set in the middle of twenty prime acres and the grounds were so well tended they looked artificial. They despised Deland because he looked down at lesser mortals. At the country club he decorated an office for himself for the little time he spent there. It was on a grander scale than his business office on the Magnificent Mile in Chicago and he went so far as to order an executive chair shaped like a throne. Seated on this throne, he deigned to meet members of the club seeking an audience.

"If I can get away with stealing priceless gems it should be a snap to steal a tree. I'll do it the evening Deland and Lila are having their annual party at the club. I bought a razor sharp hand saw over in Naperville today and that's miles from here. Tested it out in the forest preserves and in thirty seconds I had a dead tree down on the ground. I wouldn't try it with a living tree because trees are precious creations of nature. Even yelled timber when it started to fall."

"If you think trees are so precious why would you cut down one of Deland's?"

"Because he's an arrogant popinjay and so are his trees; all trimmed to perfection and not allowed to grow as God intended."

"Okay, count me in. We'll cut two. I'll rent a van so no one will see the evidence as we drive home."

"How clever you are, Julia. I would have shoved mine in the trunk with the end hanging out. We'll give fifty dollars each, what we would have spent on a tree, and add it to our regular Toys for Tots donation. Would you believe Deland and Lila refused to contribute this year?"

"We should cut down all their trees."

"Just a hundred dollars worth to make up for his neglect although we could nip off that ugly topiary gargoyle he has at the front of his house. It scares children on Halloween. I absolutely adore the holidays; they're such fun."

"And nostalgic. Do you remember how every year Mel would have too much to drink at his office party and every year he would come home, stumble into the tree and knock it over?"

"You would get livid."

"And a few years before he retired I secured the tree to the ceiling with wire and wired the sides to three different points of the window frame. I made it secure enough so a tornado wouldn't budge it."

Annie began laughing until tears came to her eyes. "And Mel crashed into it anyway and the wire almost slit his throat."

"Had to rush him to the emergency room and he sure sobered up fast when he saw the blood. He came home and wanted to fling the tree into the yard and set it on fire but the girls began crying and he relented. He never drank much during the holidays after that. It's times like this that I miss him."

"I miss Jack too. I never had to rush around like a nut during the holidays because he always took care of half the work."

"And yet if they were still alive we wouldn't be doing all that we're doing now."

"I know. Can you imagine their reactions if they knew?"

Chapter 38

"Who is that good looking older man standing by the stairs," Julia asked after they entered Hope House during Christmas week.

"I don't know but if I was in the market for husband material, or even fooling around material, I'd go after him like a falcon goes after its prey."

"You'd have to fight me because I'd be there first. He's smiling at us even though we're dressed in these deplorable clothes."

The handsome man walked up to them. "I was hoping you would get here before I have to get back to the hospital." He shook hands with each of them. "I'm Doctor Robert Manning. George said you'd be here at two and I wanted to talk to you for a few minutes before you go up."

"Is George okay? You're not going to tell us bad news right before Christmas are you?"

"There's no way I can keep things light. George is going to try his best to put on a good show for your benefit. Maybe he'll succeed if you don't stay too long. You're going to be shocked at his appearance. He's lost more weight and his color's bad."

"He was too thin when we last saw him."

"You'll see some symptomatic lesions and he has difficulty breathing. He's not on oxygen now but there have been periods when he wouldn't have survived without it."

"Could you give it to us straight? How long does he have?" Annie asked. "At the time we brought him in he said six or seven months. It's been less than two."

"He must have told you six or seven not to alarm you. His disease is progressing faster than his friend Charles'." I can't give you exact numbers but from other cases I've observed, a month, maybe less. And please don't go up with gloomy faces. It'll spoil his day. He's been so happy. Yesterday he even joined in singing carols for a short spell."

"We're not going to be morose, I promise. We'll keep a stiff upper lip like the English say."

Julia put on her Santa hat before they reached George's room. "I feel like a complete ass at a time like this."

Annie donned a similar hat and picked up one of the two heavy bags. "We can do anything we put our minds to. We just proved that early this morning."

George was sitting in a chair near the window. A smile broke out on his face when they entered. He did look ghastly Annie thought. She tried to hug him but he pulled away. "Better you don't get near these lesions."

"George, when have I worried about something like that?"

"I give the orders today, okay?"

"Oh, all right but we won't be good sports about this. I did so want a hug. I'm sorry we can't be here on Christmas Eve or Christmas Day but our families expect us to continue the holiday rituals. If the doctor would allow it, we'd take you home with us."

"Your families must be super if they're anything like you. In another time I'd accept your invitation but I'm sort of tied down here. Maybe for spring break." He gave a little laugh knowing there wouldn't be a spring in his case. "What's in the bag, presents? My favorite thing is opening presents. One year Charles and I bought each other fifty presents for Christmas. It took us all morning to open them."

"We don't have quite that many but we did our best. You said you enjoyed listening to Eric Clapton so…"

In one bag there was a CD player, several Clapton discs, chocolates and a cashmere robe that George put on immediately. "I'm finally beginning to feel warm. I think I'll sleep in this. Another whole bag?"

After an hour George had to lie down. He was weaker than hell but felt he hadn't frightened his two angels too badly. They didn't look shocked so he must still look fairly presentable. "It was almost like home having you here. I won't thank you again because you will take me over your knee but I love you both, more than I've ever loved anyone except Charles. Now go home. You have a family waiting. Pretend I'm having a drink with you at the festivities. I'll be there in spirit."

"We wanted to stay overnight but couldn't get a flight back tomorrow. Everything's over booked."

He managed another gentle smile. "This is more than enough. Now get going; I need my beauty sleep."

"Yes, you should rest because there'll be another surprise this evening."

"Another one? What more could I ask for? Okay, give me a hint. I hate suspense."

"You're like a little boy. We can't tell you but this will be the best surprise you can imagine."

His eyes were closing as they hugged him. He made no move to pull away as he struggled for breath.

Julia and Annie wiped tears from their eyes once they were outside. "How astute of us to stop in Toledo before we came here. I could have smacked his father for being so bigoted but at least his mother will be here. About time she gave in. Mothers are supposed to have a special place in their hearts for sons."

"I'll bet you a hundred dollars the father will be on that plane as well."

"You're on."

"I should tell you I whispered something in that jackass's ear before we left."

"What? Tell me?"

"In clear precise words I asked the bastard, who appointed him God, judge and jury. I told him it was his little boy that's dying, the boy who still loves him very much. I also told him he's a first class shit who certainly can't be a certified saint."

"The bet's off."

In Toledo they had also dropped off two rubies into a collection box at a homeless shelter. In New Orleans they left a diamond at a home for abused women in an envelope in the mailbox. There was more to be done closer to home.

Annie and Julia were relaxing after baking batches of Christmas cookies. Annie turned the volume on her television higher. "Did you hear that? We're going to be on next, not us in person but news of our deed."

The anchor's voice held a tinge of holiday excitement as he went into the next segment. "For the past few years we've been hearing about the Good Samaritan who drops gold pieces in Salvation Army kettles but last night his, or her, generosity was topped. The Salvation Army reported this morning that a diamond was dropped in five of their kettles along State Street. According to an expert who examined the gems they're excellent quality stones and their total value runs into thousands of dollars. The organizations would like nothing better but to thank this donor in person but until the Christmas angel declares himself openly, they send out their heartfelt thanks via our airwaves. We'll have more on the story on the ten o'clock news."

"I wish people wouldn't call us angels. First George and now people on television. It sounds ominous. Angels aren't alive; they don't go around helping anyone in distress."

"Shame on you, Annie, angels are the epitome of life. They live with God the creator of life."

"I suppose you're right. I must be down in the dumps because Allan can't get a flight until Christmas Eve. There was some sort of emergency at work, a computer glitch whatever that means. I should be thankful he's able to get away for three days but I was looking forward to an entire week. I should be happy that some diamonds, along with a few of Sukie Rae's rubies are going to good causes."

Chapter 39

"Mama, is that you?" For the past few days it seemed every time George opened his eyes he experienced hallucinations. Most of them were comforting but a few were born of nightmares. Yesterday it had been Charles standing in his room, the day before, his sweet-tempered grandmother who had died when he was ten. Other times it was a humanoid creature with rotting flesh or alien features. He hardly knew what was real and what was imagination. But he had been lucid when Annie and Julia came, only because he used every bit of willpower he could muster. Now the scent of lilacs and home baked bread wafted in the air. Only his mother had that particular scent, a clean delicious smell that made you want to bury yourself in her arms. He took a deep breath, inhaling the past.

Henrietta Bernard was hugging her son, tears falling on the soft cashmere robe he wore. "Baby, how can you ever forgive me for abandoning you, my first born child? How am I ever going to forgive myself? It's been so long."

"It is you; I'm not dreaming. Did I die?"

Henny's body was being torn into hundreds of pieces, the pain she felt real and stabbing as she looked at her child. The last time she laid eyes on George he had been so healthy, so full of enthusiasm for life. The last time she laid eyes on him he was so hurt, his eyes so mournful when his family refused to understand the different lifestyle he lived. "George, I would give my life if I could take back these last ten years." She ran her hand through his hair, what little was left and kissed his forehead, his cheeks over and over as though she couldn't get enough of him.

"Mama, you shouldn't get close. My face…"

She laid his head gently back on the pillow. "Didn't I hold you in my arms and rock you when you had measles, chicken pox, the mumps? I haven't touched you for so long, don't expect me to turn away from you."

"Please don't cry."

Henny held his hand, so skeletally thin and feverish. How she loved holding his hand when he was little. It was always warm and full of trust. "George, please don't hate me. I'm sorry, so sorry."

George managed to lift his head a little as he wiped away a tear hanging on her eyelash. "You're here now, when I need you most."

"I should have been there for you always. I should have stood up for you but your father…Oh God, I was always afraid of him, not because he would physically hurt me but because he could go into a stony silence that would last for weeks. It was always easier keeping peace, to obey instead of going against him."

"He was a macho marine; everything had to go his way."

"And I was a fool for letting him walk all over me. I'm not going to lose you again, George. I'll be with you every minute. If I could only will you my health, take the burden from you. Mothers should have the power to do that. Mothers should never have to see their children ill and hurting."

"Mama, I knew what I was getting into. I knew what was possible. I have to tell you there was only Charles and one before him for a brief time."

"Hush, darling, you're so weak. Do you know I used to call you in New York? Sometimes you would pick up the phone and there was such happiness in your voice, such laughter. Then I'd know everything was all right and I would hang up, happy that you were happy."

"That was you? I thought of getting the number changed but never got around to it. Maybe it's because I would imagine it was you."

"Once I was going to talk to you but your father came into the room and I hung up. I even saved enough money to buy a plane ticket but never got the nerve to pick it up and fly to New York. My own father ruled the roost with an iron hand and I married the same kind of man. Then one day I called your number and the operator came on the line and said it was disconnected. I tried information but they didn't have your name. When I was alone I would try information in various cities. I didn't know where else to look."

"Mama?"

"Yes, George."

"No more regrets. I can't stand to see you cry. Can you tell me stories about your young days? You never talked much about that time."

When George fell asleep, Henny called the director's office downstairs. "Is it possible to have a cot set up in my son's room? I can't...I won't leave him."

"I'll have one brought up in a few minutes."

George woke in the middle of the night in what seemed like a huge bed. From the dim light in the room he finally focused his eyes and saw that his mother was sleeping in a bed placed directly next to his. She was facing him and holding his hand. He fell asleep again, feeling protected as he had when he was small and woke from a bad dream. His mother would stay in his room until he fell asleep again.

In the morning there was the faint smell of lilacs again. Mama was sitting in a chair next to his bed, dressed for the day and still holding his hand. Now she was smiling. "I promise I won't get all weepy again. We'll be happy because it's Christmas week, your favorite time of the year."

The door opened slowly and they both looked up. Martin Bernard was standing in the doorway. There was a play of emotions on his face as he stared at them; sorrow, relief, shock when he saw George.

"Dad?"

Martin's eyes never left his son as he walked to the bed. He hesitated for long seconds and Henny steeled herself to order him to leave the room if he said anything derogatory.

Martin bent down and half lifted George in a gentle embrace. "Son."

A wave of peace flowed through George. Everything was going to be fine. He could die without a trace of fear because the people he loved most were with him. But one member of the family was missing. He looked to the doorway but no one was standing there.

"Jerry rented a car at the airport. He wanted to stop and get a small tree and a few other things to brighten up your room. He...we both remembered how much you love Christmas. I wanted to come straight here so I took a cab." He took Henny's hand in his. "I'm sorry. I never thought it would come to this."

George and Henny both stared at him with disbelief. Martin had never apologized for anything in his life. He was always right and everyone else wrong. Best not to make a big deal of it though. For Martin to apologize meant a total about face.

"George and I were planning a merry Christmas," Henny said with new-found determination. George is keen to hear stories about our young days. I've already told him some of mine but he doesn't know much about your life."

"I don't see how my childhood will add to the merriment. It wasn't exactly fun with nine children in the family and a father who was more drunk than sober. It's why I never touch liquor."

George had never heard that before and often wondered why his dad was so rigid, even to the point of refusing a cold beer on a hot summer day. "Please, dad, I'd like to know."

"Should I try to recall the better times, what little there were?"

"All of it, dad. I have to hear all of it."

Chapter 40

"You have no idea how delighted I am to see you, Velvel, how happy I am that you're spending an entire week with me and of course, Julia, although she'll be busy with her family. I was feeling just a tad depressed yesterday because Allan and his family can't come until Christmas Eve and then seeing George so ill unnerved me further. It was heart wrenching, although his family came to be with him. But now that you're here, everything seems brighter. It's almost nine o'clock and Deland should be settled in nicely at the country club."

"We are going to a party there? I loved the last one, dancing all night, pool balls rolling around the room, enough cake to feed everyone on 47th Street. More excitement a man couldn't ask for."

"No, you wouldn't enjoy the party tonight. Deland Murray's parties are dull and lifeless, just like him. He's such a puffed up snob. Put on some dark clothes. What am I saying; you always wear black. But the white shirt has to go. You'll stand out like a bull's eye. I've hung a black turtleneck shirt in your closet. Put it on under your coat. Chop chop, we have to hurry."

"We're going somewhere Chinese?"

"No, we're off on an adventure. It will be another game."

"I love our games. What is this one called?"

"It's similar to George Washington chopping down the cherry tree but in our case it will be Annie, Julia and Velvel slicing through pine boughs."

"I have no idea what you're talking about but it sounds fun. I'll be back before you know I'm gone." He danced up the stairs to change his shirt and was back in an instant.

"Not that wide brimmed hat," Annie instructed. "Here, I have a knit cap. Put it on your head and don't forget to stuff in all the springs."

"Springs? Am I a sofa? Oh, you mean my hair. There, how do I look?"

"Perfecto mundo." Annie pinched both his cheeks and kissed him on the nose. "Julia should be here any minute with the van." A horn tooted out three times." And here she is, right on time."

"Explain the game," Velvel said once they were settled in their seats. All I know is we have to slice cherries."

Julia turned around. "What?"

"A slight misunderstanding," Annie explained. Actually, Velvel, we're going to Deland Murray's house to cut down two Christmas trees and maybe a hideous bush."

"We're going to commit a crime on someone's private property? You can't buy a tree like everyone else? You need trees, I got money."

"It's not the same, Velvel. The trees sold on lots are all dried out and highly flammable. If someone comes and spots us, you're to scamper over the wall and get away. I don't think Deland will press charges if we're caught but we might have to pay a fine."

"I play, Jose. A little joke. You get it?"

"Yes, dear man. The object of the game is to be fast and as silent as possible. I have it timed at twelve minutes from the time we leave the van until we're back inside. I'll saw the tree and you and Julia will drag it back to the van. While you're doing that, I'll start on the second tree."

"No, I'm the one who will saw. I saw through diamonds so a tree will be like cutting butter. Besides I'm a man and a man should saw."

"How gallant. Well, all right, but you can't start hacking trees at random, only the two we point out. No voice above a whisper. Got that?"

"I got it, got it."

Julia pulled the van into a thicket of bushes off a little used back road.

"Get in another two feet," Annie instructed. I can still see the bumper." They were only ten feet away from a low, stone wall that encircled Deland Murray's property. Julia and Annie easily made it over by finding footholds in the stone. Velvel had slippery leather soles on his shoes and kept sliding backward until Julie and Annie took hold of his arms and pulled him over the top.

"Right here, this is the one I want, Velvel," Annie whispered.

"It's big, bigger than me. Okay." He got on his knees and scrunched until he was beneath the branches. "Thicker than my arm but still butter to an expert cutter."

They heard the sound of the saw biting into wood in a rhythmic pattern. Cut, pause, cut, cut, pause, cut, cut, cut. "You're not faceting a diamond," Annie hissed. "Cut straight through the damned thing."

The tree landed with a soft whoosh and Velvel emerged, saw held high in victory. "I got the hang of it, yes I did. I feel like Paul Bunyan. Next?"

"This one right here is Julia's. You start on it and we'll drag this tree to the van. By the time we get back, we expect you to have this one down."

"Yes, yes. Go."

A took a little longer than expected to get the tree over the wall and into the van but still they weren't behind schedule. They returned to find Velvel had cut down three trees and was ready to start on a fourth.

Julia stopped him just after he made the first nick. "We only needed two. What are you doing?"

Velvel wielded the saw like a rapier. "I've never done this. It makes me feel powerful. I love the great outdoors, love it."

"But which one is mine? You've got them all mixed up."

"A tree is a tree is a tree."

"I'll have to settle for this one." She chose the closest. "Help us shove it over the wall then we have one more little job. Hell, we're here this long we might as well stay a little longer."

"I'm ready," Velvel declared after they had two evergreens tucked away in the van. I could cut all night."

"Now we really have to be quiet as mice and make our way to the front of the house. Follow me."

As they walked through the property, Velvel kept swiping at branches, loping off dozens of them as they walked along. Finally they stood before the topiary monster. "An evil sentinel?" Velvel asked."

"It's only shrubbery. Start cutting."

"Will it bring a curse to anyone who touches it? Will it turn anyone who despoils it into a pillar of salt?"

"If it does, we'll stand you in my kitchen and scrape off bits whenever we need seasoning. Please cut or give me the saw."

Velvel was down on his knees again. "I can't; there's wire in here."

"Go down further, close to the ground."

"Too many trunks, roots, whatever."

"I'm going to take the saw away from you."

"Fast, I have to go fast." He began humming Flight of the Bumble Bee. The saw burned through gnarled wood as he hummed faster and faster.

"My God, he must be going into one of his religious frenzies again," Julia said. "I can move it a little, Velvel. You're almost there."

He emerged triumphant. "Don't touch, the saw is red hot. I think I've become an expert woodsman in one night. Who said small men were milk toasts?"

Julia and Annie each took an end of the gargoyle. "Perfect, Velvel. It still stands upright. Let's put it in the driveway so Deland sees it first thing when he comes home. It'll make his mouth hang open like a Venus flytrap." Their mission accomplished they made their way back to the van.

Julia and Annie turned around to help Velvel over the wall but he wasn't behind them. "Where the hell is he?" Julia asked annoyed. "We've been here for almost an hour, way past our allotted time. The servants must be whopping it up while Deland's gone or they would have been out here." They heard the sound of the saw again. "Oh, no, he's gone compulsive berserk with this mission."

Velvel stood back to watch as a thirty foot evergreen came tumbling down. It landed squarely on top of him, obliterating him from sight." "Help, help." The sounded was muffled.

"Quiet, It's too heavy, we can't move it."

Velvel popped out from between thick prickly branches. Several pine cones clung to his hair. "Did it. I pretended I had to find my way out of a diamond."

"Let's get out of here. Where's the saw?"

"Oops, almost forgot. Never leave behind evidence right?" He dove into the tree. "One more thing, ladies. We must have a Hanukkah bush. I found one that would be perfect."

"Will this night never end?" Julia asked. "All right but just one."

They broke into a cheer when the van was on the main road. "Now all we have to do is drop Julia's tree off in her garage," Annie explained. "Her grandchildren will decorate it tomorrow. We'll park the van in my garage and clean out the needles tomorrow before Julia returns it. Now it's time for a brandy because I'm freezing and then we'll have a tree trimming party."

"Freezing?" Velvel asked, puzzled. "I was hot, hot with excitement. I could have cut down enough trees to build a log cabin. I am Daniel Boone, Paul Bunyan and Davey Crockett combined." He began singing a Yiddish song, his fingers snapping in time with the lyrics.

The lights were strung and they stepped back to look at the tree, which stood regally in Annie's living room. I hate putting on lights but with three of us it was done in no time. Now for the ornaments." They unpacked ornaments dating back forty years. Velvel left the room and came back carrying a small cardboard box he held reverently. “I had a Christmas tree once. Only for an hour but it was mine.”

“Sit down and tell us about it while I pour us another brandy.”

“I was eight years old and sitting by the window watching snow fall. Our apartment was cold but it didn’t seem so once I was lost in the pattern of flurries. The couple upstairs were arguing, cursing each other loudly. The voices rose then someone opened the window upstairs. I thought Mr. Sullivan was going to throw his wife out the window. She was screaming and he bellowed louder than a maddened bull. They were a Gentile couple, the only Gentiles I knew. All of a sudden, I saw their Christmas tree pass my window and land on the pavement below. The window slammed shut and I ran as fast as I could to the street. There was the tree lying in the snow. It was scrawny and only two feet high and some of the ornaments were broken but the star was still in place although a little bent. I carried the tree upstairs and when I plugged in the string of lights, by some miracle, they worked. I straightened out the tinsel and sat looking at my beautiful tree with lights that twinkled on and off. It was the most beautiful thing that sat in our apartment and it was mine because the Sullivans threw it away. My stepfather came home then, saw the tree and went into a rage. He threw it out the window again, all the way out into the street. I watched as a car ran over it.”

“How terribly sad.”

“I ran out again to try and save it but it was smashed, all except for this.” He pulled a painted, wooden rocking horse out of the box. “The color has faded but it’s still beautiful. I never had a rocking horse until this miniature one found me. Will you allow me to put it on your tree? It’s been waiting all these years for a new home.”

“It shall have a place of honor,” Annie declared. “Right in front where everyone can see it. Yes, right there. Perfect. Thank you for sharing this treasure.”

Velvel had tears in his eyes and he went to the bathroom to wipe them away. When he returned he saw Annie and Julia wrapping thin wisps of thread around the tips of the branches. He came closer and was speechless for a full minute. "You're putting diamonds on the tree. Diamonds."

"And let me tell you it wasn't easy trying to get thread round them so I cut tiny plastic cages from an onion bag and tied the string to them. Doesn't it look magnificent?" The diamonds caught the colors of the tree lights and shimmered back at them in a dazzling display.

"People will come in and see diamonds on your tree."

"No one will dream they're real."

"I've never seen a diamond tree. What a miracle if they would grow like that instead of workers breaking their backs to get at them. A diamond tree. How amazing."

"I'm using rubies and sapphires on mine," Julia added."

"You're both mad but I still love you anyway. We'll dance around the diamond tree, I'll sing and we'll join hands. No, we can't because the tree is too fat. We'll dance without holding hands."

Chapter 41

"I like your friend," Allan said to his mother after Velvel went out to look at neighboring Christmas decorations. Dinner was over and Jennifer and Caroline went to visit Jen's cousin. It was cozy with just the two of them sitting in the living room having coffee. "Velvel's full of the devil, mom. He reminds me of you in some of your wilder moments."

"Please, Allan, I was always full of energy but never that hyper."

"So are his intentions honorable?"

"He's a friend. How could you think it was anything more?"

"I see the way he looks at you but then I see the way he looks at Julia too. I think he's crazy about both of you."

"Of course he is. We're his first real friends."

"He may seem like a scatterbrain at times but he sure knows his gems. I have to say you meet the most interesting people."

Annie fingered the silver bracelet Velvel had given her for Christmas. I love the blue indicolite stones and Julia's black morion. Only Velvel could find such unusual semi-precious gems. They're not diamonds but there's a fire inside."

"You know, mom, I think it's time you started seeing other men. Dad's been gone for some years now and you shouldn't be alone."

"I may be alone but I'm never lonely. There's a big difference you know. My life is so full I hardly have time to think straight. Why do men always think a woman has to have a man around to be happy? I was happy with your father but that part of my life is over. I enjoy having the house to myself now, traveling with Julia, and getting involved in some interesting hobbies. I'm in good health, thank God, and have enough money to live comfortably. What else could a woman my age want?"

"So I guess I won't be renting a tux and giving you away at the altar?"

"No, I looked in my crystal ball and romance isn't in my future. Fun, excitement and travel but not romance."

The phone rang then. Allen picked it up. "It's for you. Someone named George. You sure get around."

"I'll tell you about him later. George. Merry Christmas, dear."

"Merry Christmas, Annie. Just talked to Julia. Her house sounds like bedlam."

"It probably is. How did the little surprise go? You were surprised weren't you?"

"Dumbstruck. How did you manage it?"

"The thought occurred to us when we couldn't get a direct flight. We had a choice of a stopover in Atlanta or in Toledo. The minute the clerk said Toledo, we knew it was meant that we stop there with a four hour layover."

"I don't mean how did you travel there I meant how did you talk my family into coming to New Orleans?"

"Your parents can't be all bad if they raised a son like you. All we did was tell them about your situation. I think your mother acted the way she did because she was afraid of your father all those years. I think she's lost that fear because she said she was going to New Orleans with or without him. After she cried a bit she became very forceful."

"You're right, my father always has been domineering. I told mom years ago she should stand up to him and she finally has. Better late than never. It must have shocked the hell out of him." He had to stop to catch his breath. "Mom insisted on staying with me for a while. They put in another bed. I told her not to but…"

"But she's your mother and mothers can do whatever they want. Seems she's just found her independence, George, so don't take it away from her. Let her be the boss for a change."

"Yes, ma'am. Is that an order?"

"Indeed it is and you'd better obey in this newly formed women's army because we use very severe disciplinary actions."

"My dad came too, and my brother."

"That's wonderful. How did it go?"

"They were a little stiff at first, especially dad but then he started crying and we were all in tears. Annie, I never saw my father cry. He was always the Rock of Gibraltar."

"It means he's finally come to his senses and remembers he has two sons."

"I talked dad and Jerry into taking mom out to dinner while I slept but I can't sleep. I don't have long, Annie, I know the end is coming soon."

"I could try to sugar coat your words and lie but I don't lie to people I love. Do you want to talk about it?"

"I'm not afraid, not with mom around. And sometimes I think I see Charles, as though he's waiting for me to join him. I must be hallucinating."

"Not necessarily. Personally I think loved ones are there to meet us so we have a peaceful transition. Loved ones, then angels and at last God."

"You're my angel, Annie; you and Julia. Remember I'll love you always."

"And I love you, George. You see, I was right. You've started a ripple of love and I have a feeling that love is going to go on and create something great."

"Goodbye, Annie."

"Goodnight, George. I'm sending you a hug and a big smack on the lips."

Annie explained the situation to Allan who had been listening to the conversation. "You're something else, mom. I'm proud of you."

"Would you be proud if I did something awful?" Would Allan find out one day that she was a thief? The chances were fifty-fifty. It was possible she would tire of the escapades and quit quietly with no one the wiser but she also knew every caper sent the odds against her. For the time being she hadn't tired of following this particular dream so she wouldn't worry about the consequences now.

"Always. Don't think your son can't put two and two together? Deland Murray is having a major fit because someone got on his property in the dead of night and sawed down some of his best trees plus that gargoyle he prizes. He employs two full time gardeners to see that his grounds are nothing short of perfect. I've always hated that green gargoyle and it was no easy feat cutting it off at the roots. And voila, you and Julia have perfectly manicured Christmas trees, fresh, not like the ones that come off the lot that were cut weeks ago. They're shaped like they came off an assembly line. When I worked every summer with Deland's gardener, many a time I wanted to destroy that gargoyle because it grew bigger and more ugly by the year. I felt like it was a demon watching my every move. If I stopped to rest for a few minutes after cutting the grass or weeding, the thing seemed like it was glaring. Deland deserved to be taken down a step or two for his arrogance."

"Oh, Allan."

"I'll be proud of you, always.

Chapter 42

In all his years of coming to the United States, Tsvi Frenzel had never been beyond the boundaries of New York City. Diamonds were his business, the diamond district the only area that held any interest. Yes, he was invited to various restaurants and parties but they meant nothing unless diamonds were the main topic of conversation. Tsvi had two loves in his life, his son, Joel, and diamonds, in that order. If he was ever told he had to make a choice between the two he liked to think his son came first but yet there were times he lost sight of Joel when he gazed down at the special beauty of a magnificent carbon crystal. In any case, he would never have to make a choice between the two. Joel was at Oxford in England receiving the best education money could buy. He would not follow in his father's footsteps but would rather help run Israel one day. Not only was Joel Frenzel highly intelligent, he was personable, charming and had a sense of compassion that evaded Tsvi all his life. He wanted to love other people, wanted to love God but the emotion evaded him. Why was it he could love his son so passionately and not his wife or daughters? Because Joel was made in his image? Did that therefore mean he loved himself above all others? Probably. He was proud of his accomplishments in the diamond industry. He had amassed a fortune that would one day help his only son become prime minister or equally important official in government affairs. His wife and daughters were fine upstanding people but he couldn't feel for them what he felt for Joel and diamonds.

He had returned to New York last week and studied Zim's report. At least the detective was capable of compiling information if not solving a crime. There were three thefts that caught Frenzel's interest. He had been about to fly to Boston to talk to a society woman in her forties who was forced at gunpoint to open her bedroom safe. Several pieces of jewelry were stolen along with five thousand dollars in cash. Just before he ordered his airline ticket, Zim called to say the thieves had been apprehended that morning, three men who had records for armed robbery. There was nothing unusual about the theft. The men wore no disguises, didn't tie or tape the woman. More importantly, the total worth of the jewelry had been under a hundred thousand dollars.

The second case involved a woman in her eighties who claimed she was robbed of two diamond rings worth a quarter of a million dollars at a gala affair at the Art Institute in Chicago. The police weren't taking that too seriously because the woman had reported robbery twice in the past year and in each case it was discovered she had misplaced the rings because her mind was failing.

The third case struck a chord. Sukie Rae Fremont of Dallas was the victim. Ridiculous name, Frenzel thought. How could anyone with a name like that be taken seriously? He would see her personally to get a first hand version of the theft. Getting off the plane in Dallas, he felt out of place wearing a dark business suit. There were other men in suits but they also wore boots and big hats. The difference in dress codes was unusual seeing Texas was part of the United States. And everyone he ran across was smiling, overly friendly, sickeningly polite or all three. Frenzel didn't like being out of his element. Instead of staying overnight as planned he would take a plane back to New York tonight.

He expected to see an estate similar to those on the east coast, instead there was an enormous amount of land with hardly any greenery until one got closer to the house. And when he was there he didn't see a typical mansion but a ranch house that spread out in all directions. The house had no defined lines, it just sprawled out like an oozing porridge pot. Large but not similar to other homes he admired in the States.

Sukie Rae waited for him in the living room where the focal point was a huge set of horns set above the mantle. The animal that once carried them must have been enormous. Frenzel's heels clicked across highly polished plank floors and quieted when he walked over native Indian carpets. He took her hand. "Mrs. Fremont, I'm Tsvi Frenzel. Thank you for seeing me." He inwardly shuddered at her attire; a fringed skirt, boots, white cotton shirt and a vest so heavily fringed it swayed in perpetual motion over her more than ample bosom. A woman this heavy would look much better in a solid colored caftan.

"Never met anyone from Israel before," Sukie said. "Don't understand how you can live there with all those terrorist attacks going on night and day. I'm having a splash of old Jack. Will you join me?"

Frenzel was puzzled. "Pardon me?"

"You never heard of Jack Daniels?"

"I'm afraid I don't drink liquor."

"You don't know what you're missin…can't pronounce your name, it won't roll off my tongue easy. Okay if I all you Vee?"

What an ignorant woman. "Please do," he said between clenched teeth. I should have stayed in New York and let Zim handle this he thought. Is she trying to be coy or is she intoxicated?

"Don't know why you wanted to talk to me in person because I can't tell you any more than I told the police. And if you've come to see the rest of my jewels, you're too late. Sold them all because I was afraid to sleep in my own house fearin those jackals would come back and get the rest. We have a very good auction house in Dallas and I made them advertise the sale so everyone would know I don't keep jewelry in the house anymore. Only thing I kept was the wedding ring Bo gave me and I'm even afraid to wear that seein there's three diamonds in it. Bo loved to adorn me with expensive geegaws and after he died and I learned what I had to pay in insurance premiums, I felt I was better off sellin the lot and savin money. There I go again, talkin a mile a minute. You said you were robbed in New York. You think it's the same people?"

She was finally going to let him get a word in. "I'm not sure but it's a possibility. Forty of my diamonds were stolen from my hotel room. At first I thought it was two women who accosted me but later I felt it was two men dressed as women."

"You wear that much jewelry? You one of those guys that swing both ways?"

"Frenzel wanted to slap her. "No, I sell diamonds. I was in New York to make a sale. Was it women or men who took your pieces?"

"Damned if I know, Vee. After that bat with a human face hit my windshield I wasn't payin much attention to anythin else. I hear the sheriff's makin fun of my story but I told the truth and I'll swear to it on a stack of bibles."

"I believe you."

She was totally surprised. "You do? Well you're about the only one who does. I can't tell you much about the other two cause they were dressed all in black, even their faces were black but I did see that bat even if it was only for a few seconds. Aren't bats supposed to be equipped with radar so that they don't fly into things? We must have been goin too fast for his radar to kick in cause we sure hit the damned thing."

"Could it have been a man, perhaps wearing a cape?"

"Sukie Rae took another sip of her drink and thought about that question for a while. "I suppose it could but I don't think it, or he, had anything to do with the robbery. It disappeared after we hit it. It wasn't what forced me out of the car and into six inches of Texas mud."

"So there was a bat which could have been a man and two others?"

"That's what I've been tellin you, Vee. You people from the other side of the world sure need a lot of explainin before you catch the drift."

"You must remember something about this bat's features." The best course of action, Frenzel decided, was to go along with Mrs. Fremont's ridiculous belief. "Can you remember the eyes, nose, mouth, birthmarks if any?"

"You have to keep in mind it was rainin like a bitch and the thing's face was plastered right up against the glass. You know how that distorts features; the nose gets flattened, the mouth gets all squishy. I do recall the hair was plastered down way past his forehead. And he did have fangs. Both me and Oakie saw em."

"Then he had rather long hair."

"I guess you could say that. Shorter hair wouldn't have gone down that far."

"Where were his hands?"

"First they gripped the wiper blades but the blades were running at a furious pace because of the rain and his arms, or wings, kept flappin back and forth. Maybe that's what made me think it was a bat. It let go of the blades and pressed its palms against the window. They were black so I couldn't tell if they were hands or claws, but the blades kept hitting them. Then he disappeared."

Could a long black coat have given you the impression of a winged creature?"

"Vee, you're startin to get on my nerves. That scene only lasted a couple of seconds. I wasn't watchin a video that I could stop, rewind and play again."

"Did the police check for fingerprints?"

"The rain washed everything away, even footprints left by the thieving varmints. You ain't ever seen a Texas storm, Vee. We get some doozies where it feels like you're underwater. Everything's big in Texas especially our storms."

"There was another robbery in New Orleans in November. It took place while a costume party was in progress and one of the guests came dressed as a bat."

"You gonna go round suspectin everybody in a bat costume? Last Halloween, I had twenty bats come knockin at the door and two of them were grown up critters. It was only neighbors with a truckload of kids. Neighbors here don't come walkin down the road for trick or treat cause they'd have plenty of miles to cover. Now what were you sayin about the New Orleans bat?"

"He wasn't a suspect but he does work in the diamond industry. He was also out of town the night you were robbed. His name is Velvel Chavivi and I have a photo."

"All you diamond guys got unpronounceable names? I swear you're makin my tongue twist just thinkin about it. Let me see the picture."

It was a shot taken of Velvel walking down 47th Street. He was facing the camera but the features were a little blurred. "This guy?" Sukie Mae asked pointing to the man in the forefront. "He must be a little runt because the guy standing alongside him looks like a giant."

"He's five feet five inches tall."

"Well, it couldn't be him. This guy looks pathetic; the face on the bat was menacing. This guy's all in black though. Is he in mourning?"

"Most men in on 47th Street wear black."

"Looks like he belongs to one of them strange cults that worship the moon or space aliens. Well, to each his own I always say. First of all, whatever landed on my hood appeared a lot bigger than this little guy. Second, what I saw was evil. This guy's hair sticks out every which way. He should get a crew cut if he wants to control it. This guy doesn't look evil, he looks funny, more like a clown without makeup."

"I'll leave a card with a private detective's number. If you think of anything new can you call him?"

"Okay, but I doubt anything else will come to mind. I go over it every night before I fall asleep and it's always the same, just like I told you."

"One other question. Did one of the thieves say Mazel und Brucha before they left?"

"Amazin how those foreign words just roll off your tongue. Like I said, Vee, I was nervous and scared so I wasn't payin much attention. Say those words again."

"Mazul und Brucha."

"Sounds a little familiar. Maybe one of them did but I can't be sure."

"Stupid cow," Frenzel said to himself as a taxi drove him back to the airport. "But it's still possible Chavivi knows something about the thefts. Instincts tell me he does."

Chapter 43

"You said you had no emeralds and I think I know where you can get five or six. I wish you would let me buy you a few instead. It's much safer."

"You're not calling from a cellular phone are you, Velvel?"

"I'm at a pay phone and some woman is waving her umbrella at me. I'll come to you but I'm not flying. Only fools fly in winter with blizzards, ice storms and zero temperatures hunting for airplanes to attack. Why should I add more disasters when I already have a fleet after me? The train I'm taking."

"Julia and I will pick you up at the station."

"Trains are always late. A taxi will get me to you. I arrive on Wednesday. Ouch. Stop."

"Velvel, what's happening?"

"That crazy woman hit me with her umbrella. I have to go."

Velvel booked a compartment on Amtrak, a luxury he seldom allowed himself. He had no idea how he would occupy the hours it took to travel by train versus the speed of a jet where you hardly had time to think because of the worry of crashing. He figured if his exuberant energy got the best of him he could walk up and down the string of cars all the way to Chicago.

A mistake, he knew it was a mistake when they were in western Pennsylvania. Much too long, no productive way to fill the hours. He lay down on his bunk and morosely stared out the window. The least the railroad could do is to run the tracks through interesting scenery. He either saw dismal back yards or fields. And the blowing of the train whistle every time they passed a railroad crossing was sure to implode his brain. "Snow, now it's going to snow." Fat flakes of moisture hit the window, obliterating what little there was to be seen. He stared anyway preferring that to looking at the walls. Suddenly there was a terrible shrieking noise, his car shuddered like a giant elephant in the throes of death and the next thing he knew he was flying off his bed. When he opened his eyes his compartment was dark and the window was above him, a frame depicting the fury of the storm, applauding the havoc it caused. Flurries swirled in devilment, laughing at him. Velvel shook his fist at them. "I'll kill you, dybbuk," he screamed. I'll have the Rebbe exorcize you into a bottomless pit." All was suddenly silent. Cursed, evil dybbuk found me again, Velvel thought. Not even on a train can he leave me in peace. Screams and moans from fellow passengers broke the silence. Velvel stood. No bones broken although here was a lump forming on his head. He smoothed down his hair and winced in pain then clambered to the door, which was partly open and bent out of shape. It wouldn't budge any further but he managed to squeeze through. Awkwardly, he crawled to the end of the car where the connecting door was also hanging open. He jumped to the embankment nimbly, mounds of snow cushioning his fall. Other passengers were beginning to do the same, milling around in shock while Velvel paced through knee-high drifts. "What do you want, God, that I take a horse and buggy, that I crawl?" God deigned not to answer.

"I said Wednesday and here I am although it's very late Wednesday."

"You poor dear, you shouldn't have traveled in this storm that's socking the entire Midwest," Annie said. "Don't tell me you were on the train that derailed? We heard about it on the news a few hours ago and prayed you weren't on it."

"Of course I was on that train, where else would I be? A train doesn't derail without me, a taxi doesn't carry me unless we hit a pedestrian, a plane doesn't fly but bounces with turbulence whenever I take one. A bus gets a flat tire, elevators stop where they're not supposed to stop. They have to show me who is boss like I can't figure that out for myself."

"Did you board another train?"

"No, I flew from Pittsburgh but we couldn't land in Chicago because the runways weren't clear so we went to Nashville. From there I took another plane to Chicago because Chicago runways were clean. Back and forth, forth and back. I could have flown to Europe and beyond during the time I spent traveling here. And here I get and what happens? The storm decides to come back and welcome me. The taxi had to crawl and slide all the way."

Julia was drying his hair with a towel. When Velvel walked in he was covered with snow from head to foot. "You've gone through a traumatic time, you poor thing. You should get in bed. Anything you have to say will wait until morning. You have a goose egg on your head."

"A goose has made a nest on my head? Well, why not? It only adds to the drama. I thought geese flew south for the winter."

"A bump, Velvel. You have a nasty bump."

From when the train flew off the track. No one was killed and there were only minor injuries. That's because the dybbuks aren't after anyone but me. But no, they won't kill me, they only torment me. Annie?"

"What?"

"No game tonight, please. My head has the ache of a man who just jumped off the Brooklyn Bridge and landed on a rock instead of the water."

Chapter 44

By morning Velvel was back to normal as he sat at Annie's kitchen table after breakfast. "I say you should forget about emeralds since you already have green garnets and you don't plan to set emeralds into jewelry mountings. "

Julia disagreed. "We took diamonds, rubies, sapphires and pearls and the only precious gem left on the roster is emeralds. We have to have to real thing."

"What about black opals?" Annie asked. Aren't black opals considered a precious stone?"

"Oy vey," Velvel moaned. "Will you never be satisfied? Your treasure chest is filling nicely. As costly as a good black opal is, it is not considered a precious gem except to those who covet black opals."

"If you want to get technical, we don't have any of the champagne colored or cognac diamonds from Australia either or the slightly green ones from Aikhal in Siberia. But maybe you're right. We could be satisfied once we have some emeralds."

"Then you insist on going ahead?"

"Yes."

"Okay, okay, here's what sounds easiest. Every other Friday, Moishe Bloom delivers five or six emeralds to a car wash in Perth Amboy, New Jersey. Don't ask, all I know is it's a front for another business. A fence? Maybe. Moishe tells me a lot of goods travel that way. You wouldn't have to come to New York but waylay him somewhere along the line, before he gets to the car wash. He won't offer resistance because he doesn't believe in violence. He's a pussy cat. But you have to stop him close to the car wash because Moishe likes taking different routes so the ride doesn't get boring. He drives a dark blue Cadillac, license plate SAM ONE."

"If it's a vanity plate what does it mean?"

"Sam Cunigdorio is a ruler in New York. Moishe uses Sam Cugnidorio's car because he doesn't own one. Stuttering Sam is the one who gets the emeralds. He owns a small restaurant but he makes his money elsewhere. Doesn't deal in gems so he passes them along. Sam stutters but don't tell anyone or he'll kill you."

"But how can you be sure he sends out emeralds every two weeks?"

"Because Moishe tells me, tells anyone who listens because he loves to talk. The emeralds come from Colombia, as a little bonus, but the main shipment is coke. Why they ship Coca Cola from Colombia is a mystery when we already have no many bottles here. Anyway, that's what Moishe says and I trust him. He makes a fast hundred every time he goes to New Jersey. Moishe is a compulsive gambler. He's forty but still lives with his mother who feeds and clothes him but refuses to give him money to burn. Moishe's very superstitious; maybe you can use that information."

"We'd have to go to Perth Amboy a week earlier to check everything out. Velvel, you are not going to get involved in this one. No more of your little tricks."

"I can't go anyway because I'm very busy. Holdheim gave me two of his best champagnes to cut. I've done one and the second has to match perfectly. It's much more difficult to match than cutting only one stone. One little mistake and pouf, no one will take you seriously again and I'm just beginning to be taken seriously. Okay, now I wash my hands of it. I gave you what you need to get the emeralds. If you fail, that's it. Then I really wash my hands. I refuse to keep helping you entrap yourself in danger."

"You've been a great source of information, Velvel."

"Now I'm ready for games before I go home. What do you have in mind?"

"How about some tobogganing today?"

"You want me to fly down a steep hill and get another goose nest?"

"You'll love it. When we get cold we can go into a nice little restaurant at the bottom of the run and have hot chocolate with whipped cream. And when we're on the sled you can sit at the back so you won't get hurt. Tonight we'll go dancing at the Greek club. You can lead the line holding a white handkerchief in the air and move around very arrogantly."

"Greek music, very similar to ours. I'm going to love it. Oopa, Oopa."

Chapter 45

"Mrs. O'Neill? This is this is Adam Schuldt from Hope House. I'm sorry to be the bearer of bad news but George Bernard died last night."

"Oh, no," Annie cried. "I knew it was coming but one always hopes for a miracle to intervene." Annie had been hoping against hope that somehow George would recover or go into remission. It was a small hope but one that could be just barely possible. Now she knew she only wished that because she didn't want to face the inevitable.

"His passing was very peaceful; his family was with him."

"Where are the services being held?"

"They've taken George home to Toledo. Before the end he asked that I call you when he died. His mother offered but was so bereft I said I would do it. She left the name and address of the church and chapel."

"Of course we'll fly out."

"The service is being held on Tuesday at noon. George spoke very highly of you and Julia. He left a note, which I gave to Mrs. Bernard. If you planned to go to the funeral she was going to give it to you afterward. If not, she would mail it back to me and I'd forward it on to you. As you requested when we first met, I kept your address confidential."

"Thank you for calling, Adam."

"You also have a full week's refund coming. I'll send a check."

"No, please, we wouldn't hear of it. Use the money for the home." Annie called Julia next. "George has died. Do you want to fly to Toledo for the services?"

"You know I will. I'll call Velvel and tell him our arrival in Newark will be delayed for a day."

"Can I go to the lavaya?" Velvel asked sincerely. "The funeral?"

"But you didn't know George."

"You were his friend and I am yours. It would be proper."

"You hate flying."

"Since it's a funeral, a most solemn event, maybe the dybbuk will leave me alone. Give me your flight number and I'll meet you at the Toledo airport."

"You must think I was a terrible mother," Henrietta Bernard said after Julia and Annie took a seat in the chapel after saying a prayer for George. The coffin was closed but there were a dozen photographs covering his life until he graduated from college."

"Mrs. Bernard," Julia said, "we don't pass judgment. You were there when it counted and I know it made George very happy. When I spoke to him on the phone he said the only thing that would make him happier would be to walk out of Hope House and go home with you."

Henny's eyes were red-rimmed from crying. "I hate myself for listening to my husband when he cut George off. He ordered Jerry and me to stop all contact and like fools, we obeyed. You see, Martin always gave the orders. He was in the Marines and always acted as though he was still part of the corps. I was under his thumb ever since we married and so was Jerry after he was born. George was the one who had the courage to live life his way. When you came here and told me how sick my son was I finally found the inner strength to defy Martin. I would have divorced him if he tried to stop me but when I saw how good he was with George near the end…well, I just couldn't throw forty-two years of marriage down the drain. He's a changed man, not that counts for anything now that George is gone but father and son spent many hours together. Martin actually turned into a caring, loving father. Thank you so much for coming today. George talked about you for hours. Oh, the priest is here already. Time is going by too fast, I don't want to let George out of my sight."

Velvel had been standing off to the side, avidly interested in everything that was taking place. He had studied the photos, watched as some mourners cried, eavesdropped on conversations. Now he came over to the sofa where Julia and Annie were. He was in a somber fame of mind.

"You look like a rabbi now that you've grown a beard again," Julia said.

Her words distracted him. "If I were truly religious I would rather be a rebbe."

"Am I mispronouncing it?"

"No, no. A rebbe possesses remarkable powers, a rebbe inherits his title, a rabbi is appointed. The rebbe only concerns himself with spiritual matters while the rabbi focuses on things like fund raising, temple activities and such. A rebbe commands the highest respect, his prayers unhampered by those of lesser mortals. There are times when I wish my stepfather believed more in God than in diamonds. Oh well, no use crying over milk now. When I was looking at George's pictures I almost felt his presence in this room. Maybe he was a lamed vovnick."

"Velvel, you know we don't know what that means."

"Somewhere on earth there are always thirty-six saints. They go about their business disguised as ordinary people unaware of who they are. It is why we must always treat a stranger with kindness. I remembered a rebbe told that tale when I was young and would sneak into his home with the other children. I sometimes wonder who those saints might be. Could your friend have been one or is it you?"

"We're not saints but that's a touching belief, Velvel."

"The holy man standing before the coffin, what is he doing?"

"He's blessing it with holy water."

"You will excuse me, I have to pay attention." He went closer to the coffin, nodding as the priest said prayers. In the church he took on another dimension. As the choir and priest chanted the Dies Irae, he raised his arms and swayed his body in time with the centuries old song.

The short ceremony at the cemetery was over in ten minutes. How quickly a person who was once a living being was hidden beneath dirt. A group of thirty or so young men arrived just before George's coffin was being lowered. Each of them carried bouquets of brightly colored balloons. Martin was holding Henny tightly.

So little time with him these past ten years she mourned. So many things we could have done together if only…She wished she could sink into the grave with George, keep holding his warm hand as she had been doing these past days so he wouldn't be afraid. George was afraid of the dark when he was little and he always had a night light until he was twelve. Only Martin's strong arm held her upright. Without his support she would have gladly sunk into the darkness. Her peripheral vision caught movement to the right. She saw dozens of balloons and was puzzled as to why there should be balloons in a cemetery. It was such a contrast to the snow covered fields.

Annie, or was it Julia, came up to her. "Take one, Henny."

She looked at the bright colors. Her eyes briefly left the sight of the coffin and she chose blue. "Blue is George's favorite color. He would ask me to frost the cupcakes with blue icing and on his birthday he always wanted blue lemonade. I would add a tiny drop of blue food coloring and make a big pitcher. And when he got older he would look up at the blue sky and say he was going to soar there one day." Henny wound the ribbon tighter and tighter around her finger until it cut into her skin.

The young men, some George's friends from New York and others from Toledo, had passed balloons around to the other mourners. As one of them let loose his balloons the others followed suit and set theirs free. A crayon-hued panorama of colors splashed against the blue sky drifting higher on gentle breezes. Still, Henny held hers tightly.

"You have to let go," Julia said quietly. "You have to let George free to soar."

They watched as Henny's balloon tried to catch up with the others. The wind swirled it into a tight spiral and it dipped down until it hovered over the gathered throng. As another gust of wind scurried across open field, the balloon bowed and zoomed high into the air, catching up to the others, which were still within sight. Henny watched until they were all gone. "I'll be all right now, really I will. George is soaring now; I know he is. I can help others can't I? There must be others who have lost their…lost their families."

"We can both help," Martin said.

Martin Bernard finally acknowledged Julia and Annie, visibly ill at ease. "I know you paid for George's stay at the home. I'd like to reimburse you."

"We wouldn't think of it," Julia said. "It was done from the heart."

"I'd like to think I paid for my son's care."

"You can make it up in other ways. Donate the money to a worthy cause. It doesn't have to be earmarked for Aids; there are so many other charities begging for funds."

"Thank you," Martin mumbled. "We have an orphanage here in Toledo. I pass their playground every now and then. I'm sure they have financial needs."

"And a great need for volunteers. All orphanages need volunteers."

A spark of interest shone in Martin's eyes. "A chance to make up for my omissions. Thank you again."

They read George's note at the airport.

> *Dear Julia and Annie,*
>
> *The day I met you was one of the happiest of my life, even though I tried to run away from your generosity. You befriended me, loved me and most of all, intrigued me. I wanted to hear your full story but then changed my mind because imagining your escapades was more fun. If your journeys help others like me, then I'm with*

you all the way. If it's at all possible I'll be watching over you, cheering you on.

Love, George

They had tears in their eyes as they said goodbye to Velvel since his flight was leaving earlier than theirs. "A most interesting day," Velvel said. I wonder if this means someone has to die so I can fly without incident. The ride here was smoother than riding on a featherbed. Does this mean I should pray for Gentile souls before God looks with favor upon me? I have much to think about on the way home."

Thirty minutes before landing, just as they were beginning final descent, a flight attendant accidentally spilled a cup of hot coffee on Velvel's lap. She began apologizing, tears in her eyes, but Velvel waved her off. "It is nothing. Better than having the plane go down or blow apart."

Chapter 46

No one stays in Perth Amboy, New Jersey at this time of year, or probably any time of the year," Julia moaned. "How do we explain a six day stay in this motel to the desk clerk or a waitress?"

"A niece's wedding and if anyone has the gall to get that nosy, we give them a rude mind your own business spiel."

"After we have the emeralds I don't want to drive into New York traffic. Atlantic City's not a good idea either. Philadelphia seems the most promising route. We can turn in the car there and catch a plane."

"I leave the getaway entirely in your hands."

"We'll have to spend three or four days driving around so we know the streets as well as we know our own back home."

"I think I've come up with an ambush spot," Annie said. "Two blocks before the car wash there's an area of factories, which should be deserted on Sunday. What man wouldn't stop for ladies in distress?"

"One carrying illegal emeralds."

"Velvel says Moishe always tries to give a little change to the bag ladies in New York. Whenever he does, he usually manages to win at the track."

Five days later Velvel called the motel. He had been instructed to talk in code. "Now, now to the car. The homing pigeon is flying, the goose has flown the coop...whatever."

Julia and Annie checked out of the motel so they wouldn't have to return and made their way to Atlantic Street and then the turnover to the car wash. Julia parked the car down a side street where they gathered things from the trunk. Good, no one had touched the rusty shopping cart they managed to find yesterday and shoved under a loading dock. "Annie was exhilarated. "In a little while we'll have our emeralds. So what if there's only five or six, they're still emeralds."

Velvel watched as Moishe Bloom made his way to Stuttering Sam's Cadillac. To calm his nerves, because he would be on edge until Julia or Annie called, he stopped in to talk to Nathan Grossman at the Diamond Trading Association, which was across the street from the Diamond Club after he called the women. Nathan dealt in sapphires and Velvel wanted to know if a rumor that salmon hued sapphires were coming out of Siberia lately was true. As of now they were only mined in Sri Lanka. With hostilities brewing in Sri Lanka, a find in Siberia would have a lasting effect on the market and end a monopoly. He emerged five minutes later after learning the rumor was false. The first person he saw was Moishe talking to man across the street. He ran. "Moishe, I thought you were on your way to Jersey."

Moishe was disgruntled over losing the hundred dollars he would have made today. "Sam pulled me off at the last minute. Sent Crush instead."

"Crush Vanelli, the giant?"

Moishe came closer to his old friend, Velvel and whispered. "Must be something big going down today if they sent Crush. He's the muscle man. You don't need two or three guys when he's around. Saw him chew through a rubber hose with one bite once. They say he can bend a steel pipe in no time, tear a telephone book in half. I would never want him mad at me."

Velvel paled. His girls were going up against Hercules. He had to stop them. They might still be in the motel. "Have to run," Velvel told Moishe. "Busy hands make a busy day. A diamond to cut." The pay phone on the corner was out of order. He ran to another one down the street. "Room 212," he shouted after the connection was made. "Emergency."

"Sorry, sir, the two ladies checked out."

"Look in the parking lot, they must still be around."

"They're gone, almost ten minutes now."

Velvel slammed the phone down. How was he going to save them? According to Moishe, Crush had left a little later than the usual time but how much later? "Think, think," he moaned. His feet flew as he dashed away from 47th Street looking for a ray of hope, a sign that would tell him what to do. An ambulance pulled up to the curb in front of a restaurant. One man got out while the other stayed in the driver's seat. Velvel pulled his hat low over his face and ran over to the driver, careful to stay back of the window. "Your partner, they're beating him with a club in there." Let him run to the rescue, he prayed. You have to help me, God, I'm on a rescue mission.

The driver jumped out and hurried to the restaurant. Velvel climbed into the ambulance. Bernie Liebowitz had tried to teach him to drive twenty years ago. It had been a disaster, naturally, but he remembered the basics. He put the stick in gear, stepped hard on the gas pedal and the ambulance shot out into the street, narrowly missing a bus. Velvel was so low in the seat several people thought the ambulance had burst off under its own power. Shaking and frightened out of his wits, he pressed one of the gizmos on the dash to start the siren. The windshield wipers went into action. Another button and lights began flashing. The next set the siren off and the noise startled him so he turned a corner without meaning to. He sped on, swerving through traffic. None of the drivers he passed had ever seen an ambulance driving at such high speed.

How many times had Moishe gone on and on describing the various routes he took to Perth Amboy? At least fifty. Velvel had to remember one of those routes now. He looked up at a sign. No, he was going the wrong way. He made a hard right and came upon another sign seconds later. Okay, yes, he had to cross the bridge. Holland. That sounded familiar. Holland Tunnel. Now he must go west. "Please Lord, no dybbuk today. You can send a dozen the next time I get on a plane."

Garden State Parkway. Moishe had mentioned that. He had to raise himself up on the seat because he could barely see over the wheel. There was a medical bag on the floor of the passenger side. He leaned over to get it to use as a cushion and swerved into the next lane, inches in front of a Porsche. After some miles another sign; State Street. Velvel hummed. "On State Street, that great street. No, no, that's in Chicago.

Chapter 47

Julia and Annie stood next to the derelict shopping cart dressed in layers of thick clothing topped by army fatigues. Over their faces were translucent masks that distorted their features. Knit hats covered their heads; gloves their hands. They were two blocks from the car wash on a street that hosted two factories. Come Monday, there would be more activity in the vicinity, today all was quiet except for a few bums standing around a fire on one of the side streets. They waited for a dark blue Caddy to come up the street.

Annie shoved the binoculars to the bottom of the cart fifteen minutes later. "Here it comes, plate SAM ONE."

"I don't know how I'm going to use my karate expertise with all these bulky clothes," Julia complained.

"You won't have to. Moishe is supposed to be anti-violent."

"Supposed to be isn't the same as isn't. I hope he doesn't turn out to be a once in a lifetime hero."

"Do you have your mini bat?"

"Right behind my back. Ready or not here we come."

Julia stood in the path of the oncoming car holding a sign that read *WILL WORK FOR FOOD* in bright red letters so Moishe would be certain to see it while Annie ran to the driver's window. Sun bounced off the windshield so Julia couldn't make out the driver but Annie was right on top of him. This couldn't be Moishe. Moishe was supposed to be smaller than Velvel. The man sitting behind the wheel was immense. Oh well, it was too late to call it off now. She tapped on the window. “Spare a little change, mister?” she said in a low gruff voice.

The window rolled down. “Get the fuck outta my way,” the giant roared.

Not one to be intimidated, Annie cracked him over the head with her bat. “Spare a little change,” she said with force. “If you don’t have change we’ll take whatever you do have.” The blow didn’t phase him. In an instant, he was out of the car standing over six feet tall and half as wide. He grabbed Annie by the throat. Julia went after him with her bat but he clamped a huge hand around her neck without even bothering to turn around. “You’re dead meat, you shits.” Annie couldn’t scream because she could barely breathe. Things weren’t going at all like they planned.

Chapter 48

Sitting up higher on an extremely uncomfortable perch, Velvel spotted Crush Vanelli shoving Annie and Julia into the trunk of the car and then slamming down the lid. "I came in the nick of time but my aim must be perfect," Velvel moaned as the massive man walked along the side of the car to the driver's seat. "Okay, dybbuk, help me for once. None of your tricks. You're my dybbuk so work for me for a change."

Crush was sure the ambulance would give him a wide berth as it passed so he didn't bother staying close to the car. During his entire adult life everyone he met gave him a wide berth rather than face his wrath. The ambulance nicked him on the left side while the rear view mirror cracked into his forehead forcefully. Crush went down. Velvel slammed on the brakes and sprang to the street. There were keys lying next to Crush, who seemed to be out cold. Not dead, Velvel hoped, just stunned. He picked up the keys and opened the trunk where he found Julia and Annie lying on their sides. They looked up in surprise. "Hurry, into the ambulance. Julia, you drive. I don't know how much longer my luck will last."

Annie looked down at Crush. "He's starting to move."

"Hurry."

As Annie ran past the open car door she spotted a gray canvas bag on the front seat and grabbed it before climbing into the ambulance where she landed on Velvel's lap. She looked down at the bag. It couldn't be the emeralds because the bag was too heavy. It must contain rocks. It could be used as a weapon if that monster came after them again. She felt like kicking herself for not taking the time to go though the brute's pockets but now it was too late.

Three men were running toward them from the other end of the street. "A u-turn, a u-turn," Velvel shouted. It must be the men from the car wash. Moishe once said they wore yellow jackets."

Julia spun the ambulance around expertly and sped away with the same verve as an Indy 500 driver. "I've always longed to do this. I'm finally driving a getaway car. Whoopee. Now we'll see if I have the right stuff."

"It's stolen, we have to get rid of it soon. They'll be following any second."

"We must think," Annie said. "Julia, shut off the siren and the lights. We can be heard a mile away."

Julia complied and began making right turns down several streets. "Don't worry, I think I know where I'm going." Annie and Velvel were pressed against the door with what felt like g-force pressure.

"Oy, stop," Velvel cried. "All these turns make my head spin."

After a few minutes more Julia stopped the ambulance in a bank's back parking lot. They stumbled out. Annie peeked around the corner. "There's a car heading this way and it's coming fast. Run." Fleeing down a narrow street they came to the side of a two-storied building. There were two choices; either try to get inside or turn left and risk being seen if they tried to run down a cross street. Annie turned the handle and the door opened. "Inside, quick." She locked the door behind them. Voices of women could be heard coming from a nearby room. The voices grew louder as they tried to catch their breath.

"I really didn't want to come for the bishop's sermon today. He puts me to sleep."

"Hush, Sister Edwina. The pastor said we must have fifty nuns for our fifty year celebration and fifty nuns I had to find. God will reward you for participating in this celebration. We have to hurry. We're the last and the processional will be starting soon."

Annie looked up and saw a crucifix on the wall. "We're in a convent." She looked through a window and saw dozens of nuns milling around a courtyard. "When in Rome, do as the Romans do. Find some habits."

"What habits?" Velvel asked. "I don't have habits. Maybe I do. I always fold my blanket just so, I never put pepper on my food unless I put salt first."

"Habits, the clothes nuns wear. These must be bedrooms all along the hall. Hurry and check the closets."

"Oh, I get it. Not bad habits or good habits but clothes habits."

Julia and Annie peeled off layer after layer of clothes and shoved them into a huge hamper. They were just putting wimples on their heads when Velvel walked into the room carrying an armful of clothes. "The gown is on but I don't know what to do with these."

"Here, let me help," Annie offered.

Julia looked out another window. "Three men approaching in yellow jackets."

"Quick, into the courtyard."

A lone nun was checking for stragglers. "I thought everyone was assembled. I'm sure I counted fifty but I must have miscalculated. The procession is going to start any second. Get inside and take a pew."

"Take a few?" Velvel asked, puzzled. "Take a few what?"

"Just do what we do, Julia ordered. "It's important that you don't call attention to yourself."

There was room for all three of them in one of the middle rows. A forbidding nun was seated next to Annie with Julia at the end and Velvel in the middle. "Do you have your programs?" the nun hissed.

I'll perform my best role ever, Annie promised herself. An Academy Award performance. "No, we're late. Car problems."

"At the end of the pew. We begin with the hymn on page two as soon as Mother Superior gives the signal. She's in the front row at our end."

Julia passed out programs.

The forbidding nun took one and looked closely at Annie. "Why is your face dirty."

"Oh is it? I had to change a tire and we were running late. I didn't think to look in a mirror."

"Here take my handkerchief and get that smudge. There, right under the left side of your nose. Why is the nun sitting next to you wearing a large black shawl up above her mouth. It's not cold in here."

"Sister Albertine has a viral infection. She doesn't want to cough and spread germs."

"I trust she won't disrupt the ceremony."

Annie had enough of this martinet. "I was taught to be silent in church, to talk only to God. I have special prayers to say before the entrance hymn." Mother Superior stood up and raised her hand, the signal for the organist to begin. The first song was Holy God We Praise Thy Name. Annie vaguely remembered it. As soon as the others started she should be able to join in.

Velvel's eyes darted everywhere; up to the altar, the vaulted ceiling, statues, stained glass windows. As the hymn began he looked down at his program book, listened to the first few lines and suddenly burst out singing in a rich tenor voice which was a little muffled because of the shawl.

Julia pinched him. "Softer." He lowered his voice but began swaying with the music and she had to give him a second pinch. "We're not doing gospel music. Stand still."

Velvel could hardly contain himself. Oh, how he wanted to take part in the ritual. Was standing in a Catholic church and singing their music a sin against God? He thought not. Wasn't God supposed to welcome all worshipers? But did they worship the same God? There was a mural of angels. We have angels, he said to himself. Questions swirled around his head. He watched in fascination as priests in ceremonial garb walked up the aisle with great pomp followed by a finely dressed bishop who carried a stick just like the one Moses used to climb the mount to receive the ten commandments. The bishop's was more intricately detailed. He wore a funny hat on his head and Velvel tried to figure out its significance. If he had a hat like that he would be a foot taller, he thought.

The trio finally figured out St. Bede the Venerable church was celebrating their fiftieth anniversary, which began with the church blessing to be followed by a brunch in the school hall. The bishop's talk was boring to most of the listeners as he droned on and on about problems confronting the church in modern times. One of the nuns behind Velvel began snoring but Velvel remained mesmerized. When a great chieftain of a religion talked, everyone should pay attention lest God smite them down with a mighty fork of lightning.

The sermon ended and Mother Superior stood, motioning to the assembled nuns. The grouchy nun sitting next to Annie poked her. "We're to stand in front now, face the congregation and sing Amazing Grace while we receive the Bishop's blessing."

Annie and Julia managed to maneuver themselves and Velvel at the back of the group standing before the altar. Velvel looked to the far end of the church and saw Crush standing with three men, evidently the car wash men without their yellow jackets. His hands began to tremble as the men began walking down the two side aisles looking at everyone who was seated. Velvel couldn't stand still even when Julia squeezed his arm. He wanted to run but his feet seemed to weigh a hundred pounds. The nuns sang the song with gusto as holy water splashed everywhere. A drop fell on Velvel's nose. His eyes crossed as he tried to look down at it. He was in a most serious quandary. This sacred water must be for Catholics only. The drop slid further towards the tip of his nose. He began mumbling in fear. "If it drops to the floor, should I catch it? If I catch it, will it leave an indelible mark on my hand? If I let it fall to the floor, does it mean I dishonor God? And if it falls to the floor, do I try to pick it up? If I leave it on the floor and someone steps on it, it would mean that I look down on God and think myself better."

"Stop it," Julia rebuked losing her patience.

Velvel became so agitated he tripped on a metal stand holding dozens of large, round, fat candles. The stand crashed to the floor sending lit candles in all directions. One landed against the hem of a blue and gold banner of the Ladies Altar and Rosary Society. The flimsy material immediately burst into flames, which passed on to the Daughters of Isabella banner, which then caught on to the Knights of Columbus and Our Lady of Guadalupe standards. A fiery chain reaction with a domino effect burst across the width of the church. Screams of panic erupted as people rushed through the front and two side doors in an attempt to escape what they believed was an inferno. Actually it wasn't bad as it looked. Three men from the car wash were trampled while Crush hid in a confessional so as not to be hit by a sea of humanity.

Mother Superior ran up to the trio who were trying to beat out one section of the flames with Velvel's black shawl. She looked at Annie and Julia and then at Velvel. "Why does this nun have a beard?" Sirens could now be heard in the distance.

"Four men are in the church looking for us. They'll kill us."

Mother Superior, a.k.a. Sister Veronica, was extremely cool and calm under the circumstances. What should she do; denounce these three or help them? They were genuinely frightened and the nun with the beard was shaking terribly. "Are you the bad guys or the good?"

"Definitely the good."

"There's a passageway behind the altar. Go through the sacristy and turn right to the fourth panel. Press the middle rosette. Wait for me there.

Sister stepped on the last of the smoldering ashes of the first and second banners and began tackling the third when firemen took over. Ten minutes later it was ascertained there was no damage except for a sooty marble floor. A voice came over the loud speaker. "The bishop will conclude the ceremony in the school hall."

Julia, Annie and Velvel found themselves in a passageway beneath the church. Low watt bulbs sparsely spaced barely lit narrow corridors leading off in four directions. "We'll be lost forever if we take one of these," Velvel said.

"We're not going to move very far unless those men come crashing through the panel. Whatever happens we stick together."

"Isn't anyone ever going to come and rescue us? We've been here for hours."

"Velvel, it's been ten minutes. Keep cool."

"How can I not? It's freezing in here. Do you think bodies are buried here? What if the church burns down to the ground and we're sizzled, like pigs at a luau? What if the nun forgets about us and we're never found? Are these catacombs or medieval torture chambers?"

Chapter 49

Sister Veronica stepped down into the church basement twenty-three minutes later. Annie knew exactly how long it took because Velvel kept asking every thirty seconds. She led them down one of the passageways to a door set in stone. When she pressed the light switch, a fairly large room emerged from the darkness and chased away gloom. There was a double sink, several long tables, benches and masses of flowers. "This is where we arrange flowers for the church but I'm sure you're not interesting in chit-chat. Now would you care to sit down and tell me what's going on? I knew something was amiss when I saw fifty-three nuns after I had counted fifty earlier."

They looked to Annie as spokeswoman. "A man tried to kill us earlier and now he's joined by three others. They were all in church earlier; the big one was hard to miss."

"I saw him. He's down in the school hall where the buffet is being served. The other three are stationed around the convent, school and church. I know two of them, not personally but of them. Thugs, who should be behind bars. I believe this is the first time they've set foot in a house of God because they certainly mock the good we try to do. As soon as I saw those men and three unexplained nuns I began putting two and two together so when you said you were the good guys I believed you. I asked myself why would four known thugs be after three older women, or rather two women and a man?

"I didn't mean to set your temple on fire," Velvel apologized nervously "but I saw those men coming slowly toward us and my nerves exploded. I would never bring destruction in your temple."

"No harm done that a little soap and water won't cure. At least the diversion stopped the bishop in mid-stride. Without the disruption he could have gone on for another forty-five minutes, repeating himself until the church emptied because of boredom."

Velvel pulled several bills from an inner pocket. "I'm responsible for this disaster so I'll pay for the damage." He handed the nun five one-hundred dollar bills."

She looked down at them. "Soap and a little polish only costs a few dollars."

"No, I insist. If you try to give it back, it would be a great insult. The person responsible must always atone."

"Well, in that case I'll put it toward food and clothes for the poor."

Julia and Annie added a few more bills. "We feel like fools but there was nowhere else to run. We came to your side door and it was open."

"Open? The side door hasn't been open in years. Now how did that happen?"

"I can't begin to thank you enough," Annie said contritely. "Had we known it was a convent we never would have gone inside and…"

"And you'd probably be history by now," Sister Veronica finished. "Well, you're here and that's that. The next question is how do I get you away?"

"You're not going to ask why we're being pursued by killers?"

"My instincts tell me it's better that I don't know. I have no idea what you've done to incur their wrath but that's a problem you'll have to solve on your own. In good conscience I couldn't let you be captured by those men and have your beatings or deaths take place on church property. Moe, the light haired man, served time in prison for manslaughter. It should have been first-degree murder but somehow justice was lost in a legal maze. He beat one of our parishioners to death twelve years ago.

The victim was an older, defenseless man. His wife still belongs to this parish and is very ill. If her husband were alive I'm sure things wouldn't seem so bleak."

"Why was her husband killed?"

"I don't know all of the details except that he went to the police because Moe, I can't recall his last name, beat and raped his daughter. After her father was killed, the girl refused to testify. So how am I going to get you away? First, you'd better take off those habits. If our parish nuns see they're missing it could cause a stir of questions. I'll just take them back to the convent and say three of the visiting nuns borrowed them because theirs were soiled." She looked at Velvel. "Goodness you do have a full head of hair."

"I should introduce myself. I am…"

"No, please don't tell me your names. The less I know the clearer my conscience."

"We left some of our clothes in a hamper in your bathroom."

"I'll take care of that. All right, everyone grab as many flowers as you can carry. Several florists donated them and we had far too many as it was. Follow me." She led them down another lengthy passageway.

"How do you know your way so well?" Velvel asked struggling with a dozen huge bouquets.

"I've been here fifteen years so I know every inch of the parish like the back of my hand."

"You're not frightened down here?"

"No, unless I see a rat. One gets in occasionally."

"Oy."

Sister Veronica stopped. "This door leads up to the parish garage. Stay here while I see if all's clear." She was back in a few minutes. "This is the only escape route that comes to mind. I can't let you into the convent. There are five nuns plus myself and two of them get very crotchety when anything out of the ordinary occurs. They're quite old but rather like ferrets in checking out the unusual. And I can't let you stay in the church basement because our two janitors come and go. They're at the brunch now but they'll be back to check the furnace, sweep and put some things in storage. And our pastor certainly wouldn't welcome you into the rectory. He's rather stiff-necked. So if you'll all scrunch in the back seat of the car, I'll pile flowers atop you. If I'm stopped I'll say I'm delivering the excess to a neighboring church."

"You're putting yourself in danger," Julia interrupted. "We can't allow that. We'll hide somewhere until it gets dark."

"At first I thought the same but don't you catch the drift when I said a few minutes ago that the side door to the convent is never opened? It couldn't have been open because I have the only key and I carry it with the others on my belt. This morning that door was locked and I never left my keys unattended. Seems to me it was open by divine intervention. Not a miracle mind you, just a strange happening. And because it's so strange I feel compelled to help you.

"The dybbuk could have opened the door." Velvel said.

"Pardon me?"

"My personal devil who torments me whenever he can. But he did help me rescue the women, so he still must be in my corner. It's quite unusual but I'm sure he'll make up for it later."

"Personally, I feel we're in charge of our own destiny."

"Then how would you explain the disasters that find me?"

"You expect bad things to happen and they do. Change your attitude and I'm sure your dybbuk will vanish."

"Easy for you to say, you're protected by God."

"Those men must be certain you're somewhere around or they would have left by now. As soon as they see you're not with the crowd of people in the school hall they'll start a thorough search. Best you're away from here. All right, one of you lie on the back seat and the other two scrunch on the floor." She began stacking flowers over them until they reached the car roof. Parking was at a premium with the anniversary celebration and Sister was thankful no one had been so thoughtless as to block the garage.

The three in back listened carefully but no one stopped the nun to ask questions. She pulled over three blocks from the church. "Change of plans. I saw one of the men going into the church and another toward the rectory. Don't worry, neither of them looked in my direction. I didn't use the main driveway and not many know there's another narrow one in between two of our buildings. I'd better get back in case they try to search the convent. The sisters are in the school hall now but they could go back and get the fright of their life. Take the car and get away. I'll report it stolen in three hours."

Julia scrambled out from a mass of chrysanthemums and crawled over the seat. "I hate taking your car but it's the only way. It will be found in…"

"No, don't tell me. It will either be found or the insurance company will have to pay."

"You know, sister, we are not without sin."

"Who of us are? Go. God be with you. I'll just take this sleeve of roses so it looks as though someone handed them to me recently." She tapped on the roof. "Go."

"A saintly woman," Velvel complimented as Julia got under way.

"Sister Veronica is in tune with the times. I've known a few nuns in my day who thought they still lived in the eighteenth century."

Chapter 50

Annie and Velvel popped out from beneath flowers when Julia announced they were on the New Jersey Turnpike heading toward Philadelphia. "We should be there in an hour and a half," she announced.

Velvel resembled an angry bee amidst a heap of daisies. "I am sneezing, sneezing one after another. Too many flowers. I'll throw them out the window."

"Don't you dare," Annie warned before he could roll the window down. "Do you want to leave a trail so the bad guys will know where we're heading?"

"My eyes are watering, the sneezes hurt my ribs."

"All right then. Julia, can you pull off somewhere, just long enough to get rid of the flowers?"

Julia exited on the next off ramp and saw a bridge down the road. There was a gravel turnaround near the river. "This is perfect. The water will carry all the flowers downstream."

They were tossing the last of the bouquets when a truck driver stopped and leaned out of his window. "Anything wrong?"

Annie was startled. "No, that is, our parents were killed on this spot eight years ago. We're just putting our annual memorial in the water." The man drove off and Annie unhooked the canvas bag from her belt. "Do you realize I've been running around with these rocks under my jacket? Might as well toss them too. They're starting to clunk against my leg and it's annoying. I only hung on to this to use as a weapon if that heap came after us again." Annie undid the knot and the bag fell to the ground. Two grass green stones spilled out, twinkling in the sunlight. She knelt and opened the bag wider. "Velvel, you said five or six emeralds. Look inside. There must be hundreds, all faceted and in different sizes."

"I was trying to tell you but…I thought Crush would still have the gems. Oy, much deeper trouble this makes."

"We have no time for a pow-wow now," Julia snapped. "It's at least another hour to Philadelphia with this traffic and Sister Veronica will be reporting the car stolen in less than two. We have to be well away from it, we have to buy decent clothes."

"The clothes you had with you in New Jersey?" Velvel asked.

"Got rid of them this morning. They were thrift store items and we left them in a Salvation Army bin. Will you please get in the car and stop yakking?"

"Do stop blathering," Annie ordered. "You said five or six emeralds. This bag must weigh a pound." Her hands were trembling as she held it.

"Probably more than a pound. I called the motel but you already checked out. Sam took Moishe off the job at the last minute. I ran and ran and I saw the ambulance so I stole it knowing I had to reach you before…well, I was only a little late."

"You said you didn't know how to drive."

"I don't. I had to think back to my one and only lesson years ago. Sam will leave no stone unturned. No one steals from him and lives to get away with it. Five or six emeralds he wouldn't mind but a bag full? What are we to do? Better to put a bullet in our heads than let Sam torture us until we die. Oh, dybbuk, are you laughing now?"

"Quiet, we must think. There's always a way out of a problem if you think long enough."

"We don't have that long; we're doomed. Why did I follow you to the airport that day? Why didn't I mind my business? Better to be alive and poor than rich and dead."

The women never paid attention when he ranted and raved. "Did anyone see you take the ambulance?"

"I stood so the driver couldn't see me, not even in the rear view mirror. When he jumped out he didn't turn around so I don't think I was seen."

"How about people on the street, other drivers?"

"No one was walking close at the time. Other drivers? I don't know. Before the sirens came on I heard one woman scream that a hat was driving. You see, the seat was pushed so far back my feet couldn't reach the pedal. I had to slide down low to stretch my right foot. The crazy, screaming woman only saw my hat."

"How did you find out Moishe wasn't making the run?"

"You're like the inquisitors from old Spain. I ran into him on the street. The minute I saw him my heart started pounding. At first I thought Sam had simply canceled the trip. It wouldn't have been so bad then. You would have waited and Moishe wouldn't arrive and you would leave. No harm done. Oy, your rental car. They'll find it and trace you. We are truly doomed."

"Oh for God's sake, Velvel, give us a little credit for having brains," Julia said angrily. "We're not scatterbrains. When we were in Dallas, we had more than a few hours to kill so we drove through a few unsavory neighborhoods and in the last, a man approached us, a very well dressed man since everyone else looked rather shabby and unkempt. He asked if we were looking for anything in particular and he said he could supply anything for a price."

"You walked down dangerous streets in a city you didn't know?"

"You forget I'm a brown belt karate expert and Annie's been taking lessons."

"And where was that expertise when Crush was pushing you into the trunk?"

"He was bigger than my instructor so I couldn't make much of a dent there. How as I supposed to know I'd be meeting a man built like a mountain? Anyway, I said Annie and I were writers looking for a bit of realism. Told him we were working on a spy novel but we were stuck at a crucial chapter and we had to know how our heroine could go about getting a fake I.D. and credit card. The man answered that he could do exactly that for five hundred dollars. I told him to get two since the heroine would be escaping with a Russian double agent and Annie and I were going to trace the route personally."

"Oy, oy."

He said to come back the next day and he would have what we wanted. I told him not to bring back hot I.D.'s because our main character needed something good enough to get out of the country."

"You went back to that terrible street?"

"Velvel, I said we're not stupid. Told him to meet us at the Galleria and he was there on time. Annie stood to the side to see if anyone was following him but the coast was clear."

"It could have been the police coming to arrest you once money changed hands."

"But it wasn't so why are you worrying? The supplier said the I.D.'s were forged and not stolen."

"And you believed him?"

"It got me what I needed. I'll have to get rid of the set I used in Perth Amboy. I dressed as a man since the license was made out to a man. The other one is made out to a woman and I can be Lusanne Frost if I have black hair."

"Which brings us back to clothes," Annie interjected. "Since we dumped ours, we can't very well walk around in combat boots, khaki pants and camouflage jackets. We'll have to stop at a mall but we can't walk into a mall looking like this."

They found one just outside of Philadelphia. "Look, there's a J.C. Penney store. Velvel, you'll have to go in."

"Me? I know nothing of women's clothes."

"Ask a sales clerk to help you. Tell her you're in a terrible hurry and say they're gifts for your wife or girlfriend. Here, I'll write a list; two coats, two nice hats, two sweaters, two skirts and two mid-heel pumps."

"I have to buy all that?"

"You have exactly thirty minutes. Julia and I are both size twelve but Julia's taller. Keep that in mind. And she wears a size eight shoe and I'm a seven. I'll write that down too. Wait, let me comb your hair. If it sticks up like that everyone will stare at you."

"I have no money left. I gave it all to the sister."

"We have more. Remember to be back by the car in thirty minutes. Maybe Annie or I can walk into Walgreen's and pick up a few more things."

"You're going in there looking like that? If you are, why can't you buy the clothes?"

"Buying clothes will take longer and any saleswoman would remember us if we walked in dressed like commandos. To the store, Velvel. Shop till you drop."

Chapter 51

Velvel turned round and round in the women's department, more confused than he had ever been in his life. He had absolutely no idea where to start. Vivid colors assaulted his eyes wherever he looked. When he needed a new pair of pants or a shirt he went to Hymie Brodsky's store near his apartment. Hymie would select just what he needed in white shirts, everything else black. All he had to do was take money out of his purse and pay. He stopped turning when a saleswoman came up to him.

"Can I help you, sir? You seem lost."

"An angel, you must be an angel. So much here, I don't know where to start. I have a list and I must hurry."

The middle age woman took pity on him. "Let's see, two coats. That's easy enough. I work in the coat department. What did you have in mind; wool, leather, down, corduroy, faux fur?"

"So many choices? When they say a coat there should be one kind. Whatever you think best." She looked at him strangely and he had to come up with an explanation. "For my two cousins. Fire destroyed their home. They need clothes to go out and talk to the insurance people tomorrow, to find another house, to shop. They have nothing." His face flushed. "No, I don't mean they are naked but all was lost except what they now wear and that's dirty from smoke."

"How dreadful. Wool. You can't go wrong with a smart, black wool. Do you want identical coats?"

"No, no they must be different. Twins my cousins aren't."

She laughed. "Here's a rack of size twelve. I have one with a flared black and the other is a straight cut."

"Fine, fine. Now, the others things. Hurry."

"The other items aren't in my department."

Velvel was stricken, ready to cry. "You must. Please, please don't leave me."

Hadn't this man ever shopped before? Why he was truly terrified? "All right, if the supervisor questions me I'll have to stop and explain. We'll leave the coats here and bring everything else back to this register." Miraculously, the woman led him in a dizzying foray around the departments, asking his opinion on everything. Velvel was overcome by the choices and simply nodded at the first or second item she held out for display. The last stop was the shoe section. "Bernie, would you please bring out two pair of those black leather pumps? One size seven and one size eight." She turned to Velvel. "You'll have to pay separately here. I'm not allowed to ring up shoes."

Velvel pulled the money Julia and Annie gave him. "Hurry. I'm late, I'm late."

The saleswoman laughed again. "For a very important date?"

Velvel stopped fidgeting. "What?"

"It's a line from a song. I guess you don't know it. Hose?"

"Why would they need a hose? The fire is out."

"Hosiery, nylon pantyhose."

"The items on the list only, don't give me the trials of Job. They can go without the hose. Why do they call it hose when they mean stockings?"

"Robes? Nightgowns?"

"It's on the list?"

"No, but since your cousins lost everything I thought they might need those articles."

Velvel looked at the stack of clothes already piled on the counter. "I don't know. How much does all this cost?"

The woman rang up the items. "You're in luck today; there's a fifteen percent off sale. Six hundred and ninety dollars."

He counted off the money. "I have two hundred left."

"Then you'll want robes and nightgowns?"

"Yes, yes, but you must remember to hurry. Pick anything, I'll wait here."

The coats were in two plastic garment bags and he struggled to hold those plus three large shopping bags and two oversize hat bags. He walked out the door he thought he had come entered, still dazed and forgetting where the car was parked.

Julia was parked just off the entrance. "Annie was about to walk in, combat boots and all to drag you out of there. What took so long?"

"You sent me into a viper's nest. I had no idea what I was doing. Never, never again will I do this."

There was just enough room in the back seat for him to squeeze in since everything they bought was stowed in back. "I can't wait to see what you selected, Velvel. Hand me things one by one. I'm going to change while Julia drives. We have to make up for lost time."

"You're going to change in the car, for all the world to see? Brazen woman. Have you no shame?"

"We're in a fast moving car so no one's going to pay attention. Sweater please."

"This is an abomination. I thought nothing could be worse then being in the middle of so many clothes but this is much worse."

"Hand me the sweater and then you can close your eyes if you're feeling squeamish. Goodness, it's black with a gold lame tiger's face on the front. Skirt, Velvel. Leather? With a slit? My, this makes me wonder what goes on deep in your mind. Thank goodness you didn't buy a whip. Forget that last sentence, it'll only drive you crazy."

"It's imitation. Real leather was four times the price."

"What a discerning eye. Shoes? Well, these are normal." Annie stared at the hat. "I do believe Ingrid Bergman wore something similar in Casablanca. Coat? Very nice. It'll hide all the sins."

"Sins? You're hiding sins? How can a coat hide sins?"

"Just a bit of humor. Julia, pull off at the next exit. I'll drive while you change."

Julia slipped into a form fitting red ribbed sweater and stared down at herself. Annie went into a fit of laughter. "My, what big boobs you have. You look like a tart."

"Stop, stop," Velvel cried. "Such loose talk. You burn my ears."

Julia's hat was a head hugging black cloche. She looked at herself in the mirror. "I can use the other I.D. to rent another car. You can't tell what color my hair is with this. You did good, Velvel."

"I did? You're all done changing? I can open my eyes now?"

They were traveling down Philadelphia streets by then. "Annie, pull over to the curb every time you see a trash basket. I'll start dumping some of these old clothes a little at a time. Where should we leave Sister Veronica's car?"

"How about the airport? We can rent another there with your other I.D."

"Why do you throw away clothes? Oh yes, they could be remembered. Where do we go next?"

"Annie and I came up with a brilliant plan while you were shopping. I told you there's a solution for everything if only you stop and think. We're going to New York, to return the emeralds to Mr. Cugnidorio."

Velvel screamed. "Insanity. He'll kill you for sure."

"Think of it as another game, Velvel. This one is called Honest Injun."

"Honest engines? You make no sense."

"I'd appreciate it if you'd keep your mouth shut for the next hour. There are still a few things to go over in my mind."

"Just one more question. Why do you carry so much money?"

“For emergencies and today was an emergency. Why do you carry so much that you gave Sister Veronica five hundred?”

“In case a good gem comes my way. Many sellers want cash on the line.”

Chapter 52

Darkness fell early because of the heavily laden sky as they reached the outskirts of New York City. Annie was finishing up the questions she had for Velvel, her mind working at a rapid fire pace. "Just a few more, dear. You'll be at your apartment in no time and you can finish cutting that diamond you were commissioned to do. Tell Holdheim tomorrow that you stayed up all night. You have an alibi of sorts since Moishe knew that was your plan."

Annie went on and on while Velvel barely said a word. They had never seen him sullen but he was brooding and silent now except when he had to answer a direct question. His lips were clenched because he had to swear on his brother Avi's life that he wouldn't interfere with their plan to return the emeralds. The women had found his weak point. He could never act against that promise because to swear on Avi's life and then jeopardize it was unthinkable.

"Do you think Moishe told anyone else he was replaced for the run?" Annie asked.

"I know he's already told half the district by now. By tomorrow more will know. Moishe enjoys moaning and complaining about everything."

"Let's go over how Stuttering Sam Cugnidorio spends a typical day."

Velvel wanted to remain silent but yet he had to help. Julia and Annie could be killed if he didn't reveal everything he knew. He could be killed as well but they were more important. "First of all, you must never call him Stuttering Sam to his face. Everyone does it behind his back but say it to his face and he will make you a lifelong enemy. He goes into his shop for an hour and then his assistant takes over. Then he drives to his small office on 48th Street for another hour. He has a late breakfast at the deli in the district. At noon he goes to Cafe Roma in Little Italy. It's where his real business is conducted, in a back room. Roma is a neighborhood sandwich shop. Anyone is allowed into the restaurant but strangers are looked upon with suspicion. No one gets in the back room because two men usually sit outside the door and act as guards."

"Men like Crush?"

"Just as tough but not as large. Crush is usually inside the inner office. Sam stays there until dinner time. I don't know what he does after that. Goes home I would think."

Annie and Julia smiled at each other as Velvel fell into another brooding silence. Normally he would have continued talking a mile a minute. It was like watching a waterfall come to a halt and hang suspended in mid-air. "Here you are, Velvel, one block from your apartment. We'll follow you slowly to make sure you get in okay."

Velvel huffed as he opened the door. "I am not a child or a helpless woman that you have to watch me."

"Chauvinist. Please don't be angry."

"You tricked me. Now any time you want to keep me in the dark all you have to do is make me swear on Avi's life. You know I couldn't refuse."

"We promise we'll never use that trick again."

His face brightened. "You swear?"

"I swear on Julia's life," Annie answered.

"And I swear on Annie's life," Julia added.

"Okay, okay, now we're back in business. You'll call me as soon as it's over?"

"Yes."

"If I don't hear from you by two o'clock, I'm coming to rescue you again, promise or not."

Chapter 53

Deeply engorged veins stemmed from rage stood out on Sam Cugnidorio's balding head as he sat in the back room of Cafe Roma. Sunday nights were earmarked for his family, not business. He knew something had gone wrong when Crush didn't come back on schedule and only a catastrophe would make him late so he had to wait around for hours, which only made him livid. Crush finally returned and they were having a private meeting. Normally Sam didn't deal in gems but an unexpected opportunity came up and he never passed up a deal that could net him a couple of million.

"It had to be a set-up, Sam," Crush said for the third time. "Why would two bums be waiting on a deserted street for me?"

"You s s said they asked for a little change. Because of that you assume it was a s s set-up? Damn you for making me say words I always avoid."

"Why did one hit me in the head if it wasn't planned? An ordinary street guy wouldn't bop me. Not that it bothered me. I had both of the shits in the trunk of the car in seconds. It was the fuckin ambulance that knocked me cold. When we followed it, we were less than a minute behind. They had to go somewhere on the church grounds cause we looked down the only other street open to them."

"There were buildings down that s s street?"

"Yeah."

"If there were buildings on that…road, they could have hidden in one. Admit it, you fucked up Crush. Instead of looking in all the church buildings you s s should have checked the…damn it, you know what I mean."

"I'll find those two, Sam, and when I do I'll tear em to pieces."

"Oh, we'll find them all right. No one can hide deep enough when I'm looking. S s send Moishe in now."

Moishe was trembling from head to foot. "Whatever it is, Sam, I didn't do it. Okay, so maybe I was a little pissed because my regular Sunday run got taken away but I didn't have anything to do with stealing your goods. You know me for years, Sam, and I never stuck it to you and I never would."

"Take a chair, Moishe, because we're going to get to the bottom of this even if it takes all night. Tell me who you told about being taken off the run."

"Nobody, Sam. I didn't tell nobody."

"You're a blabbermouth, everybody knows that. I let you make a little extra money every week cause I feel…"

"Sorry for you." Crush finished.

"I promised your brother, God rest his soul, that I'd take care of you but you're making it hard for me. He was my right hand man and I thought you took after him. Knew I was wrong that first run you made but a promise is a promise. I'm warning you, Moishe, keep your lip buttoned or you're fish bait. Now you're going to…"

"Start giving us names," Crush said.

"Or we'll break your fingers one by one."

"Okay, let me think. I walked out of your place and bumped into Lefty Klein. He was with Schnozz, the goldsmith. Maybe I mentioned something to them."

Crush got up from his chair with a menacing look.

"Okay, I did mention it. Then Buddy Guy came walking along with Sal Grassano. I was going to have coffee with them but Toots Hallal had a tip on a horse and then Chavivi came across the street but he didn't stay. Had to hurry home to cut some diamond. Went into the restaurant and sat with Billy the Hammer and Oscar. Malone joined us for a minute but he had to drive to Queens. Started to walk home and met Izzy Bern so we talked for a while and Joe Kramer stopped his car. Went home and had dinner with my ma and I must have told her cause she finally parted with a sawbuck. After dinner I went out to place a bet with Hobie. The nag lost so I was broke again. Then…"

Sam's fist pounded on the table so hard even Crush jumped. "You told the whole fuckin world s s something big was going down to Jersey. Why do I give you a few extra bucks every week when I know you're a big mouth? Your brother would be rollin in his grave knowing you're s s such a s s screw up. Crush, you handle this before I lose my temper. I'm s s sayin words I never use without even realizing it."

Sam always tried to avoid using any words that began with an s but when he really got riled, one or two slipped by. Crush usually caught his meaning in time but not all the time. He and Crush were friends since first grade and only Crush understood him. Crush had only gone wrong once when Albie Alonzo flew to New York from L.A. Crush wasn't sure who the guy was because Sam forgot to tell him. He thought Albie was the enemy. Crush had walked in a little late and a conversation was in progress. Sam was looking stone faced and was saying "Albie, you're a real…"

"Shithead," Crush finished.

Silence for a long minute. "I was going to say s s sight for s s sore eyes. Damn you, Crush." But that was years ago and now he felt he knew Sam's every thought.

Sam stood. "Have to get home to kiss my grandson goodnight and read him a…fairy tale. Keep Moishe here and write down all the names he s s spits out. Don't let him go until he's finished."

Sam walked out to his car and kicked the tires in rage.

Chapter 54

Julia and Annie swept into the Plaza Hotel as though they owned it. When they reached the front desk Julia looked the clerk straight in the eye. "Mrs. Julia Devlin and Mrs. Ann O'Neil. My cousin, Senator Rolf DeWitt, made the reservation." There wasn't a person in the country that hadn't heard of Rolf DeWitt, the Senator from California being slated as the next President of the United States.

Fortunately the hotel always kept a number of rooms free in case of an emergency like this. To the general public, the hotel was booked solid. For relatives of the senator, a room could be found. "Will the Senator be visiting again soon?" Julia flashed him an imperious look and the man flushed with embarrassment at his forward question. "Pardon me. Yes, there's a room. Number…"

"I believe it was a suite."

"That's what I was about to say. Rooms 1601 and 1602 comprise one of our nicest suites."

"I'm ready to drop," Annie said as she came out of the bathroom with a towel wrapped around her. "We have a busy day tomorrow so I'm off to dreamland. Where's that nightgown Velvel bought and why do you have a stupid grin on your face?"

Julia began laughing so hard she couldn't speak as she threw a flimsy piece of material at Annie. Annie shook it out. "He bought this, a white sheer teddy? The man who says a hundred words a minute but never uses a cuss word, the man who blushes at the mere mention of sex, a man who says sax instead of sex because the real word embarrasses him? His little dybbuk companion must have clouded his judgment for a spell."

"You haven't seen mine," Julia said wiping her eyes. She held up a flesh colored satin long gown with a neckline that plunged to the waist and a slit that would reach her derriere. "He probably never looked at what he was buying. I'm taking mine home with me. Some day when he's visiting I'm going to walk out wearing it and if he dares blush and says I'm brazen I'm going to smile coyly and tell him: Velvel, I thought you were throwing a hint to play a new game.

"He'll go into convulsions."

"It'll serve him right for not moving with the times."

They were in the hotel beauty salon as soon as it opened and out an hour later having left generous tips for speed. "I shouldn't have said black, Annie. Claude is gong to have a fit when I get home and ask him to bleach it out. I'll probably wind up with orange hair or maybe it'll all fall out."

"How do you think I feel with a mahogany-burgundy blend? It's atrocious but hopefully, Sam won't pay much attention to our faces if we bombard him with other focal points. Saks Fifth Avenue next?"

"Definitely."

They dropped the things they had been wearing off at the hotel and took a taxi to Cafe Roma telling the driver he would earn double if he waited, no matter how long it took. He agreed in an instant. Julia was dressed in a simple black long sleeved dress topped with a shaggy white lamb vest. Three chains of faux pearls hung from her neck to her waist. A hat with three black feathers swept to the back of her head. She was convinced she looked like Winged Victory. There had been a sale on fake gemstone jewelry and Julia wore three rings; one a five-carat diamond, another four carat and a three carat glass ruby. All three cost under a hundred dollars and they would probably lose their luster in a few weeks.

Annie was resplendent in a dark burgundy dress and matching coat that was a very close shade to her hair. Her hat was a tapestry-patterned fedora and she carried a large matching bag. On her fingers were two diamond rings that if real, would have cost over a hundred thousand each. They were twenty-five dollars each at the sale.

They strolled into Cafe Roma as though they had been thrust from Versailles into a soup kitchen. A waiter wearing a stained apron approached them. "Ladies?"

Julia twitched her nose as if the delicious aroma of sauce and pizza affronted her. "We're here to see Mr. Sam Cugnidorio. We were instructed, no forced to come here."

"No one here by that name."

"Summon him immediately," Annie ordered. "We have a hectic day ahead of us, one fraught with numerous engagements. You can tell him we may have something he mislaid."

The waiter fled to the back room. "Sam, there's two ditzy broads out front saying they've been laid or somethin. Or maybe they said mislaid. Must be society dames cause I can't understand half what they're sayin."

"I'm in the middle of a manhunt and you interrupt me with this…"

"Silly shit," Crush finished.

"Wait, I think mislaid means lost."

Sam's impatience turned to curiosity. "Bring them in."

Julia gave the waiter a sneer. "So he's here after all." She turned to Sam. "Your employee said you weren't here. You should be cautious about hiring a mendacious maladroit"

Was this woman throwing foreign words at him? Sam was at a loss and forgot he was mad. "Mario does that to keep out undesirables."

"Do we appear undesirable?"

"No, no, have a chair. What can I do for you?"

"Something very strange happened last night as we were leaving a performance at the Philadelphia Civic Center. We had remained a little longer than planned to discuss a charity function with Armand

Koshinsky, the ballet master. The crowd had already dispersed as we waited for our car when two ruffians approached us."

"Ruffians? You mean Russians?"

"Thugs."

"Oh. What does that have to do with me?"

"I'm getting to that point, Mr. Cugnidorio. Please be patient. We stood there, terrified that we would be accosted, battered, even raped. One of the men thrust a dirty bag at me. I was so stunned I took hold of it without meaning to. The other thug began talking in a most menacing voice. His breath was foul and he reeked of sweat. Give me a second to recall his exact words. He said we should take the bag to Sam Cugnidorio at the Cafe Roma in New York, that we should get it here today or he come after us and...oh, I can't bear to finish."

Annie took up the story. "He also said if we didn't, they would come back and slit our throats, that they could do it because they knew who we were and where we lived. He saw two defenseless women and took advantage of us." Annie reached into her large purse and pulled out the canvas bag, holding it gingerly as if it might contain a bomb or worse. "We had no other recourse but to follow his instructions. He also said to tell you they were sorry and that they made a terrible mistake and it would never happen again. Our first thought was to call the police but the threatening words deterred us. What consequences would befall us if we didn't do as he ordered? I live alone and I don't relish waking in the middle of the night to an intruder with a knife."

Sam looked in the bag and grinned.

"Mr. Cugnidorio, what is going on? We're respectable women who have followed the rules of society all our lives. To be confronted in such a manner is disgraceful, frightening and humiliating."

"Call me S S Sam."

Crushed looked at his boss in amazement. What the hell was going on?

"Ladies, it's all a terrible mistake. Those two…two thugs stole my property. They must have realized their mistake and didn't have the guts to return it personally. I'm s s sure they picked you at random. You won't be bothered by them again."

"How can we be certain of that?"

"I'd s s stake my life on it. When I give my word, it's written in s s stone."

Julia deigned to smile. "And I daresay I'd stake, not my life because that's a formidable wager, but I would stake my reputation that you have a remarkable singing voice."

Crush was ready for an explosion as he stood, ready to intervene. Sam was going to lose his temper and kill these crazy broads. The police would come and there'd be hell to pay.

"Why do you think that?" Sam asked waving Crush back to his seat.

"Most people with a stammer can sing just as well or better than professionals."

Crush went to escort the women out but Sam stopped him. "Leave us alone for a while," he ordered.

Julia continued. "My uncle, Lawler Smyth, stuttered every third word he spoke yet when he sang arias from his favorite operas there was never a hint of the flaw in his speech. One day he recorded himself singing an aria from Madam Butterfly and as he listened to his voice repeatedly, an idea swept over him. If he sang without fault he should be able to speak without fault. He began recording conversations he might have if talking to a friend but instead of saying the words, he sang them. Naturally, he wouldn't think of doing this in front of anyone. He practiced in the privacy of his library. He began with simple sentences such as I'm so pleased to meet you. Gradually, he eliminated the music until there was only a trace of sing-song in the recordings. In another two months, voila, he was speaking without a stutter, except when he became agitated over the stock market. The family was stunned that Thanksgiving when he greeted us in a clear perfectly enunciated words. Dear uncle continued entertaining us on holidays until he was well into his nineties when he died rowing down the Charles River in Boston. He remains our hero. He proved that with determination anything obstacle can be conquered. Even if it didn't work in your case, Sam, a stammer is nothing to be ashamed of. Every single person ever born has at least one flaw. There are no perfect human specimens. Let's try an exercise shall we? Who is your favorite singer?"

"Frank S S Sinatra."

"I adore him as well. Such an exciting entertainer. I hate it that he died. Do you know his song New York, New York?"

"I do, it's one of my favorites."

"I'll change the words slightly. I'd like you to sing start spreading the stars instead of using start spreading the news. As you go along you can substitute other words that begin with an s. Ready?"

Sam burst into the song replacing dozens of the original words with words beginning with an s. He continued, going through the entire song. Crush, the two bodyguards and workers stopped what they were doing and listened, their mouths agape at this phenomena. It couldn't be Sam singing his heart out. None of them ever heard him even hum. And why was he singing Su Sork instead of New York?

"Excellent," Annie and Julia applauded. "Dear me, I feel like swooning just as I did when I was a teenager. "Once again, Sam, but this time you're not fully singing but rather talking out the song with just a hint of a melody."

Again Sam burst into song. "Hey, not bad," he said when he finished. "I amazed myself."

"You can't go directly into speaking after only a short practice, dear man. You'll only be disappointed but you have to remember you've only just begun. Practice whenever you can and when you feel total confidence sweep through your soul, say one or two words you couldn't manage before and only pretend you're singing them."

"You two are okay in my book. I can send someone to Philadelphia to look after you if you doubt my word about those thugs never bothering you again."

"Goodness, Sam, we're not going back for ages. We leave for Washington D.C. later today. Our good friend, the ambassador from Argentina, has invited us to stay with them for two weeks. After that we're off to visit Senator DeWitt and his family in California. We're staying there for three or four weeks, to help him with his campaign strategy. He's going to run for the presidency you know."

Sam opened the bag and spilled the contents on the table. "I want you to have a reward for returning these. Go on, take a few."

"We couldn't," Annie answered sweetly. We simply returned property to its rightful owner, which any dutiful citizen would do. You can do one thing for us though."

"Name it and its yours."

"Will you keep quiet about this? Any hint of a scandal and our friends will ostracize us."

"Ostra what?"

"Cut us off, stop inviting us to their parties, turn up their noses when we walk by."

"Any bitch tries that and you call me. I'll cream them. You have my word this goes no further than this room. Don't worry about Crush, he can be as quiet as the dead."

"Thank you."

"Could you describe those two guys?"

"Well, it was dark and the outside lights at the Center had already been dimmed but I'd say they were of average height and they wore some kind of jungle garb."

"Jungle?"

"You know, what soldiers wear to blend into the scenery."

"Camouflage?"

"Yes, that's the word I was looking for. You're such an intelligent man, Sam. They wore dark knit hats pulled down low. One was a little overweight. He had a protruding stomach."

"Protruding?"

"He had a pot belly and the other had a swarthy complexion." Julia saw Sam's look of bewilderment. "Olive tinged skin. A car went by at that moment and the headlights reflected against the glass windows. In that instant I saw he had one dark eye and one golden, like a cat's, a coppery shade."

"Two different eyes?"

"Yes. It was so eerie but I'd say that was a very noticeable feature. Sam, it's been a pleasure but we're running a little late. The mayor's wife is hosting a tea at the Hyatt and we have a taxi waiting."

"Why'd you do that? One of my guys can drive you."

"No, no, our driver is looking forward to a generous tip."

"I insist you take a reward. Grab an emerald. I insist. If you don't, my feelings will be hurt."

"Well, if you put it that way." Both Julia and Annie selected three-carat emeralds.

Sam was upset. "Those puny little things." He picked up two that had to weigh at least ten carats each. "How about these?"

"No," Julia protested. "Anything bigger than what we chose would look gauche."

"Gauche?"

"Overpowering, much too much. In our circle less is better."

"I like that phrase; have to remember it. Less is better."

"It's been an interesting visit, Sam. I must confess at first we were a little leery about coming to see you but you're a perfect gentleman and a superb crooner, not to mention that you have an extremely sexy smile."

"I'd like to know your names but I understand about scandal bothering you. If you ever need anything though, you know where I am." He yelled out. “Crush, escort these ladies to the taxi and pay the driver. Make sure you give him a generous tip.”

“We couldn’t accept,” Annie said.

“I insist. No one turns down a gift from S Sam Cugnidorio. Hey, I only had one stutter there. How about that?”

“You are going to succeed because you’re a man with determination. Perhaps one day we shall come back and play a game that uses only s words. We’ll take turns making up sentences like Silly Sally sulked on Saturday, smiled on Sunday, sailed in September.”

Crush returned to the back room. “Two dizzy old boards. I thought you were going to smak em.”

“Ladies, Crush, high society ladies. Very intelligent and interesting. Tell the guys out front they were never here. Everybody gets the word that the emeralds were never missing. It was all a big misunderstanding.”

“But Sam…”

“I know we didn’t nail them yet but we will. Let the word go out to a select few that we’re looking for a goon with one dark eye and one gold or copper colored. Makes me think they’re from out of town because I’ve never heard of somebody having two different eyes around here. Saw a dog like that once but never a person. The other thing that makes me feel the thugs were out of towners is that they told the ladies to apologize for them. If you find them, don’t ice them. A few hard knocks will do then bring them here. You never said anything about different colored eyes.”

“I wasn’t paying attention to the eyes, Sam. I was so surprised they had to balls to stop me, I saw red.”

“From now on pay attention to details.”

“Sure, boss. Sam, was that you singin?”

“Get the fuck outta here.”

Chapter 55

"Chavivi, wait a moment." Frenzel caught up to Velvel just as he was crossing 47th Street. "I just left Holdheim. He showed me the two diamonds you cut. Good job."

Velvel was affronted. The Torah dictated that you should never hate a fellow man and sometimes he believed the holy scripture, sometimes he doubted. His see-sawing belief came from never having known strict religious upbringing. His was more a mish-mash, sneaking into schul whenever he could. How could one love or even respect this arrogant piece of dreck standing before him? "It wasn't a good job, Frenzel, it was a masterful job. Only thirty percent waste. Naturally some of that was due to the diamonds themselves but a good portion is due to my expertise. With a brilliant cut as Holdheim wanted there would have been fifty percent waste. I cut pears and saved most of the diamonds."

"Wasn't that taking a great chance, Chavivi? One wrong move and all would have been lost. Holdheim would have been left with two stones under a carat each."

"I walked inside the labyrinth of the stones, Frenzel, touched their weak spots with my mind. The diamonds spoke to me as I coaxed their secrets from them."

What was this; Chavivi so cocksure of himself? The stones were cut brilliantly but two didn't make a master cutter. And there was the rumor that Chavivi had cut a ten-carat rough though no one he knew had ever seen it.

Velvel turned away, practically dancing to be off. “I have an appointment.”

“Wait. “Did you hear Cugnidorio was robbed of a fortune in emeralds?”

“I’m much too busy to listen to street talk. Holdheim wanted the diamonds this week.”

Frenzel’s suspicions grew. Normally Chavivi hung around to hear all the latest news on the street. His work for Holdheim was finished so why was he so anxious to get away? “Chavivi, Cugnidorio’s loss might have been your gain.”

“I seldom deal in colored gems.”

“Yet you sold several rubies last month.”

“Only as a special favor to a friend. I made no commission on the sale.” He had sold a dozen of the smaller rubies from Sukie Mae Frenzel’s collection but Isenberg was supposed to keep his mouth shut. Was there no limit to gossip on the street? Although the rubies were Burmese, they couldn’t easily be traced because they were small and none were marked with a serial number.

“Cugnidorio got his emeralds back yesterday.”

“Why are you telling me this? They were stolen now they’re back. The drama is over.”

“Too bad he was able to retrieve them. Someone would have made a nice profit. Cugnidorio has millions I’d say. He makes his profits dishonestly, not like us who work hard for our yearly revenue. Do you have any sapphires for sale, or perhaps a few more rubies?”

Was the man mad? “I said I don’t deal in colored stones.”

“Word on the street is that Cugnidorio is looking for two men; one a little obese and the other with one brown eye one gold. Most unusual.”

“If I see a man with multi-colored eyes I’ll be sure to pass the word along. Now let go of my arm.”

“I knocked on your apartment door Sunday. There was no answer.”

“A half dozen people knock on my door every day. Some are selling cleaning supplies, some try to sell me books and magazines. Some even urge me to join a bible study group. If I opened my door to everyone who knocked, I might as well put on a uniform like the man who stands in front of the Waldorf and direct all those crazy sellers to a special waiting area." Velvel spun away and down the street.

Annie and Julia were safe at home and that was all that mattered. He had spoken to them last night and got the full story. His little angels were so clever they were even rewarded with an emerald each for their honesty. What a performance they must have put on. Too bad he wasn't there to witness it.

Chapter 56

"Julia, I think it's time to call a halt to thievery. We have quite a lot of gemstones now and we can afford to buy any semi-precious stones that catch our eyes." They were lunching at their favorite restaurant, Tuscany, and were seated in a quiet corner.

"I was thinking along the same lines, Annie. I don't normally get frightened because I can defend myself but with a man like Crush I couldn't last twenty seconds."

"It must have been fate warning us that if we continue, gems won't come to us easily any more. I don't mean to imply that if a perfect situation arose we shouldn't take advantage of it but we should stop planning grand thefts. Spur of the moment opportunities only. Beside, I think we're giving Velvel an ulcer."

"I'm going to use a portion of our emergency money to treat the kids to a vacation in Acapulco. They were taking about it two weeks ago but couldn't afford to go so I'll pay. Maybe I'll even go along. I'll say I won some money in a lottery and that I'm giving them half."

"Allan will be moving into his new home this week. He asked me to fly out and I said I would. We'll go shopping for a housewarming gift. With the big family room he has now I'm sure he could use one of those giant screen televisions. And I could furnish a dream bedroom for Caro. All little girls like to pretend they live in a fairytale setting."

"Does having all these jewels make you happy, Annie?"

"Deliciously happy. When I wake up in the morning I open the chest and it immediately brings a smile. It was a good idea to divide them in two. When the entire box was at your house I missed having them close by."

"And how odd that I was able to find a chest similar to yours at the thrift store. I think mine is in better shape."

"Someone must have taken better care of theirs but I don't mind all the little dents in mine. Makes me feel the chest was buried under sand for a hundred years. Okay, Julia, we'll take a bit of a breather and devote some time to our kids who think we're losing our marbles by hopping on a plane so often without explanation."

Chapter 57

Velvel didn't want to answer the door but whoever was on the other side began pounding, making a terrible racket that would wake everyone in the building. Probably the man upstairs, he thought. Whenever Rusov had too much to drink he went from floor to floor until he found the right apartment. The poor soul had recently lost his wife and now drowned his sorrow in cheap wine so talking to him for a minute was the least he could do, as long as the man didn't pass out on his doorstep. "Frenzel, what are you doing here? It's late. My bed is ready and I'm about to go to sleep."

Frenzel shoved the door open and slammed it shut behind him. "It's time we talk seriously, Chavivi."

"Talk? Talk about what? If you came to talk about emeralds lost and found I have no interest."

"A red surfaced in Tokyo a few days ago, worn in a ring on a industrial tycoon's wife. It was surrounded by baguettes in a starburst pattern."

"You almost broke down my door to tell me that? I'll never own a red, therefore, I don't think about them."

"Reds are a rarity, as I'm sure you already know. There aren't more than twenty known reds in the entire world. You went to California shortly after I was robbed. To sell my red and most likely my whites? Japanese are buying up the greatest gems on the market today and most of the deals are conducted in secrecy."

"So maybe they found another red. Do you think you had the only one?"

"What were you doing in California?"

"I went there on business."

Frenzel snorted in disbelief. You, the bumbler of the district, had business in California? You were also out of town when Mrs. Fremont's rubies were taken. You sold rubies to Isenburg."

"They were small rubies not part of anyone's impressive collection."

"Mrs. Fremont's necklace and tiara had smaller rubies along with the larger ones. You were also in New Orleans when sapphires were stolen."

"Again on business. And if I am such a bumbler, why was I given Holdheim's best champagnes to cut?"

"I don't know; he must be getting senile."

"I'll show you why." Velvel pulled out the diamond he had cut, the ten carat royal. "This is why, to avenge the dubious reputation I earned years ago when my stepfather walked in and made my hand slip."

For a moment Frenzel was sidetracked. The royal cut diamond shot out a spectacular fire, a fire that glimmered into his very soul. He pulled out his loupe to examine it closely and saw perfection. A great urgency to possess it swept over him. He dropped the royal in his pocket. "I'll just keep this to make up for my loss. You can hem and haw all you like but I know you had something to do with the theft of my red."

"Your loss was covered by insurance."

"But not the fame of possessing a red when everyone would know I had one to sell. It was a once in a lifetime happening."

"Give me my diamond," Velvel demanded, flailing his fists ineffectively.

Frenzel was enraged that this little pipsqueak dare touch him. He hated it when anyone put their grubby hands on his immaculate clothes. "You can steal all you want from others, or get involved in hundreds of thefts but no one steals my diamonds. No one." His fist shot out and Velvel's nose gushed blood as he fell to the floor. While he was down, Frenzel kicked him savagely. In his mind he was beating the two who had robbed him. His surroundings turned black as he struck out at a substitute. Velvel heard his rib crack and was overwhelmed with a burst of excruciating pain. He tried to stand but Frenzel twisted his arm around his back. "Should I break all of your fingers next so you'll never cut another diamond, so you won't even be able to hold one in your hand again?" He shoved Velvel and sent him flying across the room. Velvel's head hit the steel frame of the sofa bed. He thought more words were being directed at him but he blacked out.

"Bastard," Frenzel shouted and stormed out of the room without noticing Velvel lying in a pool of blood. He had slammed the door behind him but it didn't latch. A draft flowing down the hall swung it open wider. Ten minutes later a neighbor coming home after working late got off the elevator, stared in surprise at an open door and went a few steps closer. He saw Velvel lying on the floor in a crimson pool and called the police.

Chapter 58

Julia was tanned and fit as she bustled around Annie's kitchen helping her bake six Lady Baltimore cakes for the church bake sale. "I had a marvelous time in Acapulco, Annie. Swam for an hour every day, took the little ones for long walks down the beach collecting shells. I even went parasailing once so now I know how you felt when you sky dived."

"That was years and years ago. I doubt I would do it now. My partial would probably be sucked out of my mouth and I'd land on the ground looking like a pumpkin with a missing tooth."

"How was Seattle?"

"Allan's new home is awesome. Lots and lots of windows with a glorious view of the water. Jennifer's expecting again, in August."

"Congratulations."

"They have four large bedrooms. Allan asked if I'd like to move in with them so I could be near family."

The spoon Julia was holding fell to the table sending out splatters of batter. "That's…that's wonderful, Annie. Will you be moving then?"

"The surest way to ruin a beautiful relationship between daughter-in-law and mother-in-law is to live together. I'll go back for a week or two when Jen has the baby but I'm staying right here in my own home."

Julia began to cry.

"What's wrong? I said I wasn't moving or would you rather I did?"

"For a few seconds I thought you would be leaving me, that our friendship would be separated by hundreds of miles, that we would only call each other on the phone now and then and over time lose track of each other."

"Silly goose, I'm not giving up my life here. I believe one of your tears fell into the batter but it'll make the cake taste better." Annie gave Julia a hug. "We're friends forever. Don't you remember the pact we made when we were teenagers?" The phone rang and Annie wiped her hands to answer it. "Avi. Goodness what a surprise. Are you calling from London?"

"I'm in New York; flew in the day before yesterday. I just found your numbers. A friend of Vel's called to tell me Velvel was severely beaten. He's in a coma." Avi burst into tears. "I don't know what I'll do if he doesn't come out of it. He's all the family I have."

"My God, what happened? We'll come out immediately. Tell me about his injuries." Julia came to stand next to Annie so they could both listen.

"He has a severe concussion, a broken nose and two broken ribs. There are some contusions but nothing else was damaged. The concussion is most serious. The doctors can't predict if he'll come out of the coma or not. And if he does regain consciousness, they don't know if there'll be brain damage."

"We're catching the next plane, Avi. What hospital?"

"Mount Sinai."

Annie hung up. "Julia, would you call for plane reservations while I throw a few things in a bag for us? Oh, and call for a taxi."

"It had to be Frenzel. I don't think Sam Cugnidorio found out anything. I could understand Frenzel's thirst for revenge but the man collected insurance for his loss."

"He also lost the prestige of being one of a very few on earth to possess a red diamond. It has to be a great honor to be internationally known for obtaining the near impossible."

"If it was Frenzel, we'll go after him. We bested him once and we'll have to do it again. If it was Cugnidorio, we'll get revenge."

"We're the ones who got Velvel into this mess so it's only fair that we get him out. But we can't undo the beating and pain he's suffering because of us. Oh, Julia, I feel terrible. I never thought our adventures would come to this. We have to pray like we've never prayed before. How do we make amends for what we've done?"

Chapter 59

"How is he?" Julia asked as she and Annie rushed into a private hospital room.

Avi looked undone as though he hadn't slept in days, which he hadn't. "The same. I asked that the best doctor be brought in but he can't do anything more at this point. It's in God's hands."

The women went to Velvel's side and were horrified. Velvel's face was one massive bruise and twice its normal size. He looked grotesque. Julia took his hand and began crying." "This is all our fault. Oh, dear God."

Annie was in tears as well but she had to keep some control. "Julia, stop it. Some people say coma victims can hear. Talk to him positively while I speak to Avi in the hall." They went no further than Velvel's door. "Avi, do the police have any idea who did this?"

"No. There was a diamond on Vel's work table and a few thousand dollars in a drawer. I looked but couldn't find the special diamond Vel carries for good luck. But he could have put it in a safe place. If it was robbery, the thief would have taken everything of value."

"You look terrible. Why don't you try and get some rest? Julia and I will stay with Velvel."

"I can't. I must be with him."

"Please, Avi, we won't leave him, not for a second. Go to his apartment and get a few hours sleep. I promise one of us will call, even if he blinks. You won't be much good to him if you collapse."

He was like a zombie, eyes glazed, exhaustion and fear etched on his face. "I can't go to his apartment, it's not close enough. A nurse did say I could lie down in an empty room at the end of the hall. I'll go there, just for an hour."

Annie watched him walk slowly, steadying himself with one hand along the wall. She went to the nurse's station. "Velvel Chavivi's brother is going to lie down for a while. Could you take him a sleeping pill? He's on the verge of collapsing, mentally and physically."

The nurse was sympathetic. "He hasn't left his brother's side in over forty-eight hours and there was the long plane ride. Every time one of the doctors or a nurse suggests he rest he becomes enraged.

Annie returned to Velvel's room where she pulled up another chair and sat across from Julia. They each held one of his hands. "Velvel, come back to us. Do you have any idea how much we've come to love you? You're family. There are so many things we still have to do together, things we can't do without you. You're here because of us and I swear we'll make it up to you. I know you can hear. I'm going to keep telling you I love you constantly, until you take notice." She began repeating a mantra. "I love you, we love you."

Julia took over as tears slid down Annie's cheeks. "Who's going to dance with us, go to special parties? If you don't come back to us, Annie and I will turn into old, old ladies. You're the one that keeps the spark in our lives. You have to wake up and say who did this to you. If you don't, we'll go after every single person who ever said a cross word to you. We'll even take on Cugnidorio if he's responsible, or even Crush. Dear Velvel, just open your eyes, move your finger. Please wake up."

They continued their loving words for six hours without result. Avi burst into the room at ten. "I've slept for six hours. What did they give me? The nurse said I would feel relaxed not pass out." He rushed to the bed. "Anything?"

Julia shook her head.

"I'll take over. Go get something to eat."

"We're not hungry but could you get some coffee from that machine out in the hall?"

He was reluctant to leave but getting coffee would only take a minute. Annie and Julia seemed to read each other's thoughts. Annie kissed Velvel's soft lips and whispered in his ear. "We're going to turn ourselves in to the police. Our dream has turned into a nightmare. Never will we steal again, never. We thought it would be a lark and instead it's led to this. Oh, Velvel, we're going to throw away every damned jewel we have down the drain. None of them are worth as much as you." One of Velvel's eyes opened slightly. "Julia, look," Annie cried. "His eye is open."

Avi returned, spilling coffee as he saw the two women hovering over Vel's bed. "What happened?"

"He opened his eye. The other is so swollen I don't think he can open it."

"Oy," Velvel moaned. "Such a headache I have." He tried to take a deep breath. "Oy, oy. Dybbuk, get off my chest." He glared at Julia and Annie. "Such a beautiful dream I was having. I never wanted to wake but you kept calling me. Angry I was getting but then I said to myself I can't get angry at my girls."

"You did hear us," Julia cried. "You really did."

"On and on you went. Velvel, Velvel. My name I wanted to change. You both said you love me?"

"Yes, we do. You'll never know how much."

"You also said you would never steal again?"

"Never again."

"What's going on here?" Avi asked. "Steal?"

"You swear on my life?" Velvel asked weakly.

"Yes," Julia answered.

"Yes, "Annie agreed.

Avi ran to get a doctor.

"Velvel, in another minute doctors and nurses are going to charge in here and they'll make us leave. Who did this to you? Cugnidorio?"

"No, no. Frenzel. He said I was somehow involved in the theft. He took my diamond as repayment. Gotenyu, you must leave New York. Nothing I admitted but I don't know if I said any words once the blackness came. You must run, hide."

"Don't excite yourself or you'll do more damage."

He was becoming too agitated. "Go, go. Hide."

"We will. We're leaving now. Please calm down, darling."

Two nurses and a doctor came into the room. Annie and Julia waited in the hall where Avi joined them a few minutes later. He hugged them both. "He's going to be fine. The bones will mend and the bruises will fade. I was terrified that his mind...that he would never regain his senses. Already he's telling the doctor his name, age, all pertinent information. The doctor made me leave because I kept hugging him. I forgot his ribs were cracked. He kept asking about his fingers and wouldn't believe they were okay until we held them up to his eye and he saw them move. He whispered that I should make sure you get away. Will someone tell me what's going on?"

"We have to learn as much as we can about Tsvi Frenzel," Annie finally said. Do you know anyone in the district who knows him well? You've been gone such a long time you probably can't tell us much."

"Frenzel did this? I'll kill him."

"Will you please calm down?"

"I will not let my brother's beating become a triviality."

"Your brother was beaten because of us and we're the ones who demand revenge. We need to know as much as possible about Frenzel."

"All right. Although I live in London, the diamond industry is relatively small. I know most of the buyers, the big dealers. Two hundred and fifty are invited to the sighting each year and when they come they bring gossip with them. In the diamond industry, word travels fast."

"Does Frenzel buy there?"

"He did at one time, until he raised a big fuss and refused to take the box allotted to him. He demanded to talk to the head of DeBeers. Of course he couldn't and he was never invited again. To refuse what is offered is reason enough not to be invited again, to insult the heads of the syndicate assured he'll never be invited again. Frenzel is not respected in London, not liked in many cities. I met his son, Joel, one evening in London at a party. He's a most honorable young man, nothing like his father. I hear Tsvi is grooming his son to lead Israel one day. It's his burning dream. Wait, I heard you say something about not stealing any more. Good lord, you don't mean you're the ones who robbed Frenzel?"

"Avi, right now your sole responsibility is to take care of your brother. Tell us more about Frenzel."

"There are only two things Frenzel loves; his son and diamonds. Some people wonder if his wife and daughters mean anything to him."

"Velvel once said the family danced with joy whenever Frenzel left on business."

"I can well imagine the truth of that statement. He's a very demanding, outspoken man with no compassion for anything save his son and diamonds. It's also said he's amassing a stockpile of them, that he sells three-quarters of what he buys and sets the rest aside for Joel's future. Not that he lives poor. His wife and daughters may go without luxuries but not Frenzel. His house is fairly large but the family lives frugally. When Frenzel travels, he stays in the best hotels, eats at the finest restaurants, withholds no personal comforts. I can find out more tomorrow from a man named Bishoff. He's friendly with Frenzel but not a friend."

"When Velvel asks, tell him we're gone, that we're hiding. If we're not around, he'll stay quiet and calm. Can you come to our hotel tomorrow evening and tell us what more you learned? We'll be at the Knickerbocker."

"I'll spend the morning in the district and the afternoon and early evening with Vel and then I'll be there."

"Avi, be certain you're not followed tomorrow. Eventually Frenzel will know we're here but we don't want that to happen until we're ready."

"Such mystery but I'll do anything to help Vel. I love my brother. His hard work is what kept our family together when we were young. Without him we would have been on welfare because Solomon earned very little. Vel gave me my start, even helped our two older brothers. Now Jacob sits in Miami like a prince forgetting Vel sacrificed for him."

"Avi, for some reason we thought Velvel was poor up until a short time ago and yet you say he had money to help everyone."

"He was poor because he gave what he had to us. Even though he was ostracized because he ruined our uncle's diamond, there's always money to be made in the street if you're a hustler. He finally admitted he went on a downward financial slide for a couple of years but now he's doing fine. I should have visited New York but I believed him when he said he would rather come to me. He said his latest lucky streak was all due to you."

"You'll hear the story soon, Avi, but for now just find out what you can about Frenzel. It's top priority, that and keeping Velvel calm so he can heal. We'd love to stay with him until he's recovered but he wouldn't rest unless he thinks we're far away and safe."

Chapter 60

Plans were formulated, some to be expanded, some discarded. Julia and Annie felt they had been fortunate when they first set upon Frenzel with the element of surprise in their favor. He would be more cautious now, watchful, prepared for the unusual and yet it was the only way to succeed since they weren't experts in the field of kidnapping. They settled on two ideas that might work. There were items to be purchased and places to be checked out thoroughly with little time to do it since Frenzel could suddenly decide to leave the country or go after Velvel again. They wanted desperately to see Velvel but couldn't until this matter was put to bed.

When Avi came the next evening their first concern was for Velvel.

"He's doing much better," Avi assured. "His head is clear, the swelling in his nose is beginning to go down and it only hurts when he takes a deep breath. And he walked a little today. A guard is posted outside his room twenty-four hours a day, at my expense. Frenzel will never get near him again. When Vel is recovered, we'll talk about going to the police."

"We'll help with the expenses naturally."

Avi laughed for the first time in days. "Dear ladies, I am not a poor man. I've been thinking of moving back to New York. My fiancée is agreeable so the move should proceed smoothly and soon."

"You're engaged?"

"To a lovely woman named Analise. I vowed to remain single but the day I met her, my resolution fled. I neglected to mention her when you were in London because Analise hadn't quite made up her mind as to marrying again and she took a few days holiday to shoot some photos in Greece and think the matter over. Ana also designs jewelry; it's how we first met. She already loves Vel just from hearing about him. I was saving my engagement and the move to New York as a surprise for my brother. I'm telling you now but don't mention it when you do see Vel."

"He's going to be delighted."

"Another thing I should mention is that over the years I've collected quite a lot of old jewelry, mainly from estate sales in Europe. More came from people who decided to get rid of a piece or two because they needed money. I'm not talking about costly precious stones but lesser antique items like jet, garnets, malachite, aquamarines. One woman sold me dozens of jet pieces and I have garnets of every size and color in old-fashioned, intricate settings that are beginning to come into style again. People are coming to me on a regular basis to sell their things and I can't afford to buy them all. Then came the brilliant idea. Since I have hundreds of items why not open an exclusive shop right here in New York where I could be near Vel again? The older I get, the more I miss family ties. Talking to Vel isn't the same as being near him. I can buy roughs for him to cut because we will carry some precious stones set in mountings. Ana would design the newer pieces. She's keen on the idea of creating her own signature line. When I get back to London, I'm giving notice at the syndicate. I won't lose my contacts and I'm sure my friends will send referrals our way. I have a feeling I'll be getting more jewelry than I can handle but if the store is a success, we'll buy all we can get."

"Your brother will be thrilled with this good news."

"Enough of my plans; let me tell you what I've learned."

"Do you know more about the son? Better to know a man's weaknesses than his strengths."

"Joel attends Oxford University and lives in an apartment nearby, a second floor front flat. He gets excellent grades without having to keep his nose to the grindstone constantly and so he has time for parties, dates and friends. He's not seriously involved with anyone, or at least that's what Frenzel said to several people here. Joel supposedly promised his father he would one day marry a woman who would be an asset in his political career. He's a thoughtful, kind young man who received a commendation six months ago when he went into a burning building to save two children. He covered them with wet towels and carried one in each arm down two flights of stairs. Wound up with some minor burns but the children were fine. Frenzel was furious at first because he risked his life but after a while began to see the bright side and said Joel could use that rescue for publicity purposes later. And that wasn't the first time Joel jumped into danger. While visiting a school friend's estate in Scotland last year, he saved a man from drowning. The man was fishing in a small boat when it tipped in a sudden storm. The man panicked and fought Joel off but Joel was stronger and finally brought him to shore. He's known for his kind heart, especially with women and children. If he sees children looking wistfully in a candy shop window, he'll take them inside and buy them all a treat. I'm told it all comes from the heart but with these unplanned, kind deeds he'll be a sure winner in politics."

"To get back to Frenzel, he buys his diamonds from various sources; the Russians, Australians, and some lesser figures in the trade such as small time miners who aren't affiliated with DeBeers. He takes great care to see all that he sells is legitimate but I can't say for certain if that's true about the diamonds he keeps for himself. On a more personal note, his eldest daughter married last year, to a man Frenzel didn't like. She simply ceased to exist in his eyes. She has a new baby, a daughter, and visits the mother whenever Frenzel's away. His family seems to be glad Frenzel travels for longer periods of time. The majority of his time is spent here in New York. On the way home he always stops to visit Joel. He goes home for a few days and then might take a plane to Sydney, Helsinki or South American cities, wherever he hears there are fine diamonds for sale. I'm sure he has contacts searching out diamonds and he probably pays them a finder's fee."

"Damn, we need someone in England," Julia said, "a woman, one who wouldn't think twice about doing something out of the ordinary. There wouldn't be any danger involved but just any woman wouldn't do. She'd have to be a little nervy, like Annie and me. You wouldn't happen to know anyone like that would you, Avi? No of course you wouldn't. Everybody you know must be proper English gentlemen and ladies. We might have to switch to another plan but I really thought our first was best."

"Ana's mother is what you would call zany, flighty. She's always involved in the most bizarre situations. She and her friends take the Orient Simplon Express once a year and plan a murder on board, not real of course but if there was a real murder, it wouldn't phase her. By the time they arrive in Venice, half the people on the train are involved and they all become great friends who invite her to the oddest places. In the summer, she rides in a hot air balloon from England to France so she can lunch in wine country with Henri Gautier, a man she once dated. One would never believe she was sixty because of her vitality, her daring, her fearlessness."

"Do you think she would do what we have in mind? I don't know. It's going to sound insane coming from perfect strangers."

"We adore each other and she would do anything I ask."

"I wonder if she's good at acting out a part."

"As a matter of fact, she did act for two years before she married. At Christmas, she puts on a holiday play in her ballroom. Everyone in the village is invited and everyone accepts the invitation. There's never an empty seat. The plays aren't always related to the season. Last year it was Cat on a Hot Tin Roof and she played Maggie the Cat. It was redone for a mature woman and an older man playing the leads. I must say it was hilarious."

"She sounds like a woman after our own heart. Here's the plan, Avi. The day after tomorrow, could she get inside Joel's apartment by using some pretext? I mean we wouldn't want her to break in but be invited inside somehow. She could pretend she's having a fainting spell and ask for a glass of water and a place to rest for a while, or knock on his door saying she's confused and doesn't know where she is. Anything as long as she's there when I call. The only thing is I can't give an exact time frame. She would have to hang around for a few hours. Annie or I could fly there but this job will require two of us here in New York."

"Olivia will do it. May I use the phone? I'll call her now."

"There's only one problem left. If I can't get Frenzel to go with us, everything would have to be postponed."

"What do you mean get Frenzel to go with you? He's dangerous."

"Avi, we know what we're doing. We've been in far worse situations. This is for Velvel."

"He would never forgive me if something happened to you and I knew about it beforehand and could have prevented it."

"The worst that could happen is a postponement and then Olivia would have to change the scenario, somehow get on Joel's good side so she could pop in again. But I swear there's no danger for her."

"Let me call her. The worst she can do is refuse."

Chapter 61

From Avi, Annie and Julia learned that Frenzel left the hotel promptly at ten every morning when he was in New York. If he was carrying gems, he took a taxi, if not, he walked. "Do you think we positioned ourselves early enough?" Julia asked.

"The police would only move us along if we came earlier and we could wind up missing him. Look, there he is, only one minute after ten. He surely is a creature of habit. He's not signaling for a cab. I think that will make it a bit easier." Annie walked up to their target. "Mr. Frenzel?"

"He would have walked right past the insignificant woman but she grabbed his arm and recoiled. "Let go of me. How dare you put your hand on me?" He wasn't sure if this woman was Jewish or Gentile but either way, he felt he had to take another shower. A hard object poked into his ribcage before he could do anything.

Annie smiled as though they were long lost friends. She held his arm with one hand and shoved a gun firmly against him with the other. "Try to be a hero and your son gets iced. So nice to see you again, Mr. Frenzel. What you're feeling is a 38 caliber revolver and I have no compunctions about using it, even in the middle of a busy street because we're willing to die for the cause. There's another woman with another revolver at your son's apartment; 18 Colfax Square, second floor front."

Frenzel forgot his aversion to being touched, especially by a madwoman. He had been ready to spring but at the mention of Joel, he froze. How did this woman know exactly where his son lived?

Annie continued smiling although she would prefer inflicting a great deal of pain in retaliation for what he did to Velvel. "Get in the back seat. I'll be right behind you."

He had to learn more before he overpowered this hag and the other who was sitting in the driver's seat. He would make a move soon and see them arrested and sentenced.

"Before you begin to get any bright ideas, Frenzel, let me warn you that if our contact in London, the one who's with you son, doesn't hear from us at set times, you might have to mourn Joel. Now, why don't you hold out your hands nicely while I handcuff you as a precaution against your violent temper. If you doubt my word, we'll prove it to you as soon as we reach our destination."

This was happening to him again? Impossible. He was a man for God's sake and these were two old women. No matter, he could break one of their necks even with his hands manacled when the time presented itself. The Israeli army taught him that. And if they were lying about someone holding Joel captive, he would kill them slowly and painfully.

Julia merged in with the traffic, zipping in and out of lanes far better than most cab drivers. She was timing herself to see if she could make it to Muttontown, New York in under an hour.

"I know what you're thinking, Frenzel, but would you risk your son's life?" Annie asked.

"What foolishness. Joel is safe in his bed."

"As I said, when we reach our destination, you'll have the truth. You can call and talk to him personally from our cellular phone. I must say we have nothing against your son; I hear he's a fine young man. Makes a person wonder how a devil like you could have fathered him."

"Who are you and what do you want? Ransom money?"

Annie laughed. "Everything has a price in your mind doesn't it? No we don't want money."

"Diamonds? I've already sold the lot I brought to New York but I can get more."

"I'm sure you can but we don't want diamonds, not any more that is. The ones we took from you before are quite enough."

"You?" Frenzel laughed with derision. "Now I'm certain you're insane."

"Would you like a little duct tape to remind you or should the woman sitting up front give you another karate kick where it hurts most? Should I put on my black wig; should she put on the red curly wig? Your little poster was hilarious. When you depicted us as two strong men, did it soothe your ego? Didn't think two women could get the best of you did you?"

"Crazy, old bitches."

"Watch your mouth, buster, you're skating on thin ice. We're mature women who have a defined purpose in life."

"You're also insane."

"Maybe a little but we're not the only ones in our group. We have almost a hundred women just like us scattered around various countries. As a matter of fact, there are three in England, four in Israel, some in Australia, Brazil. Don't try kicking out at me, Frenzel, or I won't make that important call to England."

He didn't want to believe the woman was telling the truth but on the other hand, he couldn't risk Joel's life.

Chapter 62

What a fascinating son-in-law Avi would make, Olivia thought. There he was, not even married to Analise yet and already he was involving her in the most fascinating intrigue. Analise had selected good husband material this time around. She was sorry they would be moving to New York but she had enough money to travel around the world for as long as she liked, first class every time. And what magical adventures might await her in the Big Apple? Analise would be helping her out in a small way tonight and that surprised Olivia no end. Analise usually steered clear of her mother's shady dealings though she was not a prim and proper girl. Well, every person had their own interests in life. Analise's were photography and jewelry design and hers was making every waking moment as exciting as possible.

Olivia looked at the second floor windows. Still dark. She had called Joel's number ten minutes ago without success and assumed he was out. She thought her ploy would work much better if she met him in front of the building rather than try to explain her appearance in the foyer, which was kept locked. Of course she could have used a plastic credit card to get in but realism was the prime objective here. If she were in the hall, Joel might think she know someone in the building and go knocking on doors. Two men were walking up the street. The shorter of the two patted the taller on the shoulder and walked across the street to another apartment building. The taller young man coming toward her had to be Joel Frenzel from the description she was given. She clutched the iron fence and gracefully fell to her knees moaning.

Joel hurried to her. "Are you all right?"

Olivia took fast short breaths. "The dizziness is coming on. Oh dear, I can't walk until this passes and at times it takes so long."

"Do you live nearby?"

"Unfortunately no. I was on my way to visit friends but I forgot to ring ahead and they weren't home. The housekeeper said they were on holiday. I would have rested there but I was fine ten minutes ago. Oh my, everything is spinning." She clutched Joel's knees.

"Here, let me help you up. I can't have you sitting on the cold pavement. Come up to my flat and I'll call a doctor. We can take the lift."

"No doctors, please. My spells pass given enough time and the doctor would only want to put me in a hospital for a check up. I vowed I would never go into another hospital, ever since they removed my spleen instead of my appendix. I almost died you know."

Joel sat Olivia on his most comfortable chair once they were inside his rooms. "Can I get you anything?"

"A cold towel on my head always helps."

He was back in seconds. "Can I take you anywhere? My car is in the garage down the street."

"No, thank you. You've been so helpful already. It's not often a young man comes to the aid of an older woman. If I can just use your phone I'll call my daughter and she'll drive out."

"It's really no bother getting my car."

"My daughter knows just how to handle these spells. She has a magic touch."

Joel brought the phone to the chair. "Analise, dear, I'm in the middle of a dizzy spell. Can you pick me up? You're such a dear girl." She turned to Joel. "May I have the address?" She relayed the information to Analise. "I'll be waiting." Olivia completed the call and swayed a bit as she turned to Joel again. "I hope you don't mind me waiting here. What is your name?"

"Joel Frenzel."

“Analise lives about an hour away if traffic is light. I do hope this isn’t an imposition.”

“Not at all. Are you feeling a bit better now?”

“The room is still spinning but at least I know I’m seated and won’t fall. Joel, can we talk? Talk always distracts me from these silly bouts.”

“You said the doctor removed the wrong organ. Wasn’t he a good doctor?”

“The best surgeon in London. How was I to know that the night before my surgery he caught his wife in bed with another woman, his first cousin, as a matter of fact. I don’t blame the doctor for being distracted but he should have taken time off. Goes to show you even a genius has his bad moments. Just as I was going under I heard him say all women should be burnt at the stake. I tried to cry out but the anesthesia kicked in.”

“Fascinating.”

“Strange things have happened to me all my life, Joel, ever since I can remember. I could tell you some stories.”

“I love hearing stories, ever since I was a child and my mother would relate Jewish folklore. Can you relate a few of the most unusual so I can add to my collection?”

“You see, I’m starting to feel better already. Talking always helps. The spins are slowing down a bit. Let’s see, where shall I begin? I have hundreds. I fell in love with a German spy during the second world war. Naturally, I didn’t know what he was at the time. Such a gentleman but I should have known something was amiss when he ordered bratwurst in a restaurant. Yes, Conrad dazzled me all right although that wasn’t his real name. After I was dating him for two months I came home one evening and found two members of the secret service in my house. They told me who Conrad really was and gave me proof. What else could I do but help capture the man? I still loved him but patriotism is more important in times of war. We found Conrad a few miles from Dover, ready to board a boat to take him across the channel, where he planned to deliver troop positions to the Germans. I called out his name, he hesitated and that's when one of our men winged him in the knee with a bullet. Good shot. The boat sped away and Conrad was left on the shore. I'll never forget the look on his face as they took him away. He would have killed me if he could. He spat out a single word to me in German. The English officer standing next to me got flushed in the face and refused to translate. That's when the love I felt drained away. Two weeks later I had a private meeting with the Prime Minister and he complimented me for performing my patriotic duty under very stressful circumstances."

"You must tell me more Mrs…"

"Olivia Coco-Stoddard."

"An unusual name."

"My mother's surname was Coco. She was an exotic dancer before she married my father, who was very wealthy and entranced with her movements the moment he saw her on stage. Naturally, she had to give up her career. It wouldn't do to disrobe in public after marrying a member of Parliament."

"Your father was in Parliament?"

"For a time although after he met my mother he spent less and less time there. He was besotted with her, you see. She used to dance for him privately in their bedroom. When I was ten she thought I was old enough to know her story and performed the dance of the veils for me one rainy afternoon. I tell you, Joel, I was thunderstruck that day. I immediately understood why my father hated leaving her, even for an hour."

Joel was enchanted. "One of my passions is hearing unusual tales." He looked at his watch.

"Am I keeping you from something? I can always wait on the front stoop."

"No, no, it's just that I don't want your daughter to get here too quickly. You mustn't leave until I hear more."

"You're such a dear. Do you know of Agatha Christie the writer?"

"I've read two of her books."

"At one time in her life she simply disappeared. I think it was for an entire year but I'm not quite sure about the time frame. She was having a severe case of writer's block and I happened to bump into her in France and we soon became thick as thieves. We plotted a murder mystery together: Murder on the Orient Express. You may have heard of it. I believe it was made into a movie although I haven't seen it. Never saw her again after those three weeks but in her memory I travel on the Orient Express once a year with friends and every year we hatch up another plot to keep us amused on the train. Such fun. Dozens of people ask to go along but I always keep the number at ten after another one of her stories; Ten Little Indians."

Avi was enthralled. What a remarkable woman compared to his mother who enjoyed staying home. Not that staying home was bad; he loved her for her domesticity but this woman probably experienced more excitement in one year than his mother would in a lifetime.

"About five years ago I went skiing in Gstaad during the season and who should I run into on the slope but Prince Philip. I mean I literally ran into him full speed and knocked him into a snowdrift. The man was practically buried in it and was livid. I didn't mean to slam into him but I misjudged a little hill. Never thought a member of the royal family could cuss using words even I'd never heard before. I was having a hot toddy in the hotel lounge later that evening and in revengeful spite, he pretended to drop his drink, right on my lap. Bumping into him was truly an accident but when he became spiteful I decided to give tit for tat. When he was seated at dinner, I casually walked by and quite by accident, my slice of lemon meringue pie fell right on top of his balding head. Needless to say, I don't think I'll ever be invited to the palace. I must be on their black list. I'm rattling on and on about myself but you haven't told me a bit about yourself. You have such nice, olive tinged skin, like a Greek god swimming in the Aegean. The people I know in

England are all so pale and pasty unless they holiday in the sun. Where are you from, Joel?"

"Israel."

"Shalom and Mazel Tov. I've never been there. I keep meaning to go but something always pops up at the last minute. I'd like to float in the Dead Sea, sit in on a few Mossad training sessions, work on a kibbutz for a week, sit under a tree and eat a half dozen of your delicious oranges."

Avi laughed. "Not the usual tourist things."

My dear boy, I never do what tourists do. What do you want from life?"

"My father wants me to train for a career in politics."

"I don't mean what your father wants, I mean what you want."

"I always obey my father. I'm his only son; all his hopes are set on me."

"If that's what you want, fine and dandy but a young person should always follow his heart. Before you know it, you're old and regret not doing the things that excited you when you were young. Thank God I have no such regrets. Whenever I took a notion, no matter how bizarre, I followed through on it. Analise, my eldest, wanted to go off in the wilds when she was young to shoot exciting photos and I never tried to stop her. She chose tamer locations after she was attacked by a lion in Kenya."

"Good lord. Is she all right?"

"Now, yes. The nasty creature nipped out a chunk of her shoulder although a plastic surgeon reconstructed it beautifully. But she'll always bear some scars. She would have gone back but she doesn't relish pain. And when she married that gambler, I never tried to dissuade her. If I had, it would only have encouraged the romance. But she married him anyway and came to her senses five years later when she had to pay off an enormous debt to the owners of a private gambling club. She kicked Nigel out but paid his bills so he wouldn't commit suicide, which he threatened on a daily basis. I always say if a person threatens to kill himself, he won't. If a person wants to die, he does it without announcing his intentions to the world. A truly suicidal person simply slips away and puts a gun to his head or manages to find a cyanide capsule or leaps off a tall building although I find those ways rather commonplace. If one is going commit suicide, may as well do it with panache. Analise changed profession about ten years ago. She designs jewelry and only takes photos as a hobby now. She's engaged to a man I simply adore. He's an arbitrator for the Diamond Center."

"How coincidental. My father deals in diamonds. He travels to New York often since half the world's production of diamonds finds its way there."

Olivia was disdainful. "Personally, I don't own expensive jewelry. Spend my money on exciting things rather than putting pebbles around my neck, fingers and wrists."

"My father would be shocked and outraged at your words.

"Think of it, Joel. What if someone had decided centuries ago that gray slate was valuable? We would discard gems as so much garbage and crave slate instead. I do have a malachite bracelet a dwarf presented me when I saved his life. He was too short to leap over a fence so I gave him an alley oop. But that's another long story. You haven't told me if you want to spend the rest of your life working for the government."

"You'll never tell anyone what I'm about to say?"

"Of course not. Once a person tells me a secret it stays a secret even if I were to be drawn and quartered, or hoisted by my own petard, whatever that means."

"Sometimes I think I want to be an actor. I see all the plays and movies I can in London. I visualize myself playing the parts."

"Well, I must say you have the looks to be a star. You have an interesting face, so sensual and at times sad, as it is now. And such soulful eyes. I do believe a camera would be extremely kind to you, not to mention the fact women would go gaga."

"I don't care about my looks, I care for the emotion I would feel with each part. I would love to be in front of a camera or on stage and entertain the entire world."

"I for one say you can do it. The least you should do is give it a try to see how far you can go. A casting agent would snap you up."

"You really think so?"

"I'd wager a thousand pounds. Do it, Joel, follow your heart."

"My father, the disappointment would kill him."

"Let me tell you something, dear boy. I'm a lot older than you and much wiser when it comes to life. From what I've heard you say, it's evident your father enjoys working with diamonds. Well, hooray for him. If he wanted to be in government once and thinks you'll take his place in that dream, he's not playing fair and square. Each and every person born has the right to choose the course of his or her life. I didn't tell you what my other daughter does, did I? Her name is Joanna and she drives racing cars. The girl's fascinated with speed. She's dating a test pilot and sometimes begs her way aboard when Johnny's flying. I wouldn't dare forbid her to follow her dream. It's what she chose. If speed is the death of her, at least I can say she would have wanted to go out in a quick, fiery ball."

"You are a remarkable woman."

"You have to take a stand before too many years pass and you're stuck in a quagmire of boredom. I always did what I wanted and I always will. No one would dare stop me."

"Your husband?"

"Regis, rest his soul, was zanier than me. He went off on safari once and didn't return for a year. I think he took up with a native although I never questioned him specifically. If that's what he yearned for, I say God bless him in his quest. When he finally did return, he was always staring at black girls, ogling them with wistful eyes. He was so pale, I think the contrast in skin color excited him. I asked him once if he wanted to return to Africa, that if he did he had my blessing but he decided to stay in England. Eventually he got over the African attraction and went on to study penguins in their habitat. Came home minus two toes he lost to frostbite. He locked himself in the library afterward to write his memoirs but when he died I only found one sheet of paper with a lot of gibberish. He must have had a terrible case of writer's block. Regis really wanted to be an astronaut but he had three strikes against him. We don't have a space program in England and he was overweight and overage. Dear Joel, I adore talking to you. You're such a refreshing young man."

Chapter 63

As Annie and Julia neared Muttontown, it began to drizzle. Perfect, Annie thought. They were pretty sure they had chosen a desolate area outside of Muttontown but if the weather had been fair, there might be a hiker or two. In a month or two that certainly would be the case. Julia drove down a dirt road and parked the car between the boughs of a giant evergreen. Annie prodded Frenzel out of the car and instructed him to walk. They stopped when they came to a narrow river. "Sit under the tree, Frenzel; we don't want to get soaked."

Julia tied him to the tree in no time. "Are you going to kill me?" Frenzel asked with sarcasm.

Julia raised an eyebrow. "We prefer toying with greedy men. Sometimes we agitate them for years before we tire of them. First of all, we want the diamond you took from Chavivi."

"So he was in on the theft. I knew it."

"He wasn't in on anything. We forced him into talking about the more notable people on 47th Street. In fact, when he spilled the beans, he was tied just as you are now. We left him no other choice because we said he would leave him in the wilds of northern Canada if he didn't tell us about every important man in the district. The minute we saw you posturizing and posing to lesser mortals on the street we chose you as our candidate."

"Will you stop this stupid nonsense and tell me what you want?"

"Chavivi's diamond. The least we can do is return it him after what we put him through. I must say we didn't hurt him as you did. Basically, he's a kind man. You, on the other hand, are evil. For that you deserve to be punished."

"It's at the hotel."

"I think not. You don't trust hotel safes."

"I sold it yesterday."

Julia took the phone from her purse. "Do you want to dial Joel's number or shall I? I think you can manage to punch in the numbers even with handcuffs. Just ask him how he is, Frenzel. No funny stuff or double talk or we say the secret word."

Chapter 64

The phone rang in Joel's flat and he went to answer it. "Papa, you just called yesterday. Is anything wrong?"

"No, no, I just wanted to talk to you. Joel, is there a woman in your place?"

"How did you know? As a matter of fact, there is. She practically fainted on my doorstep so I invited her inside to rest. Her daughter will be picking her up."

"Does she have gray hair? Is she old?"

"Well...yes. Are you clairvoyant?

Annie motioned for him to hang up with her gun. "I must go now, take care, Joel." The line was dead.

"How strange my father sounded," Joel said, perplexed. He asked if there was a woman in my flat."

"Wouldn't that be a normal thing for a boy your age?"

"No, he asked if the woman had gray hair."

"He must have had a psychic experience. I've had a few myself. One day I called my sister and asked if there was a fire in her house. She said no but then she screamed. Smoke began pouring out of the kitchen from a grease fire. Normally I don't gamble but once when I was in Monte Carlo, I got a deep urge to play the number three, three times. It came up and I won a bundle. Since I didn't need all that cash I gave it to a struggling young man who wanted to open up his own business. He suggested I become a partner but I declined. Seems he thought up a computer program that revolutionized the banking business. Sold the rights for three million pounds. Since I refused to take any part of the profits, he sends me cases of the most expensive wines every month. My cellar is overflowing."

The phone rang again. It was Analise asking for Olivia. "Okay, mother I'm right outside or should I say I'm still miles away?"

"You're here already? Time passed so quickly I didn't realize I've been here over an hour. I'm sure this nice, young man would like to get to bed instead of listening to me rattle on and on. I'll be down directly."

Avi helped her from the chair. "Can we talk again one day soon?"

"Any time. I'm listed in the directory. As a matter of fact, I'm having a party next week. A séance will take place. We're going to try and contact Lord Byron because some of my friends and I disagree on whether or not he was a homosexual."

"I'll be there, with your permission."

"No one ever needs permission to visit; people are popping in and out all the time. If I'm away, Hepzibah will tell you when I'm expected."

"Hepzibah?"

"My housekeeper. She's from Haiti and knows thousands of voodoo stories. Extremely fascinating woman. If I'm not home ask for some of her delicious fresh ground coffee and brioche. She'll take you into the kitchen and keep you entertained for hours. Too bad I didn't find this treasure when Regis was alive. Her dark skin and winning ways would have kept him out of the library and he might have lived longer."

Analise was waiting at the entrance door. She smiled at Joel. "I want to thank you for taking my mother in. It must have been awkward."

"Not in the least. I had a delightful time. I'm going to a séance at her house next week. Will you be there?"

"I tend to stay away from her spiritual get togethers. Eerie things have been known to take place. I'm hoping my fiancée will be back by then."

"Yes, I heard. Congratulations."

Olivia was settled in the car when Alalise turned to her and laughed. "All right, mother, how much lying did you have to do? Avi will be asking for a full report."

"Hardly had to lie at all, dear; only about the dizzy spell and that you lived so far away. And the call came sooner than expected. I could have gone on talking for hours. Such a delightful boy. My new goal is to get him out from under his father's thumb so he can be an actor. Fortunately I know two directors. Have you ever known me to fail, Analise?"

"Never."

Chapter 65

Julia put the phone back into her purse. "A young woman is coming to pick our contact up in an hour. If we don't call back, she's to use her own judgment on what to do with your son. I should tell you her late husband was a Palestinian. He was shot several years ago by Israeli soldiers."

"Chavivi's diamond is in my top left pocket."

Julia removed it and examined it closely then closed her fist around it. "Maybe we won't give it back to Chavivi after all. We've learned owning diamonds promotes greed and greed is what destroys the world." Julia opened her hand so that he could see the diamond. Without warning she flung it into the river, which was only a few feet away.

Frenzel strained against the rope. He watched as the flashing gem went sailing in the air, emitting one last spark before it fell into the water. "You threw away a ten carat royal cut? It's worth a fortune. How could you? My God."

"A little lesson, Frenzel. The diamond is almost the same as a worthless lump of coal, a chard of crystal. You still think we stole for profit don't you? Diamonds mean nothing to us unless some good can come from them."

Annie reached into a pocket and held thirty gleaming whites. "Nine missing because one paid for a poor woman's taxes, another sent a child for medical treatment. The other seven went toward good causes. She put two into her right hand and held them in front of Frenzel's nose. Recognize them?" She reached into his pocket, took out his loupe and put it next to his eye.

"Two of my perfect Siberians. Not a trace of the usual green tinge." He wailed in agony.

Annie put all the diamonds in one hand, reached into another pocket and took out a red. She held it temptingly close to Frenzel.

"My God, give that to me. My red."

Annie flung the entire handful into the water."

Frenzel moaned, then cried out in despair. "No, no. They're lost forever." A sense of desolation swept through him, far worse than when his parents died.

"Frenzel, how will you meet God when the time comes? They say you're fifty-nine years old so how many years do you have? Thirty at most, probably less. It all depends on your health and luck. But men are felled by so many diseases nowadays; prostate, heart problems. And you smoke so there's the lungs to worry about. You're a despicable man, Frenzel. Joy and laughter come to your wife whenever you leave Tel Aviv. Your home becomes a real home when you're not there. You have a granddaughter you never acknowledged. Maybe God will decide to make her an Israeli leader one day. Instead, you've put all your eggs in one basket. What if your son decides he wants something different in life?"

"How do you know all these things about my son's future?"

"We have a dossier on you and your family."

"My son agrees with me in all things."

"Because he's afraid? Have you ever let him speak about his wants, desires? You're putting yourself in God's shoes and I don't think God finds it very amusing. He always wins in the end you know. And when you die I doubt there'll be ten men to form a minyan unless someone in your family pays them to pray. You're despised, Frenzel, by so many people. You'll be a lonely old man one day with no one around to comfort you. I hear you have high blood pressure. How fitting if God were to fell you with a stroke. Would your family care for you or put you in a nursing home with strangers? They'll spend the fortune you've accumulated while you dribble, unable to move, dependant on someone for your every need."

Frenzel was afraid of death, terrified of sickness. If he could make a pact with the devil for another fifty years of life he would give up half his diamonds. "Stop this talk."

"Here's what we want, Frenzel," Julia continued. "You have the insurance money from the theft so in reality you haven't lost anything."

"The magical red. There won't be another in God knows how long. It was a special creation of nature."

Julia was going to take a chance. "Come on, Frenzel, how about the other one you have socked away, the one you kept for yourself?"

His face paled. "How did you…?"

Bingo. Julia and Annie were almost certain there was another. A man so obsessed with diamonds wouldn't sell the rarest of them unless he was desperate for money and Frenzel wasn't a poor man. "You have a strongbox full of diamonds, safely hidden no doubt. If you ever go near Chavivi again, there will be no warning but one of our group will strike. Chavivi is our problem and for the information he gave us, under force, we gave our word he wouldn't be bothered again. He's served his purpose. We must have your word that you'll never do one single thing to harm Chavivi again or we'll simply forget to call London at the prearranged time. And your word better not be empty."

"You have my word."

"If the day comes when you start forgetting that word or become too complacent, start paying attention to older women, not that you'll be able to discern which of them belong to our organization. It might be the grandmother pushing a baby carriage, a bag lady on the street who appears homeless and hungry, a waitress at a restaurant. Right now we're only watching two others so adding one more doesn't create a problem. We could easily have fifty women watching you constantly if we so choose."

Annie took off the safety catch on the gun. Frenzel's eyes widened in fright. "You said I would live."

"Women have such changeable minds." She shoved the gun into Frenzel's mouth and he stared down at blue-black, gleaming steel, watching in horror as her finger squeezed the trigger. If he died, no one would find his diamonds. Years and years of hard work would be lost. The woman's finger pulled back all the way and he closed his eyes waiting for death. Please, God, he prayed. Don't let me die like this. I'll change, I swear I will. He felt a rush of something cold and sweet in his mouth. Grape juice. He was swallowing grape juice. Annie let loose a maniacal laugh. "The next time it might be a bullet, or a deadly poison. Stay greedy if you must, Frenzel, but don't let that greed interfere with our plans or you'll be seeing us or someone like us again." Annie unlocked the handcuffs. "A former Israeli soldier should be able to free himself from the rope in fifteen or twenty minutes."

"You'll make the call?" Frenzel pleaded. Insane people were too unpredictable. Would they call off their watchdog from Joel?

"Annie looked down at her watch. "In exactly eleven minutes.

They walked down the wooded path and minutes later he heard the car pull away. He had no problem undoing the knot at the back of tree now that his hands were free. He had to find a phone and call Joel to see that he was safe. He hesitated as he started down the path. Should he look by the riverbank to see if some of the diamonds didn't make it to the water? What was more important; his son or diamonds? This was a decision he never thought he would have to make. He turned around and headed for the road with heavy steps.

Julia watched with a pair of binoculars. Good, he was walking toward the road. If he had headed toward the river she was going to frighten him further speaking over a bullhorn.

Chapter 66

Gaily colored balloons and flowers and festooned Velvel's small apartment. Catered food was set on the table and a chocolate whipped cream cake lay waiting for the celebrants in the refrigerator. Avi ushered his brother inside. Velvel looked half crazed when he saw the decorations and Julia and Annie. "Oy, you're supposed to be in hiding, not standing near to the lion's mouth." He began lamenting, his body swaying to and fro.

"It's over, Velvel. Frenzel will never bother you again but if by some very slight chance he does, you have to swear to tell us immediately because we have a hold on him. He knows dire consequences will follow if he even looks at you the wrong way."

"You handled him; just like that?"

Julia snapped her fingers. "Just like that. We also have your diamond back. He gave it up willingly."

"What did I tell you, Avi? They work wonders." His eyes glistened as he saw the royal.

"When he saw us throw the red and the rest of the whites into the river he went berserk."

"Red? Whites? You threw diamonds into a river."

"All fakes except for two of the whites that Frenzel originally had. What's the loss of two whites compared to guaranteeing your safety? He has another red, you know. It finally came to us that he would never give up the only one he would see in a lifetime. We used that as our ace in the hole."

"Ace in the hole? Is that like golf?"

"Somewhat."

"Of course he would have another red. I wonder if he got them in Brazil."

"Is anyone going to enlighten me now?" Avi asked.

Julia looked to Velvel. "It's up to you."

"I'll tell Avi everything," Velvel decided. "After all we're going to be one happy family. Avi's moving back to New York with his bride. We're going to own a store together. I shall cut and polish diamonds and other precious gems and find some good buys now and then while Avi handles the business and buying end. Happiness has come from the tragedy. Avi, sit down, this is going to take some time."

Almost two hours later Avi was astonished. "All I can say is one thing. My future mother-in-law is going to love you two. Maybe it's better that you never meet though. I dread thinking of the results."

"Well, we can't wait to meet her," Annie chirped. "Velvel, we will no longer dabble in gem theft. We have more than enough jewels in our treasure box. We'll think of something else to keep us amused. We made you a promise and we intend keeping it."

"What will you do instead? Tell me."

"Nothing outrageous. We're not sure exactly because it'll take some thought. Right now you have to concentrate on healing because you'll be busy planning your store opening."

"You must at least tell me how you dealt with Frenzel."

"Only if you stop bouncing around the room before you hurt your ribs."

"I can hardly feel them. I'm healing so fast my doctor is going to write me up in a medical journal."

Chapter 67

Annie disguised her voice into a nasal whine. "Mrs. Fremont, I have good news. I know who has your rubies and they're willing to return them, no reward whatsoever, no questions asked. The settings are gone but the gems are all there. The two men have repented and want to make things right."

"Who is this?" Sukie Rae demanded.

"Just a woman who wants to see that justice is done."

"Never call me again, do you hear? If I got the rubies back I'll have to repay the insurance company and then I'll have to reinsure them, which would cost a fortune. Mind your own business. Burn the damned things for all I care."

"But Mrs. Fremont…"

"Swallow em, throw em to the dogs but don't you dare come here with rubies or I'll shoot you with my husband's rifle. I'm an excellent shot. Buzz off, you hear?"

"She doesn't want them." Annie told Julia, surprised at the vehemence in Sukie Rae's voice.

"My turn to call Claudia Fanchon." Julia dialed the number. "Mrs. Fanchon, please. Claudia? I heard about the theft of your sapphires and I can get them back for you. No reward, no publicity."

"Is this some joke?"

"I thought it was a shame your beautiful jewels were stolen. I know who has them and I can get them for you."

Claudia's voice dropped to a whisper. "Forget about it. Louis isn't buying me any more jewels because he found me in an embarrassing situation with…never mind. If someone returns the sapphires he'll take away my diamond belt and I'm the only one in Louisiana who has one. Tell whoever has the sapphires to keep them." She hung up.

"Well, so much for her too. Neither one of them wants their jewels back. How utterly strange. I guess we'll have to hang onto them, unless we manage to sell more. Annie, do you realize what we've accomplished in less than two years?"

"Amazing isn't it? I'm going to dig out our old notes and see what other dreams we had in high school. I know becoming a brain surgeon is out. By the time we got through medical school we'd be ready to perform our own autopsies. And of course we can't be astronauts; they won't accept us at our age but we must have pages and pages full of dreams. We have to cull out the impossible."

"It really was two years to remember wasn't it?"

"We'll have to find something new soon before we're tempted to delve into criminal acts again."

"As long as we don't do old lady things again I'm game for anything."

Epilogue

Late September was heralding in the fall season in New York, a brisk wind blowing away the last of summer's heat. Annie and Julia emerged from a cab in front of Avi and Velvel's shop. A discreet bronze sign was posted to the side of the doorway:

Chavivi Brothers
Fine Jewelry

The women had to stop and admire the window display. "Look, Annie, could that be a black opal ring? It is. I'm going to buy it."

Velvel burst through the doorway. "What are you doing out here? Come in, come in. It's been too long." He kissed them both.

"You have such soft lips, just like a baby's. We should have kissed you more often. It's been a long summer, Velvel. You've been busy with the shop and we took our grandchildren on several vacations including a train trip across Canada and to Disney World."

"But you're here now and that makes me dance with joy. You must meet Analise. Such a girl; just right for Avi. I have another angel for a sister-in-law. You didn't make hotel reservations did you?"

"You told us not to. Are we going to camp out at your place and have another pajama party?"

"Yes, yes, but now I live in a bigger place; three bedrooms, and each has a double bed. I walked into the store and asked for three doubles and that's what the man sold me. One is brass, one is French and one plain. I don't need a fancy place to sleep. Another pajama party I planned. I miss the games."

"I can't wait to see your new place and I can't wait to see everything you have for sale."

"Just give me a hint about one of our games and I won't ask any more questions."

Julia grinned impishly. "How does this one sound? The case of the transparent teddy?"

"As usual, I don't understand but I'm sure it will be fun. Here's Analise. Ana, these are my two dearest friends, my only friends Annie and Julia."

Avi's wife was a distinguished woman in her early forties. Her hair was sun streaked, her eyes the color of fine sapphires. She was tall and slender and wore a mauve suit to perfection. Analise warmly welcomed them. "Finally. I was beginning to think you would never come to New York again. I feel I know you though since Velvel's tells so many stories. And don't worry, I'll never repeat a word of them, not even to my mother, because it would only give her ideas and she has enough of them as it is. She's going to be visiting for three weeks in November and I do hope you can come here then."

"Wild horses wouldn't keep us away. We have to thank Olivia for a job well done. Oh, what striking murals on the wall."

Velvel praised Analise's work since she was shy when it came to touting her talent. "Enlargements made of photos Analise took. Now she designs jewelry that mere words can't describe."

"May we see some of your work?"

"Come in back. Avi's getting it ready for display. He's been waiting for your arrival as anxiously as we have."

Annie and Julia hugged Avi. "My dear, you look so happy and content. Both of you do," Julia praised. I can see it's a perfect match."

"You two look like a diamond advertisement for DeBeers," Annie added. So distinguished and in love. I can see the picture in my head, you putting a big rock on Analise's finger and she gazing at you with adoration while a five-carat, perfect diamond glistens in the forefront of the ad."

Avi laughed. "Thank you but don't start embarrassing me. Let me show you some of Ana's work. Our first two weeks was a huge success but only time will tell if the sales will continue."

"I know they will. At times I think I have second sight," Annie said. Oh look, Julia. Is this your work Analise? I thought I wanted the opal in the window but now I think I'll change my mind and buy this Egyptian bracelet."

"You'll each select a gift," Avi insisted. "Whatever pleases you."

"No, let's not start off on the wrong foot. We're paying customers. It's either that or we walk out the store and shop elsewhere."

"All right but you'll have to accept a discount."

"We'll accept a discount but only because we know the markup on jewelry is high."

"Agreed. Browse to your heart's content while I finish setting up these trays."

A salesman they had hired was taking care of a customer when Frenzel walked in. Velvel stared. Frenzel had certainly changed in the last months. He was stooped and all traces of arrogance were gone. He looks old, Velvel thought but looks could be deceiving. He was ready to pounce on his enemy but Frenzel spoke first.

"I come to you in peace, Chavivi, to wish you luck in your new endeavor."

"I don't need your wishes of luck. Get out."

"Chavivi, listen to me please, only for a moment. I also came to apologize for taking your diamond, for hurting you. My actions were despicable. I would return your diamond but it is gone, wasted, thrown away but not by my hand."

Velvel couldn't tell him the diamond was safely in his pocket where it would stay until the end of his days. "You took it and beat me like an animal. God dictates I must forgive you but I will never forget. May you live to be a hundred and wish you hadn't."

Frenzel took a briefke from his inner pocket. "I come to repay you. God also dictates a man responsible for an evil deed must atone." He opened the folded paper. "Six salmon roughs from Sri Lanka. Brought out just before the country fell into turmoil. Look through the window that's been ground away."

Velvel automatically reached for his loupe. Immediately his mind slid inside one of the diamonds as he browsed through its corridors. "Fine diamonds. Unusual color."

He tried to hand them back but Frenzel wouldn't accept them. "They're yours, from my personal collection."

Velvel spat. "You never touch your collection."

"I have been and will continue to do so. My hopes and dreams are lost, Chavivi. Nothing is as I thought it would be. My only son wants to be an actor. No, he is an actor and several people predict he will be famous. I talked and talked until I was blue in the face and still he defies me. I have to tell you this now so my humiliation won't be overwhelming when the movie opens in a few months. It was made in England but already Hollywood is sniffing after him. He will play a politician instead of becoming one. I will refuse to watch this waste."

He'll see it sooner or later, Velvel thought. How could one not see a son and be proud?

Frenzel's eyes clouded as they often did these days. He had called Joel immediately after he walked to a small town and found a phone after he was kidnapped. Joel was fine although sleepy. The woman was gone. Frenzel said a prayer of thanks, the second time he had prayed that day, the second time he had prayed in years. He called Joel every day after that. He wanted to fly to England immediately but pressing business had him scheduled in Rio de Janeiro. Three weeks later, he did fly to England. He had rushed from Heathrow to Joel's flat and held him in trembling arms. Father and son sat down to talk. "Joel, I want to talk to you about that woman who was here when I called."

"You've been calling every day for weeks."

"Don't be impertinent. Three weeks ago, the gray haired woman."

"You mean Olivia Coco-Stoddard. What a remarkable old girl. I've been to her house twice and she's totally fascinating. I meet the most amazing people there."

Frenzel was aghast. "You've been to her house? No, you must never go there again. She's evil."

Joel laughed. "She's not evil, she's funny and lives a most unusual life. You wouldn't believe the stories she tells."

"I tell you she's dangerous."

"Evil or dangerous? Which?"

"What's come over you? I forbid you to see her again."

"You can't forbid me, I'm a grown man."

"And I'm your father and must be obeyed in all things. I'll take you back to Tel Aviv with me."

"And if I refuse to go, papa?"

Frenzel sank back in his chair with astonishment. This was his son who always obeyed him. "You'll have no money to continue with university studies, to pay the rent on this flat, to gad about with your friends."

"Then I'd have to earn a living instead of studying."

"Doing what?"

"As an actor. I think I can be a good actor."

Frenzel flew into a rage. "Do that and you'll be dead in my eyes."

Joel was shocked but refused to back down, especially after Olivia introduced him to Harvey Cotswald, the award-winning director who offered him a screen test. He would be taking it in two days. Everyone he met at Olivia's had been optimistic at his plans for the future. "Did you want to be important in politics, papa?"

"No, of course not. I wanted to deal with diamonds since I was a young boy, to step into my grandfather's shoes."

"Then you went into a career you loved, a career of your choice?"

"Yes."

"Acting is what I love. I don't like politics or government affairs. I find it all tedious and boring."

"You never said anything to that effect before."

"Because I didn't want to hurt you and yet I've watched you inflict hurt on my mother. You hurt mama when you act like she's invisible, when you make demands on her and never give her a loving word. When I marry, I would never treat a wife the way you treat my mother. And my sisters; you hardly know they're around. You don't know that Sharon graduated with honors that Adriana begins teaching next month and that Ruth is expecting another baby."

"I devoted my life to you, my son."

"Doesn't God teach that all children are equal? You don't even talk of God any more. You used to when I was little."

"I…I…"

"All you think about is diamonds, useless little stones used for nothing more than adornment. How do diamonds make the world a better place papa?"

"They bring mysterious beauty to those who gaze upon them."

"A child looking up at you in trust is more beautiful, a old woman beaming with pride at some little thing her grandchild did, the ocean pounding against the shore, a flower blooming in glory. These things are much more beautiful."

Frenzel had no argument because he knew this to be true.

"A chance, papa, that's all I ask. If I fail, I'll do as you say."

Frenzel was certain at that moment that Avi wouldn't fail. He had too much fire, to much spirit to fail at anything just as diamonds would never fail to shoot off dazzling hypnotism. If he forbid Avi his dream, in essence he would be destroying him. "Take the chance then but you must stop seeing that woman."

"I don't see her often. She's older than my mother and I have friends. I simply say she's an interesting person."

Who would have killed you, Frenzel thought. He would have to tread carefully if this woman was watching him through Joel. "I must return to Tel Aviv tonight."

"Bring mama a gift. You never bring her a gift from your travels."

"She never wants anything."

"She does but you never notice."

"I have no idea what a woman likes."

"Anything as long as it's from the heart. And maybe you could get something for my sisters and the granddaughter you've never seen."

"My plane leaves in…"

"Four hours. You have plenty of time. Mama would love Austrian crystal. I bought a present for the baby. You can take it and I'll buy another."

"What is it?" Frenzel felt he was sinking in quicksand. He was losing control here and didn't know how to stop it.

Joel opened a drawer and removed tiny diamond stud earrings. "They're small but just right for a baby like Ariel. I'm sure Ruth will have her ears pierced."

Frenzel took the box. "Thank you."

He had gone home with gifts and his family was shocked speechless. His wife had cried. She was a strong woman who never resorted to tears and yet she cried like a baby and all over a cluster of crystal grapes done by Swarovsky. And little Ariel had smiled at him. There were never many smiles in his house but Ariel smiled. She would grow to be a beautiful woman one day with her raven curls and blue eyes.

Frenzel remained at home for four months and watched his family as they tiptoed around him. One night he kissed his wife goodnight and she stared. What was so wrong? They had made love before, how else to account for four children? He went to temple and everyone stared at him. In four months he only looked at his diamonds once. After that he flew back to London where Joel's movie had wrapped up a week before. Joel had just returned from a trip with Olivia and her friends. To his horror, Olivia was at his son's apartment when he arrived.

"Mr. Frenzel," she gushed. "We just returned from a most enjoyable train ride on the Orient Express and I must say your son was a big hit. He kept my friends amused and even solved the murder. So exciting. Everyone on the train participated even those who couldn't speak English. We managed to converse in sign language. What's wrong? Why are you staring at me?"

"I warned my son it's not wise to be friendly with you."

Joel was mortified. "Papa, please."

"It's all right, Joel," Olivia said with a hint of fire in her eyes. "Mr. Frenzel, I didn't force your son to go along and neither am I an old woman looking for a young companion. I'm only here to give Joel a set of the photos we took. I don't appreciate your glare."

"Who are you, Olivia? What organizations do you belong to?"

"Organizations? What an odd question. I belong to the Hot Air Balloonists Club, the Hospital Aid Ladies, the Society to House Unwed Mothers, the Tory Women's Guild. Should I go on?"

"I mean sinister organizations?"

Joel was too shocked to speak. Was his father losing his mind?

"Sinister? Let's see I'm not a spy although I almost gave it a try once. I'm not a double agent nor am I a member of the Irish Republican Army or a satanic cult. There's the Klu Klux Klan but that's in the States. I might look into some other organizations when I visit my daughter there."

"Nothing associated with older woman trying to rid the world of greed and corruption?"

Olivia was still perplexed. "I don't sympathize with greedy people, Mr. Frenzel, but I don't know of any organization devoted to that cause.

Maybe it's a good idea though. I'll have to look into that as well. Goodnight." She whispered in Frenzel's ear at the door. Take heed, diamond man. Loose lips sink ships you know. Big sisters are watching."

Joel walked her to the elevator. "Don't fret, dear boy, I can handle myself in any situation. Frankly, I think your father's become unhinged. You might tell him I'm a charter member of the English Geisha Girls in Great Britain. I forgot about that although I do have a certificate somewhere."

Joel was angry when he returned to the room. "I don't like my guests treated rudely."

Frenzel put his head in his hands. Had he gone to far in insulting a woman who belonged to a terrorist group? Would she report this affront to those two madwomen? "I don't know what's happening to me. I see gray haired women walking on the street and I think they're out to kill you."

"I think you need professional help. I'll fly home with you and we'll find a good doctor."

Velvel was getting nervous as Frenzel's trance continued. He poked him. "Frenzel, snap out of it."

"What? Sorry. You'll accept my gift?"

Velvel was in a quandary. What else could he do? It was that or argue with the man when Julia and Annie would be coming back into the shop at any minute. "Yes, yes, I accept."

"And you'll forgive me for beating you?"

"Yes. I'm busy."

"I wish to buy a gift for my wife."

Was the man going mad? Frenzel never mentioned his wife much less bought her gifts. "I have just the thing," Velvel said hurrying to a display case. "Italian gold bracelet, etched by a fine craftsman in Milan."

Frenzel stared without really seeing it. "You think she'll like it?"

"I guarantee she'll love it."

Frenzel pulled out a wad of cash and Velvel dashed to put the bracelet in a box. Julia and Annie were just coming out of the back room as Frenzel was leaving. He looked at them for a second. Could they be the ones who held him captive? He rubbed his eyes. No. He was seeing kidnappers in every woman that passed him by. Only yesterday he had spilled coffee all over himself in a restaurant when an older woman walked toward his table. She was actually meeting friends at the next table. In the hotel, a gray haired woman came out of the elevator and he shrunk back in horror.

Velvel waited for an explosion but Frenzel walked out the door. Julia and Annie hadn't even noticed Frenzel because they were too busy looking at other items in a display case. He bounced over to them. "Today we celebrate an official end to your stealing. Maybe I should find out what you'll do next? It may be worse than stealing."

"We had so many dreams when we were young but we have managed to narrow them down a bit. We're considering conducting tours for seniors to out-of-the way places like the tundra, or diamond bearing sites Russia or Australia. What a way to travel far and wide. But we have to deliberate our next move for a while longer."

"You'll include me in whatever you do?"

"We could never leave you out. You're one of the Three Musketeers. Ready for that pajama party?"

"Ready, willing and loving it. Tell me what games we're playing besides the teddy bears."

"Have you ever done Pin the Tail on the Donkey?"

Velvel stopped fidgeting with excitement and was suddenly nervous. "Julia, Annie, a jackass they don't allow in my apartment. It's a ritzy place."

0-595-13876-4